# Coltrane, AZ

## CHRIS DIETZ

**HNS Publishing | Bisbee, Arizona**

# Coltrane, AZ

ISBN: 978-1-7335729-3-4

Cover Image: Randolph Dietz, *The Red Chicken* (2022)
Book Design: Bill Dietz

HNS Publishing
Bisbee, Arizona

*For Billy and Tami*

# THE DAY BEFORE

**Clay Mason**

> *blood of a butterfly*
> *I be blood in a butterfly vein*
> *I'm a cell*
> *I'm a trillion cells*
> *like a galaxy*
> *with a brain in the center instead of a black hole*
> *in the center of that*
> *that lumpy gruel brain*
> *a magnet*
> *like a single secret raisin*

The brain inside, in the corduroy folds, a magnet points straight to where I'm going. Direction, no problem, nothing bad about that. Us retards got a natural inclination for finding our way home. Our brain pleats are awry. But exactly where I am corrects straying. But I can do correct. No talking out loud to myself. No jiggly cat's cradle finger play. No scary grimaces. No mind control Trilobites! I be clod clopping down Mule Canyon, through the pea soup fog, dawn's early morning mist, heading down from the Time Tunnel to Main Street here I come, Coltrane, Arizona.

Had to check for sign up at the tunnel, near where I found this fine piece of hemp rope coiled round my neck. I was hanging around, now I'm hanged ambulatory. Now I'm in the drainage ditch that runs down the middle of Mule Canyon – cover is critical, below Mule Canyon Road. Above the road, past a layer or two of houses, the highway bypass cuts its own lanes, straight around the mountain to the tunnel. It's one of only two ways out of Coltrane now. Down here in the ditch, cement walls ten feet tall, I feel one foot tall. But I'm not, I can pass. I'm a big boy. Beware of ambush. It's a trap! Choose clear. Choose clean input. Easy greasy to be trapped down here, pelted with caliche clods and stinky trash. The war continues. Never lets up. Never get caught below – seek the high ground. Enfilade! Seize the high ground! The Trilobite War never ended!

No sign to report.

I like to challenge the odds down here. I dare the world to –

But this mist, this fog – does fog go in tunnels? I didn't dare go check. Is all the fog one thing, or lots of little things – like molecules? Fog goes round the whole canyon, a white thickness line I can't see through, where everything stops, or ends, but fluffy, where sky damps down. A white wall starts just past the top houses, but no pea soup. Isn't pea soup green? This is white white. What's that from, pea soup fog? Sherlock Holmes?

Careful! One foot after the other finds the exact dry spot to go. It's a flow. Don't slow down. Hip-hop juggle, like a puzzle, keeping to the jumpstones.

Drainage ditch's mainly mud weeds volunteering out a living between rains. Will it rain? Will the fog coagulate to dry, dirty drops? No rain this October, before Halloween, one month to my fifteenth birthday. Duh parental units (PUs) flew the coop – the parental units have left the building. Well, I can celebrate with my friends. One month to make friends. One month swerving in the closed town's nerving. How many kids on their own now? We divorced our parents! We made our choice. Irreconcilable differences. Direction. We decided to stay. Clop clop straight through a teeny puddle, and little sulfur butterflies rise in swirls of daintiness. I like it down here. I say all fancy, goldfinches chip in the mud, searching for seeds too small for me to see. Not many birds, but some. A towhee hops away like a question mark, its note rising in a pitch to query. Nobody asked the birds if they wanted to stay. I hear a crow calling my name: 'Clay! Clay!' Helixes of colored light, fractals of polarized light, atop a smear, mean poison. Direction. Decide –

PUs? I miss them. Sure, I do. Ma's casseroles...ha! Ma hadn't cooked in eons. Everything came out of the nuker. They decided. My limp parents: burned out, battered... Baby Boomers toted, bummered, not good for much anymore. I was like their mistake. We wandered for years, looking for work and a home, before ending up in Coltrane. Mom drank too much. Dad read science fiction and drove a truck. Not at the same time. They didn't care if I stayed. They just wanted some comfort, some down time. They didn't want to worry any more about anything. Consolidation was the perfect fit.

The canyon swells above me, and I like saying 'swells.' The topography swells complex, looks like a bunched up blanket from above. On my left, to the north, the swells meander into offshoot canyons, each with a name, each with its houses' encrustation. Each with a privacy I have tempted. To the right, the south, the swells bellow steep to the bypass, then climb up to Baldy Peak, tallest of the Apache Mountains, which you can't see now on account of the fog. Houses on both sides of the bypass. Houses built over houses, houses on top of houses. Then houses literally built around and over older houses. Layers and levels. Houses loaded up the side of rocky canyons, in the cocked position, with elaborate walls. Everywhere walls, retaining walls, holding walls, arty walls. Then the spider webby steps, binding trails and shrines and cliffs. Paths. Runways. I know all the steps. I know where they go. I know where they hide. Checking my feet, avoiding some dog dirt. The swells decide the drainage. Swells dotted with junipers and pinon, up to the fog. No run off today. What's with this fog? Dry fog? Heart throb. The mountains used to be covered in pines, until the miners came and the Apaches went away. The rain went away, too...it hasn't rained in –

At the Circle K, climb out. Bearings! Direction! Readings say, this way. Going downtown! Circle K looks paralyzed like a goner. It's differently-abled. Am I taking too long? Gotta focus. Convenience store at the end of time with an empty parking lot. There is no gas. Is it open? Tomorrow the power goes off. Everything closes without THE power. Humans shine lights, run alarm clocks, watch TV, vacuum, recharge devices, use electric can openers, electric toothbrushes. Besides, no money anywho – if there's no do re mi, there is no purchase. No money like suddenly we're on Mars. There's nothing to buy on Mars. Legal tender zilch. We'll barter. Today is the last day of electric, moneyed Coltrane. The powered town is powered down. Then, the THE FUTURE is here. They call this dump Art Town, tomorrow it'll go Tomorrowland Art Town. I never understood what Art Town meant. I know there are artists around, but is it their town?

I wind around, scan. Almost a bad breath comes from Circle K, then, no, old factory olfactory, it's coming from air tousling the dreads of Ewoks across the street, lined up at a stone wall's bus stop bench. No buses for a long time. A Wook comes over to join them. They move their heads. Faces in a row, smothered by hair. Lives in a row, smothered by stank. They didn't want to leave. Can't waste water on baths. First, we will learn each other's aroma, then we will cherish each other's aroma. They decided to stay. I decided to stay. Then, I decided to stay, too. My scan is complete.

Pass by. Going my way? Maybe they've been up all night? Their alarm clock broke. Their power has been off a while. I acknowledge the Ewoks. They go, 'whoo.' The Wook shows no teeth. Please, close that trap! We are all chums now, doing the air nod. We stayed.

Ewoks are the back to the land types. They land in abandoned cars or broken down mining structures. Nature freaks. While the Wooks are on the pipe. Their hair falls out, they have acne. With the Ewoks you can expect peace signs and goofy smiles, but the Wooks have melty eyes, like their faces are peeling off.

I gotta keep going. Wind cars are the answer! Desert flyers sailing over the caliche! But nobody's going anywhere. No one's leaving now. We've been told not to. All my life, been told not to. Gotta stay in Coltrane now. It's the rule.

Besides besides besides the border is death now. Mad Max cartels. Viral outbreaks, disease in the dust. Weird fungus infections. Besides, there's no water. It doesn't rain. Why would anyone want to stay? Why would anyone want to go? This is the 'after' picture in the text book I'll never use.

Up Mule Canyon on the main drag, seal my invisibility. Sidewalks have rules: no expectoration, keep it to yourself. This way leads right to the vertex vortex. My home town. My last home. This is the last place I'll ever live, because this is the place for sure I'll die. I'll never see a Trilobite! Mule Canyon opens, propagates, populates, goes sophisticated.

The canyon's like a big L. The long arm, Mule Canyon, becomes Main Street where it eventually pivots, turns left, north. The pivot is a plaza, hub, heart, from where Coltrane throbs. The short leg of the big L, heading north, moves up the Gulch, a whole other canyon crack. Earth talks back in Coltrane. We get landslides, rock slides, cave ins. Plumbing disasters are legendary. I can hear the rocks in their faults, in the down deep deep, this steep wrenching pulse and shudder, as the Earth tears at itself. The old hippies say they can hear dinosaurs stomping around down there late at night.

Small houses, mainly of wood with metal roofs, line the street. Some come up to the curb, jumping the spotty sidewalks. There are mini-windmills on mini front lawns. Others have sun dials, a gnome or two. I've counted fourteen plastic pink flamingoes at one place. Here is the house of the old guy who stayed who cuts his hedges in animal shapes – topiary. Across the street is a purple house. Here's a pink house. Peeps like to decorate. Now what? Who will keep up appearances? Most of the houses are empty.

Still, signs signs signs, tacked, nailed, glued, all over the place, on walls, on telephone poles, wrapped around stop signs. Trying to communicate. Political signs, government stuff – on border trouble, on consolidation. The new official rules and regs everybody must follow. Warnings warnings warnings. Kind of pitiful: posters with push pins from another world, and what about all those cell phones peeps were so proud of, now, today, their last day? After today, there will be no appeal. There can be no appeal.

Hey, it's a free country. Decide! Choose! Decide to stay, decide to go. Free speech easy cause no one cares. It's the constant emergency. Just stay out of my way. PU's excuses for consolidating in Tucksoon or Phoenix. Which what most did. Save the posters for toilet paper – everything getting scarce.

Giant cottonwoods now, pretty shaggy this time of year, shoot up up up. Vultures used to roost up high in the branches, those black hooded figures, total reapers, then they migrated, or died. They never came back. We have some birds. We have some mice and rats. We have rabbits. There are still pigs around. Near the base of the thick trunks, this hobbit house with fancy windows and skylights. Move my sorry ass. Dead cars and trucks in the street, in driveways. A lawn the size of a yawn has a couple Volkswagens on top of each other like sculptures. Metal armatures would make super weapons. Here's a wall of solar panels that looks like space communicators. Electric equipment litters the lawns and driveways, the empty lots.

Used to be, you'd walk up the canyon and every other house had a porch of yappers – snappy, scrappy, little toy dogs. New rule: no little yappers wasting resources – that's how it was explained. Rules seem so random. But it's got to be better than consolidation. No kitties either, but for a different reason rule: they are competitors for food. I guess when we're all hunting mice and rats. A few guard dog types remain. Big fellas. Work animals, to protect and serve. Two women on bikes go by me. They don't glance my way because they don't see me. A guy on a horse comes clop clopping along from a side canyon – Moon Canyon? He touches the brim of his baseball cap, but not to me...he's adjusting the angle. A car goes by slowly, running on fumes.

Who stayed? Old hippies, retired people, some Mexican folks, artists, weirdoes, a bunch of PUs with families...Wooks, Ewoks, kids. No one stayed who was retarded or in a wheel chair.

More Ewoks now, as I get downtown. A Wook or two. What are they waiting for? What's everybody crowding up for? Something cooking? What are they looking at? It's early, misty, but always-time now, now-time now, when clocks don't mean anything. PUs scuttle about like whirly bugs on top of a puddle. Old hippies gristle about, come pouring out of their hidey holes in the walls like cockroaches. Conversations! Loud voices! Another big meeting for sure. Everyone haunted. So many meetings and palavers to get here. Now, everybody pointing and looking. The great debate! What are they looking at? Up ahead, center of town, where ley lines meet, where people meet – convulse...the gist. People are badgers dogging road kill. People are roadrunners taking care of snakes with spearheads. And I am a radio station playing static.

There's the last policeman on Earth trying to deputize old hippies. What's going on? The old hippies will have none of it and besides beard tugging, they point. Retired men, golf shoes and gold pants, nice sweaters and jackets, keep their arms high, fingers out – they point. Two city council men, last of the official Old Town government, are drumming hand signals with the mayor. They are pointing, too. Some kids are hanging nearby with broom handles clutched in their opposables. The kids are looking the direction of the points. Up.

I have to turn, I have to look, I have to see. But it has to be perfect. I have to see...when suddenly suddenly suddenly, speed riot bloom: there she is! High school girl with startling gray eyes and ruffly brown hair. She pings! She rode my bus when school was still going. She's got like jeans on, a sweat shirt. She's barefoot. What is she doing barefoot in Coltrane in October on the last day? Not good! If she cuts the sole of her foot, I'll have to carry her home. She could get Tetanus. What was that story about the man who showed up barefoot would kill the king and marry his wife? She's standing on bare feet, watching, pointing. Monkeys point. We all point. Now I look –

– and there it is!

I would not choose to look until ready.

Above the center of town, 'bout one hundred feet on top of us, but I'm a lousy guesser, is a huge, metallic sphere, big as a bus... but... a sphere... of shine... a mirror rounded... floating there... maybe one hundred feet up... up –

Balloonacy? It's perfect! Just what we needed. We can see ourselves.

More Coltrane folks, so make a throng. The gray-eyed girl is busy with the worker bees, the PUs, the kids. She talks, offers her views, counters her points. The kids watch her. She stirs them. I watch her. Maybe she saw my rope and figured I was going to hang myself. We're thinking in extremes. It's official now. Mi gente will freak now. And the kids will reign. Must be hundreds of people, all ages and planets, and carapaces and tentacles. We are the last! We stayed. Ugly people every one. Except for her. She is not ugly. She has the gray skill cool of an anime ghost.

We see it all. On top of us. Mirror sphere. Our first challenge. And she and I will be friends. Her and me. When, exactly on time, crazy old guy, Jacob Derry, in his jungle fatigues, like a great white hunter, who is said to have been an actual 'great white hunter', strides right up to and through the throng. He whistles and weasels his way to the center of command, and whoa! He's got a compound bow and I know he knows how to use it.

I say like a hillbilly, adults move back like slugs on a trail of salt licks. Kids stay where they are, sticks and knives and forks ready for action. The high school girl with gray eyes is scanning methodically, from Jacob Derry to the silver sphere to the crowd. She's taller than I thought. Her feet are small and dirty. The mayor and the policeman are pleading with Derry. But not that hard. The council men have teleported to safety. And Jacob Derry powers up the compound bow and lets loose an arrow into the shiny –

"That does it," blurts the mayor.

The policeman goes, "We're committed now."

The high school girl with gray eyes is a few feet away from me when the shiny sphere whooshes like a giant vacuum cleaner and the sphere collapses in on itself, snapping away fast and erratic as it deflates. A wave of human surf sound then, from people's special angry fear whine, as they flee. And she's gone, too, running up the Gulch on bare feet.

I want to show her my rope.

## Daisy Piper

*father is Geisha, mother is Ninja*
*I am a girl at the end of the world*

The balloon takes an arrow through its eye, and that calls for running straight through Grassy Park then up the Gulch. Poison gas released from the balloon? Poison gas that'll pacify us? I choose oxygen. Breathe deep. Tickles. Cool, gray October air. I choose live, and run, and stay alive another day. Misty. Fog bank all around on top. Veils to our vision. Be not shy and hesitant now. People – adults are spreading out, running, scurrying, in and out, they go. Many carry guns. Or makeshift weapons. A woman my parents bought Tofu from is clutching a pistol like they do on TV, with two hands out front, just feet away from me, as I run past. But I am confident, ready for anything. Everyone who stayed had to be a certain amount confident. Right now, I choose to fight another day. Poison gas, nerve agents, hypnotics – what was with the balloon? They're trying to scare us. The Gulch clamors with Ewoks and Wooks, shaking that way they do when they're stoned and trying to keep it together. But everyone knows each other now, so why cringe? Recognize. See what it is. In the same lifeboat. I think they said seven hundred stayed. Sigh, stop running. My feet are dirty as rocks and achy with cold. They look like animal parts when I check for blood.

I had no intention of giving up my shoes. I left my parents' place this morning with my old sneaks on. When I got downtown, the sphere had just appeared. This old hippy lady was crying beneath it, pointing, trembling. I asked her if I could help. She said her feet were bleeding. She said she was getting the stigmata. I said maybe her shoes were too tight. I gave her mine.

The square, red brick house on the Gulch has gingerbread trim – where's the witch? Coltrane has plenty of witches. It's an empty house kids use. Red bricks seem to breathe out, then heave in. I'm panting. When I knock on the wooden door, so flimsy a fairy could kick it down, I hear commotion inside. Where the wood of the door meets the bricks, I can see right in. Movement! Bennett Tilson opens the door and steps aside quickly. He pushes up his glasses, smiles. My eyes go clear to the faces huddled on blankets and jackets on the floor. I enter. The gutted red brick building is filled with kids and mirrors. Up against the wall, tall mirrors in wooden frames, as tall as some of the kids. Where did they come from? What are they doing here? From some store or beauty parlor? Mirrors and kids look back at me. Eight kids who decided to stay, three boys, five girls. Where are their parents? Some left. Some stayed. No one can say why what we decide now seems so important. I mean that kids can get their way over parents. That seems important to those of us who decided to stay. No one knows what to do. Kids are no different. No better. No worse.

My hands do a big wave to the kids. I look into each kid's eyes.

Bennett explains, "They didn't know what to do. Or where to go. But knew they had to get away from the balloon. But they like it here for now."

Maybe it was an eye, an all seeing eye balloon? Maybe surveillance makes us act funny. Was it a balloon? A weather balloon! We're paranoid monkeys, and that's good. Some freaky gizmo! But they said we'd be left alone.

The kids are solemnly nodding. I know their names: Scott, Cassie, Samantha, Amy, Roland, Biker, Aliana, DiDi.

I shrill, "Good! Everyone's safe. And we're all friends

now, looking out for each other. We'll figure this out, where we can go. Some of your parents stayed, so you need to tell them where you are. They'll be worried after the balloon, or whatever it was." I shrug, pause, dance in to their midst. "I know a place. At the end of the Gulch. That last house? I'm checking it out. For us. A kids' house. Why not? What you should do is hang, be koolio, talk to your parental units if they stayed, chill."

Bunch of the kids run up, hang on, grab tight, hold hard. Hugs all around. Gotta go! Gotta go!

What now? What are we going to do? Tomorrow, power and water and phones – off! Cell phones may work until their batteries go but cell towers, kaput. We decided to stay. I decided to stay. These kids decided to stay. I step back into the street into a pothole. I'm standing in a pothole wondering if my toes made it, when I break into a skip up the Gulch. Pass City Park where bunches are gathering. Farther on, the Gulch opens wide, a big scoop. A bowl in the canyon surrounded by a hat box? No, a layer cake! Houses stacked up, one on top of the other. The canyon narrows, Luria's grocery is closed. No one around, everybody downtown. End of the world tense quiet, which is an expectant sound. A few kids run by, yelling at each other, ignoring me. This is gonna turn ugly without my shoes, in case I have to skedaddle.

"Hey, Daisy," goes Brian Hobart and waves a dirty mitt.

Where did he come from? Allies appear out of the mist! I grunt.

He tries again, "What's the rush, mush?"

I come over by him. "I'm checking out some stuff. Getting ready for tomorrow."

"Oh, yeah. What's to get ready? Me and my ma got a whole box of protein bars and a big bottle of sleeping pills."

Now the Gulch begins to thin, fewer houses, and they are older, droopy. Cars plunked along the single lane are dinosaur carcasses being worked for their parts. A couple boys, older than me, deep in the metal innards. We have to learn to take things apart, then we rebuild them, then we use them right. Another kid, up on some steps, a boy, with a stick. They all glance at me warily. Boys' Club. I say 'hey.' None of them utters a sound.

I want to go to the very end finally, to the last house on the Gulch. It's been empty a long time. It has a fire place and an outhouse. On the side, around back, there's a well. It'll need work. And ta-da! There! There it is. There's the house, with a pomegranate tree in its churned up front yard. Some trash but not too bad. We can clean up –

I like this house. I love this house. I look it over. I dream saying 'my house.' Windows, eaves, door at an angle. What will break off first? Who cares? It's ours for the time being. What more can we need? Roof heaped with leaves and dead branches. Ancient metal roof – leaks? Get a bucket! Basically the place is intact. For now. So why not? Me and the kids can move in, start our own shenanigans.

Saunter on, go past, filled with plans for the house. My feet are okay or I am so exuberant, or in shock, they don't hurt. Until, finally, the Gulch road ends, runs right in to the wash, makes a path there, sorta. Shiver pleasantly, pick my way through rocks. Plastic shit everywhere. Gray bright off, casting embarrassed light. Fog bank filter. Easy to find houses in Coltrane now. I count three old mine shafts from here, but can't tell if they are occupado. The canyon is narrow, now, cracky rocks then sheer formation walls. I love it out here. This is the edge of my universe.

Bushes and weeds in the wash. Mesquite along the steep hillsides. We are the weeds who refused to leave. They told us we'd die, and we said not yet. We are the nondescript, the unimportant, the goofballs who stayed. In all the universe, right now, the only ones who care about us are us. This is a fine, fine tuning that calls for skipping. Skipping, hopping to a cottonwood clump – shedding trees making a mess, in a widening pocket that opens to Bone Canyon. A rock wall, opposite the trees, s wall of cracks, strata, sutures, like a 3-D cragginess map.

Staccato atoms! Make me go to slow array – all eyes. We've been practicing for this all our lives. How to stay alive? How many movies and TV shows were about taking a stand? Rugged individuality stuff. Now, I feel the watcher. I feel like molasses – I'm cold, I'm hot. Bend to grab up double handfuls of rocks. Lean into it. Arm back –

Where are the eyes –

In the cottonwood?

Is it an animal?

"Up here!"

Let loose projectiles into the topmost branches of the tallest cottonwood.

"Nice! Real nice!"

"I'm a Ninja, my muscles are faster than my thoughts."

"I want to show you an item."

The cottonwood trunk has bark in hand holds. Walk straight up to the first fork. "Item? If you show me your dick, I'll cut it off." The cottonwood feels warm, alive. I need a knife. Everybody is accumulating weapons.

He laughs with genuine, good natured goofenjoy, which means he probably has a real 'item' to show.

Climbing is scrapey and scratchy. Toes are perfect. He's pretty high up on a limb. He's leaning into the trunk to hang on, not too dangly. He rode the bus. Kids thought he was a retard. They didn't like the way he dressed: white t-shirt and baggy work pants, with big ugly work boots. Now he's got a denim jacket on. His face is red. He was worse than poor, he was a Coltrane street kid.

He's right next to me. He has to scoot over to make room on his branch. He can't go far because he has to keep a hand on the rope he's holding.

"Item," says the nodding, glowing boy. "I climbed up this tree to have a look see, few minutes ago, and across the way, across the canyon, see there?" He points with a hand but very quickly, in spurts, as it's his holding on hand. "See there?" he repeats. "Three bald guys in white, maybe pink, jumpers came in from Bone Canyon on some kind of ATV and set up that machine, then left. Minute before you got here. You know, with the sphere thing going on, then this. They weren't from Coltrane."

"What am I am seeing? Do I need X-ray vision for this?"

"Right across from us, the canyon wall there, where the rock makes a nook, do you see it? What they left? There's a flat place with something in it? A machine?"

"Black thing."

"It's a machine gun."

"It's not a machine gun."

"Okay...item: I figure they'll be back, right? So we gotta move fast. I bet a person could grab on this rope and swing over there, check it out, and swing back."

"You do it."

"Too big. Not enough, you know, Galileo."

"Like a pendulum. Like a swing? You think I can swing over there and check out that item. Before those guys get back?"

The rope after a few firm tugs seems secure around a limb near the tippy top. The branch bends out and over, almost across the canyon. Long enough. Tall enough. In theory. How did he get the rope up there? How hard can this be?

"If I do this thing?"

"Knowledge! Knowledge will come to you."

"You fucking with me? Who were the baldies? Like police, you think?"

"Never seen 'em before. Didn't look civilian."

I guess we're all active duty now. Get my body in gear, I can do this. Awkward take off, kicking back on the tree trunk, then the full swing throttle smacks me into the wall.

At the exact same second, he yells, "Hurry!"

I'm flattened to the rock wall like a bug, holding on with fingertips, bare toes, climbing. Pull up and into the cracky craggy spot, keeping the rope wound around my arm.

What's he saying?

Metallic black, this clunker bunker machine, with what might be a muzzle sticking out front. It aims out, towards us, towards home. No trigger I can see. No switches or dials or buttons. I don't see any bullets or even where to load them. Why does it say machine to me? What else could it be? Manufactured. A foot or two across, four feet long, but tapering, blocky parts, with lines that might be seams, and a couple stubby legs to rest on: machine poised at the notch in the rock wall, barrel out. Under its legs, then extending out, some kind of pad. Stepping on it, it feels funny, scoopy soft. The pad – the way it makes a flooring, it could be for the machine's users to sit on. The baldies?

Maybe it's a musical instrument? A totally new kind that makes music for leftovers, the guys who stayed?

Wind the excess rope around the machine's midsection. Tie it as tight as I can. Get behind the machine, on the padding, start pushing. Is it heavy? The machine teeters. A shove, a heave, one more shove, and the thing flips forward, over and out of the notch, dead weight straight down the wall. The rope catches, twangs, holds, swings, snaps.

The machine falls into the wash.

The boy screeches, "My rope!"

Blue jays squawk and come right over to see what's going on. Life in the wash. A few bird stragglers. There's not a lot, but the birds belong here. They're not stowaways: they're connected to here, too, like us. We are not alone. My heart won't stop drumming, so I take a cue from the birds, check it out, see what I gotta do now. I gotta get down. I'm climbing down the wall, slip a couple times, scrape my hands grated. Poor feet! Strong feet. I feel like my hands and feet are gonna tear.

He's standing by the machine in the wash. It doesn't look broken. He's poking it with a cottonwood branch. He's fidgety, red faced, growling. He stammers, "The item is not a machine gun."

"What's going on?"

"The sphere in town. Now this. You tell me. Gotta be – I mean, it can't be a coincidence, right?"

I shrug. "The balloon? It was a weather balloon. People will check it out now that it's...crashed. I don't know! Someone will know what it was for."

This boy is wound tight. He goes, "We gotta get outta here! Help me get my rope."

"Up in the tree? I think that's lost. I don't think you can get it. Besides." I shrug. He makes a face –

– drops the stick, takes off running up the wash, then he starts jumping rock to rock. He stops. He looks back. What are we doing? I guess he wants me to come with. We walk together now, not talking. I can tell how hard it is for him to hold back. Pretty soon there's the last house – my house, our house. There's a bunch of kids there.

He pulls up, a little spitting, with jerky arms and body tremors. He goes, "We gotta go back and get that thing!" Now he's fixed on the house, the kids, so he slows his breathing and arm waving, and he says, "Kids' house?" His hands drop to his sides, but I can see the way his fingers are crooked.

"Who are you?" I venture.

"Clay Mason."

"I'm Daisy. Daisy Piper."

"What's going on?"

"Bennett Tilson! What's going on?"

Bennett Tilson comes over grinning huge. He wipes his drippy nose, pushes up his glasses, and blasts, "We're moving in! Why wait? What you said. The kids figured go for it. The kids are getting their stuff and moving in. We got brooms. We got tools and supplies. We're cleaning up. We got water, supplements, chips. Doing it smart. Kids're smart."

Clay Mason says, "I got flash lights, candles, a box of power bars."

I go, "Some of these kids have parents who stayed. We don't want any trouble. What are they going to say? Your parents stay, Clay?"

Before he can answer, Tennyson Luna is in the front yard with an aluminum baseball bat slung over his shoulder that he begins swinging about, pretending to hit and clobber. Practice. Baseball cave men never get it right.

He goes, "Hey, Daisy Dee!"

I say, "Your parents stayed – what are you doing here?"

"Everything's different now. Starting tomorrow. We may as well make the most of it."

Cassie and DiDi run over for hugs. The house's front door is held open by a box of food and water bottles. All the windows are open. The misty mountain air will go in and scrub it down. Through the open windows I can see kids squealing and laughing, arms filled with boxes and clothes and chairs and dolls. A couple kids saunter up the Gulch with back packs on, one girl carries a suitcase.

Tenny says, "Your parents stayed, Daisy. You're just worrying about yourself. Everybody made a choice to stay, that makes us all equal."

Clay pushes in close to me and goes, "We gotta get back there! The item."

I go, "Tenny, give us a hand a sec. You, too, Bennett. Up the Gulch. We found something."

Bennett says, "Oh, koolio, can I bring my rockets? I been dying to try these new babies out!"

Clay goes, "I'll meet you there. I gotta get something, too." He zooms away, running.

I spot kids with a little red wagon. I go, "We could use that." I point it out.

Tenny ends up commandeering the little red wagon after he helps the kids unload its toys and fruit roll ups. Bennett's back, ready, backpack protruding with rocket heads. The payload? What do you call the top? The warhead? He's been making them for years. Once, he took me to a secret place to watch them take off. He was more excited than I was. He's younger but he's my friend. He explained the mixtures for fuel, how he tried different things. We made a lot of 'ah' sounds, when they shot away into the sky to pop. He can shoot them off by remote control, too.

When we get to the black machine in the wash, Tenny kicks it, saying, "It's too big for the wagon." He leans into it, pushes aside some rocks, gets his arms around it, gives it a heave. "Not that bad," he says with relief.

Bennett says, "What the heck, Daisy? What is it? Where'd you get it?"

"Up there, in the rocks. I'll show you."

Bennett says, "I am not climbing up there – scorpions. All sorts of nasty critters. Vinegaroons. Solpugids. I want to set up my rockets. I need a clear, open spot, so I'm gonna go over there." He points back the way we came, some rock formations. "In those rocks. Perfect cover in the rocks." Bennett takes off, hustles around in the rocks, disappears from view. He calls, "This is good."

Tenny spits, exhales with, "Well, I can't carry your machine back by myself, Daisy."

Clay Mason comes tearing up the wash, rock to rock, hopping, panting, sweating. He's holding his left arm out and in its hand he's holding a pillow case. He says, "Got here as fast as I could. I dropped my box off at the kids' house." He shakes his hand with the pillow case. "I got something for up there in the rocks."

"What?" says Tenny. "A Trilobite?"

"You'll see."

Clay goes over to the wall, leans back to study it. He's very thorough, I figure imagining his handholds to the notch, where I found the machine. He starts climbing with one hand, the other hand with the pillow case held out. I go over to climb, too. This guy is good! He's climbing with one hand.

At the top, there's not much room, so we go through the notch one at a time.

Clay says, "You didn't tell me about this." He's running his free hand down the weird cushioning.

"Item,' I answer.

Clay says, "'Smart weave – you know? Maybe it's alive?" He drops his pillow case at the corner of the pad where it's pushed up against the rocks. A small western diamondback comes tumbling out. The snake gets oriented, pulls itself together, makes a nice spiral, head on top, tongue flicking.

We can hear Bennett calling, "Set!" "Set!" He's ready to blow up Bone Canyon.

Glancing around, farther back into Bone Canyon, where it's trees, and a trail, a vehicle appears on that trail, three bald guys on top of it. They look naked. Or all in pink. Pink, for sure. Clay sees them, too. Have they seen us? Clay starts down. The vehicle is a square platform with one big wheel below, set right in the middle. I've never seen anything like it. ATV, my ass!

Clay's already down the wall. I fling myself over and only slip once. My left pant leg at the knee rips. These are my favorite jeans. But my feet are okay. Clay's telling the others about the weird bald guys.

Tenny, Bennett and Clay pick up the machine. They are stooped, grunting. I position the wagon for them. They lay the machine across the top. We drag it into the rocks where Bennett's set up. We huddle up close. We hunker down like we do this all the time.

Clay's on all fours, scuttling back and forth like a crab. He has to see. Hiding to the side, using rocks for cover, the rest of us gotta see, too.

Three big bald heads, white or pinkish, at the notch in the wall. They move funny, or they're flustered, looking for their machine. They jerk about, heads coming into and out of sight. Their heads, their faces, their eyes – something's off about them, but too far to tell what. Finally, from up there in the rocks, a scream like none I've ever heard.

The heads disappear.

Clay orders, "The rockets! The rockets! Fire the rockets!"

Bennett has his remote control in front of himself, both hands on it. He pushes the buttons, the sequence, the code, and the rockets roar!

# THE FIRST DAY

**Oscar Wargo**

Everyone hates Nyquil: the epitome of white privilege in over the counter succor. It's packaged, it's pricey. It's the fabled remedy that just happens to be a fabulous 'sleep aid.' Without sleep, everyone is punished: I poot out, bloat, clutch about like a three-toed sloth. This is my secret, nobody knows I'm on the juice, the luxury combo of antihistamines and Dextromethorphan that does the trick. Right before bed, before I brush my teeth, I take my cap full. In bed, there is a flush, then I settle. Quiet down. On the verge, I know everything is working out, particulars cosseted away. Eyes closed, I see wakefulness replaced. Matters of attention stroll through, then away, images of the day, bye bye. Then images from movies. Scenes – they fit! The mind is a catalog. The cascade of imagery goes on and on. This so-called life in the in between zone, state of reverie, no choice required. Nyquil sleep secret...

What will I do when my Nyquil runs out?

I made my choice. My direction is my choice, and if people want to call my attire 'hippy robes', so be it. Hippy scholar! Rogue scholar! Here, at the edge of nowhere, precarious sleeper, we came seeking independence at the bottom of the map. Nowhere else to go. We were independent scholars. Now we're hollerin' scholars. Control is not what it used to be. We refuse to settle for inertia. Consolidation be damned! We depend on humanity's illogic.

First day, so I must get out! I simply must. I haven't been out in days. I missed yesterday's balloonacy! Ha! Downtown needs my acumen. Not since the Trilobite Wars have people been so fraught.

We who stayed have a different brand of hope. We present visceralism, offshoot of delightism. We live without control. We can learn to live without Nyquil. When they cut the lights, we can even learn to live without movies. All the images are buried away in the cranial portfolio. Folders for TV, folders for movies, folders for special broadcasts. TV as penology. Humans began the process a long time ago, collecting pretties, now it ends with consolidation. Some have gone...some have stayed. We are alone. We had to watch, we had to plug in, we had to get our dose. Guilt? No guilt at all? The images read like maze passages now. Sage stage surpass surreal – one cap is all you need –

There are ten doses per bottle. I have two cases. Or I could have a liver collapse. 'They' would like that, wouldn't 'they'? To see another breakdown, freak out, in those who stayed? The people who stayed decided to go with fidgeting. But all the pervs are gone? What about preachers? What will the preachers say now? Will the bars stay open? Nyquil is ephemeral. Brandy is eternal. Everything will stop, then fall apart.

I'm up. I'm prepped. I'm popped. Out the window, high fog over, on top of the Apache Mountains, sky island sights, the stark desert mountains. Sere. Tumbling terrain terror. I can see here, I have a view, as opposed to the temperate zone. Here is wide open, easy to pry. In the temperate world of suffocating green, one's view is curated, curtailed, pressing in with awful pressure. Coltrane is an island of canyons and parks. No black and white in the American Southwest. Dry Grasses and brittle weeds and stocky shrubs tend to the white gold, camouflage in plain sight. Green is a dream of the palpable in the desert. Living in the blast zone, red granitic uplifts shatter my cracker jack box house that smells like a scorpion, that oily aftertaste when I smash one.

My shack sits back from Main Street in a clot of close-set houses. Not much room for a wood pile or a garden or a cistern. But there are other ways to hold and store water. We will innovate. We will invigorate, proving that when you close down amenities, neighbors don't automatically go bestial. Ha! Scavengers afoot! Looting, the hot new sport! Who will eat a child first? Two million years of foraging before agriculture makes tomorrow not a return...but a re-investment in basic skills. There are bunnies in the hedges. I see them winking at me. They know their time has come. And the funny acorn woodpeckers go goofy hiding nuts in the eaves. But I read woodpeckers are nasty to eat – too many ants in their diet. But what about the nuts? Who will care for the acorns? The gathering? The bleaching? The grinding?

At death everybody knows the same thing. Finally, there are no choices to make. Even the kids made their choice. Now the kids are onto something. Neuronal emancipation? New brains! Always gets down to this: crux of change is thrust of brains. Brains act up. Power's off, brains come on. Punctuate. The new retinue! This is the proving ground. I have wasted my life worrying the unassumed. I never cared about publishing, teaching. I am accused of inconsequentiality. Now my brain is along and no one will discover I was right, I was wrong. It all amounted to a hill of beans. My neurons flash failure's unique ubiquity. Here in Art Town, waking full of attention, success in seclusion, everything would be dandy if I had enough Nyquil.

Before dawn, I cleaned house, everything spic and span. New day: new way. The last time I have 'excess' to clean like that. No water for cleaning any more that's for sure. Then I spilled tobacco on the floor – inevitably I do this after cleaning, and the shreds can't be picked up...only smudged deeper. How much time do I spend picking up lint? How much time before all the tobacco is gone? Well, there's Indian tobacco that the hummingbirds favor.

Rationalize the message...ratiocinate the messenger: today I walk, I seek. I wander downtown, slow as a poke –

The fog looks Japanese. The Tavern – my favorite watering hole...it has foggy panes. Will it stay open? Lukewarm beer? Is it open now? Today is the day. Everything is free now. Ownership is slavery. Dressed this way, I putter by, along my mantra trail, leaking good vibes, dripping karmic band aids. Downtown! By the post office, you can see and feel the town's vortex, the stolid old buildings, the mighty souls mustering. Picture perfect *gravitas.* Beyond the post office, Main Street moves on only to merge with the bypass, the highway out of town. Nothing's there! The world just stops. The road into town emerges from a white cloud bank. Here, and up at the tunnel, are the only ways in or out. No traffic. But watching, testing, stewing, glimmering, pondering, plotting, the heat meat of town residentials. Cassandras, every one! Now vehicles are pulling in from up town. More pedestrians. Bikes, motorcycles, couple guys on horses. Everyone's bundled up in layers in the chill dawn air. Many carry weapons. Kids, too, packing, swarming past my position as post office sentinel. They wield sling shots, slings, bolos, sticks. Anybody can pick up a stick. Mojo rising: and the children shall lead them!

Vehicles are all banged up exiting Main Street to the bypass. They're inching out onto the highway. What are folks thinking? New parking lot? Metal beasts running on fumes! The parking dream of the golden spot...they line up. Today, everybody gets the golden spot. It's not really parking if you can't move again. Parking implies the end of parking. Everything temporary. On time, no time. Someone is driving a school bus up Main Street, then exiting at the bypass, then onto the highway. Now that's a waste of gas.

Mayor John John Placido stands with Officer Oscar Latta and Councilman Jimmy Martinez.

They're over by the convention center keeping track of things. That's right across from where I am. I go over to assuage. Other notables who stayed are with them. Men, women, kids. The new leadership! This was all decided – yes? What?

"Why all the nukes?" I say.

Oscar Latta goes, "Oscar," and nods.

I go, "Oscar," and nod.

Councilman Martinez, a successful businessman, ran an auto body shop – what will he do off the grid? He challenges with, "Don't start, okay? We're doing the best we can. What we decided."

Officer Latta, the only cop who stayed, says, "You guys have it covered here. Just don't let anybody shoot each other. I'm going up to the tunnel to make sure it's copacetic."

Mayor John John says, "Enough folks up there?"

Officer Latta shrugs. "The folks up the canyon are ape shit about holding the tunnel."

I pounce: "What can this mean? 'Holding'? 'Holding' from? 'Holding' on? What are these cars doing on the bypass? The natives are restless. Neighborhood watch on 'roids! Why? Why all the alarums?"

Mayor John John glares at me, puckers and rattles, "Closed town. You voted for it. Closed. Period. They said we'd be on our own. No interference. We better hope the neighborhoods get involved." He shakes his head, looks forlorn a second, confidence drizzles, then adds, "That balloon, whatever it was, got folks nervous."

Councilman Martinez puffs, says, "We'll see. We have to keep talking, everybody involved, keep our options open. We'll have a confab at the park or the convention center later. We have to be ready for anything. It's the first day." He shrugs, says, "We chose this, remember?"

"Like herding cats," says Officer Latta and totters to his squad car, muttering, "I'm off."

What's on his mind? Why is he so sullen? Or pensive? He's a good guy, well liked. Coltrane is small enough for everybody to vaguely know everybody else. Now, it's critical. Know your neighbor as yourself! Officer Latta puts on the colored lights, no siren though. Lights in the gray, they slash and bash, push back the fog. Color!

He heads up the bypass to the tunnel.

People keep barging in, coming right up to the mayor and councilman with advice and warnings.

"It's our town!"

"We decided!"

"No turn backs!"

"We're staying!"

"We can't keep them out!"

"They're keeping us in!"

"Are the bars open?"

"What are the cars gonna do?"

"John John, what's with the bus?"

"We need more cars if we're gonna make a roadblock. Get all the beaters, line 'em up here, two or three deep. Same at the tunnel. I mean, if we are gonna go that route."

"Nobody talked nothing 'bout any 'roadblock'?"

"What if we have to get out?"

"Nowhere to go!"

"They won't let us out now."

"They won't like it we close the town."

"We should cannibalize the roadblock cars. Harvest batteries, tires, oil, gas, all like that. Stuff that's not too old or funky."

"What if everybody starts shooting?" I add.

"Who's shooting? Why would they?"

"Nobody's shooting!"

"Oscar," says the mayor, his eyes open...open wide, "that's not going to happen. We're reasonable people." His eyes say we're not.

I say, "But it's the end of the world. So for us to decide to stay means we're unreasonable. See how that works? This gives them license."

The mayor tsks. "Listen to you! That how you gonna help us hold together? It's not the end of the world."

Voices:

"The beginning."

"We decided!"

"Closed town!"

About a quarter mile east of us, where the cloud bank wins, where the disappearing highway comes into town but does not go out: a stir, a stab, something happening, or else a seizure. All of a sudden, colored lights from the cloud bank! A Coltrane police cruiser slowly emerges from the fog followed by a sheriff's vehicle with its lights going as well.

The leadership junkies move up the road without hesitation, approaching the oncoming. To deal is all! Boom! I go, too. The great crowd has a migratory fix now, though many singletonians are hightailing it out of here. Set off by law enforcement's appearance. Other singletonians get into defensive positions behind dumpsters like they've seen on TV – behind broken walls, behind telephone poles. Kids hide behind the bus. Cars on fumes vibrate. They know what comes next. They're going to charge the cop cars, like jousters? Demolition derby at the end of the world! This is the future? This future has a line drawn in cars, starts here, ends here: this is the new border. The police car and the sheriff vehicle stop, pulling over to the side. Welcoming committee ready to greet them. The mayor and Officer Latta yell for folks to turn off the damn cars and clear out.

Coltrane Chief of Police Siskin must have a megaphone app for his radio outfit. We hear his voice call out, "What the hell is this? You can't do this! Mayor Placido! Mayor! There you are. I don't know what the heck you folks think you're doing, but this can't be. You can't block the road. And all these folks with guns, gimme a break. What're you doing?" He pushes a scrawny neck out of the window, a small squarish head with an ugly look. He glances around, takes in the view, says in to his mic, "Safe to get out?"

Adults and kids start yelling, "Closed town!" and, "Our town!" and, "Go back the way you came!"

Siskin throws open his door, swings his legs out, stands. On the other side, the door opens and a white man in a dark suit steps out.

The mayor actively cuts through to the police chief. Entourage intact. He shakes Chief Siskin's hand. Chief Siskin is tall and skinny with dusty brown hair and wire rimmed glasses. The mayor is short and fat. Round as a cupcake! They are about the same age. More people are yelling from hidey holes.

Chief Siskin glances around, ready to spit, then he

slams a fist in to his opposite open hand and yells, "Enough! Okay – you decided to stay. We told you the consequences. You made your decision even though this whole border country is being evacuated. You chose. Consolidation is the only responsible way now, but you said no to it. You know that, you decided to stay. Okay, fine, stay, you and all these kids. But that don't mean the highway gets blocked. It stays open, it has to, in case of emergencies. We gotta convoy coming through pretty soon. That means today. Right now."

The mayor stutters, "I-I don't think so. Don't think folks will allow that." He shakes his head, looking embarrassed and sad at the same time. "It's because of the balloon. Whatever it was. That silvery sphere...that came in yesterday. No one said anything about that. You said we'd be left alone."

The suit says, "Mayor Placido, I'm Stan Mankin, government representative, and that balloon, as you call it, was for monitoring. We wanted to keep an eye on things. Make sure you're ok. And now it's gone, destroyed by your people."

Mayor Placido grunts.

Sheriff Veeland, who is a broad, big fella, younger than the others, has since gotten out of his vehicle and now he ambles over to nod and say, "Mr. Mankin, Chief Siskin, Mayor." Then he begins: "What are these folks doing with all the hardware? There's kids out there!" He raises his voice: "You gonna start a war?" He raises his voice some more: "Come on, people, think about it! We don't want any trouble and neither do you."

Mayor Placido answers loudly enough for the people around to hear: "'Monitoring'? You said we'd be left alone. You said we wouldn't have any recourse at all.

No emergency services. Once you turned off the power and gas, we were on our own. So monitoring what?"

"You're right," says Chief Siskin, "but National Guard and Homeland Security operations are still active through the border country. They have to be. You know what the border's like now. This road stays open."

Sheriff Veeland announces, "We're growing donkey ears, Chief. We been through this a thousand times. They decided to stay. All right, stay! But the road stays open and we will make sure it stays open." Then, confidentially: "Wadda you say, Chief? Give 'em 10 minutes, then we run the convoy through?"

Mayor Placido quakes with it: "You said we'd be on our own. Now you say we're under your orders."

Someone, a woman nearby, sounds like a woman's voice, yells out: "No way! Closed town – our town!"

I am proud of our cupcake mayor. He is four square in our moment of tribulation. He has absorbed the body politic. He knows how we feel.

Chief Siskin says, "You're still subject to national law."

"Not here, not now," says Mayor Placido. And it's as if something snaps, and there is a thick, heavy, delicious, pregnant silence punctuated by revving engines. When the government decided people could turn down consolidation, there was no going back.

Now the cars are bugs, scattering around, soft parade. Cars wait their turns to get in line. There's some honking but it's very organized parking. It looks like old trucks and cars on their last legs, the beaters of town...creeping onto the highway, assembling, forming up.

Sheriff Veeland moves towards the cars waving his arms. "Stop, stop!" he calls.

They have their windows rolled up and don't stop. On the highway they form a road block. The roadblock congeals.

Mayor Placido shouts in a lusty voice: "We decided to stay because we know we will die here. *But on our terms.* That's better to us than consolidation."

Chief Siskin goes, "Where's Office Latta? He should be here. I need to talk to him. He's still under my jurisdiction."

A woman says, "He's holding the tunnel." A cheer goes up.

Mr. Mankin laughs in that phony laugh all bureaucrats do, then calls Sheriff Veeland back. He says to the crowd, "The convoy is coming. The Chief and the Sheriff gave you 10 minutes. Time is counting down."

Chief Siskin almost sighs, but gets tough: "Most everybody has agreed to consolidation. Viruses, terrorists, mutants – you up to that, John John? It's hell out there. You know that. There's no water. You got kids here." Now he exhales heavily. "How they ever figured to let kids decide. Even against their parents' wishes. Never heard anything like that."

Mayor Placido says, "It's a done deal. Some kids refused to go no matter what their parents said."

Chief Siskin says, "So you let kids *divorce* their parents? That's nuts!"

Mayor Placido shrugs extravagantly. "It's been decided. Some of these kids would have killed themselves, rather than go for consolidation."

Chief Siskin grunts, shrugs too. "But-but...I'm glad I'm moving to a consolidation apt. And it's not too late." He calls out to the crowd: "People, if you want to come with me, tell me. Let me know. Step forward. I can help. You, your kids, everybody. Anybody who wants to come, can. My whole family is consolidated."

Mayor Placido says, "We didn't agree to continued harassment."

Mr. Mankin says, "This is unacceptable." He's staring, open mouthed, like all of us, at the road block solidified. Plus, people, young and old, men and women, are rushing out to the vehicles with weapons in hand. They're taking up positions.

I say loudly enough, "Last act of freedom is suicide."

A kid calls out, "What was that balloon?"

"Tell the truth!" insists a little girl.

Chief Siskin says to the mayor, "How long can you last? Seriously. You think these canyons can support folks? What if one of the plagues gets in? Do you have a doctor? What about looters? What are you going to do then?"

Sheriff Veeland piffs, grunts, then: "You can have your fucking old town, but the highway stays open."

A woman says, "What does that mean?"

Chief Siskin's voice is strained: "It's so dangerous

now. There's no water." He shakes his head.

Mayor Placido is looking at Sheriff Veeland. He says, "You're saying you still have control. Uh-uh." A hooting holler goes up. He continues: "That negates are choice, our decision. It's all or nothing. If we stay, it's our place. We decide who goes through."

Mr. Mankin implores: "Please, folks, we're not here to cause any trouble. The convoy is coming through to save time. You know this is a short cut across the valley. And they're hauling crucial equipment that's needed ASAP."

Now Chief Siskin hangs his head and retraces his path to his vehicle. Mr. Mankin follows to his side. They get back in the car. The swirly lights are giving me a headache or else packing in photons too tight. Interact! Sheriff Veeland returns in his cruiser. They back away slowly, the way they came, keeping to the side.

The roadblock is 2-3 cars deep in places now, with the bus lined up in front.

The law enforcement vehicles stop at the cloud bank, half in, half out. They are going to wait then. Lights on.

The mayor and councilman and some of the other men and women, who have tried to supervise and suggest and advise start exhorting, declaiming into the dawn. Some encourage a return to homes, to check supplies, to assess moisture collectors. Others go on about violence – avoid at any cost. Share. Respect. We chose!

Who knows how long suicide takes? How long did the Trilobites last? What happened to them? What will happen when the Nyquil runs out?

Everyone's jostling.

We were told we would not be able to leave Coltrane. So why should they be able to enter Coltrane?

The roadblock bristles with gun barrels. And kids are snuck in among them with bb guns, pellet rifles, the odd 22. Sling shots and slings! Men and women with rifles race across the highway, pass the road block, and climb up the side of the mountain to position themselves up high in the rocks. What are they thinking? Here comes Jacob Derry with a handful of young men pushing up Main Street his famous homemade catapult on wheels. They exit. They push it in among the vehicles of the roadblock, keeping behind the road block's front. They swivel the catapult around.

Minutes go by when there's no time. No power, no money, so no time. Everything is new constantly. We are in a state of eternal raptness. New experience leads to new attenuation. Everyone is paying attention as never before. People are not beasts. They are sharp warriors learning alternate ways. We chose this. Kids, too. We're up for discovery. We decided to stay.

Someone is yelling that the kids should get back. No kids should be up here in harm's way. The kids laugh and jeer. A young woman, a brown-haired girl with gray eyes that stands like a dancer, or an avatar of Diana, strides up from her hiding place in the road block and spits out, "We decided to stay, too. This is our home. We protect it, too."

Mist means rain, doesn't it? This fog, the white fog bank seems portentous. The erudition of humidity.

The law enforcement vehicles are off to the side enough, so when the big black matte juggernaut emerges from the white clouds in a rush of mechanical throbs and blue smoke, they're out of the way. It's huge! Some kind of SWAT vehicle? Got to be 10 feet tall and covered in smooth, black paneling so no surface features, seams or breaks, are visible. Totally enclosed! No windows, no doors. It looks like a big black wedge, and it's moving steadily, straight for the roadblock, towards the center, where the bus is. The thing is speeding up. It's front end is shimmering.

It's going to ram the bus!

People run for cover.

I duck down by a friendly dumpster.

Jacob Derry lets out a war whoop! Small voices rise in a cascade of ululations, kids at war. I hear little voices cry: "Big babies!"

The exact moment the black wedge hits the bus, about a hundred weapons open up. All sorts of pistols, bb guns, .22's, shot guns, rifles. Sling shots. The wedge literally breaks the bus in two, then stops. Bullets are whizzing in all directions, deflected or ricocheted off the black wedge. People are yelling to stop firing. Kids keep pelting the black wedge with rocks and sticks. It slowly backs away from the bus. It's going to have another go for sure! This time it will complete the bus's break up and push through the rest of the cars. And bullets don't affect the thing.

Then three or four kids snake through the road block's cars and trucks, moving closer to the wedge machine, but not too close. Little tousled heads rise, fall, as they peek, hide, peek, hide. They let loose with paint ball guns. Paint balls splatter all across the front of the wedge. Paint drips and oozes over the black shiny, shimmering front.

The black wedge hesitates. It doesn't bash forward at all. Instead, it backs up some more and stops again. The top of the wedge in the front, pops. A panel slides open, a rectangular space, and a silver tube extends. The tube starts spraying thick, viscous stuff, shooting it out 10-15-20 yards! The gooey material puffs up when it strikes a surface. It's aiming for the kids! It's trying to stop the paint ball attackers. But it keeps missing.

Guns go off. People shoot at the silver tube and the open portal around it. Can't tell if someone is in there firing the silver tube. Maybe the whole thing is robotic. Maybe the paint messed up the sensorium back at HQ?

An old pickup charges up Main Street, takes the exit, gets behind the road block. In its back two guys are hovering over a wooden box. They hustle the box over to Jacob Derry and his catapult.

Bee hive! A huge box of bees!

They muster the bee hive on to the catapult. Trigger! Erupt! Let loose! It's flying through the air –

– the bee hive lazily, sloppily arcs over the road block and the defenders, lands *splat!* on the silver tube at the top and front of the black vehicle. The bee hive is caught on the tube, hanging there. The luckiest catapult shot in the world! The gooey spray stopped immediately. Now a swarm hovers at the tube. Can the bees get in there? The black wedge backs up. It moves jerkily. Something's wrong: it's backing up, stopping, starting. It jolts with speed, swings to the side wildly, backing right towards the sheriff and chief of police vehicles. The police chief and the sheriff and the suit are out of their vehicles before it hits. They back away. The wedge vehicle stops.

There's a frozen moment so everybody can gasp. The wedge's rear end pushes into the law enforcement vehicles, whose metal sides collapse like butter.

The police chief and sheriff, standing nearby, hands on devices held to their faces, blabbing uncontrollably, start batting at their faces with their hands. Now they're flailing their hands in front of their faces and bodies. They make a mad dash into the fog and disappear.

The wedge seems to have shut down. No pushing. Is it dead? One for the bees! Bugs rule! Invertebrates forever! Back behind the tube area with the slot on top, something pops up. A roundish cover? Emergency exit? Some big bald pink guys climb out – three guys, three pinky baldies jump to the ground. They, too, are batting their hands in front of their faces and bodies. Are they naked? Just all over pink? Pink uniforms? Skin tight jumpers? They, too, make a mad dash to the fog bank and disappear.

Now we're all alone, except for bees and roadblock warriors. Silence reigns for a few counts. The holy buzz of the bees lingers, then slowly dissipates. Disbelief and wonder are the chosen emotions. Cheering starts! An eruption of cheers and yelps and screeches envelops us. People emerge from hiding places. More shouts and hurrahs! People are waving baseball bats and .22's over their heads. Glee is palpable. Jacob Derry has done it again! Our world needs heroes...so it seems. Luckily, no one was hurt...on this side. No stray bullet or ricochet bullet caught an unsuspecting bystander hid behind a dumpster. No foam goo caught a child in its soggy mess. Not even a bee sting.

People are heroes because they make choices. We

decided to stay. Our town! But me? I step out. I am the watcher, the gadfly, the conscience of the unaffiliated. Nyquil hero!

Groups are congratulating each other. The mayor and the councilman are shaking hands. Kids are running back and forth, between groups, between the road block and town. Three little boys in yellow shirts whiz past me chanting, "Our town, closed town, our town!" Teenage boys hug teenage girls. Hippies go into trances with arms held high. The victory dance is luscious, mandatory. Street people whoop with full throatiness. Looks like it's all Wooks. That brown-haired girl with the gray eyes stands up from between some cars in the road black. There might be thirty cars and pickups, and a broken bus in the road block. I haven't counted them. Gray-eyed girl is looking around, scanning. What does she see? What does she seek? She is touched, I can tell. I'm watching her so she knows and glances my way. Females can always tell when they are being worshipped. I see she's holding a large pistol. Our eyes meet and she seems contrite, but she may be unsure how to hold such a monster. Maybe she wants to shoot me for practice. Finally, she tucks it into the front of her jeans and scampers off. Little ones follow her. Jacob Derry and his catapult are surrounded with back thumpers. People start yelling out questions to the mayor and councilman:

"What was that?"

"That was no SWAT tank I ever seen!"

"What do we do when they come back?"

"Closed town!"

"We done it now, folks!"

"Holy bees! Saved our ass!"

Spectacle! The final hurrah of the last free people, Planet Earth. Too impetuous, too ambitious. No poem here. No ode to victory and necessary violence. Too quick to count a victory. The arrogance of our sanctimony tastes like a sickly-sweet cotton. The sun shines on a new world today. If we could see it – the sun, I mean. Our closed town has taken control of this day. We re-invent wonder. We re-invent modern. We re-invent liberty. We change categories now. We invent new expectations. We assume the new order of possibles.

A small helicopter thrusts out of the fog bank, coming right towards us. Total surprise! Superfast, the helicopter zips past the bee-in vehicles, including the wedge, and flies towards the roadblock. It's on us before we can react. It's only about 30 or 40 feet above the ground, so it has to watch for lines and telephone poles. It's small, maybe 10-15 feet long, compact metal body. All those super new alloys. Pure power drone! This thing has no windows, and its flashing rotors blur in motion. Some kind of drone – no one could fit in it.

Drone attack!

People rush back to cover. The roadblock crowd, too. But the helicopter has slowed and heads into town. It's over town now, right over the center of town above the post office. It's hovering. It starts circling up, moving higher, climbing. I watch, standing in the open, wondering if this is it. Our own big bang?

Counterattack?

Violence begets violence.

Unleash the dogs of war!

When Jacob Derry steps away from the catapult and his admirers, and he has his compound bow in his hands. And a man I don't know is helping him with a special arrow. For the arrow seems to be tied to wire that is wound around a large spool. Jacob Derry takes the arrow, adjusts it in place, insures the wire is clear, steps into it: fires the arrow.

The arrow cuts by the helicopter at an angle. Clean miss! It's not going to hit the helicopter. But the trailing wire is just so...and the true purpose of Jacob Derry's shot is clear: because the wire quickly entangles itself in the top whirling blade. The helicopter bucks, shakes, rotors screaming. It starts to fall. The thing, the drone helicopter, explodes. Rotor blades fly through the air and through the top floor of the Silver Queen Hotel. Meanwhile, the body of the helicopter beast simply collapses...plummets...straight down into the center of the road by the post office.

People scatter. No screams. No shooting. The helicopter pushed in, we pushed out. Case closed. Closed town. People are running over. The folks at the hotel must have had a surprise. Guns are held in the ready. The defenders at the road block look grim. What's next? More helicopters, but this time with machine guns? Who will decide? What are 'they' thinking?

Actions, this chill autumnal morning, have set things in motion?

Where's the damn convoy?

Hypothesis? Melioration is real. We can... we will take charge of our lives and community. Step 1: We organize the kids. Get them off the street. Not school per se – an Academy of Desire. For sure the basics are instilled, but then each child is encouraged to find his/her own motivation...and attention. They will arrange their own expectations. Step 2: We organize a Peace Militia. No weapons. Our truth must be our only shield to debate and prove our autonomy. Step 3: Share everything. No more looting. No more segregation. Beware enclaves.

We begin anew.

# THE SECOND DAY

## Josh Ryan

*some*
*times*
*everything*
*works*
*right*
*if I move*
*it'll shatter*

First dawn. As a scout. Don't open my eyes. Pressed tight. Slept some. Chilly night. Chilly now. Finally, fell asleep, I guess in the middle of the night. I kept going over what happened yesterday, what I would have done. Everybody was pretty freaked. But Frankie Lucien had already gotten the militia set up. Experience counted. Strength and health. Me and Marley picked as scouts first watch. All the way out here in the Apache Mountains, the rough slopes on this side of the tunnel. We are the defensive edge. The forward sensors. We know these slopes. On the north side where I am, rocky uplift, scraggly brush with hardly any green. On the south side, where Marley is, oaks and madrone and mesquite, not as steep. Couldn't have a better partner on the other side for like back up, than Marley. She's tough, good with a firearm. Ms. Lucien says everyone has to do his or her part. I could tell Dad was proud, but Mom not so proud as terrified. Mom worries. She's been unsure maybe about her choice, our choice. But me and Dad are certain we don't want consolidation. No way. Hate that word. The world falls apart and what? We run off and hide in rodent boxes?

Everything falls apart. The warrior knows which way it falls. I will have no fear. I will open my eyes and this will be real. Input. What do I see? Gray rocks. Mist, misty. This time of day, critters out, like ringtail cats – their curiosity scoots them in. One of my favorite animals. But Ms. Lucien says they're not good to eat. No ringtails this time. Probably too rocky up here for pigs. Pigs'll head back to their dens now. Raptors? Where are the raptors? Lost in the fog? Up so high in the sky, watching? I can't see squat in that sky. No vultures now. A few hawks – I've seen them! Eagles gone? Forever? Can you eat a vulture?

I make sure I know what I'm doing as dawn's early light touches my cave. Well, it's more an overhang. It's gray overcast – dim. October, Halloween weather, and I'm bundled up like a papoose. Fit perfect. Not really a cave, it's a rock slide rock pile, making a wedge of cover. Cuddled in this last moment, the moment before action. Next, I move, and everything happens.

Little camp stove heats up some water. Tea and oatmeal with honey and raisins. Mom would be proud. Clean up. Stow the gear. No ringtails, no badgers, no porcupines come calling. Who knows what's left?

Dad says humans are wrapped in plastic today, inside and out. In town, plastic bags, plastic wrap trashes everything, like it's the basic stuff, this universal material we couldn't do without. No plastic out here.

Warmth fills me. Take my weapon. Weapon ready: the twelve gauge, crack it, check it. Pocketful of shells. I have ten shells. Safety on. Dad taught me. Head out. Head down. Here I go.

Because something is bound to happen today. All the action yesterday was downtown. Missed it, training. So now it's logical they'll try from this end. At least no convoy showed up yesterday.

Not many can cover these slopes the way we scouts can. When I move, part mountain goat, part mutant ninja warrior. Scouts are loners. Keyed up. Ready for action. Trained by Warcraft and Halo. Hard knocks trained. End of the world trained. Power up. Wish I had a phone. Or one of those old fashion walkie-talkie dealios. Phones dead now. The whole point of a scout is to relay intel. Get our observations to whoever.

Avalanche this! Boots grip, stop a slide. Catch myself. Hold still, breathe, get it together.

The tunnel goes under the divide of the Apache Mountains. It's supposed to be the longest tunnel in Arizona. Above me, sheer rocky cliffs, rock formations like pink battleships thrusting from the Earth, in to the fog. Where Marley is, is woods. I like this side's dangerous steepness.

The fog's rolled back. Receded. Some. Move down, roll with it, fall into it, controlled crash, my natural gait. Geared to adjust, adapt to the terrain step by step, jump by jump. Close up: rock surfaces break down to handholds and foot jambs. Take it in, memorize a path. Pass a squirrel midden? No, pack rats. The Apaches would ram a stick right through a big fat pack rat, mouth to bung, then cook it over the fire. Nibble like corn on the cob, once the fur and yuck burned off. I place an X in my memory map.

I can see directly below me. I can see around me. The two-lane highway goes right down the middle of the canyon, until it hits the wall of fog. Surrounded by fog. Sky's low, ceiling presses in. The highway runs into the fog and bam! It's gone.

I always wanted to be a scout. I read that video games trigger those parts of the brain keyed to the particular physical action going on in the video. That means I am super trained. L33T! My eyes slide down the elevation, taking it in.

Stop.

Huddle. Find cover. Peek. They're coming! I can hear – engines?

Like a big ATV, a vehicle rolls out of the fog, cruising straight up the middle of the highway. One guy on top, riding it. He looks real white. Those his clothes? Maybe he's more a pink? Behind him and his weird vehicle, out of the fog, another vehicle emerges. This one is bigger, bulky, more like a truck with two big wheels. One big wheel on either aside – that's all it's got. Looks like a truck that's all front end. Kind of silvery. No windows. Slot in front.

Nearest signal fire is close. Pull away from my cover, skip low to the signal fire. Pull away the trash can cover and plastic bags. Get the lighter fluid sprayed, and dry matches light it up. The old cottonwood chunks, slightly damp, make plenty of white smoke. But they burn so fast. Pile it on! Plus, they're stinky. Will they see my smoke up at the tunnel? White smoke, white fog –

Marley! Race for the road. In and out of boulders, slide down scree of red pebbles. The ATV thing is too close. I brace, aim the twelve gauge straight up to the sky and blast it. The kick is hard, the sound deafening, resounding from the cliffs. The ATV stops.

Breathing hard, twelve gauge out in front, I reload, then I make it to the road, bunny hopping, but hang back. Where's Marley? The ATV is about twenty feet from me. The dood has a pinkish bald head. Pointy. Some kind of skin tight uniform? Big guy. Sitting atop a flat surface. Underneath, only one wheel on the thing, but it's a big wheel. The pink guy sits on his butt, legs out, kinda lazy looking. Ha! No feet, so he is wearing some kind of a suit. No steering wheel. No joy stick. Now the truck thing shows up, gets in close, pulls up to a stop behind Mr. Pink Head.

Marley comes crashing through the oaks on the other side of the highway. I hear her, then I see her. She stays in cover. She's got a .22. We stand up, eye each other, walk out, over to the middle of the road, facing Mr. Baldie. Marley's got her .22 on a strap around her shoulder. What are we doing? Wish I had a 'nade! What's that truck thing doing? What are we doing out here in the open? Marley's only fifteen, so I'm almost two years older than she is. What should we do? What's that guy doing over there? It's like he's staring, but not at us, he don't meet our eyes, his eyes look, see, but not what we see. He looks doofusy, stupid. Retarded, maybe. He doesn't have a weapon or anything. We're scouts. We're scouting. Marley's a good shot. Her dad was in Viet Nam. Her mom's a MILF. I know she was really into Grand Theft Auto training.

We're a fine couple of trollers! Standing out there in the middle of the road. When the ATV, or whatever the heck it is, starts inching forward, moving again. Real slow. It rolls towards us.

The ATV thing comes to a stop in front of us, and this big black thing, like a machine, maybe a weapon, slowly rises beside the guy, comes right out of the flat top by where he's sitting. He gets up to cradle it in his arms. He's on his knees now, and he's aiming this black thing at us. It's big! But it doesn't look like a machine gun. Then, Marley and me check on the signal fire. It's burned out already. We let him have it.

**Oscar Latta**

> *I remember reading about Wyatt Earp when I was a kid*
> *someone had to walk down main street in Dodge City*
> *of a Saturday night*
> *when the cowboys were in town*
> *and face them*

I never was much of a public speaker. Or leader. Up until recently, I never had to do much public speaking, so it didn't matter. But I'm the only police officer who decided to stay. Automatic respect, right? Or something close to it. Really, it seems to imply only expectations. Now I spend my time watching out for looters going after abandoned homes. I check on the firearms safety classes. I keep apart people at each other's throats, over water, or their toilets, or their lot boundaries.

I wouldn't have chosen this gig for a monkey on a rock. I don't have a wife or kids. But this is my home, darn it. Why should I consolidate? Give me a break! I didn't destroy the world. And, now, if it is the end of the world, I'd just as soon go out my own way. I decided fair and square. Is that selfish? Being a cop is not selfish. Father O'Meara made that clear to me. Father said police were altruists. Then the Church cleared out. Orders from the Vatican. Who knows? Consolidated Church? Sleeping up here in the tunnel is very altruistic, or else it's all the biggest fuck up ever.

There's gotta be fifty-sixty people in the tunnel. Bunches of kids, too. Pretty close to the middle of the tunnel is the main road block of old cars and pickups. Some boys have been draining their oil and gas, removing their batteries. Looking for anything we might be able to use. We'll have a common store for all that stuff to be used as needed by folks. People argued the road block should be at the end, on the town's side. Other claimed it'd be better at the entrance. Frankie Lucien and Michael Ramsey pushed for the middle. Frankie Lucien was some kind of commando from one of the defense contractors. Security all her life. Her push for the roadblock down the middle of the tunnel obviously won out. A few old cars were placed strategically from the middle to both ends. On account of that way nobody could make a charge straight to the roadblock. These extra vehicles could be rolled together if need be for cover, too, making barricades for security teams. Lucien said, 'a layered defense', whatever that means. We have experienced hunters and vets with weapons. I have to trust their common sense. Because we got all these kids, too, plus hippies. We got bb guns and paint ball guns, pellet rifles, spears, nun chucks. I'm afraid there's going to be an accident. A couple retired doctors and a few nurses stayed, but we don't have an operating room or much in the way of emergency medical supplies.

Should I deputize some men, especially the ones with experience and cool heads? We could make it official, have some authority. But what would that do to me? Make me the leader? What would Lucien say? Or the mayor for that matter. No, little point in deputies now. For right now, everything is informal like. Maybe too informal? Gotta move slow, take it as it comes. Let common sense rule? Is that what we want? It's going fast now –

On this side of the roadblock, which is the town's side, I slept in the back of the squad car. This end of the tunnel, all along the side, along the sidewalk there, is the tunnel camp. Cots and mats in a line. A mess with hot food and drinks. To go to the bathroom, you have to walk out of the tunnel. After some more coffee, weak as tea, and a pop tart offered by an old hippy lady, I take one last look at the camp, and I head for the other end. I have to start cutting around old cars, then push through the roadblock.

A kid yells to me, "Oscar, you think they'll try the tunnel today?"

"Ah, don't worry about it. We're set. Maybe they'll just leave us alone for now. We ain't looking for trouble that's for sure."

An older woman, all bundled up, carrying a trident shakes a finger at me. "One, they tried downtown yesterday; two, they'll try the tunnel today. They said a convoy was coming? We made our decision. No use freaking now."

"Thanks, Mrs. Ramirez, you're right."

Several men are helping out at the roadblock, parting out the wrecks. Tom Dillon has his big pick up there to load the parts and oil and gas, so he can get them out of here. Wonder how much gas they've collected. And when the gas runs out? Some of the men are hippies that look like those Rainbow People we used to get through Coltrane every winter. No judgment! Everybody helps. Everybody necessary. Bunch a hippies even showed up over the last weeks. Couldn't tell if they were Wooks or Ewoks – like the kids say. How they got through border security is anyone's guess. Lucien said, 'agentry', whatever that means. How could we keep them out? We still don't know what to do with them. They found squats fast enough. Lots of folks moving around, in to the vacant houses, a source of major squabbles. The closed town is an open town. Is it? Everybody is equal now. Pulling his own weight. Well, we'll see, as it's only the second day.

The tunnel entrance on the mountain side has a ton of folks with weapons. Groups of two and three cluster all over the place. Buddy system. Plenty of cover. Supplies stacked to the side. Young men and women are outside the tunnel, on the road's shoulders, back in the rocks and trees. Some sit and stand on boulders with binoculars. Can't see far with the fog. But it's pulled back. It starts way down the canyon, where it becomes solid. Fog covers the peaks. It could be heaven up there. We could be ghosts. Arizona doesn't get much fog.

Frankie Lucien and Michael Ramsey wave me over. Lucien is a middle-aged woman with short gray hair. Councilman Michael Ramsey looks like a used car salesman in camo. They each carry a rifle. 30/30 looks like, with scopes. Fucking deer rifles! And in regular hunting gear. Their eyes are red and glossy, like they've been up all night. Or else they're stoned immaculate, which I seriously doubt is real.

Michael Ramsey says, "You heard the latest from

downtown?"

I answer, "No, what? Is there a problem? Did something happen?"

"Not funny, Oscar. No, there's no problem. Nothing new, anyway."

I say, "Geez – don't I get a good morning?"

Ramsey is tense. Intense. "We lucked out yesterday. You know that. It just depends on how tough they want to play this. Maybe they'll just shrug their shoulders and go away. Leave us be. No convoys. That's what they said they'd do. That we'd be on our own. What we want."

Frankie Lucien chuckles. "Amen! So why we been up all night watching this picturesque mountain canyon?"

Michael Ramsey keeps looking at me, as though I should know what to say. But I don't. He goes on, "We missed the action yesterday. But sounds like the mayor and those guys had it covered. Still don't know what to think of that drone copter."

Lucien says, "Human terrain. Eye in the sky. Intel is all."

Ramsey says, "So maybe it's our turn up here. You know, the enemy likes to test the fortifications. Test the perimeter. Right, Frankie? Funny thing, about Coltrane, the way it's laid out. Big elbow in the Apaches. Natural fortifications. Not many ways in – "

"Or out!" Lucien gasps, spits, pffts it all together. "Enough blather!" She laughs. "It's Brigadoon, don't you know, and we're about to disappear for 100 years!"

I go, "Okay, okay, so no news from downtown?"

"Nothing," says Ramsey. He sighs and pulls his rifle forward. "Communications! We haven't heard a word. Cell phones." He grumbles, shakes. "We got a couple radios we might be able to figure. We got a couple good walkie-talkies. After that, I guess it's gonna be runners."

Lucien says loudly, "Smoke signals!"

"What? Where?" says Ramsey.

People start yelling, moving fast.

Two little kids come up to us. The little girl taps a finger into my leg. "We're runners! We can get messages anywhere you want. Back and forth. He's got a skateboard!"

I say, "Thanks, Sweetie! What's your name?"

"Amy. This is Roland."

Roland goes, "We're super fast!"

Lucien adds, "I like your spirit. Good for you." "I can't believe you said that." Ramsey is fidgeting and won't look at the kids. "Don't encourage them! Can't have kids in harm's way." He gasps. Then: "Smoke signal? Where?"

Lucien points with a long arm snapped out, fingers out, down towards the canyon.

We move out of the tunnel, straining to see, amble over to folks with binos.

An Ewok outside the tunnel with a spear made

from a broom handle runs up yelling, "Smoke! Smoke!"

Someone else yells, "Could be dust!"

Lucien grabs someone's binoculars and takes a look, says, "White smoke. For sure. From the scouts." He raises his voice: "Okay, this is it. Something's happening. You kids spread the word."

"I will," says Roland. "She better stay in case there's more."

I say, "You guys be careful. And if anything happens, get out of here fast as you can. Got that? I'm not kidding. Get away as fast as you can. Understand?"

The little faces are set, not scared at all. They look intense, too, as they nod to me. I don't know what to do or say to them. This can't be right. But it is −

"How old are you?" says Ramsey.

Gah, I don't want to know!

They both go, "Eight," and run off. Lucien, too, moves off fast, to join the guys on point.

Where are my kids? I'll never have kids now.

What have we done?

How could we have known it would come to this? Of course, we knew. We're human. We take responsibility. To see this out. To carry this through. Altruists! Nothing is ever as it's expected or wished to be. No utopian 'closed town' at the end of the world. Expectations, anticipations turn out shit. Relations, work, sex never as good as − we are so fallible. Humans − complex, contradictory, impossible. It unites us. That, and fear of phonies.

Michael Ramsey says, "Now what? Now what?" He's glancing all over the place, checking out people taking positions. He does a fast, kind of jumping in place. He grips his rifle and I can see how white his knuckles are.

We're all like that. But we decided. We chose. Which turns out to basically mean, deciding to defend our decision. We're all the same now. No fakes. No phonies. They would have left by now. Still, we got nerves, we worry. We been so spoiled by pleasantries.

Put my arm around Ramsey's shoulders. "Let's get into cover. See what's happening."

A guy in the rocks outside the tunnel pops up and waves. "Gunfire! I heard a blast. Like a shot gun. Now more, for sure."

Ramsey and I get behind a green panel truck that was built during the Kennedy administration. I draw my weapon. Hands on the hood, we watch the road.

A few hectic minutes later, here it comes. The oddest looking truck comes into view, rolling right up the middle of the highway. It's fat. And like all front. Tall, silvery, but no windshield. Across its front, a long slot. Big squat thing.

Ramsey says, "Looks like that thing that rammed the bus yesterday. I saw a film, someone filmed it with their phone."

I shake my head. "That's all those damn smart phones are good for now. Hell with that! This thing looks serious! Thought the thing yesterday was black. All black.

Thought that's what I heard. I don't know. That's what I heard." I'm rambling.

Ramsey squeaks, "What do we do? What do we do?"

Lucien, across the way, calls. "We see what it does."

"If it tries to enter the tunnel?" somebody shouts.

"Let's see what happens," Lucien confides.

Suddenly, Lucien's voice bellows through the tunnel: "Don't fire until you see the eyes of their whites! Everyone chill! Take a breath."

The truck, or whatever it is, slows as it gets closer. Can't tell if anyone is on board. It doesn't look like any of the SWAT vehicles I've checked out in police journals. It stops about thirty feet from us.

There's a sharp popping sound and three white discs shoot out of the slot in front.

Ramsey and I duck. Nothing happens. No explosions.

I peek over the hood at the discs, which are still airborne, but slow, like white dinner plates, sailing in to the tunnel, about twenty feet off the ground. Not going very fast. They're floating in. Are they are spinning?

A man's voice cries, "Wadda we do? Wadda we do?"

Ramsey and I huddle behind our panel truck watching the three discs.

Lucien comes out of her hiding place and struts right over to below a disc. She follows it, sticking to it, gets beneath it. She yanks up her rifle, straight up, braces herself, and fires at the disc. The disc bursts. No explosion. No puff of deadly gas. Pieces everywhere. Lucien bends around, eyeing the pieces. She kicks at them.

Lucien straightens, hollers, "Take them out!"

Gun blasts pound through the tunnel. Deafening booms echo. The other two discs are shattered, bits to the ground.

"Be careful! Be careful!" Ramsey yells. "Make sure you know where you're aiming!"

From the front, a man calls, "More!"

The truck pops out more discs, in threes. Rows of threes are floating in to the tunnel. Slowly, the discs fly or float in – they seem uncertain.

I screech, "Don't shoot each other! Watch what you're doing!"

Frankie Lucien yells, "It's like skeet practice!"

Gun blasts take over. Discs get knocked down. The truck quits popping them out and begins backing away from the tunnel, down the mountain. Ten groups of three. The guys up front are cheering.

Lucien and I start following after the discs, the ones no one has managed to hit. They are a tricky shot unless you're pretty close and right under them. We're trotting along, yelling out 'careful', and 'don't shoot me', when Bob Pauley, standing up in the back of a pickup, a great big man, hoists like an open dog cage straight up to a passing disc. He nails it, swinging the cage to the side fast to catch the disc and hold it. He plops the cage to the back of the pickup, quickly swings its door shut. Closed! He bellows, "Got one! Caught the motherfucker!" He starts tying it down to the back of the truck.

It's at the top of the cage, hovering there. No sound. No movement. Hovering there inside the dog cage.

Bob Pauley jumps in place, big belly rolling with it, as is the whole pickup. "See what makes this thing tick. We'll cut it up!"

Lucien studies the disc in the cage. "They're delicate. Breakable. On purpose? No fuss. No bomb. What are they for?"

"Surveillance?" I suggest.

Lucien shrugs. Other people are crowding in to see the disc.

Gun shots taper off.

Lucien backs away. "Any getting through?" She takes in my worried look and goes, "We'd better make sure. And we gotta let downtown know."

**Roland Banks**

> *together*
> *me and the kids*
> *we*
> *so fast*

I can climb on top of this pickup if I want to. Get all the way up to the tip top of the cab. And I got a towel and my skateboard.

Here comes one! One of them disc things. Too far over. Can't get that one. An old guy with a t-shirt that reads 'AC/DC' blasts it to smithereens with a shot gun. Pieces fly, little pieces fall to the ground like from a smashed toy.

Another one coming –

This one is close. I can be still.

I toss my towel at the exact right moment and it goes over the disc and I grab the other end of the towel and whoa! I'm flying! It's carrying me along, skateboard clutched between my knees. That old guy with the t-shirt is watching with a big fat open mouth now. Hope he doesn't shoot me.

"Don't shoot me!"

We float down the tunnel.

A kid yells, "You're gonna be in trouble!"

Parents and teenagers are yelling, "Jump!" "Just jump!" "Let go!" But they're way too busy to stop me.

I don't want to let go. I'm floating out of the tunnel now and the disc is over my head, and I'm clinging to the towel. We drop down lower, so I get my skateboard out and under me.

Awesome! The disc is flying me down the road on my skateboard.

Daisy will be so glad I got one.

**Daisy Piper**

> *kids' house*
> *we choose this way*
> *this is the way we do it*
> *yesterday, parents seemed accepting of the fact*
> *we are here to stay*

I get ready to leave at first light, stepping around and over kids lined up in sleeping bags, I see Tenny through the window, snooping around out front.

Kids glance up at me.

I say, "I'm gonna go see what's going on. What could happen today, right? Ready for anything."

Outside, Tenny smirks at me that way boys do when they have other things on their one track minds.

Tenny goes, "That your pistol?" He points lazily with a flip of a finger towards the pistol stuck in the front of my jeans. He seems weird, out of it, fidgety. He keeps looking away from me, not wanting to catch my eyes.

I go, "You're stoned."

"Bunch of kids our own age has a house up on Star Avenue."

"Yeah, heard about it."

"It's koolio. Know what I mean?"

"You guys smoking dope and drinking all night?"

He giggles. "You should come by." He kinda falls into me, his arms going around me, and he's so cute and spacey stoned that it takes me a second before I pull it together to slam him into the wall of the house. His face gets red.

I go, "What are you doing?"

"Daisy, don't be a bitch."

"What are you guys gonna do when the pot runs out?"

He makes another grab at me. I'm close, so my knee easily goes right into his crotch. He grunts, folds over.

"Don't puke on my boots."

"What are you doing?" he pants out in little bursts. "Why you hanging out with these little kids?"

"Don't be an ass. If you don't know – "

"Then," his breath coming back, he straightens and says, "what's wrong with partying at the end of the world? One more time. For old time's sake."

"Nothing, I guess."

Clay Mason comes out of the outhouse across the way. He swaggers over like he owns the place. He's got the work pants and white t-shirt on. Big boots. Maybe he thinks me and Tenny are hooking up, standing this way, so close, up against the house.

He mumbles, "I'm going up town, see what's

what."

Tenny says, "Best show in town! Get there early for a good seat!"

Clay says, "You're being ironic."

I go, "Clay, I'm coming, too. I was just getting ready to go when Tenny showed up. He's pulled an all-nighter. Security detail. Gotta keep a handle on the pink elephants and talking toasters."

Tenny is almost contrite. "Very funny. Toasters don't work anymore. 'Less, maybe, your parents had a solar powered one. Ha! That would be funny."

Clay mumbles, "What's wrong with him?"

I go, "Stoned out of his gourd. You know how kids are today."

Tenny says, "You're the ones being ironic. You, two, are so ironic, it's all the way back to un-ironic! Besides, what can you do with a toaster at the end of the world?"

Clay and I head out. Tenny watches us leave. Clay gives him the bug eye. My big gun in my pants is pressing against my mons. I am trying to figure how to walk with it. My parents wouldn't like the gun. They have rules. We agreed.

They are cowed. They are into isolating themselves from controversy. No resistance, they say. Their generation – everybody a Buddhist. I'm being mean. They are my parental units. I say to them, what about the long run? They say, trust in human creativity. I say, isn't that what got us in to this mess? They are low down, bleak. I refuse that way. Staying put at the house with hidden supplies in the crawl spaces is not for me. No meetings for them. No weapons either. I worry about them. I'll have to check in on them. I promised. Cabin fever is going to squelch them. Mom can only read the Jane Austen books so many times. Plus, they will want to come and see me. I predict it.

Ewoks and Wookies join us in the dawn parade to downtown. Civilians, too. Clay explains how some of those Wooks are new – showed up at the last minute. Handmade weapons galore: simple clubs or shafts or spears, made from brooms, shovels, branches, rebar. The paint ball crew in yellow t-shirts skitters past. They skip and jostle, making weird popping noises. Everyone wears jackets or sweat shirts. Some security guys with rifles are by the steps to City Park. The guys Frankie Lucien supposedly trained. Their rifles are behind their backs, slung over their shoulders. They look official. Playing it up. This one guy worked for the mechanic my parents took their old Toyota to. Now he's all serious with his arms folded in front of himself all strict. He's a big man, buff. Maybe he could teach me to use the pistol. He catches my eye. That's a leer if I ever saw one –

Downtown looks like an old time movie. Like a silent film. Quiet so far. Beyond the roadblock, looks like the fog is at the same place it was yesterday. Overcast. Gray as the gray kitty Ms. Kell fed at the high school and called William Butler. The police car and the sheriff's car and the black wedge thing are gone.

People are wading around, through the vibes. They look heavied out. Maybe everyone's stoned like Tenny and his crowd. The little helicopter has been cleaned up. There must be a hundred people by the post office in the center of town. Up front, standing on the bench in front of the post office, Mayor John John. It starts to get noisy.

"I wonder if he's got an item?" goes Clay.

Is he making fun? Oh, he's trying to make a joke, a private joke between him and me.

"Clay!"

He goes on: "They'll try grunt force this time. The second time. They always do. Military strategy is so predictable. They were just fooling yesterday. Feeling us out. What are we gonna do if they come in with tanks? Tank traps! We dig tank traps like the resistance in Poland in World War Two. Do you know how to make a Molotov cocktail?"

"I don't drink."

"Very funny."

"Everybody knows how to make a Molotov cocktail. Hey, there's Ms. Kell! Ms. Kell! I haven't seen her since we closed down."

"She didn't see you. She looked like she was on a mission."

"I like Ms. Kell. She showed us those paintings of William Blake."

"'Tiger, tiger burning bright!'"

Mayor John John Placido yells, "Big meeting today. Later, in City Park. Okay? See if we can get the whole town over there. Lots of things to discuss, to decide. So spread the word!"

Someone blurts, "Had enough meetings!"

Another voice goes, "What if they come in this

morning with tanks?"

"Told you," says Clay. I punch him in the stomach.

Mayor John John says, "Now why would they do that? Come on, people. No one knows what's going to happen. People, stay vigilant. Be ready for anything. We are adaptable, aren't we? Isn't that why we decided to stay? We're in this together. We decided."

That old hippy who thinks he's John the Baptist tries to step up on the bench next to the mayor, but the mayor won't let him. His funny robes are fluttering. The mayor seems to be making faces at him.

Clay goes, "That's Oscar Wargo. My PUs liked to make fun of him. Remember when he was trying to change the curriculum at school?"

"Why'd your parents leave? I mean, were they were old hippies, too?"

"No resistance," says Clay and shrugs. "I don't know if they really were hippies. They just got real, real sad. Couldn't take it anymore, all the worry."

The way Clay's standing by me, I can see the blade strapped to his side. "That's a big knife."

"My dad's hunting knife. But he quit hunting a long time ago. I guess I shouldn't make fun. Your PUs stayed? They're still here? I think mine gave up. But I don't know. That's a big pistol you have."

"I don't know how to use it."

"I'll teach you."

"Should we trade for now?" And so we do.

Oscar Wargo hops a bit as he babbles about non-violence and being led by the nose to utter destruction. Mayor John John has retained his perch, his short round body bobbing to keep up with the robes fluttering Wargo. It looks like a bit – from a comedy show. People start yelling for them to cut it out. They're telling Wargo to pipe down. Others blab about change and choice. A voice cries out about convoys.

Mayor John John says in a commanding voice that stops Wargo, "We got it covered! We're in communication with the tunnel. So far, so good. We're doing this thing. We're taking care of business."

Now he's in full speech mode: "People, we can do this. We got teams working in water collection and storage. You all been catching water. We can do this. We got teams to check out the empty houses for supplies. No more random looting. We're on top of stuff. We got the latrine situation under control. We're doing it. Spread the word about the big meeting today. So far, so good!"

From beyond the fog where the highway disappears, two loud booms! A gasp inhales from the crowd. Everybody searches the fog. The mayor jumps down from the bench. Didi sneaks through the crowd and gets close to me to take my hand. We follow Clay, weaving through the people, then behind the convention center towards the vehicles in the roadblock.

Up on the highway, right there at the edge of the weird fog: two white tubes emerge. Slide right in. More *extrude* in. Long black tubes push from the fog. They look like tunnels? As tall as a person, the open ends face us. All dark in there. Can't see a thing. What are they? Like giant pipes suddenly plopped in!

Clay says, "Get ready to run!"

I go, "To what?"

Didi pipes in: "Away from the bads!"

Kids, Wooks, Ewoks, PUs get situated. Kids zigzag hunched over through the cars and trucks of the roadblock. People are up in the rocks on the other side of the highway. Lots of people back away. Everybody's got eyes on the tubes sticking out of the fog. They look angry empty. I hope Ms. Kell is taking cover. She seemed out of it. Whatever that means, when everybody's out of it. Who is not out of it now? We have the greatest excuse of all time, for all types of weird ass behavior. And no one could complain or point a finger.

"Here they come!" comes the cry.

I don't see – like echoes, others join in with loud voices to warn. I can see –

Clay keeps going into the road block. He's bent over, moving through the vehicles and people like a mongoose.

Didi says, "Where's he going?"

Didi and I watch pink bald men march from the tunnels one by one. They've got those skin tight leotards on? They're pink gymnasts! They fan out after leaving the tunnels, walking into town. Taking their time. No rush. Plodding. They have the emptiest faces. Maybe they're not wearing jumpers at all. Maybe they're naked and their skin is it. So ghosts? Bald. Heads a little pointed maybe. No eyebrows. They all look the same! They have eyes, ears, noses, mouths. No nipples. No junk –

Me and Didi back off.

The way the canyon opens up to the highway, and

way to my left, the north side is called Lonesome Hill and is a steep hillside of ramshackle houses a good sneeze could tumble into the bypass. Some of the baldy pinkies are fanning out that way. They're spreading out in all directions, slipping in to town. They're coming in! They want in. Here they come. If they go for those houses on the hillside –

I tell Didi to stay here and keep down. She nods grimly. I head out, straight across the open road, past the old cop shop, and take the steps up Lonesome Hill two at a time. The steps are crumbling. Before long, I have an overview of the pinkies almost at the roadblock. Others are scattering. One is coming this way.

That old hippy in robes walks through the roadblock, hands held high. He approaches the nearest pinkies. Is he welcoming them? He seems to be talking. I can't hear. But I imagine it's all about peace and non-violence. The first pinks he reaches, without hesitation grab him and start pulling at him. The old hippy screams. They're pulling too hard! Anybody can see that. They pull off his arm. They're beating him with his own arm. Blood's spurting! Oscar Wargo screams!

Sounds like a hundred guns go off at once. Most of the pinkies are hit and topple. Shouts and screams. Gunshots all over. The roadblock lets loose. When a pinky takes a bullet, it falls to the ground and leaks out clear, thick stuff over a yucky mound of skin.

I rush up to the first house, a decrepit wooden house, the Keckler's place. Old folks. Not really sure they're even here. I call out. No answer. Place looks empty. Did they decide to stay? I swing back to check what's happening. Below me, a pinky's tearing up the rocky hillside – so fast! Right towards me! Not bothering with the steps. When he's at my level, his eyes find mine for the first time. He...it gurgles.

There's nothing in those eyes! Empty eyes. Monster eyes. Drone. Cyborg. Clone. Robot. This awful thing –

– comes at me with mouth wide open. Nasty gaping lamprey dealio. I stick that big hunting knife of Clay's dad's right into its smooth chest without nipples. The blade goes right in, so I pull down with all my might. The thing turns inside out. No innards! Just splashes of gooey yuck. Clear viscous stuff. The thing falls, caves in to a squishy mess.

Gunshots!

# The Third Day

**Oscar Latta**

> *murder in Art Town*
> *pulled apart*
> *drawn and quartered*
> *for what*
> *by who*
> Who decides this crazy weather?
> *first murder in Coltrane*
> *long as I can remember*
> *but no whodunit*
> I've never seen fog like this.

Everybody's going, maybe it's not fog. Can we test it? Some kind of chemical analysis? Now's not the time to rely on science.

> *I've never seen god like this.*

I'm at the cop shop. Might as well. It's got symbol value.

The weather makes folks anxious. And they be one

ornery group – pissed off, hustling. Those who stayed! Last couple days exploded shrapnel in their heads. My neighbors! Mi gente. No one's too worried right now about when their next shower might be. Or bath. Nobody sleeps much I get the feeling. I sure don't.

Gotta figure what to do with the old hippy...in monk robes. Mr. Robes? What are we gonna do with the remains of Oscar Wargo?

What are those things?

*I've never seen death like this.*

Cremation or burial? Who decides?

Cremated those things that's for sure. What was left of them. A detail of men from security and supply raked up the mess on the highway into a great big squishy pile. Torched it. Bonfire right there in the middle of the highway. Greasy, smelly fire. One of the retired docs, some folks with science backgrounds, said the stuff was organic. Not like organic food, but organic as in made of biological stuff. No one can figure why the things had no navels or nipples. I guess that's why we call them things. Most are calling them Pinkies or Baldies.

The tubes disappeared. Not there this morning. Just vanished.

No one went to check on the tunnels. Tubes? Whatever they were. I mean, after. I sure didn't. By the time I got back from the divide, and our disc situation, it was over. I heard the last of the shooting as I drove in.

No one wants to go into the fog. What's back there? I'm not doing it.

What for? We made our decision and it was

ratified. Case closed. Nothing to negotiate. We don't have any way to communicate with them, out there. No convoy though. We can't negotiate with things or monsters. Negotiate what? We're not going anywhere.

After what went down yesterday, it's clear there is some serious shit happening beyond the fog. End of the world stuff we didn't imagine. The doc, Dr. Stevenson says they're organic, but not actually human. Dr. Stevenson managed to look over some of the bodies before they squished. He said, he'd never seen anything like it. He said they had no fingerprints. They had flaps or plugs in the heels of their feet. But no toes. He wondered if maybe they were inflated, filled, or loaded, from there?

Now folks are glad we blocked the road. What were those things?

Dr. Stevenson said they weren't clones or animated dead people. They had no brains. He said they had to be some kind of disposable soldier that was made.

He's checking out the captured disc now from the tunnel. Took it home with him last night.

What am I doing at the cop shop? Last vestige of legal authority! What does legal mean now? I can't mess this up. I can't let these people down. I have to start deputizing men. Get security tuned up no matter what Frankie Lucien says. Can't let him just take over. Like a done deal. Diversify! Ha! Multiple leaders, so multiple ways. We have to make sure people don't turn on each other. Watch where they aim all these weapons. We have to find strength in each other. We have to trust each other.

I couldn't sleep, came down early, opened up. Empty office. Sitting at my desk with my feet up on it.

Actually, it was the Chief's desk, but I don't think he would mind. Past dawn, so enough light I can see out the front window, folks coming downtown, then heading up the Gulch to City Park. Time to go! I check my weapon. I lock up the cop shop and join the parade up the canyon. People aren't talking. No shout outs 'hello' or 'morning.'

Where are we going to stick Oscar? We'll need a cemetery. That was something no one thought of before –

At City Park, people fill up the cement bleachers on the side. Still quiet, subdued. They walk slowly, carefully, in small groups. Some families. Some alliances brought on by necessity, usually neighbors. Others form a loose, buzzy crowd in front of the clamshell stage. Looks like a good turnout. Folks from way up the canyon are showing too. The divide and the tunnel are secure. Those folks from that part of town need to be here. We have contact with the tunnel via walkie-talkie but reception is poor. The tunnel reports no disturbance this morning. Scouts are good.

A couple men, a couple women are walking over to the side of the clamshell now, where the steps to the stage are. I sigh, go around to the steps. I join them on stage. We're the leaders I guess. Diversify!

Frankie Lucien is here, the mayor, both council members. Mrs. Gorey, the retired nurse, stands at the back of the stage with her arms folded in front of her. Margaret Pitka from the Episcopal Church is on the other end of the clamshell from where I stand. She's shuffling a handful of papers? Tom Dillon rushes towards the clamshell, pushing his way through folks. He's got a bullhorn. I take it from him and he says, "Good batteries!" I thank him and hand it to the mayor.

Mayor Placido takes it, starts off the town meeting

without it, "Okay, folks, looks like we got a good representation of town here. Let's figure how we're gonna do this."

Voices rise all at once, yelling right away, from close up before us, also from across the way in the bleachers. Big voices! Demanding, desperate voices. Lots of shouts about 'what were those things.' Baldies! Pinkies! Then shouts about the sphere, the wedge, the drone, the discs. We got it covered! Wails about the death of Wargo, whether they liked him or not. Or even talked to the SOB. His death brings a level of seriousness to town we've only pretended.

Now plans and strategies suggested with extra decibels. Should I take notes? Is anyone writing this down? Talk about traps, generators, missing people. Looters! 'Shoot the looters!' Then, more questions about the discs. People jostle forward to get up close to the clamshell. Some pushing and shoving. This is where I come in. Kids dart in and out of the clamoring adults. Little guys, then some teens. Mainly, I think people are yelling about those things from yesterday. A fight breaks out about 'extra batteries.'

A woman's voice cries, "Who's got cough syrup?"

Lucien's security boys break up the fight before anyone gets hurt. I don't have to lift a finger or raise my voice. Not too many guns visible. Hippies wield homemade spears and staffs. Lots of sticks, pikes, clubs. Yes, this is how we are in the future, gathering loudly, speaking at once, carrying a big stick.

"Settle down," says the mayor in the bullhorn. His voice comes out, metallic, scratchy, but carrying over the others.'

Boos ring out!

"Oh, come on," continues the mayor. "Let's get going on this. Then we can take questions. Okay? But in an orderly manner. We'll take turns."

Margaret Pitka says loudly, "We could have a sign-up sheet?"

A teacher from the high school, Mrs. Kell, makes her way to the front of the crowd before the clamshell. I don't know her well, but now she seems stiff, walking funny. Sick? Or just freaking? Is there a difference? She's in workout clothes. Yoga pants? Maybe she doesn't have any jeans and sweat shirts, the fairly standard uniform. She turns away from us on stage to face the crowd, and yells, "I don't think that's fog!"

"What is it?" "What is it?" over and over, comes back to her.

Mayor Placido interrupts, gets back to basics, "Okay, this is what we got. We got four committees, Security, Supply, Health, and Water. Each committee has a leader and anybody can help out in any committee. Right? That's what we agreed to. So we got Frankie Lucien as Security. Councilmen Ramsey and Martinez in charge of Supply, with Ramsey focusing on the upper canyon and Martinez down here. Mrs. Gorey is heading up Health, and she's got Dr. Wasson and Dr. Stevenson helping her. Tom Dillon's working on Water. We're moving all leadership and command activities to the convention center. Every committee will have its own office. And every day these folks will meet and figure what the day's duties are. If you want to help, and if you have any experience in a particular area, you should volunteer. Get your names in. Sign up."

A high school girl, with brown hair and gray eyes, up front, presses to the edge of the stage. She's tough looking – strong girl. She calls out to the mayor, "We need a kids' committee!"

Kids start cheering.

Mrs. Kell has made her way onto stage. She marches up to the mayor, gives him a stern look, her hand extended in front of her. He hands her the bullhorn.

Mrs. Kell is a nice-looking woman, maybe in her 30s, maybe 40. I've never known her to be so fierce looking. She looks really pissed off. She takes the bullhorn and brings it to her mouth. The opposite arm not holding the bullhorn is held straight up, forefinger pointing at the sky. "People," she calls in the amplification, slightly echoey, slightly distorted, "I think the main thing on everyone's mind is what happened yesterday. What were those things? Those things that ripped Oscar Wargo apart yesterday were not human. They came out of this fog. The police chief and the sheriff came out of the fog, then ran back in to it. The same fog that's here right now, and that doesn't seem to dissipate. So we know something's going on out there. But what if it's not fog? Has something drastic happened out there since we closed town? I know it's only been a couple days, but what's going on out there? In the last couple days, has the world changed? Is it war? Is it just the regular crazy weather meltdown of climate change?" She pauses. People listen intently. "Maybe – are we still on Earth? Have we been kidnapped and moved, and don't even know it?"

Frank Stanley is up on stage now. And he pulls the bullhorn from Mrs. Kell, and she pulls back a fist to let him have it. The mayor slaps at his big thighs nervously, jostling around on stage by them, like a referee, chiding, 'no, no, no.'

Frank Stanley lets blast, "Great, super list of choices there, lady! Hey, I just want to say, a lot of us prefer neighborhood organizations rather than this sorta taken for granted central command idea. Hey, I know, you and the fog, it's a good point. But. Each neighborhood, High Road, Mule Canyon, Zacatecas, the Gulch, Quality Hill, what have you, each takes care of its own stuff. Its own needs. Neighborhood emergency centers are better than having to wait for help from downtown. Especially when time is of the essence. Why not neighborhood centers that elect their own representatives, then those reps from all the neighborhoods can meet together up here – "

Michael Ramsey yells, "Fred, you're way out of line – we already voted on this. We decided. You know that. You need to go back down there and wait your turn to talk after the mayor."

Fred Stanley goes, "You let her talk."

Mrs. Kell leaves the stage. Her lips are pressed together so tight they're a thin pink line. I need to get Lucien to station a few security guys at the steps to control access. But the mayor and Ramsey are arguing over the bullhorn with Fred Stanley. Frankie Lucien joins in, makes a grab for the bullhorn –

"Look!" she cries. "Look, look! Above us!"

"They're coming!" is the response from the crowd.

Boy – wish I never heard that sentence again!

People shout, pointing straight above us. Now the decibels run ragged, as it becomes a full blown screeching match. Bleacher folks stand and point, too. They start the awkward, steep step downward get away. The crowd's moving!

I can't see because of the angle of the clamshell, so hop down from the stage and move off a ways for a better angle. My head aims straight up into the gray overcast sky.

Directly overhead, but way high up, a shape. Not a plane or a helicopter. Doesn't look round either, like a balloon. But it's definitely descending. Getting bigger. Long, triangular shape. Delta wing shape. But not that big. The bottom of the sinking object is smooth and gray.

A few people have binoculars. Others cluster around them demanding to know what it is. But the binoculars don't seem to help much. No one can tell exactly what the descending object is. People head out. Frankie Lucien consults with her security people. Pistols and rifles are drawn and brought around. Kids popping everywhere. The girl with gray eyes is giving them orders?

Mayor Placido has the bullhorn again and pleads: "Easy, easy. Take it easy now! Security's all over this. But we're still gathering info, so maybe it's best to go to your homes, wait to see what's up. When we can figure what we got here."

The people from the bleachers mix right into the main crowd getting away. People stream out of the park entrances, but getting bottle necked. There's only so many ways out of the park. Pushing, angry words, curses start up.

I keep my hand on my weapon and move through the crowd near the stage trying to reassure folks. Lucien's people do a good job breaking up the knots of people that are slowing folks down. Rifle barrels over their shoulders, security is making sure people leave. Lucien and a couple of her guys huddle up by some ornamental trees in the park's corner by playground equipment. I got one eye on them, one eye on the crowd, a third eye scanning up high. No idea what this thing is. But it's low enough now to see a little more clearly that it's some kind of flying craft. I mean, it's not falling down on us like a missile.

It's about a hundred feet above us. Right over City Park. Maybe twenty feet long. Sharp 'front' like a prow. Triangular. Can't see much on top or its sides because of the way it's descending. Can't tell how big it really is.

**Daisy Piper**

> *death, murder*
> *gross murder*
> *I think the murder of Mr. Wargo*
> *has knocked us one*

So many of us have pinkybaldy blood on our hands. I keep seeing the way my knife went in to the chest of the thing. I keep remembering how it felt pulling the blade down, like cutting a watermelon. The way the ooze gurgled out. I don't want to get used to that. Ever. No matter what a pinky is. Now this –

Over by the playground equipment, kids hide. As if the plastic slide and jungle gym is a good place to hide. It is. Kids can melt into the background. Like desert animals camouflage. Ms. Lucien's back there with two of her men. Whatever the thing is, descending on the park, it can't be scrutinizing playground equipment. Unless they want the kids? No point in speculating: we don't know who or what this is. You gotta see the deets to figure it out.

We gotta be ready for anything. Think on our feet. Shift, adjust, adapt. Isn't that what people do? Isn't that what a leader does?

People keep leaving the park. Wooks. Ewoks. PU's with families. They're afraid. I stick with the kids. I go over, sit in a swing. Push back, feet straight out in front of me. Let go –

The long triangle suddenly tilts or angles so we can see its top side. It's got like a clear dome curving over the top. Now it's so close, we can see in it.

Didi skips over to me and tugs at my hand. She's got a Smurf sweat shirt on. Her nose is a little runny and she swipes it. Does she want a turn on the swing? She sings, "'Meet George Jetson!'"

"Wha – "

"Looks like George Jetson's car!"

"Didi, I got four things you can do at once."

"I can do six impossible tings." She holds up her hands, fingers extended for six. She loves me reading *Alice* at night.

"Tell all the kids here to keep down. That's one. Is Roland around? Get him to go up to the tunnel at the divide. He can take his skateboard. To tell the people up there what's going on."

"What's going on?'

"Just tell him to say a space car is over City Park. That's two. Then I want you to get another kid over to our house to tell those guys what's going on."

"That's only three, Daisy. I need a weapon."

"Number four is you come back and tell me when you got it all done. Okay? I'll get you a stick. Like make you something from a broom handle. Okay?" I get off the swing, poke a finger in to Didi's tummy.

"I don't want a stick!" She looks stubborn. She folds her arms in front of her, then flashes a smirk and takes off running.

The floaty/flying thing is low enough now and angled so inside the dome is plain as day: there they are: two, or is it three, yes, it's three ugly people sitting on some kind of sofa in the clear dome. Can't see a lot of detail. The floaty flyer bobs about so changing the angle but allowing glimpses. The ugly people are not baldies! They look like gnarly old skinny people, dressed in white, but I can only see the top halves of them. They sure aren't pinkies. What makes them so ugly is their exposed flesh, like their hands and necks and faces, are covered in like balls. Look like puffballs. Maybe they're tumors. Puffballs tied to white ratty frames, of thin, thin skeletons. They're moving! They look out, glance down at us, scanning around, checking us out. They seem excited, the way they bend their heads and point at us with those bumpy arms and hands. Tumors or pustules. Just gross. Can't really tell what they're doing, can't see anything else under the dome. No controls or steering wheel. The smooth surfaces of the gray outside show no protruding barrels. No missiles. No exhaust tubes. No weapons I can see. But you never know.

A woman screams!

What's up? Where is she? She needs help! I can't see her.

Didi gets under the slide with the little ones. Other kids take off. Clay's over by the stage. He crouches by it with that pistol in his hand. Tenny and some of the other high school kids climb up the bleachers like monkeys. They hoot and giggle. Maybe they can get a better view from up there. Tenny's got his baseball bat. He was a star hitter at one point. One of the other guys, I think it's Sam Bean, has a .22.

Why is that woman screaming? I still can't find her. People freaking!

Cut away from the playground equipment and hunch in by the stairs to the stage at the side. Cover. Get a better view. Most of the people have cleared out. Security types have taken the meager cover afforded at the park. They're in the corners, behind benches or trees. Clay stays where he is, right out in the open, in front of the stage. Frankie Lucien gives out orders from her new position over by the picnic tables in the ramada.

BOOM! A beam of pink light shines down from the floaty and hits Clay. It totally covers him.

"Clay! Run!"

I almost attack, launch myself straight to him, but, like the Ninja Geisha I am, I flatten out again the wall, and reach for my knife. What? I'm going to throw it at the thing? No!

Clay!

The pink beam shuts off. Clay looks the same. He's

blinking, turns to me. Doesn't look hurt at all.

I call out, "You okay?"

"Think so. That was weird."

Frankie Lucien hurries to Clay. Three of her men are behind her, all with rifles. Ms. Lucien says, "You hit? You hit? You okay?"

Clay says, "No, I'm okay. Didn't feel a thing."

One of Lucien's men points at the floaty above us and goes, "Check it out!"

It's about twenty feet above us so when it slightly dips to either side we can see right in. And right now, under the dome, and before the three uglies covered in boils, for sure I can see three, all with tumors, and there's a pink shimmering outline of Clay in front of them. But mini. The uglies have these long straws in their hands, one end in their gross mouths, and the other end in the shimmery pink of the Clay image.

Cackling replaces the screaming woman. Peeps watching from hidey holes, peeps freaking. Frankie Lucien kinda hugs Clay away from the stage, making for the picnic tables. Bunch of Ewoks runs up the steps from the street and into the park screeching. They get right under the floaty. They have sticks and spears and slings and brooms, and they taunt the uglies. They sing! Maybe, they're trying to communicate with them? Ms. Kell strides up from the back of the park. She must have been hiding. I'm still scrunched down by the side of the stage. The pink light shoots down again. This time it takes over Ms. Kell, envelops her. She's covered in pink light. Her arms shoot out. Her mouth is open. She looks creepy covered in pink glow. Silent scream!

Security guys yell for everyone to get back. Ewoks start throwing their sticks at the thing.

The pink light goes off.

This is as weird as anything that's happened since the Trilobite scare. Definitely extraterrestrial.

Ms. Kell stands there looking up. She raises a hand to her eyes and touches her forehead. She looks the same? She's checking herself, her thoughts, to see if she's okay.

Sure enough, a shimmering pink image of Ms. Kell appears under the dome. In miniature, about half size. The uglies use their straws!

Someone shouts. Someone shoots. Must have been a rifle. I see exactly where the bullet hits the dome.

Frankie Lucien shouts, "No shooting! No shooting! Everyone stay back!"

I can see where the bullet hit because it's sending out ripples through the dome material. Circular shock waves. Then the bullet gets through the dome, like it burrowed its way in like a tick, and falls to the floor in front of the uglies. One of the uglies reaches down to retrieve the bullet. The ugly bounces the bullet in its hand like a person would do with a hot potato. Bullets are hot? Maybe it'll keep it like a trophy.

I slip away to the stairs out of the park. Fly down the stairs two at a time and hit the street, weaving myself through people hanging around in clumps. Everyone's trying to see what's going on. But they're scared. I can tell from their faces, that extreme cackled look, like something's broken. Maybe fear means you have no clue what to do next. So you're really truly empty, not just empty in some kind of metaphor sense. Empty of hope. This provocation is like nothing we expected. But we decided to stay.

Head right over to the red brick house where I saw all those mirrors. The door's unlocked so I go in. No kids. Mr. Nobody. Empty, but for the mirrors leaned up against the walls. I take a big one with a wooden frame, and I haul that piece of furniture back up the way I came. Hurdle up the steps, so when I'm back in the park, I'm panting.

City Park with a floaty on top! Security guys and Ewoks, right under the thing. Security is trying to get the Ewoks out of there. Men and women trickle back in, keeping down, rifles in their arms. The teens up on the bleachers are still shouting suggestions and cuss words. Tenny stands at the top howling, then he heaves his baseball bat at the floating whatever. Clean miss!

I get right under the floaty with the few remaining Ewoks, skirting my way through the security guys. No one notices my mirror, I guess. There's a gypsy woman next to me and she's dancing. Bare feet in this cold? I know all about that. She's writhing about with her arms and hands making all sorts of signals. The pink light shoots down and covers her. Gun shots explode – pistols, I think. Now rifles go off. The pink light stops. The dancer continues with her strut as though nothing happened. Still, the uglies must be pulling something out of people to sip at it that way up in their vehicle.

I keep by her. I can hear Ms. Lucien's yelling. I wonder if Clay is still over there with her.

The pink light comes back on and hits me, but I'm fast, already raising the mirror.

I angle the mirror. Easy! Don't feel paralyzed or

anything. No Satanic tendrils slithering through my brains. The mirror catches it, sends it straight back to the floaty.

Sounds like a sizzle –

The floaty jerks. A loudness of machinery we all recognize as broken machinery. The floaty starts ascending at about the same speed it came down. It's going away. The folks at City Park give off a giant, "Hurrah!"

Didi runs over to me with a baseball bat clutched in her hands. She's holding it out in front of her. It looks so big, half her size. Her big stick –

She goes, "Daisy, Daisy! I got a stick!"

# THE FOURTH DAY

**Tennyson Luna**

> *foul*
> *foul ball*
> *fast ball right side over the plate*
> *he swings*
> *he hits*
> *thwack*
> *looks good*
> *good connection*
> *solid hit*
> *high center field*
> *back, back, back*
> *oh, yeah*
> *it's good*

Limber, limber, limber. Stretch it out. Bend. Squat. Gotta stay in shape. Ball or no ball. We can still play catch, throw some scrimmage at the park. Now, I'm camping, we're all camping, and camping is not a sport. Camping out forever. Camping out inside. Camping out – and I'm a troll. We're on guard duty. Who wants to be a scout? Not me! Who's an imbecile now?

Blazed!

Over the hill to grandma's house, we go! Battle axe over my shoulder, I am Cave Man ready for the big game. Now's the time. Team's depending on me. Gotta get this done. This isn't baseball weather: there's not a cloud in a blue sky for a million miles. Only gray, gray. Sneaky fog sky, out of reach. Will it ever clear? Will it ever rain?

Rained out! Ha! Baseball is my game. I can hit. I can run. I can catch. I can field. What can't I do? America's past time. This is the real me. Baseball and apple pie. In the future, baseball bots for sure. Apple pie pills for sure.

In the future, no room for stars. The whole high school hierarchy collapses without athlete heroes. Then what? Anarchy? Religion? Meltdown?

Sam Bean says, "At the end of the world, we're like gompers. Gomping across the mountain, gomping across town. Schlubs. No wraiths attacking in the darkness in this version of the end. No heroics, no dragons. Just fog and fog and pinky baldy phonies. Never as bad or dope as it should be. You know how you see an ad on a screen for a giant burger layered with onion rings? Then you order that shit, try that sucker...it's not – "

I go, "Don't! We may never see a burger again for the rest of our lives."

Sam whoops. "The bads have such depth compared to the goods. New rules. Who do you think's pushing the buttons on this weather? If it was a game scenario, there would be big fat Easter eggs, that once you got, the weather would clear. No spoilers! No way out! Uhwelluh.

So wadda we do? Change the rules. Bend the rules. Break the rules. Isn't that why we stayed?"

He whacks a bush with his sword, but it's dull, ceremonial, and the bush shakes in a worry then springs back in his face. Sam spits and yelps in an annoyed voice. He's talking to bushes again. Shrubberies! He's awkward outside. Not a nature dood at all. Never an athlete. Strictly a gamer. Total old movie freak. Never played ball. Stoner nerd ...geek...all the rage – side order of klepto –

I go, "When's the last time you slept?"

"Why do you have to go see her?"

"You look like a wraith!"

"Well, look at you, Mr. L33T, when's the last time you slept?"

I got no juice left. Up and down the steps in an afterglow. Move into it stronger and stronger, then gradual like, like when you're warming up for the big game. Second wind. My second wind to do this dirty. I can do this. Each step – been down these steps a zillion times. Sam, too. Well, maybe...not. He's not a hiker type either. But we know this town. We know where we're gonna die. Sam knows it different from me: he's kinda loud, 'husky', a big voice, but he's strictly an inside man. Indoors supports the way of the lay of the game of those who stayed. Par-tay! Still, we clamber the steps, up and down, over the hill. I keep my axe out of the way. He watches his sword. We are unstoppable.

The thing about Eliani's house where we're all staying is it's right in the middle of town, the old part. Right up School Hill, off of Nowell, this big ol' house, totally cherried out, like a freaking lighthouse on that hill.

The ratty miner's shacks clustered around it like dirty piglets. The house is like a bull's eye in the center of town. Eliani doesn't know why her parents left. It was their decision. Her brother and two sisters left, too. She decided to stay.

We started getting together at her place with her peeps. I brought Sam. Sam brought Eileen. Eileen brought Tom Tom and Weed. Andrea showed up. We shared what we had: water, batteries, canned goods, power bars, weed. Eliani likes being the center. She never was before. It's her place, so she gets to be boss. Parents in consolidation don't care. People in town who stayed don't care. I mean, what are they gonna do? Call the cops? Tell our PUs? None of that matters. No one cares. There's only so much care. Like a finite amount. People got all cared out what with the Trilobites. They ran out of care. Maybe peeps on the consolidation high are like ultimate caring. Here, all we got is survival. Three days later –

The thing about volleyball is if everyone decides to go with the flow, it becomes a power dance, not just drama dunks to freak out opponents. Working together, making every move count, moving right into the exact spot necessary, is the decision every player must make. The team thing: we are bigger than the sum of our parts. Depends on total telepathy. That's what coach said. But coach left.

It was right before school was closed. After practice and cleaning up, I saw Sam lingering by the playing fields where a bunch of girls were playing volleyball. He wouldn't go by himself to watch. I led the way. That's when I saw her play. She was in cut offs, t-shirt. Every time she moved, her long muscular legs, dirty and streaked, would clench and unclench. She was sweating and laughing, having a super time. Any fool could see how strong she was. Any fool would want those legs wrapped around himself, in pure girl power.

Over the hill into the Gulch, we go. But now we're off the stairs, and bushwhacking on pig trails. Sam tries to use his sword. I tell him to cut it out. He gives me the finger. I can see he's sweaty, panting. I've barely broken a sweat. This should take us right to her door step. The kids' house is at the end of the road.

"Let there be light!" he cries.

"Thank you, Lord! Light that phattie!"

Sam tucks his sword up under his arm to light the doob. He sucks on it a bit, passes it over. Athletes aren't supposed to smoke. But most of us do. We don't smoke cigarettes.

"You think ET wants to eat us?" he asks.

I inhale like a turbine and go, "Dood, they want to suck out our brains!"

"Dood, those baldies had no guts."

"It's a thing, like a new diet."

Opposite the kids' house on the side of the hill from where we spy, I exhale, imagine she's getting up. It's quiet at the funky little place. Not even a mouse. And she's all stretchy and curling up her toes, waking up. Morning pee – wow! They have an outhouse! Very very! The kids have weapons. We have weapons. Ready for anything! Sam and I toke away and Sam is ready to burst. I can see he's shaking. Maybe he will explode? I stab out the joint, put it behind my ear. I shake my head and want to suggest a good workout routine for him but think better of it. I want to see Daisy!

"What's wrong with the girls we have?" asks Sam.

"Nothing. But, shoot, drinking and smoking and doping, three days straight: 'man needs a little variety.'"

"Woody Harrelson. *Natural Born Killers.*"

I go, "Woody's L33T. Even in those old movies. You always say Joey Ramone was the best. What are we gonna do for tunes when the batteries die?"

"They say in 'consolidated zones', people have incredible band width. Totally virtual, man. Whatever – "

I disagree: "This is better!"

"How?"

"Well, it's like real sex is always better than beating off."

"That is so profound."

"Getting high at the end of the world, it's like extra awesome bonus high. 'Say hello to my little friend.'"

"*Scarface.* Al Pacino. There she is."

I whisper, "It's like our whole world was on Channel X, and suddenly we've switched channels: we're on Channel Z, dood."

"*World War Z.* There she is."

"That which is not here does not exist." Now, I'm shaking. He heads down the hill.

Sam calls, "That which is here exists. Go for it! Got your back, man!"

I go for it: "Daisy Chain! Daisy Chain!"

Daisy looks mad – tough, mean. She mutters, "Shut the hell up! You'll wake the kids. You guys are up to no good. Your eyes are like chicharrones. Your skin like pancake batter."

We join her, nodding too much.

She goes, "You smell like dirty ass."

Sam cries, "What are you? The smells inspector? We wash? 'Hey, ho, let's go!'"

Spring into action, take her in my arms: "Kiss me!"

She slaps, pulls away, belching: "Snap out of it!"

Sam cries, "*Moonstruck*!" Then: "This is it, man. Got what you wanted. Want me to should run her through, boss?"

Daisy says, "You guys are so wasted. When the cat's away, the mice play."

"How is this rodent?" asks Sam.

She stares at me. She is so intense. I swallow. Have to keep this going. I go, "How many teenagers you got here?" She keeps staring. "What happened to the big black machine gun thingee?"

Her eyes the color of fog? The overcast sky is in her. And I can't say a thing. Googled that shit, too, before, about gray eyes. Lot of your famous gunslingers had gray eyes. I want to do the right thing. I chose to stay. I blurt, "Where's that big pistolero you got?"

"Tenny, nobody has any idea what's going on. You

were there yesterday? You guys saw it. Maybe Miss Kell's right." She shrugs, dances in place, away from me. "Maybe, we're playing this loose, cause no one's sure what to do. But got to, because it's never been like this before. We have to be ready for anything." She studies my face like she's going to grade me. Like she's going to slap me? "I'm serious. We chose to stay. When you're serious, you pay extra special attention. How else will we know what to do?"

Sam and his sword sulk.

Clay Mason comes out of the house. He hasn't changed either. White t-shirt and work pants, work boots like Frankenstein's. He's a goof! Bet he smells –

Sam says to Clay, "Take us to your leader!"

Daisy laughs, "You guys been partying all night!"

Sam giggles. I harrumph.

Clay goes, "What's the debate? You guys having a conference out here? Some kind of symposium?"

Sam goes, "'What we got here is a failure to communicate.'"

I go, "'*Cool Hand Luke.*'"

Daisy continues in that tone, "Clay, you're gonna stay here with the kids for when they get up, right? I'm off to the convention center. Mayor John John said they're gonna have a meeting. So I should be there. Tenny, come back when you guys are ready to rock. Not this shit. The real deal. It could be fun."

She finally smiles at me and I glow from the inside out, grin back. Sam notices and I think he will puke.

"Like real reals?" goes Sam.

I go, "You representing <u>all</u> the kids?"

Daisy smiles again at me - bam! bam! Those smiles hit hard. At last she says, "It's a dirty, ugly job but somebody has to do it."

What movie is that from?

**Clay Mason**

> *item item item*
> *item in my noggin*
> *item in my noggin*
> *in the morning, morning, morning*
> *canyon wren, cactus wren, house finch, quail*
> *Cat's cradle finger play!*

This is the way the world ends...we shall not cease from exploration...this is the way the world ends...we shall not cease from expectoration –

Those boys? What are those boys – what are those boys doing?

They stink of love. Entice. Lure. Allure. Jazz it all up: jocks get the babes. They're after Daisy. I can see it, I can feel it. Daisy, Daisy, Daisy. They are so ripe. If they take one step – ta ta for now jocks!

If they make one move –

Bean and Luna go over the hill. They are the size of gerbils now. I could put them in my pocket.

I am an observer, the *observatron* which can't stop seeing. Discern. Scrutinize. Tunnel to the Gulch, Main Street to Zacatecas I know where the shiny things are.

Item, item, item: discs! What are they? Uglies! What are they? Baldies! What are they? Big black machine – wazzit?

Did the pink ray –

Did the pink ray do its duty? Have I been compromised? All my secrets laid out before the uglies? They know everything?

I know so little –

I know nuttin –

Shall I tell Daisy to put a bullet through my noggin, noggin, noggin? Cause I'm compromised? Is she compromised? The pink light hit her...she fought back.

Keep an eye on me, Daisy!

Her eyes on me, like butterfly wings. Palpable flutter. But she's a one track, one trick girl: survival. I choose to survive. I stand at her side. I choose to make this –

A little girl comes out on the porch. She looks around. Her little feet are tensing, grasping. Her little fists mortar into her eye socket pestles. She says, "I'm not going to ask what time it is? That doesn't matter. Now, all there is, is now. But it's not a time machine. Just because something doesn't matter, doesn't mean it doesn't exist."

"Right, right, right."

Daisy goes, "You are one heavy chickie!"

So gray and overcast. What sky is this? Whose sky is this? Up, up, up!

She asks Daisy, "No such thing as a time machine, huh Daisy?"

Daisy shrugs, hugs, makes a mewling sound. Daisy takes off...up the Gulch...she is in all sizes, formats, scramble suit blazing, like that girl going down the staircase.

"It's early, isn't it?" says the little girl. I can't remember her name.

"It's early."

She scratches her neck's dirt rings. "Tell me a story?"

**Mayor John Placido**

*I'm going to lose weight*
*I'm really going to*
*serious weight*
*like I never have before*
*I will look the leader's part*
*I will make the right decisions*

What will the missus do? She will be unable to

resist me. If I live through this –

What were we thinking? Closing the highway? That wasn't in the bargain. But we decided to stay. It's our place. It's what we have and know. It was a spur of the moment thing. It was a think on your feet type of deal. We will survive. We have chosen this way and I will lead them.

But that implies this...situation...has a beginning, middle, end. Like, eventually, some kind of resolution.

Like how else can it go? I don't think we are destined to –

We've settled in the big basement room of the convention center for headquarters. If that's what you call it. It's a big square room with windows along the top edge. We've pulled together tables and chairs. I'm first one in this morning, wandering down the stairs, letting myself in, with a camp light. That's what a leader does, comes in early, takes charge. I have the key.

What about keys? Can we make new keys?

The committee heads should be here shortly.

Let there be light!

I find a chair at a table, spread out my materials. Not much light gets in through the narrow slots of these basement windows. Maybe if someone washed those babies, we'd get more light. Oh, I see: delegate authority. I could do it myself. We'll need lanterns here before long. Something. I aim the camping light better, so my paperwork is clear.

We're hanging on here, folks, by our toenails! We will not collapse. We will muster. We will stockpile. We will follow our slim new leader!

One day at a time. I am a natural born leader. No choice. Am I kidding myself? Too late for that now – me and the wife decided to stay. Trilobites be damned! All the corruption in recent years, government and industry, toxic as poison, means everyone's got a built-in BS detector. Everybody so sick of being a victim, being a loser. We know what's right, right now – this moment in time.

Bodies barge down the stairs to the basement. I can hear them coming. Councilman Martinez enters, swings open the door, checking the corners – we're all SWAT team ready now. He's going on nerves alone. Probably hasn't slept. Eyes wide. He's a good guy but never expected this. Look at me! See how calm I am, even after yesterday. He looks terrified.

I ask, "What?"

Martinez says, "You know, Paul Greer? From Peterson-Hodge?"

"The mining guys?"

Martinez says, "It's dark in here."

"Got any lanterns, camping lights? Stuff like that?"

He shakes his head, comes back to focus.

I go, "What's up with the mines?"

"Should I go get him?"

"Where is he?"

"Standing outside. I wanted to check first. I can go

get them."

"Bring 'im in."

Martinez goes back to the door, hurries through, closing it behind him.

I select a clean legal pad, put aside the one with my notes for today's meeting. Gotta stay organized. Everyone has a job, a responsibility. We have a system. We can do this. I know the caliber of folks who decided to stay will make sure of that.

Plus: funeral today. For Oscar Warga. Figured we'd bury him up on city land by the community pool. Something odd and spooky about an empty pool. But there's room up there for more. Don't think that. Focus. Doc Stevenson's working on the disc. It's just been a few days. We're still working out the kinks. Conjectures on what happened yesterday are pouring in. Everybody has total knowledge! People so used to TV and movies, those crazy scenarios, they think they can figure what's happening. I don't believe that for a second. I think people watched too much TV before.

A girl walks in. It's that high school girl from the park yesterday. She got hit by the pink light, then did the mirror thing. She has gray eyes like a gunslinger.

"The light hit you! You okay?"

"I guess. I don't feel any different. I represent the kids. You said there'd be a general meeting of committees this morning so I'm here."

Martinez and Paul Greer and two other men walk in.

Paul Greer is a tall man, florid, receding hair line,

glasses. He's wearing nice clothes, under a nice jacket. He and his wife decided to stay which is weird to me, but there's no figuring out how or why a person decides one way or the other. Maybe the mines wanted to keep a hand in here, in case things come back? That's crazy. Never happen! Work, pay, jobs? No way! Bills canceled. No mortgages. No liens. The Big Repo Day took care of that, people forced to give back all the stuff on credit – losing cars, trucks, freezers, sofas.

Paul Greer goes, "This your daughter?"

"No, I'm the kids' representative for the meeting."

Councilman Martinez seems embarrassed, shuffling, avoiding looking at the girl. The other men are the same. He manages, "Now, listen here, young lady, we're in the middle of God knows what, and this is no time – "

The girl giggles! "I agree. Totally."

Martinez insists, "John John, tell her! I've seen little kids running around town with guns, crissakes."

"None of us been hurt," says the girl.

Martinez says, "Tell her to get serious! Go home and listen to your folks!"

"Maybe her folks are gone?" I mumble.

She says, "No, they stayed, but they're not interested in the town's organization. Stuff like committees doesn't mean much to them." She shrugs. She looks like an athlete. "We're serious as you. And, besides, all that's going on, you have no clue about what's happening any more than we do. Kids can help. Kids decided to stay, too. They are here whether you like it or not. It's not about age or experience now that everything's gone crazy. We have a right to be part of all goings on. We've proven our worth. Who stopped that black wedge thing that broke the bus in two? Kids with paintball guns. How many baldies got squished because of kids? I used the mirror on the uglies yesterday. You didn't think of that."

Paul Greer and the other two men look nervous, worn out. Maybe they have kids?

I cut in, "Enough!" Time to get serious. Time to lead. "She's fine. She stays. She stays because she's part of the town. "

The gray-eyed girl looks serious like a statue, her features clear. She says, "Young people haven't been given a choice for a long time. Maybe a few generations. We made up our minds. If we get shit from older people, we'll fucking go live in Bone Canyon. That's all."

I go, "She's right. This is a weird and different world. Everybody made a choice. Kids, adults. We have no secrets from each other. We're all in this together. Now what's this about, Mr. Greer? What's with the mines?" Paul Greer says, "This is Roger Mead and Ray Groves. Mr. Mead is chief mechanic. Mr. Groves knows the underground well as anybody. Here's the dealio: we thought we should let you know: we got our own gasoline-fired generators, so we can use the lifts to get down in the mines in an emergency. Okay? So, during the Cold War the upper level was classified as a bomb shelter. Did you know that? Actually, I let it skip my mind. But, then, Mr. Groves runs into me on the street and reminds me: at the upper level of the Czar shaft, where it'd be easy to get to, we got a room stocked with emergency provisions – water, food. Civil Defense stuff. Sitting down there cozy and ready for an emergency. Sure seems like this qualifies as an emergency."

No one says anything. I finish nodding to Mead and Groves who I know slightly. Mead is short, compact. He's tough and strong, and the sweat shirt he wears stretches over his big arms. Groves is a regular Joe on the verge of skinny. He has a long face that can't help but look questioning. The girl is looking at Greer. Councilman Martinez is fidgeting.

The girl says, "Daisy Piper. My name. No one asked me."

Roger Mead says, "I live near your folks."

Daisy says, "I know. So Cold War, huh? That means the stuff has been there since what – the 70s?"

Greer says, "The 60s."

"Still good?" asks Councilman Martinez.

Greer says, "Why not? Fifty years." He shrugs. "Right?"

I sum it up: "You think we should go down there and retrieve those supplies?"

"Sure," grunts Greer. "Why not? Food, water – who knows what else? Frankly, I'm not sure. But they could go into the community pile. Emergency rations. Might as well."

Daisy says, "But right now we got food and water, and that gas might be better used for something else. Don't you think, Mayor? I mean, especially if the supplies turn out to be rotten and full of maggots."

Paul Greer says, "Only one way to find out. Mead can run a fork lift. Groves knows exactly where the stuff is."

Groves nods, says slowly, "Not exactly hidden. The supplies are fenced off to the side of one of the big tunnels at top level. Been there so long most of the guys don't even notice anymore. I don't even know who has the key."

Mead says, "There's a forklift at that level, too. So we got one on top, one below. We can easily load the elevator, bring that stuff up, then, here, load it on trucks."

Paul Greer says, "Me, my two guys, a couple volunteers, we can do this. We can at least check it out. If it's no good, we come right back up."

Councilman Martinez says, "I'll go."

"Me, too," says Daisy Piper.

"You are not going," says Paul Greer. "The mining company cannot allow a young person such as yourself entrance to a potentially dangerous – "

"What mining company?" asks Groves.

**Clay Mason**

*follow me with roses*
*follow me with rhyme*
*I will not follow her*

*I will not*
*follow, follow, follow*
*I am back up*
*I am procedural*

Kids are up, safe, doing their thing. I tell the story about the witch with snakes for hair. Boom! Time to boogie!

When I get to the convention center, there's one of those big official looking pickups with a backseat. It's black. I want a black truck. All kids want black trucks. Black is the color of children's dreams. I should know. The little ones tell me everything. Probably more, too, as I learn their names.

I hang back, watch, assess, get the feel of the matter. These mining doods are getting in to the truck. PUs for sure. Then Daisy. What is she doing with them? At first I think she's under arrest, but that's stupid. Then Councilman Martinez climbs in the truck with her. Mayor John John waves them off. They head up the main drag, turn into the road block, staying behind it. Security people wave them through with rifles and shot guns held over their heads. Guns make a party. Guns are a challenge. Every toy is a weapon.

Energy increases my glands' hurry up, follow up. Where they going? I didn't bring my pistol. Daisy's pistol. I was in too much of a rush. The black truck takes the dirt road on the other side of the highway that leads to the Czar shaft. I know the short cut –

Straight up!

Look, look! Lookey lookey!

I flex my way through rocks and brush, barely

touching ground. I am made of rubber ribbon, bend, duck, around the stabs –

Thorny, thorny, thorny.

I fly up the mountain to see –

### Councilman Jimmy Martinez

*dad worked underground 20 years*
*thought I would*
*I got my mechanics certificate*
*he was ready to pull the proverbial strings*
*Momma didn't want me underground*
*no way*
*she figured one in the family, twenty years was*
*enough*
*she didn't want to worry anymore*
*men down below, underground*
*wasn't natural to her*
*made her think of men descending to hell*

When Dad entered his retirement paperwork, they made him an offer he couldn't refuse: a cushy gig as night watchman at the pits, on account of he was loyal and trustworthy. Then he'd be a double dipper. He was so proud of being a double dipper. Drive around all night on service roads, watching for pit pirates. That's what he thought.

No more pirates. What's turquoise worth now? Just a shiny rock now! Now, no more mom and dad. Mom and dead.

That's gross.

I didn't want to go underground any which way. Anyway. The surface, up top, good enough for me. I wanted to work on cars. On trucks. On the surface.

Something about desert light on the surface seems right where I belong. I don't want to go underground. You either love the desert or you don't. You either fit into this place or you don't. I'm glad it's not for everybody. Some folks can't adapt. Born and raised here, the desert is under my skin: that quality of light always lets me know where I am. Or maybe it's summers. When the great big summer sun comes down and takes over. I had my own shop by the time I was twenty-five. Married, couple kids. My mom was pleased to beat all when I got elected to the city council, but my wife not so much. What a time to get involved! They all decided to go – consolidation. My kids. I knew my wife was unhappy, scared. I guess none of them thought about the desert the way I did. But now, come to think of it, I'd be stupid to think about *that* desert, the one I imagine, cause it's gone, turned to poison and dust. Out there. But here. Then, so, I guess, it's my last stand. I sure never thought of myself as a hero. And now I'm heading underground.

Mead and Groves get the generator buzzing, a noisy thing. It's big, has to be for that kind of power. I guess in case of emergencies they had to have a reliable back up. Well, this is an emergency. Green lights come on. We've all been outfitted with helmets with lights and backpacks with emergency supplies. We get in the lift, a tall boxy thing maybe twenty men could fit in...if they had to. It's me and Greer and Mead and Groves, then the girl and her pal. On board! A shudder from the contraption, then a wail from a piercing whistle. Chains start bucking. The kids are right. If they want to help, they can help seems to me. But – but, still. I guess I adapt.

When we had it out about the girl wanting to come down with us, Mayor John John explained, "This is about all of us. Crazy demands all of us. Involved. In case all the adults," he went on with a lisp in his speech, "are gone. They need to be self-reliant. We need them to learn how to survive." That made sense. Then the big boy showed up at Czar shaft, insisting he had to go with his friend.

Short trip. First level. Lots of clanks and buzzes. A jerk, we're there. Mead adjusts the controls. Underground: dark, dust, flat air, gas smells. Not too bad. The kids are brave. Or have no fear. No common sense? Nah, just kids. They got no other way to be. Groves yanks open the front of the lift's cage door. Like a giant squirrel cage.

Everybody clicks on the helmet lights. This huge space, like the biggest, scariest basement ever, and our little lights don't help.

Mead goes, "I'll get the lights." He hurries ahead. The kids go next, following him, then stopping, looking around. We adults hang back. Carved out of sheer rock, tunnels and equipment every which way. Our lights don't show much. Then the bulbs hanging on wires strung around the walls, about a man's height, come on. We turn off our helmet lights.

Four main tunnels take off from this lit up central hub. Because they're on different light bulb strands, they're not turned on. You can't see in to the black tunnels, so those tunnels look like entrances. Greer is going over particulars for us. There's a tool area where men would check out what they needed for the day. Plus, there's an office and latrine down here. Groves goes over to a mini fork lift parked to the side and starts fiddling with it. Mead heads over to help him.

The rest of us keep following Greer who won't shut up. Safety protocols until we'd just as soon not know. The ceiling is close. Ribbons of quartz run through the black and gray rock. Heaviness. Like a pressing down. The kids look excited. The boy is fidgety. The girl seems careful. Along the side, an area's been fenced off, making a long narrow room tucked in to the rock. Floor to ceiling chicken wire on a wooden frame with those Civil Defense yellow and black signs across the front. We line up before the fencing to check it out.

Four fifty gallon barrels – must be water. Then stacks of boxes clearly labeled emergency. Boxes stacked high. A couple tons of stuff at least.

The girl says, "It's gonna take at least two trips for the elevator."

"That's fine," says Greer. "That's fine. Generators are good for ten trips. Loaded." He pulls out a ring of keys from a pocket and flips through them. He tries a key at the padlocked door. No luck. He flips some more, tries another key. He undoes the padlock and the chicken wire fence door is pulled open.

The forklift's engine rumbles to life behind us. We see Mead driving the little beast our way, with Groves holding on to the side, hitching a ride. Mead stops the thing, forces it in to a reluctant neutral. Groves hops off. The fumes are tough. Mead yells over the engine, "Can't get this thing inside there. You're gonna have to bring out the stuff. Barrels first. I can take one at a time."

Groves and the girl and boy tackle a barrel. Groves shows them how to heave it up on its side and kind of roll it, guiding it out the door. It takes a while until they get it. Greer and I stay off to the side to give them room. They get it out and I go help. Mead brings over the fork lift, the fork down all the way. We walk it, slide it, roll it in place. Mead has it! He backs up and starts for the shaft elevator. I think, this ain't so bad. I can do this. In and out like the wind!

Greer and the boy start hauling out the boxes, stacking them outside the fencing. Groves and the girl work on getting another barrel out. I go help them. Mead calls back to us, "Little help here!"

Groves runs over to the elevator to give him a hand.

Greer says, "There's a dolly, I believe, in the equipment shed. We could load the boxes on it and double our time loading." He hurries off to fetch it.

Mead comes back with the forklift and takes the second barrel, Groves working with the girl to get it on right. Mead and Groves go back to the elevator to unload. Greer comes back pushing ahead of himself a wheeled dolly. Greer and the boy start loading the boxes on it. Greer says, "Not too tall or it won't move. Floor's rough in spots." He takes off his jacket, hangs it on a nail in the chicken wire frame.

The elevator can hold most of the boxes and two of the barrels. The rest of the stuff will have to wait. Two trips, for sure. The fumes from the forklift are bad. The ceiling has not moved. That's just nerves.

We can't get everyone in the elevator once it's loaded. But we'll have to come back anyway for the second load. It'll take a few minutes but not long. Some will have to wait down here. For the next trip. The boy and the girl and Greer agree to stay and wait. While Mead and Groves and me go up. We'll unload the stuff fast as we can. And I'll go for more help and another truck to haul the stuff to storage. Mead says there's a forklift up top so that will help. Mead pulls closed the elevator door. We're all scrunched together, leaning over boxes and barrels. Mead hits the switch. We start climbing. I admit I want to gasp. But it would look foolish. No one says bye or anything.

**Daisy Piper**

> *Clay Mason shows up in the nick*
> *what is the nick*
> *do nicks bleed*
> *do they get infected*
> *when I killed the baldy*
> *split him almost in two*
> *that was a nick in his time*

They gave us backpacks. Mines got a filled plastic water bottle, power bar, gloves, and a flashlight.

It takes forever to go down in the elevator. Clay talked his way in! He's a smart guy, knows stuff, knows people in a way. He reads people and sees things differently. I argued he should come as we needed the extra hand. Kids are represented on this trip. Clay's a big dood. He can help. He said he'd been down before. Sometimes, I wonder if he makes up stories. No. Maybe that pink ray did something – to both of us? How would we tell? No one seems to notice anything about us...different?

Clay works harder than anybody. I do what I can. Mr. Groves shows us how to wheel around the water barrels. Water is heavy. The boxes of supplies aren't bad. The space is like a scooped out edge of the tunnel. Mr. Mead likes wheeling around on the forklift. Mr. Greer seems nervous. Mr. Martinez I can't figure. Nervous? Exhausted? Afraid? But everybody adapts in his own way after making the choice.

By the time the first load is going up, my hair's wet and sticky, under my hard hat. Stuffy down here. The light seems thinner with them gone. Forklift's quiet. I can see dust particles in the air but only from the side, like I have to sneak a peek to see them. We're standing there, quiet, a few moments. We already got the two other barrels out, ready for the second load. Most of the boxes went up in the first load. Clay is doing those weird finger motions.

Mr. Greer says, "We can load the rest of the boxes on the dolly and take them over, ready to go. Save some time."

Clay goes, "Maybe one, maybe two dolly runs."

The three of us on top of it, then the three of us pushing and pulling the dolly. We're set. Two dolly trips did it. One big, one small. We get all the boxes stacked up by the elevator shaft. We're sweaty. Mr. Greer glances around. I can tell Mr. Greer is looking for something. At least when he's talking we know he's okay. Clay is shimmery. He did most of the work. He makes little pipping noises.

Mr. Greer takes us over an area where there's a table and chairs. Plus: a five-gallon water thermos. We have a drink. Whew! Stale, dirty water, here since the Cold War, too?

Greer says, "You know, we got a lot of tools down here." He's talking slowly. He goes on, "You know, like shovels and picks. We might as well bring them up. We can have a common tool shed at the convention center. Folks can, I don't know, check them out when they need them."

I go, 'That's a great idea."

Clay mumbles a bit, making these odd pipping sounds, then: "Lotta work for this hunk of supplies. I hope it was worth it. I hope they're good, better than that water. Maybe they'll get back up and open the boxes and find out they're no good. They might figure, forget the dumb dumbs underground. We'll become like zombies down here waiting forever for the elevator."

Greer shakes his head, rubbing his dusty hand across his mouth. It leaves a mark. "What are you talking about? Don't be ridiculous! Not likely. Don't worry one little bit. Let's go get those tools. We'll load them on the dolly."

I go, "I'm gonna look around. You mind?"

Clay shakes his head, smiles, grunts.

Greer looks at me, looks at Clay – he frowns big time. "Go for it," he says.

The lit light bulbs on the wall wires stop just past the emptied chicken wire cage. The tunnel next to it plunges deep to who knows where. It's black. Walls look smooth. The floor is uneven. It's like the walk-in closet at the center of the Earth. Put my helmet light back on.

I walk. I'm not very far when I can tell the temperature is dropping. It's been kinda pleasant, warmer than up top, but now it's cold. Plus, even with my light, it's hard to see, like it's fuzzy. The air dissipates the light. I don't even know what that means. We're so paranoid. I wonder if light can be absorbed? The tunnel is a raw, black, corridor...hallway in the dark, to the dark, and I can't see very well.

Ahead of me, my light makes shadows. Forms ahead. Structures? Shapes? My light shines over like a toll booth? A long pole across the tunnel, blocking egress.

This isn't fuzzy. This is fog. Fog. Thick. White. Is this what's on top? Do they get fog in caves?

– same fog as on top...

...I'm backtracking fast as I can, trying not to breathe. Walking backwards so nothing can sneak in. We are surrounded, top and bottom. Underground. Overground.

I stop and turn, walking back the regular way. I try to slow my wild breathing. I'd be dead if it was poison gas. I guess I'm starting to see something happening, like a pattern, in Coltrane, that's happening to each of us. Wall bulbs! I'm back. That's the edge of the fencing to the closet where the supplies –

The space is full!

The exact same supplies – four barrels of water, stacks of food boxes – are right there.

## Clay Mason

*shovels*
*picks*
*rakes*
*axes*

The adult shoots tendrils out of his noggin: blab...the rules? His whole being radiates mucky suggestions. Daddy stuff: responsibility, duty, conformity. What the – I pretend. Because, also, he's struggling. Old people need to do the right thing so can't resist acting as though they are doing the right thing, which comes out to young people as advice. I already made the right choice. I watch my fingers. I contain the noises that leak from my pie hole. I am not talking to myself. I want to want to want to... Daisy.

Dolly was the name of the first clone. A sheep.

We push the dolly back to the elevator, bump the thing along, not nearly as heavy as before. I unload by the elevator. He stands there. Now, he won't talk. I don't want to say – my left hand signs to my right hand, like little animal puppets having a private secret language discuss. I feel a growl percolating through my bowels.

I am not on fire. I am going to let this PU know how to do it.

I squinch my eyes tight when I hear Daisy huffing to us. Open wide! Her light's on. I can see her eyes.

Daisy's in front of us. She's looking from me to him. She announces: "All the stuff – all the supplies, they're back!"

Greer whines, "What – what are you talking

about? Come on!" Even Mr. Official can read Daisy now. He's gonna go with freak out. "What do you mean? What are you talking about?"

"Let's go!" I lead the charge back to the Civil Defense cage. We hustle along. Daisy snaps off her hard hat light. There! The exact same barrels and boxes are there.

As if –

Greer groans big time: "Impossible!"

I go, "Believe it or not!"

Daisy talks fast: "What's going on? Who could have done it? How did they get the stuff down here? I mean, we would have seen them. Where are they?"

Greer sputters, "Impossible! Somebody's down here!"

This is beyond all expectations so's gotta be good. I cry, "We have to do it all over again? Repeat? Someone hit refresh? Redundant. Repeat."

"There must be other people down here!" Greer walks away and starts calling, "Who's here? Anybody down here? Answer! Answer me!" Then he mutters but loudly enough so we can here, "Because that would be trespassing. This is still private property, no matter what's happened. No way people should be down here." Then, loudly again: "Who's here!"

Daisy's watching me and I can tell she's charming.

I go, "Impossible possible. Go with it, Daisy. We're okay."

"How could the stuff get back down here?"

We go in, tiptoe to touch the barrels and boxes. They're really here.

Greer's back, ordering, "Go get the dolly. We'll load the boxes."

I do as ordered. But Greer is clueless, and he wanders off again yelling for the invisibles to show themselves. Come out of hiding! They've been had, he calls. They've been discovered big time. He knows!

When I get back with the dolly sheep, Daisy says, "Replenish. And you know what? Clay. Down that tunnel," she points and for a sec her arm is an arrow, "it goes to a toll booth in the same white fog above ground. Just like the fog outside on top, right now I bet."

I shiver, "*Phantom Toll Booth!*"

"I love that book!"

"Replenish," I go.

I've never seen Daisy shimmer like this, like she's my friend, and tuned in to me. She's surpassing expectations. She's avenging restraints.

I stumble, "Replenish. It means you repeat the 'plenish.' Good, good, good word. Item!"

Daisy chokes back a chortle. Then: "You are a weird fucker, Clay. But who better to have with?" Daisy lunges to the back wall of the supply space. She feels all over it with wide open hands. Those hands with the long, tapered fingers. She's got dirty nails. What's she looking for? What is she doing? She's so intent! She pulls me in.

Now she's muttering, "Replenish. We would have seen someone. It would take a bunch of people to replenish these supplies so fast. There's gotta be a passage back here." She's running her hands on the wall, stroking it like it's a cat, feeling for tell tales.

I wonder, "Where's Greer? You think I should go for him before he hurts himself or breaks something?"

"Look! Down here on the ground, behind the boxes."

I go over to Daisy on her knees, squeezed in between boxes and barrels. There's an inch high hillock of dust making a straight line along the bottom of the back wall. Unless it's not dust.

I snort. "Secret panel?"

"I don't see anything – like a seam."

"Maybe you need a magic word. 'Open sesame'!"

Greer gives a shout out and we scoot over fast to see what's up. Daisy is reluctant to leave the supply room, keeps glancing back. Maybe she's afraid the supplies will disappear.

It's the elevator. It bangs its way down, hits our level, clanks to a stop. The metal clangs vibrate our bones. We're so excited to tell it, say it. Mead pulls open the gate. Greer hangs close by to greet them.

"What's up?" says Mead. He's looking us over funny. He can tell something's up.

Greer croaks, "Where's Martinez?"

Groves comes out of the elevator cage, staring at

Greer, goes, "Dood! You look like you seen a ghost."

Daisy says, "Replenish. All the supplies are replenished."

Mead points to the tools. Mead says, "We bringing up those tools? Looks like you guys kept busy."

Greer says, "'Replenish'? Listen to her."

Groves say, "And that means?"

Greer bursts, "Someone's down here! They restocked the whole shebang! I know it sounds impossible. Go see for yourselves!"

Mead stares at him. Slowly, he goes, "Okay. Should I bring the fork lift?"

"Why not?" says Greer, hustling everyone forward, towards the wall with the fenced-in supplies.

It only takes seconds to get there.

Groves takes a look and goes, "Crazy." He saunters over to touch the boxes and barrels. Daisy is right behind him. Greer won't go in. Groves turns on Daisy: "You guys! How'd you do this?"

Daisy goes, "How could we?"

Mead brings over the fork lift spitting and coughing. He revs it. He jumps off, hurries in see the supplies. Mead calls, "Might as well should! Let's get these barrels!"

Groves, Daisy, and I roll out the barrels. We're getting good at it. It's all in the angle of the dangle. We got it down! Mead gets them back to the elevator one at a time, where Greer helps him load them on. We start loading the dolly. Those exact same actions again. Repeat. Replenish. My body remembers each box, lift and shift, deliver. We figure we'll just empty the supplies once more and see what happens. We'll wait. See who shows up. No one mentions the obvious unmentionable: freaking baldies down here? We could keep the handy dandy pick axe. Didn't bring no pistolero down here. Does Daisy have her knife? Her blade, blade, blade? Finally, all the boxes and barrels have been delivered to the elevator. The elevator is full again, and the supplies and barrels that don't fit are stacked nearby, outside the elevator's gate. Good to go. Ready or not, here we go.

Greer can't stand it. "Suppose it happens again? We should watch, see who it is."

I say, "No one is gonna come out with us standing there."

Greer says, "Damn right."

Mead says, "Martinez's trying to get a bunch of guys up top to help. It won't take so long. Why don't me and Mr. Greer go on up with this load. It'll go faster. You guys okay to wait? You kids need to get up? We could squeeze you in." No one answers. "I'll be right back for the rest of the load and you all. Few minutes."

Groves says, "What's going on?"

Mead says, "Leaving you down here? Or about who's messing with us? Come on, no one's down here. Hell if I know. Still, free supplies?" He shrugs, wipes his nose. "We got this."

Groves says, "You're not worried, I mean, I mean, I don't see how anyone could have...'replenished'...that fast, and none of us seen a thing."

Daisy says, "We didn't see a thing."

I go, "Or hear a thing."

Groves says, "We'll wait. It's fine. Go on, take that load up."

It's my turn to say something. To insert some heroic quip right here. I snarl. The elevator is engaged.

Daisy watches intensely.

**Ray Groves**

> *replenish*
> *good word*
> *new word*
> *word*

Greer's freaking. Mead's right to get him out of here. No place for freaking out underground! I remember the first freak out underground I saw. Young guy, newbie, got obsessed about the elevator getting stuck. Old timers said they'd seen guys do this before. He wanted to try the emergency ladder, the series of metal rungs embedded in the wall, up along the shaft, just in case. He really had to make sure, he kept saying. But it was strictly forbidden. Course, he eventually goes for it, and gets stuck half way up. Gets the vertigo, hanging on for dear life. Took hours to get him out of there. Had to uncurl his frozen fingers from the rungs. He was no good underground after that.

I'll stay with the kids. Don't sound right calling them kids, what with the way they pull their own weight. In the before times, kids were not equal. But now – nowadays, we're all equals. Or it falls apart. Everyone pulls his own weight. I decided to stay because why the hell not? What would be a reason to consolidate? Living in a goddam apartment complex! No way. Never wanted to check out the World Wide Web. Never had one of them damn phones. Never could play those damn video games. No interest is why. If you're not interested in a thing, then why would you want to do it? What's wrong with sticking to what you know...what you get a kick at...what you know is real? Where – I don't know, it feels like home, all like that. I decided to stay and this is what we got.

The elevator ascends. We wander back –

Right in front of us, the back wall of the supply room has disappeared. I guess that's what happened. It's hard to say. It's hard to explain. Happened so fast. Standing there before the empty supply room, and not a flicker, not an eye thing, but some kind of shift, like something my whole body felt, and the back wall is now a black window onto a huge blackness, with, maybe, a distant dim glow. Goes way back. I can't see, except for space. Seems really deep.

Daisy and Clay slide together, side by side. They take hold of each other's hands, and they start walking. They pass through the chicken wire gate sideways, keep going, heading to the back, and I'm watching, thinking this can't be good.

"Hey, you guys, where you going?"

No answer. They're walking, slowly, close now to the back. At the back, any second.

"Where you think you're going? It can't be good back there. You guys!"

My hands make fists and I shake with a wave of anger and exasperation, that I quickly realize is plain fear. They shouldn't – they couldn't. They did! I gotta go see. They walked right in!

The kids are gone. There one second, then gone into the back wall emptiness. A step and gone. Disappeared. I push through the gate. At the back wall, can't see much. Blackness. Can't see the kids at all. I call out for them. They just walked in and disappeared. All I can see is deep black space. If I had a rope I could tie myself to it and anchor the end out here, somewhere sturdy. I don't want to go in. I'm not going in.

Who could blame me? Someone has to wait for them. They're okay. They have to be. I call out, "You guys?" No answer. It was a sickly, little girl cry. No way. I holler. This is ridiculous. We've seen some shit lately but this has got to beat all.

I stand right up against where the back wall would be, just in front of the opening, an inch from it. That glow? Dim. Bluish? I keep my body and arms back and lean my head in to the space. My head goes through, very faint yielding, something easily pushed through. My head's inside –

"Daisy! Clay! Get back here!"

I can't stand what I see, so I pull back fast and sharp and hard. I stumble backwards, catch myself. Breathing heavy, soaked in sweat. I cut out the sobbing. Daisy and Clay step out from behind, or through, the space.

Daisy says, "I think we better move. It only takes a few seconds."

We manage to get outside the gate, whip around to the new vision: supplies replenished. Every last one of them. The wall is solid.

"That's how they do it," says Clay.

These guys are fearless, plus they got hit by the red light, so what's going on – like some kind of power? No, can't be. This ain't no cartoon.

What I saw when I stuck my head through was infinite space without direction. All through this space, billions and billions of what looked like evenly positioned, silvery balls, in lines I guess, some kind of geometry, stretching on and on. Silvery balls, the size of ping pong balls. Daisy and Clay were hanging around in there, like floating, in the silvery ping pong balls.

## Clay + Daisy

> *we fly empty nowhere*
> *we float space sky*
> *familiar because we dreamed it*
> *pattern of balls*
> *circles*
> *okay, spheres*
> *how many dimensions*
> *can dance on the head of a pin*

## Didi Grebe

*Charlie Chaplin went to France*
*just to watch the ladies dance*

When Daisy and Clay get back to the house, we'll all be doing chores, like clean up, and dishes, and sweeping with the broom. I have my baseball bat which is a club, which is my weapon of choice, and I'm going around the house making sure we're secure. Cassie said we should air out the sleeping bags on the line Clay put up in the yard yesterday. So she handled that chore with some kids, Scott and Brian, who are eleven and ten. Cassie is ten and can beat up anybody except Amy, who is the fastest runner. Cassie gave me a look when I was policing the living room where we sleep. We get fifteen kids in sleeping bags with pads, next to each other, in a circle around the coffee table. We don't drink coffee. We look like the spokes of a wheel. Bennett Tilson made the table. He got a big round table top and put it down on that big black thing Daisy and Clay and Bennett dragged back from the Gulch. That's a secret we can't tell. For the good of the house. This is our house, and I like it better than my other house. We all have two houses, so we get to choose which one to live in. Then, Cassie said I was a big baby, and I said, I am not. I slung my baseball bat over my shoulder. Parents love you when you're not there, cause when you're there they just worry, so probably better not to be there, and just love the ones you're with.

Then, Roland, who's nine, started giving me the business, acting real jerky, teasing me, and fake hitting, which is annoying. Why do boys act like that?

'All secure,' I say to Clay and Daisy when they come in from town looking hot and sweaty. Daisy has a new backpack. We got teams of kids going all over the place for old backpacks, plastic bottles, broom handles, for books, for all like that we could maybe use some time. We're like baby hyenas afraid of nothing. You got to be nine, you're supposed to be nine to be a scavenger. But you never know about rules around here. Daisy and Clay get home and everyone's terribly excited, wanting to know their story. Daisy thanks Cassie for taking care of the sleeping bags. At first, I think she's going to go into her cleanliness speech, but she stops in time. We all know about bugs and keeping clean. Clay rounds up Bennett and the rest, and we gather at the round table. Clay and Daisy kneel in front of it. Daisy takes off her new backpack and tosses it to the table. She said she got it from the mayor's office. She opens it and pulls out a white, plastic case. She slings it on the table like it's a hot potato. We all make 'oh's' and 'ah's' like it's a thing. For what, I don't know –

Clay and Daisy act upset. I don't think now is a good time to bring up my idea about the bouncy castle. Sighs and ponders. I love bouncy castles so thought that would be a good dealio. I better wait to discuss. Clay jumps back from the case and gets to his feet like a giant. Daisy has clenched her hands to her face like she's going to pray.

Clay shouts, "What is that? Where did that come from?"

Daisy says, "Sit down, Clay. It's safe or we wouldn't be here. I put the silver ping pong ball in the pack, and this is the first chance I've had to check it."

Bennett goes, "You guys aren't making sense. You

have to tell the whole story."

Daisy mainly tells it, of going underground, in to the Earth, to get city defense supplies from a long time ago war. And how when they loaded those supplies into the elevator in the underground mine, then went back to the supply room which should have been empty, all the supplies were back. All of them were back! Makes sense. Like that fairy tale of the Brownies? They took out all *those* supplies, then hung out to see who was doing it. Can't be Brownies as they're make believe. Then they saw the wall disappear. Clay and Daisy walked in to the beyond, the great empty space. Like outer space? No questions during story! And the space was filled with ping pong balls, and Daisy took one.

Bennett says, "And now that ping pong ball has turned into this case?" He points at the white case, then jabs it. It's still in the center of the table. It looks like white plastic and is a rectangle, bigger than an iPhone.

Clay and Daisy are nodding their heads fast. They look happy or really scared, like parents often do.

Bennett says, "Brilliant. Just brilliant. Could the ping pong ball still be in the case? But you never saw the case before, right?" Clay and Daisy look confused. I think they need hugs. Bennett keeps talking, "You touched it, Daisy, and you're fine." He leans over on his knees and picks up the case. It has a top and a bottom. The top has a clasp and Bennett pushes it, and the case opens in two. Bennett lets it fall open on the table. It's red-orange inside. Not like a fire truck. And in the middle is a silver ping pong ball. "Did the ping pong ball make the case?"

Daisy reaches over and grabs the ball. She says, "We have to find a good place to hide it." She stands up, looking all over the place.

Roland says, "There's room up the chimney where we got the disc."

Bennett says, "I don't get it. It – the ping pong ball, makes stuff?" He fiddles with the case. The red-orange innards are all different shapes, like tubes and rectangles and triangles, but sorta flattened. Looks soft and hard at once.

Daisy says, "I know!" She hurries to the kitchen and goes right to the half filled five gallon water jug, sitting on the extra chair in the corner by the back door. She unscrews the top and drops the ping pong ball in.

Bennett goes, "Contamination! Daisy, you know better than that."

"I know, I know. But it hasn't hurt us. Maybe it's inert. Just for now," insists Daisy. "There's not that much water in it anyway."

What's 'inert'? Did she say 'jerk'?

Clay's still in the living room and he calls us, "Hey, guys, check it out! Item!"

We go back to the living room. Clay's holding a red thing in front of himself. Like a long tube with triangles coming off it. Oh, it's a rocket ship.

"What did you do?" goes Bennett.

"It's a *Transformer*," says Clay. "I mean, I mean, I mean, I was looking at the red shapes and ridges, on the insides of the case, and I had the urge to bend it, twist it up, the whole thing, and it easily found this shape."

"What is it?"

Daisy says, "It's a toy?"

Roland hoots, "A toy? Maybe the disc is a toy?"

"It can't be a toy," said Bennett. "Put it down on the table and let's look at it."

Clay does and we all stare at the red rocket ship. It could be fun to play with. But a boy's toy I think. Unless you could get real small and get into the front part. That's where the pilot would sit. That's the command center.

Clay goes, "Look! Look!" He bends in, picks up the rocket ship and starts twisting. I'm afraid it will break. But it doesn't. Clay says, "I see another way to do it."

He finishes. It's a red ray gun for sure with a funny knob sticking out of the bottom half way.

# THE FIFTH DAY

**Oscar Latta**

> *gun*
> *guns*
> *riot gun*
> *pistol*
> *traditionally, a riot gun*
> *was a shot gun*
> *ten or twelve gauge*
> *standard today*
> *the Persuader*
> *I check my Glock*

Frankie Lucien's a good guy. I trust her – her judgment. Mayor and councilmen, the folks who've risen to a place of leadership just by their participation, all went along with Frankie Lucien's ideas about security. Not a lot of discussion. No one used the term 'militia.' I mean in a meaningful way. No one bothered to make a motion about how I was to coordinate, liaison, or make decisions with and/or for Frankie Lucien and her group. What's my role now?

Arbiter? Compromiser in chief? Peace maker? Sounds great, but without authority, some granted sense of trust and expectation, what? What am I then? No expert in this shit, that's for sure.

Roger Mead thinks there's something 'funny' about Clay Mason and Daisy Piper. They seem like decent young people to me. But Roger says they both got hit by the red beam of the uglies, then they went in to the dark, the unknown, whatever it was, underground. Way back in the dark reaches of that shaft. Ray Groves looked in, too. Ray thinks the kids are in way over their heads. Who knows what that pink light did?

'Replenished' bomb shelter supplies? People are watching us?

Baldies...uglies...wedges...spheres...discs –

There's no fricking water! It may never rain again. How long can we last? A year?

That's my real job: cannibal hunter!

Looting reports? Where did I put those? Can't believe I'm still having folks fill out incident reports. But the whole neighborhood movement thing is getting ratcheted up by Fred Stanley: let each neighborhood take care of itself, its own needs and requirements. That's what he's insisting. Each neighborhood would have its own central supply. Now, they're insisting each neighborhood gets the abandoned homes in that neighborhood. But we've already voted against that. We decided to do central supply at the convention center. The community supply center will be located in the basement. Course, each neighborhood has its own representatives. That's natural. But in terms of the abandoned houses: some neighborhoods don't have a helluva lot of homes at all, and few empties...so...ipso facto...those neighborhoods are not going to have much to salvage. Which means we got to keep it fair. Which makes looters of us all. We set up rules. It's a control thing –

Every man for himself?

How can you tell if you're successful now? What is of value now? What is a day's work worth now? Back to barter, simple exchange. Trade! Ms. Pitka said it was called 'reciprocity.' It's the way people made exchanges for thousands of years before money. It depends on everyone being honest and up front. It depends on everyone being willing to share. And if they're not? They call in the one and only, the last *Police Deputy* in the world. But they probably won't call with a phone, seeing how they are kaput. And they probably won't call Frankie Lucien. Least, not yet.

Every man for himself?

Every human makes a decision to how they will enter into public life. The public forum? The public arena? Us together now, stepping up to the plate, each has his or her turn, so integral members all, for the community. We need everybody. Safety in numbers. Not literally as in numbers of guns deployed, but in terms of shared abilities. There is this diversity of ideas and opinions and abilities in Coltrane. Probably always has been. Versions of coping? We need them all. Kids, too. We are on a track that requires all of us.

The cop shop is like my hideaway cave this morning. The mist outside keeps it slightly spooky. When will the fog lift? From the windows, dawn light is baffled. My man cave like a throwback space I am reluctant to quit. I'm still a cop. This is my office. It's quiet in here.

Moisture last night. A little rain. Whole town out gathering it as they could, with all sorts of inventions. Abilities! Everyone must have been up late.

Through the windows, I see a little man on a bike pedaling up fast.

They still come for me.

What do I know about wedges? Or uglies? Pinkies? Baldies? Whatever folks are calling them.

Are we being watched? The whole thing a set up?

Have we triggered some retaliation because of our roadblocks?

They come for me.

A frantic knock sounds like a woodpecker, then the little man bursts in: "Officer Latta, there's shots up by the old Arctic Circle!"

I stare at him, trying to place him. He's middle-aged, trim, receding blond hair.

"Gunshots!" he adds.

Who is this guy? I vaguely recognize him. I don't know everyone's name. Maybe we need to take a census, like keep a tally of everyone who stayed. We have an informal one, but no one knows how accurate it is. We know some folks are hiding out, keeping it remote, on the down low. We're all neighbors, aren't we?

I go, "Slow down. Tell me what you know."

"I live near there, in the neighborhood, up Mason Hill. And a little while ago I heard a pop. Didn't think much about it. Then more pops. Pop, pop, pop! It was gunfire! I went out to see what was up. There were two guys in the bushes on my side of the street shooting into a miner's shack across the way, couple doors down from the old Arctic Circle. It's a notorious dope house. Everybody knows about it in the neighborhood."

For the life of me, I can't recall his name. "Okay – so what I want you to do is go over to the convention center and see if you can find somebody from security. Ask for Frankie Lucien. Or just ask one of the councilmen or Mayor for help. Tell them I'm heading up there right now, and I'd appreciate back up."

The cruiser's fuel gauge reads under the F mark. I head up Main Street with the lights going. No siren. Don't want to cause more of a ruckus. Up the canyon, hardly anyone out. No dogs. No kids. No traffic, that's for sure. And that's good. 'Barking and parking' used to be our most common call.

It's probably an overzealous neighborhood watch. Maybe they're target practicing? Maybe they saw a *chupacabra*. Pass the Circle K and its boarded-up windows. Nobody sitting on the stone bus steps across the street as they are prone to. Not a Wook in sight. Too early, I guess. The road widens. On the right, the north side, coming up, is the defunct Arctic Circle with a small parking area. A grove of tall cottonwoods push up a mess through here. Across from the Arctic Circle, on the south side, steep gravel roads lined with houses and cancer trees up the side of the canyon. I slow down. No one visible. I slow all the way down. I lower my window. I know the shack the guy was talking about. It's past the Arctic Circle. I take a deep breath of canyon air: not a hint of bar-b-q smoke...usually, that's all you smell. We're all cooking out now. Picnics forever! I don't see anything –

That girl with the gray eyes – she's the one to watch. Thoughts of her jump out. That mirror thing was really smart. What she did underground, too, sounds incredible. I need to touch base with her. Well, first thing a cop learns is when folks are all beside themselves freaking out, it's best to go very slow and very calm, and pick out the cool heads you can rely on. I force my thoughts to something here, so I can come across all serene like, but as a pro. But that girl, thinking on her, that girl does stuff. That girl is doing stuff. I need to talk to her.

I come to a stop in the road at the end of the parking lot, pulled off to the side. I flip on the loudspeaker: "This is Officer Latta. I got a report of gunfire. I want everyone to just relax and let me know what's going on. Just take a breath. We got this. You don't want to be shooting so close to homes, and all like that. Safety first. Someone could get hurt. Everybody okay? I'm coming out. I'm getting out of my car."

Who's shooting? What's going on?

I open my door and am about to step out of the car when a scraggly haired man kinda falls or stumbles out of the trees from the south side. My legs are twisted out, but I'm still sitting in the driver's seat. He's close, and he's got a pistol out in front of himself, holding it with two hands, aiming it at me. It's a .45 1911 ACP Colt!

Damn!

I keep my voice chill: "What the hell, man? Put down the weapon before someone gets hurt. Come on now, take it easy. Put down the weapon."

He fires. The bullet hits the windshield and cracks a comet trajectory across my field of view. I duck down behind the open door with my standard police issue Glock drawn. I hear muttering and groaning. Voices screech back and forth across the canyon. Another bullet flies by me. From under the cruiser door, I fire.

He's hit. He falls. Screams of agony, now. And another guy, crying, just wailing, lurches out from back in the brush and trees where the shooter was. He's got a pistol and starts firing at the shack.

Gunfire from the shack, now, and it sounds like a rifle. Then, a second weapon fires from the shack. The new, hairy young man keeps firing at the shack. He's got what looks like some kind of semi-automatic. He keeps glancing over at his buddy stretched out in the road. I can see he's shaking. A crack from the rifle in the shack and he's hit. He spins around hard, but somehow manages to come back to face the shack. He takes a shot at the shack. The shack explodes.

The whole back of the shack goes up in a fire ball. The guy collapses by his dead buddy. Two men down!

I kinda roll back into the cruiser. Grab up the mic of the loudspeaker, hoping it was not hit.

"If you can hear this, go for help! This is Officer Latta, we have two men down and a fire. We need fire fighters and security and health workers on the double!"

I stand up beside the cruiser, door open in front of me.

The fire's not as bad as the explosion promised. Lot of white smoke. The back half of the shack shows flames. Nothing near brush or trees. Smoke. It starts raining. Swear to God, real live rain! Fat pungent drops! A light rain, a fancy drizzle. But rain for sure. The whole place takes on that desert rainy smell, over the smell of chemically smoke.

Two guys burst out of the shack's front door, hollerin' and yelping. The door bangs shut behind them. I raise my weapon. They're carrying rifles. They throw them down.

Bunch of Wooks!

The bigger of the two smolders, with smoky puffs coming off his clothes and from his big hair and beard. He's older looking. He puts his hands on his head. He yells, "Patrice is in there! Somebody's gotta go back in there for her!"

I lope over with my weapon drawn and held out straight in front of me. "Step away from the rifles. Keep your hands up!" My weapon drips. The rain is putting out the big guy. His companion is a skinny kid who can't be more than seventeen. He's yellowish and his exposed skin around his face and hands is pimply soot.

An old pick up bounds up Main Street at us. It shoves itself to a stop next to my patrol car. Bunch of guys in the back! I give out a sigh. A splutter. From the passenger side up front, Alan Ripple jumps out with his deer rifle. Bob Pauley is driving. I recognized his truck right away. The four guys in the back have rifles.

Alan Ripple heads over to me. "Wadda you got, Oscar?"

"Fire seems to be dying down. You guys, pat these two down, get 'em tied up. Get their guns out of here. Someone go check on those two on the road. For right now, just stay by them. Let's get a perimeter going. Alan, we gotta girl inside. You wanna go with me? You don't have to. Maybe you should send for the fire crew."

Alan talks to his men. I can't listen. One thing at a time right now. He turns back to me and says, "Let's find that girl!"

Alan and I go for the shack. He's holding his rifle out in front. Smoke is bad. He slings the rifle over his shoulder. Rain's pitter patter. We hunker down on either side of the front door. Not much heat. Crouching there like TV cops. I call out, "Police! Police! This is the police. We're coming in!" I grab and turn the door knob, throw open the door. We scramble in, keeping low.

Alan mutters fast, "Check it out! That smell? Chemical fire. You know what we got here."

The smoke's coming from the back. Small place, we're in the main room up front. No furniture.

Heap of sleeping bags and blankets in the corner. To the side, maybe a kitchen, dining area with a table with scales and boxes of small plastic bags. No stove. No fridge. Wish I had a wet kerchief over my face! Smoke's blowing out, getting sucked out. We head towards the back. The door in the back is closed.

Now what's the dealio? You're not supposed to open a closed door in a fire?

I hear chain saws. Heavy blows rain down on the back of the house. Firemen to the rescue!

I kick in the door and a blast of thick white smoke, like in a big ball, shoots right out at me. I duck. Alan is right behind me, and he dives into the room low, under the smoke. He yelps. It's the bathroom. It's where the explosion happened. But it's just smoldering now. Rain's coming in from the exploded roof, falling on the young woman's body face down on the floor. She's burned bad. Her size makes me figure young, but I could be wrong. All sorts of glassware blown up, burned up. Glass is embedded in the poor girl's back in several places. She's not bleeding anymore. Patrice, I think. Maybe she was the chemist. The chemical smell is putrid in here, probably toxic. Alan gags, backs out fast.

I go, "We got to get her out of here."

Suddenly, I think, the desert smells like rain.

## Alan Ripple

I volunteered for security detail. Lucien quickly made me team leader and now this: burned out corpse of a young woman in a sooty pool of her own deep fried, congealed blood.

> *Outside*
> *the rain stops*
> *Oscar plods out of the shack*
> *face pretty intense*

What makes a hero? Is that a dumb ass question these days? I'm a dumb ass.

Grace under pressure? Cliché. When you sacrifice for the good of – isn't that brave? Don't matter no more, I guess.

Burned up girl on the floor of a shack!

Cause it goes the other way, too. What if it's a sacrifice that wasn't necessary...then who's the dumb ass? We're not heroes, we're survivors. Edie and I decided to stay because it had taken too damn long to get a place of our own. We'd worked too hard, scrounged too much. Edie wanted kids. Maybe never now. Maybe we're back to square one, scrounging forever. Like that's all we know. By the time we got our house, by the time we were in our 30s, we thought we still had a chance to make it in the music industry. Then the whole damn world urped up total chaos. Haven't had a rehearsal of *Ghost Riders* in over a year. Me and Edie practice. The others took off. Not all for consolidation. Hell with them. We were never gonna make it. We didn't have the original songs. We didn't hold our mouths right. We played covers in funky country bars. Edie, dressed up as Dale, didn't cut it anymore, unless in some kind of ironic, nostalgic way.

Burned up girl on the floor of a shack!

No kids for us at the end of the world. No fabulous riches and celebrity. We see it for what it is: the penultimate adventure for scroungers. Scroungers!

I mean, seriously, what kind of people would want to get consolidated in some cement high rise in Tucson? There, to await obliteration...instead of waiting for it here, in their hometown, in their own place? Makes no sense to us. Maybe, now, we'll get some requests, do some jams, community gigs. Ha! For sure we could get out the Stetsons, the acoustics. A new community needs a new sound. People like music.

I thought of a new name for the band: *Apocalypse Later.* Sure, it's smart ass irony, but it's way tough as post-apocalypse cowboy music. Couple tracks already running 'round my head...

One of the guys, Barry Hilton, goes, "Those two over there are dead. What do we do with them?"

I look over at Oscar. He goes, "Get some guys and go into the shack. Fire's out. The main room has a bunch of sleeping bags. Gather up a bunch and wrap the dead guys in them. I'll take care of the girl. Leave me one sleeping bag or a blanket. Put the bodies in the back of one of the pickups."

Oscar is stiff, talking grim: "We'll go downtown, see what everybody thinks. What we should do. We'll need a burial detail."

I nod. "Sounds good, Oscar. Barry, take another guy for blankets. We take these two live ones to the convention center, Oscar? Figure out what to do with them."

The firemen's detail leader, Frank Trevor, strides up from around back of the shack. He's carrying an axe and a shovel. "It's out. I guess a bullet went through the wall and sparked the chemicals. Nasty."

Oscar Latta says, "Thanks for your help."

Frank Trevor says, "You guys want us to stay? What are we gonna do with these two?" He motions with his head to the prisoners, sitting on the damp ground, back to back, their hands tied behind them. "A trial?"

Oscar Latta's eyes jump.

Neighborhood locals with their own weapons are walking over, checking on what's going on, forming little groups of two or three. Oscar says, "Keep folks back."

Frank Trevor goes on with his query, "A trial and what? Sentence them to jail? We got no extra food or water for trash like this. Plus, you'd need to have people assigned to look after them."

Oscar Latta says, "So what do we do?" He shakes his head. "This is not gonna be easy. I guess, we gotta see what they have to say? Maybe some kind of hearing? Whenever a law enforcement officer is involved in a shooting, there's gotta be a hearing."

I go, "We can't shoot 'em."

Oscar nods, says, "They're in bad shape. I don't know what would be best. Don't look at me like that! I'm just saying. We got no rehab in Coltrane."

"Guess not," says Frank Trevor. "Well, word'll spread. Everyone'll know what's happened. Let folks decide."

The bigger suspect, older, hairier, who'd been literally smoking, shouts, "We can hear you, you dumb fucks! It's too late! You're fucked. We're fucked. We're all fucked! Cold turkey all the way! You all be jonesing over your *Cheetos*, your brewskis, your TV programs before long. Just wait."

Frank Trevor says, "Junkies. Fucking Wookies. Don't know how cops stand that shit."

The big guy cackles, "They came after us! They were shooting up our place! We were – it was self defense!"

Oscar Latta says, "Alan, people are getting curious." He sighs, points. "Our sleeping bags, let's get this show on the road. Get the bodies out of here. Take these two downtown."

"Okay, you guys," I holler. "Let's get it going."

Rubberneckers all over the place. "Folks, you gotta keep back."

The crowd mutters. Questions come out.

I go: "We got it under control. We'll have a meeting about all this, Figure it out. Okay?"

Oscar Latta heads back in to that nasty shack on his unspeakable duty. He wears a look on his sooty face. Sad. Resigned. His uniform's dirty.

## Susan Kell

> *...slouching towards the convention center*
> *between rain drops made of syntha-tears*
> *show emotion sky*
> *stand in the face of god*
> *new sky*
> *gray beard overcast*
> *new god*
> *tears squeezed out*
> *'Rain, rain, go away, come again another day!'*
> *hurts the sky to yield its bounty*
> *booty*
> *sky hurts*
> *clouds ache*
> *air thrums*

Hello, children! Hello, citizens! Hello, downtown!

The natives are ceaseless. We've all been savoring our final idioms. Fiend memes! Now, the town wakes up.

Gotta go see what's up this day. I heard cars or trucks –
the ubiquitous pickups breed in the fall, pushing out baby
trucks and baby truck drivers. They are fertile, fervid,
febrile. As rabbis!

Lots of cottontails in town, under the landscaping
gnomes. I saw into a rabbit's eye, big and glossy, glassy,
but way back in there: flicker of life. He popped away,
under the morning glory vines in the cancer trees up
against an erosion wall. When supplies run low, when
people are hungry for rabbits' feet –

Hello, students!

Bikes, a horse, take up position in front of the
convention center. Envoys, scouts, diplomats, front and
center. The flow of info blows mofo. Here is today's
mastery. Today, we cross another limit that we assumed a
boundary, when it wasn't at all. Past town and the turn
offs, I see the roadblock glistening under gray tears. In
Van Gogh pastels. Then, up the highway, past the
roadblock, cottony fill at the end of the road – the cloud
bank still.

*Alles gut!*

Pickups! Police car! I'm just in time.

Here's Latta, Lucien, the mayor himself! Folks
gather in front of the convention center. In rain gear or
sweat shirts and light wraps. An umbrella seems funny at
the end of the world. Even women carry guns or
pitchforks. I don't. Some wear fancy belt holsters with
pistols. Many carry sticks, like mop handles scrimshawed
to staffs. The committees are about to meet? Confer on the
list of honey do's? But, no! Two guys, youngish louts, in
the back of one of the pickups. Men are helping them
down. The two's hands are tied. The game is afoot! The

moon is down!

Cry havoc!

"What's happening? What's happening?" I cry.

Mayor John John positions himself in front, then his big, fat man voice: "There's been a shooting!"

Aha! Goes the crowd with vast inhalations. Suck up the poison, citizens!

People call out for details. Question marks dazzle the air above the heads of everyone there. The mayor and Latta look worried, exchanging notes.

Daisy Piper pushes in. I recognize that glow. I know her brains are stretching to work this. How can I help? How can she help me? I look away so she won't know I know. She's on her own. Like all of us. I know she'll make it. She goes to a pickup and examines what's back there. Its contents. What's there? I can't tell. Lumpy wraps – should I go see?

Mayor John John continues, "Officer Latta got a report of gunshots up Mule Canyon at a miner's shack by the old Arctic Circle. When he got up there a young man, who has been identified as a Mr. Thomas Grayling, came out of the bushes opposite the shack, firing a weapon at Officer Latta. Officer Latta was forced to return fire. Mr. Grayling was hit and subsequently died. Another man, identified as Mr. Sergei Robinett, came out of the same bushes firing at Officer Latta and at the shack. Gun fire from the shack hit Mr. Robinett, but not before one of his bullets ignited the meth lab in the shack. There was an explosion. The fire has been contained. The drizzle helped."

He pauses, because at the word *drizzle* it hits him how horrible all of this is, yet the word *drizzle* almost makes him giggle. "Ms. Patrice Long burned to death in the fire. Or maybe it was the explosion. In any case, we now have three bodies in the back of that pickup. These two live ones were in the shack with Ms. Long, but managed to escape. Their names are Joe Nichols and Sky – no last name."

Someone yells, "Death don't have no mercy!"

Bob Pauley starts in, "They're Wookies! We got no jail. What do we do with them?"

Frankie Lucien says, "Let's get outta the rain. Let's go inside where we can talk."

Alan Ripple, from that funny cowboy punk band, says, "What about the bodies?"

Officer Oscar Latta says, "I suppose we should get one of our health people, like Miss Gorey over here to look at them. Death certificate."

Bob Pauley says, "Dead is dead."

Latta shrugs, exhales, says, "I'll head up a burial detail. Over where we put Oscar?"

Mayor John John tries to lead everyone into the convention center, but his corralling won't work. Too many want to talk it out right then and there. They want to get in close to see the wrapped bodies. The two live ones are jostled and pulled and yanked.

Frankie Lucien insists, "Get them out of here!"

Meeting in the rain! There must be a hundred people.

Dead dead children. Three dead. Bury 'em at the swimming pool. They'll swim away like seals through the secret underground passages. Free at last. Free at last! Two thousand miles of tunnel beneath us, enough to house us all.

The older of the two live ones is Joe Nichols. I think I've seen him around, hanging out at the park. He's got the male leer down. His face can't relax and just sit there, without that sinister leer. He's chubby, hairy. He looks out of it. He looks like he's on the verge of falling asleep. He looks like he hasn't had a clear thought in a million years. Clarity is reserved for those who stayed by choice. The other young man, Sky, is shrunken. Gaunt. Pimples popping pustules over his exposed skin. He could be one of my students. A student I'd be concerned with: is he eating? Is he legal? Is he hooked? Is he leaning into death? Suicide and teens. Got that covered! Teens flocked to consolidation.

Did these two choose slow suicide by drugs? Did the cooker chemist make a conscious decision – *oh, yes, this is the future: stay in Coltrane at the end of the world and make meth?* The high school kids called them Wooks, for Wookies. The way they look like Wild Men, a used paradigm at the end of the world.

Daisy Piper is talking and everyone listens: "We're not gonna shoot 'em. We banish them. We can't afford to keep these guys here and watch them 24-7. We exile them."

She was a reader at one time. I loved her reading and then need to talk it out. What's she reading now? She loved Shelley, Blake. Adored Emily. I tried to guide...just a little bit. She never needed much help. Every teacher's dream student. She believed in ideas and knew there was a way in to clarity. She adored the *Great Gatsby*, like I did. But I didn't make her like it. She delighted in books and she could write.

Frankie Lucien goes, "Clever girl!"

Sam Bean is next to him and mouths the words, "*Jurassic Park*, Part 1."

So there's that: total commitment to our alternate path means commitment to consequences. It has to be, or else what happens when someone throws a sabot into the gears of our commitment? No one figured on shootouts. We figured we humans had seen it all, so what the hey. Why consolidate? The hell with Trilobites! The only thing we humans don't know is what we humans have never known. Might as well stay. We decided to stay to maintain our familiar ignorance rather than take on new ignorance. Now with mounting monster manipulation and basic neuronal hijacking – oh, yes, our brains are being aligned.

"Where?" I go. "Where do we banish them? Shouldn't we hear what they have to say? Let everybody know and decide?"

Oscar Latta, bloody and dirty, manages to make himself known. He wants to say something.

A big crowd now, gawkers at the pickups: dead people. People like to look at dead people. Dead people don't mind. Coltrane thinkers in their thoughts and L. L. Bean outfits get an eyeful. They emit air and gas, sighs and whews. Our incipient leaders, bristling, busy, bloviating, some even in ties, vapid, not knowing the next thing.

I figured folks would be busy moisture gathering. The morning was moist. But this morning, this new day, already living up to our new tradition: new dogma: one monster per day...

...these are our monsters...surrounded by men, dragged to the front doors.

Oscar Latta says, "We take 'em up there to the cloud bank. Up there on the highway. Let them walk in. Let the so-called authorities deal with them."

Frankie Lucien adds, "They take one look at these two, they'll know what's up. I guess it could go either way."

Joe Nichols weeps now, and it's a snotty sort of tears that makes me want to look away.

Sky yells, "I ain't going in there and you can't make me! This is a free country, last I checked. I'd rather you just fricking shoot me. You might as well. Go ahead. Do us all a favor. You know what's back in there well as I do. Them baldies. And you know what they do. Tear you to pieces. Uh-uh! I ain't going. You got no right!"

Margot Pitka says, "There's no argument here. I mean about the baldies. But we don't know all what's back there. Police Chief Sisken, I bet. They can deal with you, we can't. You made a decision, like all of us, to stay. But you made other decisions that none of us made. Or agreed to. See what I mean? People are dead because of you. Do you have anything to say? What happened back there?"

Wet, ugly, they groan, foam bubbles down their chins.

Councilman Ramsey says, "Frankie, we gotta keep watch up at that shack. People will be curious."

Frankie Lucien says, "Agreed. For sure."

I go, "Have we all decided? Is this the best we can do? Does everyone in town know? Shouldn't we wait until everyone can decide? The majority? What's the rush? We can have a hearing."

Frankie Lucien says, "You guys have anything to say?"

They howl!

Moaning in the mist...

Frankie Lucien moves over to the cluster of men at the front door. He gestures at the two prisoners and extends an arm, saying, "Let's go."

Sky starts screaming. Joe pees hisself.

Frankie Lucien and a couple big men get around the two and force them into walking mode. The escort moves out, gawkers tight behind. We're following. The two are led but not without extravagant dragging, hauling, pulling. We get around the convention center, moving to the roadblock. Do roadblock guards, men and women of all ages, all with weapons, know what's happening? The crowd is strangely quiet. I can see the mayor tagging along. Officer Latta is stern faced, looking ahead, following. People are running back and forth from the convention center to the roadblock. It's happening fast.

I catch up with the prisoners and their handlers, start prognosticating, gliding along nimble and light in my sensible shoes: "At least wait 'til the whole town knows. We can wait. We can go over to City Park and the whole town can gather. The rain's stopped. We can talk then.

Not everybody knows. We got time – there's no rush."

They're walking right down the middle of the road the baldies attacked on. This very same stretch of road the big black wedge machine came hurtling. The crowd thinks better of it, starts backing up. People slip away. People in front of the roadblock glare, stare. No one's saying much.

We're there, where the clouds take over. Some of us get close to peek. I don't know if anyone has been this close before. Did anyone check it out? Has anyone gone in? Don't think so. Daisy is next to me. She's straining to see into the white. I can't see anything. Can she? We strain an inch closer. Murky foggy white. I don't want to get any closer. She doesn't either. She's got a big hunting knife on her side. Little girl! With a big knife. For sure, in the white tendrils, yes, we can barely make out shapes...forms...structures in the fog's density. We're not seeing things. Items. There's something back there –

Daisy says, "It looks like a toll booth."

**Roland Banks**

*skateboards*
*are*
*rockets*

I wish I had my skateboard right now. But I left it back at the house. I didn't hear anything was going on until the last minute. Me and some kids ran downtown right away, and I forgot my skateboard because we were talking and stuff. I can fly on my skateboard. My parents don't like it. And I don't like the helmet they gave me before they left, because I can't see good then. My parents, my PUs, are going to be so mad at me. But they discorporated –

After the two bads walked into the clouds all crying and moaning, everybody started back to town. Nobody talked. Seemed like everybody sad. We kids broke away and headed back up the Gulch by ourselves.

Daisy and Clay and Bennett were in front. Talking. Real serious. Big kids with scrunched up faces. You can tell those squinty eyes aren't seeing what's right in front of them. They're seeing ideas and words. Lots of words. I don't know what 'banish' or 'exile' means. Something to do with the druggies who walked in to the cloud bank where everything bad comes from. I can tell the big kids want a confab. That's when everyone gets together at our house and talks stuff out. Daisy and Clay and Bennett keep talking the whole way up the Gulch. Scouts follow us in a circle, not too far away. They got sticks. They can throw rocks. They keep an eye out. I'm a scout. The way we like to do it.

I'm close enough to Daisy and Clay and Bennett to hear what they're saying:

Daisy: "It looked the same, like a toll booth. Like a border crossing?"

Bennett: "It's gotta be more than that, what you couldn't see. A toll booth makes no sense. But no people? Guards? Toll booth is just the first thing you associate with what you saw."

Daisy shakes her head. No. In two places now, the same...structures. The pole across the road."

Clay: "Maybe." He shrugs, puffs. "I thought they were for taking tolls. I didn't see anybody."

Daisy: "We couldn't hear anything, either. I mean, when they marched into the clouds. Not a sound. Creepy quiet real fast. Do clouds dampen sounds? Miss Kell is right. Maybe we should have waited."

Clay: "What for? It was your idea. How'd you get so smart?"

Bennett: "Notice how smart everybody seems to be getting? No, I mean it. I've noticed it. Us, even the PUs."

Just then, huffing and puffing, comes that big boy that hangs around looking at Daisy funny, that Clay don't like.

Bennett says, 'Hello, Tenny.'

Clay and Daisy nod or blink at him. They look funny, like you look before you have to do some chore you don't like. This boy, Tenny, is breathing hard, walking along with us, no weapon, and he blurts, "Daisy, I heard what happened. You did it again! Everyone's gonna think you're magic or something."

Nearby little kids giggle hearing the words. I don't. I don't like Tenny.

Daisy says, "Everybody helps. We made a decision. We don't know if every decision is right. We'll see how it turns out. Maybe, I'm responsible for two boys' deaths."

"How do we know if it's right?" asks Tenny, stopping on the road, which makes Daisy stop to look at him. "How will we know? Funny, huh, used to rely on our PUs to tell us what was right. Now?" He snorts. "Seems to me, we're splintering, we're all splintering. Separating, breaking down to these little groups. Going rogue. Commando style."

Scouts watch. Wait. Walk along. In position.

Little kids make perfect scouts, says Daisy, because people tend not to watch little kids. They're like invisible. We take turns going out, wandering over different parts of town, keeping our eyes open for water and supplies and usable sticks. Seeing what's going on, in case some of those baldies show up.

I have a club. I got it stuck in my pants, under my belt. But I'm not on today, day off, so I follow the big kids back to the house at the end of the road.

I don't miss my parents at all. I'm glad I decided to stay. This is a lot more fun than anything. I get to ride my skateboard all the time.

Cassie runs out of the house and grabs onto Daisy. Daisy hugs her back, but Cassie won't let go of her leg. She's like a big leech on Daisy, so Daisy has to walk like a pirate with a peg leg, carrying the girl. Cassie's slurring out, "You have to see, you have to see."

I can pick up Cassie. Cassie's smart. But she's a scaredy cat. I am half a year younger than Cassie.

Didi is the youngest, and she comes out of the house saying, "My parents want me back. But I'm not going."

Cassie adds, "They came over and everything."

We go in the house. Kids come up to say hi and what's going on. Cassie keeps going, "Come see, come see."

Daisy says, "Didi, we'll figure it out. I'll go with you to talk to them. Okay?"

Didi won't cry. Daisy lets Cassie pull her into the kitchen to the five-gallon water jug we use to store our potable water, resting on an extra chair in the corner. I know what potable means.

Cassie points to it.

Daisy takes a look. She goes, "Huh!"

Bennett and Tenny push in to see. Tenny says, "It's full."

Bennett shakes his head, goes, "Kids must have scored some good water – "

Cassie goes, "No! It was half full. Member, Daisy? Did anyone put any water in it?" No one answers. "See! And the rain water from last night still needs boiling."

Daisy looks at me and nods.

Daisy rolls up the sleeve of her sweat shirt. She goes to the sink and uses the water bottle there to wash her hands and her left arm. With soap. Scrubs hard. She comes back over to the five-gallon jug and unscrews the top of the wide mouth.

Daisy says, "I better check on something."

Bennett says, "Very hygienic. I can make pincers."

Cassie goes, "For reals!"

Bennett says, "We got to take some of the water out. Displacement." He grabs three empty plastic water bottles and starts filling them from the spigot in the side.

Daisy goes, "The whole town's hurting for water. Folks'll do anything for water. That what you mean about splintering, Tenny?"

Cassie says, "I hate splinters."

Daisy laughs.

Tenny says, "It's the deaths. I think. Got people freaked."

Daisy says, "But we're good. Aren't we?"

The kids chime in with agreement.

Tenny says, "Everybody knew those Wooks were using. That's why they're called Wooks. What else could we have done?"

Daisy says, "Did we vote? Or was it mob rule?"

Tenny says, "People hang with people they agree with. Right? Don't you think, even if the whole town was there, and talked it out, it would have been the same?" He can't take his eyes off Daisy. He's staring at her bare arm, like it's a bone he wants to eat. "People who stayed have stuff in common."

"That's like saying whatever happens has gotta be right because it happened," says Daisy.

Bennett finishes with his water bottles. He says, "That should be enough. What are you gonna do, Daisy?"

Daisy sticks her bare arm into the water jug. "I washed it!"

Tenny goes, "Don't try this at home, kiddies! No contamination, right?"

Her arm wriggles and flexes, so I guess that means her hand is checking at the bottom. She says, "It's the pong, the little silver ball me and Clay found in the mine." She pulls her arm out and in her hand is a little silver ball about the size of a ping pong ball.

Tenny says, "You put it in your drinking water?"

I go, "It's not poison. It made those supplies in the underground. Huh, Daisy?"

"Which the big wigs and Pus confiscated, for the good of the town," says Tenny in a dumb voice. "Keep 'em in storage for an emergency! Yeah, right, like we can trust those douches. What if the supplies are poison? What if the water is? Maybe, it's radioactive? It could be radioactive, then we'd all start glowing at night. We need a Geiger counter. We're like guinea pigs."

"I want to see." I go over to Daisy, lean into her stomach, reach out to touch the silver ball in her hand. It's wet.

Cassie asserts: "For cute! I love guinea pigs."

Bennett goes, "It was the perfect place to hide it. You dropped it in yesterday. Maybe half-filled yesterday. Today, voila! Water. Filled up!"

Tenny says, "How can it make water? That's impossible, Bennett, and you know that." He pauses, waits, glances around at the kids, then in a spooky voice says: "Unless it's magic. Wow – maybe it can make gold? Or skunk?"

Cassie goes, "Ewww! Skunks are stinky! Can poison be magic?"

Bennett says, "We don't know what we got here."

Cassie shakes her head. Makes a frown. "I'm not drinking this water," and she puts down the plastic water bottle that Bennett had filled and given her, that she'd been sipping from. "Outer space water. I don't want to be a spaceman."

Didi says, "'Outer space water.'"

Daisy fusses with their hair, giggling with them for a second, then takes a big drink from the water bottle. She sighs. "We got a never-ending water supply!" she declares with a big, outside voice.

Tenny goes, "Don't tell the PUs! They'll take it for sure! Make it make bombs or some shit. You know they will."

Daisy glances around at the faces. She says, "We're not splinters." Everybody laughs. "We trust each other. We're in this together. For now we keep it quiet. Top super secret. Everybody got that? But we share. Anybody want a drink?" Daisy glugs a second huge swallow gulp. "We have to keep our options open."

Kids nod.

Bennett says, "Gimme that." He takes the water bottle from Daisy and drinks. Then he makes gargling monster sounds. Everyone giggles and snorts. "Tastes fine. Get me some more water bottles to fill." He drinks some more. "You're gonna put the whatchacallit, the ping pong, back in there? Maybe we should test the ball? See what else it can do?"

Daisy says, "Bennett, you're in charge of coming up with tests. Meanwhile, we leave it in here for making water. I'm fine. It's just water. You feel normal, Bennett?"

Tenny says, "Oh, yeah, Bennett's normal. Anyway, how would any of us know what normal is?" He laughs but nobody laughs with him. "We fill up water bottles all day. Boy, we'll have enough to trade."

Didi says, "We could trade water for candy." Everybody laughs.

Daisy sees her face, goes, "What, D? You got something on your mind?"

Didi says, "I think we should have a carnival at City Park with a bouncy castle."

Everybody is stunned.

Daisy says, "Beautiful! Let's do it!"

Bennett interrupts the goof: "We need a Geiger counter. Maybe somebody has one. Maybe, the mining museum?"

Tenny pokes at the silver ping pong ball in Daisy's hand. "Dood! It's inert! I took chemistry, too."

"You don't know! How do you know?" answers Bennett.

Daisy drops the ball. So that's that.

I bust out with, "What about my disc? Who's gonna test it?"

Daisy shakes her arm free of drops, then she screws the top of the jug back on.

Tenny goes, "What disc?"

Bennett says, "Everyone's splintering because everything splinters. Second law, man. It's like we take one step forward and a half a step back. Every time."

"Quit trying to change the subject," says Tenny.

Daisy says, "There have been discoveries – " Then, she stops and turns from Bennett to Tenny: "I feel bad about those druggies. No one's trying to change the subject."

"What disc? I was just asking," said Tenny. "Like a CD or a DVD?"

Cassie goes, "What is 'banish'?"

Clay mumbles, "Is he one of us?" His heads jerks at Tenny.

Daisy says, "Tenny, are you with us now?"

Tenny looks embarrassed. He gets real formal. He pops with: "Hey, she has my baseball bat."

Didi says, "Finder's keepers! It's my stick. Right, Daisy?"

Daisy says, "Tenny, you're welcome to stay. All you guys up at Eliana's."

Tenny laughs. "You mean we get to sleep here with all these little kids?"

Clay says, "No one's forcing you."

"Hey, I'm on your side," says Tenny. "I helped with the black thing that day. With Daisy and Bennett. I can help out. I won't say anything about the ping pong ball. I don't know about the other kids at Eliana's. Besides, it'd get pretty crowded here."

"Not a word!" cry kids.

Clay says, "Do we vote?"

"What about it, guys?" says Daisy.

Cassie says, "We need more big kids."

The other kids nod their heads, so I go fast, "What about my disc? It needs testing. We still haven't tested it."

Bennett says, giggling, "We got toys! We got the latest toys! We got the black thing. Daisy brought in the ping pong ball with Clay. We got Roland's disc. Those guys like the mayor, the other PUs, would freak."

"What about the disc?" asks Tenny again.

Clay says, "Tell 'im your story, Roland."

"Remember that day, up at the tunnel? I was up there like a scout with my skateboard. And this big truck came up to the tunnel and shot out those discs. And Ms. Lucien yells, 'Let 'em have it!' And they blow them to smithereens. But I caught one. It floats. Just a flat disc. Sorta like a Frisbee. But it floats, and it kinda sorta flew me all the way back here on my board."

"Wow," goes Tenny. "I heard about the discs at the tunnel. What you did, kid. Wow. Didn't they get one to some scientist guy?"

"We're doing the right thing. On our own," says Daisy.

Cassie says, "I hate splinters! We have the disc, the ball, the case it made, and that black thing."

I yell, "Let's check the disc!"

Bennett and me go for it. We needed a super

hiding place for the disc, and first we figured the chimney was it. But suppose we had to make an emergency fire? Or wanted to cook something in the fireplace? So we moved it. Alianna had brought to the house her pet rat in its own cage. Wasn't supposed to. Against our rules. She kinda had it hid in the back. Bennett and me put the disc in there and it went right to the top of the cage and just stayed there. Alianna was afraid it would mutate her rat. Alianna is ten. But, so far, the rat, Mr. Licorice, is ok. The rat is all black. I think it stinks. We put an old towel on the top of the cage as a cover and there's no way anyone can tell anything's in there.

Bennett brings in the cage, puts it on the table. Alianna's scared she's in trouble. She keeps back.

Bennett's pulls off the towel. Mr. Licorice watches us, twitching his whiskers. His eyes look like black peas. He starts washing his face.

Tenny goes, "Rat? Hello, rat."

"His name is Mr. Licorice," says Alianna and slowly slides over to unlatch the cage door and get her stinky friend.

Daisy reaches in and grabs the disc. It's wrapped with a wash cloth and an old t-shirt of one of the kids. She takes it out of the cage, uncovers it. The way her hand jerks, lifting and falling, means it's still working. She says, "What do we know about it?"

"Well," begins Bennett, sounding like a teacher, "we know it doesn't have a lot of parts. It's not like the black machine gun thing."

I jump in, "I saw what was inside the one Ms. Lucien blasted. Just junk. No motor. Little bits of junk." No one says a thing. I go on, "Maybe the big black thing isn't really a machine gun."

"Maybe this thing just wants to float around," says Bennett.

Clay says, "You know what it's doing."

Tenny says, "What is it doing? It looks like a plate."

"I don't know," says Clay. I bet he could beat up Tenny. Clay says, "Surveillance."

Bennett says, staring at the disc in Daisy's hand. "That's why we wrapped it up. Let it go, Daisy. See what happens. All the windows closed?"

Kids go yes. Daisy releases it and it floats right up to the ceiling.

Didi says, "Don't let it get away!"

Tenny says, "It just hangs there? Wanting to go up?"

"At the tunnel, they wanted to come to town," I say.

"What's it for?" says Daisy. "I guess, we know what the silver ping pong ball is for. And the machine gun that is not a machine gun – "

Tenny goes, "Clay's right. Surveillance, 24-7. The uglies figured they'd release a bunch of these so they could keep tabs on us. Like that big silver sphere dealio was supposed to. Like maybe this disc is right now transmitting pictures of us."

Cassie waves.

I go, "Uh-uh!"

Daisy says, "What do you think, Roland?"

"They're for free. They're for fun. For skateboarding and stuff."

Didi and Cassie start jerking their heads back and forth very fast, blinking all the time. They look like they're having a seizure. Cassie goes, "This is what Clay told us to do. Huh, Clay? To keep the eyes in the sky confused? Right? All you got to do is move your head back and forth real fast and blink your eyes a lot. He told us about it."

Clay says, "You got it."

The whole group in the living room, standing around the table, all eyes up on the ceiling where the disc is, start moving their heads back and forth quickly. Like we're all totally spazzing out –

# THE SIXTH DAY

**Janet Gorey**

*treat the sick*
*cause no harm*
*no one shows*
*for sick call*

My new routine – come in early just in case. Change has come. Those who stayed in Coltrane have gotten over that prevailing American myth that illness is the result of being bad. Once that's overcome, it's simple to keep healthy, because one takes responsibility for one's own bod. Maybe that realization came when we decided to stay. Maybe it's been reaffirmed with the deaths. Change comes knocking. We came to Coltrane in the first place because it was the last place. Nowhere else to go on the map. We're at the bottom of the page. We had no idea what was to come. For all its flaws, this goofy Art Town still affords a sense of community. I'm telling everyone to get naked in the rain and wash then! We can't exactly waste water on baths.

The last medical updates we received were all about the latest plagues. New viruses mutating, evolving, conquering. But they always say that. Plague or spill or infestation. Take your pick. They tell us the whole border zone is contaminated now, a dead zone making the ultimate moat, where only special border forces tread, in their hazmat suits, keeping out the mutants, the carriers. We will have nowhere to turn for help. All the little towns of southern Arizona gone, gobbled up. Except for Coltrane. Consolidation took them! My artist side burned out on the end of the world nostalgia. It doesn't help. We arrived long before it got so bad, so we have history here. We trust ourselves alone. We have little idea what we are getting into. After the past few days, we know a little: death, baldies, uglies. Is this suicide then? Suicide by experiment – the latest gray goo tests cooked up in the lab. Is that what we're doing? No way. We are here because we didn't believe in suicide.

I suppose deep down we knew we couldn't keep them out – as in military or governmental intruders. We knew we wouldn't simply break away and truly be left alone. Ever after. But still. We ended up here. We came to Coltrane for a reason: treason. We no longer accepted the status quo, which might as well mean, *we no longer accepted that reality.* Nope. Nada. Nichts. We came here and we stayed here because of treason. Our desert island, cut off by what seems crafted fog we dare not cross, has enough. No. Is it large enough to sustain us? It is large enough.

The chronically ill and disabled went with consolidation. No way we can maintain their drips and monitors and respirators. They'll have continuous care – no charge. Yay, consolidation means free health care. For the last 500 years humans had the ability to feed everyone. In consolidation, everyone lives together and everything is free. Dream come true! They make sure you have a job. Everyone works, everyone gets stuff.

Those of us who stayed tend to be healthy, at least healthier than the 'average' schlub. Chronic illness has left the building. Long term care no longer meaningful. The decrepit elderly are gone. Preventative medicine steps in. Twenty years as a county nurse, then 10 years in nursing ed at the community college have crafted a solid base for me. I wish we had more doctors. Retired docs who want to be left alone ain't much. I have sick call every morning at the convention center. Then, after, when no one shows, I work with Tom Dillon on the latrine plan. Every neighborhood will have its own poopers. That's right: calculate the poop! If there are 900 people in Coltrane, pooping every day, and a 6 foot hole can hold X amount, then how often do we move on and build a new one? The funk calculation! We can keep the odor and flies down. We have to keep folks from digging their own latrines all over the place. Or, literally, we're going to be drowning in human excrement. We have a few barrels of lye to spread. I've got basic equipment, limited supplies. We have a few room temp drugs. Lots of supplements.

I look over my domain at the convention center. A couple empty cots. A cabinet with supplies. A couple shelving units with more supplies. Bandages mainly. Alcohol swabs. The healthiest people get cuts and bruises. I can sew them up! What about gunshot wounds?

To give of oneself is a key. Not necessarily *the* key. Before consolidation, Americans didn't really have neighborhoods anymore. No sense of community at all. Many who stayed in Coltrane are singles. But even old curmudgeons knew that if they stayed, they'd have to get along.

I came to Coltrane because the Goddess told me to. Dykes on bikes don't fit in most places. Coltrane was branded as an eclectic 'art town' that was gay friendly. Goddess or no, women give energy. After *the great before,* of endless horrors, we embrace this moment, this blip in the space-time continuum, this island, this exhale. Goddess be praised!

Mayor John John bursts in my 'clinic' and very fast says, "Come on! Need you right away!" His eyes are wide and round. He's wearing a tie and a white shirt with jeans and boots. He looks grand but jumpy. He looks like a leader all of a sudden...but too jumpy. His torso makes him round, distended in the middle, with flattened top and bottom, like Humpty Dumpty.

I smile encouragingly. "What's up?"

"Those two druggies from yesterday – they walked out of the cloud bank. Just now! Security's bringing them in."

"I have my stuff here. Bring them here?"

"We need you to give them a checkup. Like a physical. They look different."

"What do you mean?"

"I'll go make sure they're brought here." The mayor exits in a flurry.

'Rehab is for quitters!' is what the bumper sticker says behind the bar at Ernie's. Drunks love that sign. Wonder how much warm beer is left. Won't it go bad? Will the bars ever open again? We have no facilities for addicts. I have nothing that could help them. I could try hydrating them.

I can't help people pulled apart. I can't help deflating gooey, baldy people that are impossible to classify. I have no idea what to do with people touched by pink rays.

Maybe I should get a runner to go for a doctor. Just in case. To alert them. Back up. A kid on a bike can be there in no time –

Mayor John John pushes in: "I know," he says triumphantly, "I'll have someone go for Doc Stevenson. He should be here, too."

"He's a physicist."

"He's a doctor, right?" asks the mayor. He hurries back out.

The door closes behind him. I push back on my wheeled chair and get up from my desk. I go over to my supplies. Saline drip? But the mayor said they look different –

I turn to face the door, opening to a good looking tough with a rifle. He's got a handful of whiskers nicely distributed over a handsome face, and he's very tanned or swarthy, with a mop of disheveled hair. "Hey, Ms. Gorey," he says. He lowers his rifle to his side, keeping it parallel his leg. "Here they are, Joe and Sky, all dooded up, sleek and pink." I can't remember his name, though I guess we've met.

He clears the way for the two druggies who enter all smiles and aglow with health. Wow: they are pink!

Another man with a rifle follows them in, then Councilmen Ramsey and Martinez and the mayor. This second man with a rifle is older and looks worn out, just tired to death, with dark circles under his eyes. He holds himself focused.

Right away, the mayor says, "Well, they're not baldies, but they're not the same guys who walked over yesterday. Janet?" He extends his arm, indicating the two, clean cut, crew cut, young men who stand there smiling broadly. They either look like they swallowed the canary and are ready to confess, or else they look like those cult figures interviewed on the net, who grin scary.

I ask, "What do you want me to do?"

Councilman Ramsey blurts out, "Are they human?" He looks away, backtracks. "We gotta be sure."

Councilman Martinez says, "What's going on? I saw these two yesterday and they looked like they were on death's doorstep."

I go over to the two young men. "I'm Janet Gorey. I'm a nurse." I shake their hands. Warm, friendly clasp. I say, "Why don't you two have a seat on the cots."

They each go to a cot and sit. They are wearing simple white pants that could pass for pajama bottoms, and white t-shirts. Wonder if they're cold? They seem comfortable. It's not that bad out. It's not cold in here, a little stuffy. They have white slippers on their feet. I say to the nearest one, "Which one are you?"

"I'm Joe."

I get out my scope, flip on its light, grab some tongue depressors.

"Say ah!"

He opens his mouth and I take a look. Pink all the

way down. No growths. No spots. What did I expect? Circuitry? Pinky space parasites? Looks good. Sweet, healthy breath. I slip on an ear cone and check his ears. Fine. Clean – no build-up of wax or secret alien probes. I feel his lymph nodes, my hands around his neck, under his jaw. No swelling. But he giggles. Ticklish? He seems relaxed. I get my stethoscope, listen to his heart through the t-shirt. Perfectly strong beat. Clear lungs.

I repeat the simple exam with the other guy, Sky.

They both seem like healthy young men. Clean, well groomed.

Ramsey says, "Doesn't prove a thing. What about hair and nipples?"

The mayor goes, "Michael, obviously, they're human. And they obviously have changed. Janet, is there any new, fancy, high tech treatment that could do this in twenty-four hours?"

I answer, "In twenty-four hours? I've never heard of anything – "

Martinez says, "They got hair. It's just short now. They got haircuts."

"Haircuts didn't do this," says Ramsey.

I go back to Joe. "Take off your top, please." He does so. He has a smattering of hair on his chest. Two normal, human nipples.

Same for Sky.

Ramsey says, "What about – what about their private parts?"

The two men with rifles standing in the back are enjoying this. Snickers! But they're holding it together.

I ask the mayor, "Maybe, we should get one of our doctors to look at them?"

He nods. "Okay. Okay, you guys, human to human now, we got one question for you guys – "

Joe speaks up, "Of course. Anything. It's amazing to us, too. But we feel responsible for the horror we brought to our community. We want to make it up to you. This whole week has been...who knows...filled with amazing things. Terrible things."

"Say that again," says the sleepy looking, older security guy.

Sky says, "This whole week has been...who knows...filled with amazing things."

The other, younger security guy blurts, "You gotta check their junk!"

I have the two young men stand and lower their pants. No underwear. Everything is there. In fact, in working order, as they both seem a bit turgid. I have them fix their clothes. They sit on the cots watching us, their eyes going from person to person, always with the big grins. Their eyes aren't exactly glassy...or glazed – they're hyper clear, piercing.

The mayor says, "So what happened?"

Sky says, "We don't know."

The mayor says, "What do you mean?"

Joe says, "It's all mixed up like a dream. I

remember we went through the fog. Then through some kind of gate, with a little waterfall pouring from a pipe. Men in uniform put us in the back of a truck. They gave us something to drink in these little ampoules. The next thing we know we're getting out of a truck, maybe the same one, back at the gate with the gushing pipe, and the same men tell us to go back and tell you."

The mayor says, "Tell us what?"

Joe shrugs, smiles at his buddy, nodding to him. Together, they proclaim, "Whoever wants to walk over can."

Ramsey says, "What does that mean? Waterfall? This is nuts!"

Sky says, "Whoever wants to walk over can."

Joe says, "Whoever wants to walk over can. This is your last chance. Now or never. For consolidation."

Ramsey says, "Get out of here!"

Joe and Sky stand and make as if to move away, but the mayor and I corral them back to sit on the cots again.

Joe says, "Hey, whatever they did to us, I feel fine. I feel great!"

"Me, too!" goes Sky.

Joe continues, "I feel better than I ever have. So, yeah, consolidation. The men in uniform at the gate told us we have to return today. Whoever wants to walk over can. Last chance."

Sky says, "We're supposed to get the word out.

You will help us."

Ramsey is agitated. "They're drugged! Hypnotized! They don't know what they're saying."

Martinez says to the boys, "How can we trust you? What about the baldies and the uglies and all that?"

Joe twists around to look at Sky. They both smile with renewed vigor. They shrug in unison. Joe says, "We don't know anything about that. I guess each person has to decide for himself. But it's today. They said it had to be today. Last chance."

Martinez says, "We need some kind of proof. Your word is not good enough. I mean, if people want to consolidate. How do they know you're not luring them back to be ripped apart by baldies?"

I add, "There's no way rehab can work in twenty-four hours."

The mayor says, "Folks need to know. We gotta tell everyone. Get the word out. We have to. It's been a crazy week. Maybe some have changed their minds."

"You gotta be kidding," says Ramsey. "You saw what those things did to Oscar Wargo. You saw the dead bodies in the back of the pickup which these guys caused. We got flying saucers shooting pink rays on people! We got magic discs! We got mining supplies appearing from nothing! Come on! Monsters, man! We can't trust them!"

Mayor John John says, "Take it easy, Michael. Point taken. What do you think, Jimmy? People have a right to know?"

"I guess," says Martinez, but he looks totally undecided or flat out scared.

"No, they don't," says Ramsey.

I say, "We can't decide for everybody. We call an emergency meeting at City Park. It'll only take an hour or two to organize. We'll get the kids to help. Let everyone know what's happening. Hey, Mayor, you can try that new wind up siren Frankie Lucien found. Get everyone down here. So everyone knows and can figure it."

The mayor says, "I don't think that siren works. Anyway, might scare folks."

I finish, "We have to let the kids know."

Ramsey abruptly changes his tune. "You didn't draw their blood."

Martinez says, "I agree."

"I have no way to test their blood. I don't even have a microscope."

Ramsey says, "We'll get you a fricking microscope. But that's not what I meant. I want to see what happens when a needle pricks their skin." Ramsey stares at me. He's holding his clasped arms across his chest, trying so hard to be a real hardass.

Mayor John John says, "That's not necessary. Come on, Michael. They're human. Not baldy replacements. Not pod people. Come on!"

There's a knock at the door. Everyone jumps except for Joe and Sky. The two guards go to either side of the door. The door opens and in walks Dr. Stevenson and Frankie Lucien.

Dr. Stevenson looks like a college professor. He still wears corduroy sports jackets with the leather elbow patches! Today, he's got a button-down shirt, powder blue. He has messy white hair over a lean face with wire rim glasses. He must be near seventy but in good health or he wouldn't be here. Frankie Lucien exudes something that says 'cop', but I don't know if she ever actually was a police officer. She's stockier and shorter than Dr. Stevenson. She's got a pistol in a holster at her side.

Dr. Stevenson smiles at me, says, "You called?"

I say, "Hey, you know these two? Take a look: what do you see?"

Dr. Stevenson has a warm presence. Maybe he's in his sixties like me. Sixty is the new forty, and both of us are ready for anything. The way he purses his lips and squints his eyes, you can tell he is thinking, looking over the two young men.

Dr. Stevenson says, "Two young white males in good shape, in their prime. How did I do?"

Ramsey says, "Did you hear about what happened yesterday? "

Dr. Stevenson replies, "The shootings? Terrible."

Frankie Lucien strolls over, head jerking back and forth from Joe to Sky, then back again to Dr. Stevenson. She puffs. Suddenly, she bends in over Joe and gives a sharp whoop. Joe cringes, but casts his eyes up into Lucien's, and when he sees it's some kind of test, he offers a big smile. Lucien turns away.

Frankie Lucien belts out, "Impossible!"

I say, "Mayor, we need to get this thing organized right now. City Park, right? You can try the siren or not, I don't care. We need to get on this. Contact the kids, get the word out."

The mayor takes Jimmy Martinez' arm and starts walking him to the door talking rapidly. Martinez is listening and twisting around to watch the rest of us.

"What are you talking about, Janet?" asks Stevenson. "What's going on? What's with Frankie?"

Lucien says, "It's them. The druggies."

Mayor John John announces, "Jimmy will get the call out for an emergency, city wide meeting. He'll get the kids to help. They can be all over town fast."

Martinez breaks away from the mayor and yells, "Wait a sec! She hasn't tried the needle!"

I explain to Lucien and Stevenson: "I did a quick exam. They seem okay. Healthy, in fact. Robust. I certainly didn't find any needle marks. But, I mean, their background – "

Lucien butts in, "You mean background, like yesterday! It's impossible! Isn't it?"

I go on, "Mr. Ramsey thinks we should check to see what happens if I prick their skin with a needle."

"Because if they're counterfeit, like the pinky baldies, they'll deflate," says Stevenson.

Ramsey comes up close to Stevenson. " There's no way those two guys we took up to the fog yesterday are these two. I don't care what anybody says. And, by the way, they said up in that fog, the cloud bank at the end of the road, they said there was a gate with a waterfall. There's some kind of gate, right?"

Martinez says, "I heard him say that, too."

Joe shrugs. "Yes. Across the road, what looked like a complicated gate. Cubicles, on either side. I don't know, like equipment? In the middle, an upside down...J pipe shooting out water like a waterfall. We guess it was water. We don't know what any of it was."

Sky offers, "Complicated gate."

Stevenson says, "So you came back? In one day, totally recovered, to make amends?"

Joe says, "What can we do to make amends? Yes – we are totally recovered."

Ramsey looks at me, "Are you going to do it?"

I go to the shelves and take two plastic insulin syringes with small fixed needles from a bin of them I have. I grab some alcohol swabs.

Stevenson says, "Why did you come back?"

Joe says, "To tell you."

Then Joe and Sky, together, utter, "Whoever wants to walk over can."

"Now, that's spooky," jumps Ramsey, backing away. "I don't know where these jokers been, but damn!"

I swab the top of Joe's arm and tap the small needle in. Joe giggles, then: "'Oh, what a world, what a world! I'm melting!'"

I pull back the needle. A drop of blood oozes out. I swab the spot. I do the same for Sky. I say, "Well, I suppose a sense of humor proves something about their humanity."

Ramsey goes, "Very funny! Yeah, they're a barrel of laughs!"

"Let's go, Jimmy," says Mayor John John.

Stevenson says, "Do you think people will want to leave now? I mean, after all that's happened this week?"

Lucien says, "I can think of a few I'd just as soon get rid of."

"Don't say that," I say. "It's not funny. That's not how we do things."

"How do we do things?" asks Frankie Lucien.

We move. We engage. We get going. It's overcast and cool, 50 degrees Fahrenheit. Not too bad. Perfect for an emergency gathering. Summer sun's on sabbatical. Had a little rain. People been collecting rain water assiduously. People don't stink as bad in cool weather as hot weather. Unless they reek of wood smoke. Folks stocked up their wood piles these past couple months. A lot of wood stoves in hippy art towns. We take what we need from what is known. Lots of shacks to dismantle.

City Park meeting assembles. Town in motion. From every canyon and dead end and cul-de-sac, people head downtown, then to the park. It's going to take a while. Folks start rolling in portable barbecues, Hibachis. Pretty soon, little fires smoky sputtering in the park. What gives? Last of the meat, I guess. Hot dogs for everyone! Gulch bars bring up cases of warm beer.

Folks must know this is important. Word is out! They've decided to party. Celebrate! A final feast that we've made it to here. They want to know what's going on, but nothing can deter survivors from one last par-tay. Everybody knows this should be good. Might as well make the most of it.

Frankie Lucien has some of her men, no rifles, bring Joe and Sky to the park in the back of a pickup. She wanted them tied up but we convinced her otherwise. The two are installed on the stage on two lawn chairs, guards at either end of the stage. There's a couple more lawn chairs leaning against the wall of the clamshell in the back. Someone brings them water bottles. They say they're hungry, so someone else gets them some almonds. Lucien arranges an arc of security people in front of the stage. No one packing. She won't let people talk to them yet.

People call out, "Who the heck are they?"

Word's out. There's a crackle in the park, then there's a cackle, then there's the sizzle of fat hitting coals. People do what they want.

Maybe this is a test for all of us: what kind of people are we now? The festive air is a displacement of the past week's impossibles. This is the human response: smoke, grease, belches. Par-tay! Grill up some meat! Down a warm beer!

We have to let these young men say their piece.

Is consolidation so bad?

The mayor and councilmen, Dr. Stevenson and Frankie Lucien bunch up near me by the stage. We're all standing around waiting and watching as people arrive. Back in the day, this park could hold more than a thousand for a concert. Those who aren't cooking fill the cement bleachers up on the side. Folks be thinking: *Look at them up there. Who are they? They're the druggies from yesterday! Did you see them yesterday?* The fires make a lot of smoke, but it smells good. People chug beer, suck down hot dogs. Kids run between the knots of people spaced across the park. The park fills up. Daisy Piper, that girl, hangs near us, watching everything. Her eyes over everything and everyone.

Margaret Pitka, like a bull, pushes in to our group. I see Frank Stanley moving towards us. Here comes Susan Kell and behind her is Tom Dillon. Jacob Derry, a crossbow across his back, gets up close among the security boys to stare at the two young men on stage, who smile back at him and wave. Kids with sticks – they all carry sticks now, get close, ignoring security, slithering on up to lean on the stage rim.

The mayor motions me over. He says, "Janet, you're good at this. You're fair. Everyone knows you pretty much. We want you to interview them in front of everybody."

"It's turned into a party."

"People are jazzed up," says Frankie Lucien, nodding, but somehow still looking grim. "Hey, not yet, just a little longer, we got folks coming from the tunnel."

Tom Dillon, a good looking big fellow, who clearly has worked outside all his life, stands beside us and says, "You'll need this." He hands over the battery-powered bullhorn to the mayor, who gives it to me.

I go around the stage to the stairs. The security guys let me through. I walk to the front and center of the stage. People start clapping and hooting. Smoke lies low across the park, then seems to be whisked away. The bleachers teem with people. They're still coming in!

Young, say, twenties to middle age. Families. Kids. Kids on their own – how we ever figured that I'll never get.

I adjust the bullhorn, make an experimental throat clearing rasp that echoes across the park. Frankie Lucien nods at me, gives me the thumbs up. Cheers now. I pull op a lawn chair from the back, set it open next to the two young men.

Let loose: "Hey, everybody! You know me, or most of you do. I'm Janet Gorey, nurse of the new Coltrane clinic."

The clapping is brisk enough to make me pause. Then, as it weakens, a man yells, "Who the hell are they?"

Someone else answers, "Special guest stars!"

Laughs and groans.

A voice goes, "They can't be the same guys exiled yesterday?"

Ready to talk, here we go: "Good question. He asked, for those of you in the bleachers, how do we know these are the same guys who were exiled yesterday? Well, I checked them out, basic physical. They're human. Definitely human. I even stuck a needle into them to see what would happen. And you can see: no deflation. But I'm getting ahead of myself. Mayor, think we should start?"

People yell out questions. Others tell them to be quiet. Many are occupied with their grills, or eating and drinking. Laughs and hoots escalate. The mayor and the councilmen walk among the people, pleading, cajoling, for them to listen, to chill, to take it easy, wait to ask questions. The grumbling crowd complies, mouths full of incandescent mustard. The clamshell's smoky, with a greasy smell.

Mayor John John gives a thumbs up.

I explain to the crowd, "We'll pass the bullhorn between us so everyone can hear."

I get situated. I'm right next to Sky. Joe is on the other side of Sky.

"Tell us your names, please." I pass the bullhorn.

"Sky – but my legal name is Skyler Chronic." He smiles broadly, too big, too much, so he looks phony. It's annoying because he ends up looking like a retard folks will immediately reject. He hands the bullhorn to Joe.

"Joe Nichols." He hands the bullhorn back to me.

"Please tell your story, what you told us earlier."

Sky takes the bullhorn and says, "Which one?"

He hands the bullhorn to Joe who blares, "Hello, Coltrane! Here's the dealio: what happened yesterday is gone, because today we are new. We were sick. Today, we are well. We were a wreck!" He giggles. "Today, we are more than better. See how this works? How easy it is? What? You folks think I'm brainwashed? Would I be saying that if I was? You folks walked us into the fog to the other side. That was the right thing to do. You did us a solid." He gives the bullhorn to Sky.

Sky continues, "We're better. We're new. We're people. Totally. Just like you guys. Something happened over there we don't understand. We have no memory of it. We went through the fog. There was a gate with this gushing pipe, then these men in uniform gave us something to drink. They put us in a truck. No, they weren't Martians, or baldies or uglies. Next thing we know, we're back at the gate by the pipe with its gush, same men in uniform tell us we have to go back and tell you."

Did it matter that the first version of the story had them given the drink *after* they'd been put in the truck? Could that be significant? Like a memorized story with a glitch?

Sky comes to his feet slowly, stands in front of his lawn chair. Joe's done the same, stands next to him. Together, speaking into the bullhorn, mouths close, they announce, "Whoever wants to walk over can."

Quiet. Quiet response is thoughtful response. Nine hundred or so noggins figuring what's up.

Joe takes the bullhorn and walks to the edge of the stage. "It's perfectly koolio. No danger. No monsters waiting to eat your face off. This is your last chance. Consolidation! Go for consolidation. It's not too late. Consolidation means safety. Health. Means security. Why not? Why stay now? After this week?"

Sky joins him up front, leans in to say, "Whoever wants to walk over can."

Bob Pauley, a big, heavy set fellow, yells, "This ain't right. What about the baldies? I ain't going anywhere they come from! 'N what's this about a gushing pipe? There ain't no water around here to gush!"

Sky takes the bullhorn, "Consolidation has nothing to do with any of that. Come with us, you'll see. Perfectly safe. We're going back. Pretty soon now. We'll take whoever wants to come with us. We're supposed to make sure you understand. You can come with us. We're going back. We just walk over, easy as pie. Hey, I haven't felt this good, so alive, so healthy, my whole life. And it has nothing to do with any of that bad stuff. Not at all. No worries. Why would they make me better, if they were gonna hurt me? See what I mean? Doesn't make sense. The only thing that makes sense is consolidation. You folks with kids, come on! Bring what you can carry. That's it. No giant loads. You'll have no need for stuff in consolidation, that's for sure. We head up to the highway. This very afternoon. We walk over. Easy as – "

Joe claps and squeals, "Easy as pie!"

Daisy calls out, "Something's not right. This is like our last last last chance? That's dumb. You can't expect us to suddenly believe anything you say." Daisy! That girl! She's pushing forward through the crowd, stopping at the security line before the stage.

I stand, take back the bullhorn. "I'm sure people have a lot of questions." We go back and sit.

Questions are mean, cautious, suspicious, some hoots, some jeers.

I say, summarizing, "Mainly, I guess, people are wondering what happened to you? What did they do to you? But you won't say. Or can't say. But you want these people to trust you. See the problem? After the week we had – " I splutter a sec. "You can't expect to be welcomed back with open arms."

A voice cuts through from the crowd, "Murderers! They're murderers! We don't want them back. Good riddance!"

Another voices cries, "Anybody who goes for

consolidation now is a fool!"

A cheer goes up. People clap. Some wild laughter. Some hollering. High on nitrates and warm beer and decision making? The people in the bleachers stand and shout and wave their arms.

Joe takes back the bullhorn. "The people who were involved in those acts are no more. Those people are gone. Today is a new day, a new world awaits us. It's our last chance. We're going back. Whoever wants to walk over can."

Questions are shouted out. I try to take them one at a time. The two young men blurt out responses with or without the bullhorn. Pretty chaotic. Questions, answers, to nowhere. I assume they're trying to tell *this* truth, to convince folks, to appear at ease. But they really don't make me feel very comfortable. The smiles, the glowing health – what's going on? Humans of my day and age did not have technology to do this. None of this! It's staged, a put on. Fake reality?

Discussion rises and falls, shouts and explanations, theories and condemnations. The mayor intervenes, coming up on stage with us. He calls for order. We take a break. People leave. Others come up close to get a better look at the prodigals. There's a lot of side talk now. Bunches of people around the park, in the ramada, up the bleachers. Hot dogs and beers are gone. The young men repeat things. Folks are exasperated, but have to get back to rain harvest. The guards escort the two to a latrine. I moderate. I watch.

"It's a trap!" screeches a man.

Ms. Kell, from the high school, calls, "They keep changing the rules!"

Concerns, complaints, worries, suppositions. Guesses. Then repeat. Then repeat all over again. What would answers look like today?

Who will go with them now? No one!

We decided to stay because we trusted in ourselves. We are our own masters. We created Coltrane in this likeness. Maybe that's not how everyone sees it. We may be snug as bugs in our little out of the way, nowhere, Endsville town, *for this moment*, but most have given up on projecting how long it'll last.

People take off. Grills are cleaned up. Bottles collected. Discussion falters.

Are people going home to get their stuff? The last hot dog burp echoes through the clamshell. I wonder what will come of this – this invitation? The whole town is a sizzle of sedition.

All we can trust is ourselves. I keep saying that, but I think a lot of folks wouldn't be here in Coltrane in the first place if they didn't intuitively know this.

Joe and Sky look tired. They stare at me, stand, nod. I stand, nodding to Lucien. The mayor nods. We all nod! I hand over the bullhorn to Sky.

He announces, "It's time."

Right now? They're leaving now?

He hands the bullhorn to Joe who says, "Whoever wants to walk over can." He hands it back to Sky.

Sky says, "Whoever wants to walk over can."

Frankie Lucien's spouting orders to her men. Now?

I thought we'd have a break. Let everybody think about it. Joe and Sky descend the steps of the stage. I follow. They don't hurry. They flow. They're met by armed guards who position themselves on either side of the two. Joe and Sky nod, nod, walk, one after the other, single file, guards on either side.

Here we go!

The park has thinned out. But on the street, a lot of folks seem to suddenly be behind us, then lining the sidewalks. We move slowly. It's embarrassing. A little girl, carrying a cage with a rat, gets behind Joe who is behind Sky. They don't look. They walk.

Another little girl runs up to the girl with the cage and yells, "Alianna, no!"

The little girl in line with the cage goes, "They were rude to Mr. Licorice." She sticks out her tongue at the other girl.

Daisy comes up behind the little girl who doesn't want her friend to go. She puts her hand on the girl's shoulder. Daisy's too young to be her mom. But she has laser eyes and thinks fast and gets things done. She moves like a Ninja. I know that look. She's taking charge. She's the ballsy chichi who's been so busy this week.

An older fellow gets behind Alianna. He carries a suitcase and has a back pack on his back. Monad. Single. Then two women get in line behind him, each pulling a wheeled carry on. A family, a mom and dad and a teenage boy, follow the women.

They're coming up on downtown, the city center. Men and women and children, then children on their own, arrange themselves in line. Couples – men, women. Then one woman, one man. Random single file parade moves steadily, purposively. They don't talk. They don't look around. No tearful goodbyes. Eyes straight ahead.

We allowed little kids to make their own decisions. The momentousness of the times seemed to call for that. So why shouldn't they change their minds now, just like the adults?

People following along, beside the growing line of departees, call out: "Do you really want to do this?" And: "Don't go!"

A man yells, "It's a mistake! Think about it."

Another man says, "You'll regret this!"

Then someone else: "It's a cookbook!"

At which high schooler, Sam Bean goes, "*Twilight Zone.* 'To Serve Mankind.'"

Straight by the convention center, head towards the highway. Pass the roadblocks. People on tops of cars, on hoods and cabs, then standing in the backs of pickups, cradling their rifles and sticks, watching without comment. People on bikes follow along, get ahead of the line and stop to watch. More people join the line. I know them. But I don't look at them in the eye and they don't look at me in the eye. I won't belabor it. We don't want you here, if you don't want to be here.

I see Paul Greer and his family. Greer boldly enters the back of the line with a stuffed pack on his back. His wife and kids are also loaded. Greer calls on a man walking nearby but not in the line. "Roger, you're in charge now. Whatever that means!" He hoots. "Good luck!"

I get an idea and scramble around looking for the mayor or councilmen. I find Mayor John John and go, "We need to get everyone who's leaving's name and address."

Mayor John John says, "Of course! Great idea!"

Councilman Ramsey is next to him, considering this. Then, he takes off, hurries along the line, shouting, "We need to get names and addresses of everyone going."

Runners go for pen and paper. Councilman Martinez and Ramsey have little notebooks out already, jotting down names, moving up and down the line, getting addresses as well.

The mayor explains to the people in line the need for their names and addresses.

A voice calls out, "Traitors!"

Then: "You'll be torn to bits!"

And: "Don't! It's not too late!"

Frankie Lucien says loudly, so a lot of the folks in line can hear: "You're not coming back. We might need the stuff you left behind. You won't need it." She's grinning, eyes shiny with glee.

Councilman Ramsey has sidled up alongside Lucien and says: "We'll have to get guards at their places before looters figure it out."

I'm thinking, goodness sakes, let the poor people leave in peace.

Lucien says too loudly, "We promise to take care of your stuff." She seems to think it's funny, and her tone, the sharp meanness is picked up by the crowd.

"Then, go! Who needs you?"

"Traitors!"

Margaret Pitka pushes up to the line, past Ramsey and Lucien, and hollers, "We need to figure what to do with the stuff left behind. Right? It's only logical. You won't need it any more. We have the right to survive and if your stuff can help. See what I mean?"

She's trying to mollify, ease the abrupt callousness. But no one in the line says a word. No tears.

Pitka goes, "We'll have a dandy common supply room now at the convention center for emergencies!"

As though these folks care –

The guy who Greer had been addressing, Roger something, is hanging nearby, walking, pacing the line. He's a thick solid looking character. Short. But looks strong. A big head. Maybe a miner? Daisy comes up behind him, passes around him closely, squeezing by. He kind of jumps, like she surprised him. He calls her over. They walk together. He's talking fast. I hang back, stay close, in front of them to hear what this guy has to say to our star.

Something about 'Christmas trees.' Yes, he's talking to Daisy about Christmas trees.

Daisy says, "Lotta people keep their Christmas trees nowadays. Instead of trashing them or mulching them. Sure, they can be fire wood now. But, also, they make great walking sticks."

Roger says, "Walking sticks?"

Daisy says, "You know what I mean?"

"You're a smooth one, young lady," says Roger. His tone has changed. "Weapons, you mean. Right? You want all the kids to carry a stick. When their protection is their parents' job."

"Now, it's all our jobs. Self defense."

"You got it covered. Ever since we went underground, and you and that boy went into that space, I been wondering."

"Wondering what?"

"Well, you also, both of you, got hit by the pink ray at City Park."

"And there's no such thing as coincidence?"

Roger clams up. We're walking up the highway, towards the gate and fog. He bursts, "Just saying."

How many people are there in line? Over a hundred at least. I'm not counting. Maybe more? Maybe less?

Roger inserts in a quick voice, "My daughter and my wife left. Consolidation. A while ago. They didn't want to stay. They didn't understand why I did."

"Must be hard?"

"Yeah, sure, I hurt. But who would have thought – geez, talking to the smart kid about my problems. You know all about grumpy old people." He makes a rasping laugh that no one who noticed would believe is for fun. He sounds irritable, strained. "Do you know about rejection? No, course not. You've had it made all your life. You can't imagine – "

"You feel rejected?"

"You making fun of me? You know it all, don't you? You feel like a pop in the mouth?"

A long pause. I glance back. Daisy has a big knife at her side through her belt. I don't know if it's a Bowie knife, but it's big.

Roger says, "Forget that. I'm sorry." He lowers his voice, mutters, "Just – I couldn't believe they would leave me. I know I wasn't the best father, or the best husband."

Daisy goes, "My parents are here. They stayed. But they don't understand anything outside of themselves. They won't have anything to do with the town, the meetings. I mean...I don't know."

"You think they're rejecting you?"

"They're just – what they're into. You know?"

"They're scared."

"We're all scared."

"Not me." He laughs heartily this time.

Suddenly, Daisy stops and says very distinctly to Roger: "Maybe you should go."

"Join them?" He motions to the line.

"It's your decision." Daisy goes on, "My parental units have a routine. It works for them. Do you have a routine?"

"What makes you so smart? Yeah, the routine. We're about there."

"What are you going to do?"

"My daughter is about your age. You in high school?"

"What's her name?"

"Melinda Mead. Kids call her Mel." He sounds like he's getting mad again. "She sure didn't talk like you. Why, I'd – "

"What? What would you do?" Daisy is walking again. I move ahead. She says, "I knew your daughter. We didn't have any classes together. But it's a small school."

"My daughter is nothing like you. She wouldn't talk to me. Now, look! Yacking it up with you?"

"I won't tell."

"You got quite the mouth!"

# THE SEVENTH DAY

**Margaret Pitka**

> *everywhere people are born free*
> *but live in chains*

If we begin with the notion that anarchy is the natural state of humans, then government must be seen as a controlled crash, civil war. If we begin with the notion that instead of a thin veneer of civilization over savagery, we humans have a thin veneer of savagery *from* civilization over our true noble nature, what then? What is possible? If we see humans as naturally good, then impossible things start happening, everybody freaks out.

A week ago, the other night, we gathered around my kitchen table in my little house above City Park. Susan Kell, Janet Gorey, Calliope Terpsichore, and I had mugs of herbal tea (*Celestial Seasons*, 'Sleepy Time', < 20 cases>). We were basically waiting for the lights to go out. My one light bulb, ceiling light, hanging down over the center of the table. Janet remembered stories from relatives when she was a girl, about folks gathering the same, about the kitchen table, but waiting for the one light bulb hanging over the table to *come on*. When it went off, what would we do? Sigh, giggle, or curse?

We decided to stay. The take away? See above! Presuppositions get a person in trouble.

Who stayed? Artists, wackos, survivalists. Rugged individualists with fiercely private agendas. And kids! Kids stayed, and I'm not sure why. I believe traumatized people stayed. Staying might be seen as revenge or suicide. At any rate, it might be construed as some kind of 'getting back' at others. I'm sure there are many who don't fit categories. Some have withdrawn, refuse to come out, refuse to see their neighbors. Not everyone likes picnics at City Park.

Who took off on the Long Parade? The soft parade? Families with kids. Singles. What I would have imagined was a good sampler of our peeps. They'd been tested this week. We all had. In an extreme manner that no one expected. Why stick around for the inevitable? But still.

> *deaths this week*
> *make us*
> *death close*
> *a new companion*

Why did artists stay? No audience anymore. Many moved to Coltrane in the first place because of the anonymity. Probably just as many people hate artists as claim to be artists. So, iconoclasm? We came here to be left alone. Now we are alone! It was the artists who warned us that this iteration was coming...big brother on steroids. Coming down the pike – those who chose to stay knew this was coming...probably knew this the last fifty years. Collapse of savagery, its last hurrah!

This morning, early, Alan Ripple and Barry Hilton and I score a pickup with gas from the 'vehicle pool' to cruise the newly vacated homes. Last night, security assigned people to each of the homes on the list. Now, we're supposed to check on those guys and gals at each house. We have a copy of the list, and we have a map. We're doing up the canyon. Other teams will visit other parts of town. We pull out onto Main, get going. People on bikes. That guy on his horse. People kept their favorite vehicles, hoarding what gas they had. Most vehicles have been donated to the community pool, to be parted out. There hasn't been much gas available for months. Vehicles make great roadblocks.

Janet Gorey figures 120 people left yesterday, including the two druggies. That turns out to be fifty homes and apartments. Several places we're to visit are in the same neighborhood.

There's no accounting for human behavior – or decisions. Decide one way one time, the next time the opposite. The only thing we ever know for sure is humans are ingenious. Pi goes on forever, never ending, but we still build circular structures. It's impossible to end, yet we act like we do. We decide to stay all over again.

Alan Ripple used to sing and play guitar in a band. He's forty something, good cowboy looks, dark hair and eyes. He's driving. Barry Hilton is younger, skinny, but apparently a vet who did a tour in Kurdistan. The gun rack behind us has two rifles, a .22 and a 30.06. Susan Kell taught me how to shoot.

Alan Ripple continues with our conversation: "I agree, we gotta have a common supply for emergencies. It's a good idea. I don't think anybody will argue with that. Except you know who."

Barry Hilton says, "Everybody – everybody just wanna be left alone. Hey, I'm here to help, my community duty, but I can see the other way. Stick to your hood! Know what I'm saying. Folks don't want no more bosses, anybody telling 'em anything."

I go, "It's gotta be based on trust then?"

Barry twists, almost like a mini-fit.

Alan says, "I guess? Soon as folks started leaving, people were sneaking around, checking out abandoned places."

Barry says, "We shoot looters."

I say, "No, we don't."

Barry chortles.

Alan says, "It's been going on over a year, since the first people started leaving."

I shrug. "Who has authority?"

Barry goes, "Damn! We all got authority now. Right?"

The only authority is doing what's right which is doing what's best. Can we depend on that? In place: security, regs, rules – control.

I say, "I think it's important to know what everybody thinks. If you don't want to be involved, fine. But that doesn't mean you can harvest empty houses any time you want."

Barry grumps, "*Harvest?*"

Alan says. "You can't be messing with someone's

stuff. We're working it out. If somebody has already taken advantage of his neighbor's empty place, so be it."

"Okay by me," says Barry. "Don't make them criminals. Nobody's saying that. But those tweakers, yesterday, that was messed up. Rehab is for quitters, as the man says. But even if they did go through rehab, they'd still be criminals. Those doods never get over the craving. I'm glad they left. And the folks that decided to go with them? Good for them. Good for us."

I'm in the middle so when Alan shrugs he presses against my shoulder. Barry is squeezed into the passenger side door. We're heading up Mule Canyon, near our first turn off, a Star Avenue address, with three abandoned homes. It's past dawn but gray – gray light. Yes, you can tell it's day, but everything's a bit dreamy. I check my list, my map. We turn right on Star. I volunteered to come with these guys. I didn't have to. Figured, see what was happening, finger on the pulse. My role as a kind of go between? Not that they needed supervision. But we all have to know what's going down every step of the way. We decide on things together, with the best info. Take a vote when and if we can. We do what we want. A leader is not really needed.

Star Avenue is steep, a hilly side canyon with narrow roads. Three houses coming up – all small, remodeled jobs, with garages and driveways. Cherried out by loving home owners! Who now have flown the coop. The houses are set back, with yards. The flower beds have turned to compost. The hedges look healthy. Rose bushes going to hibernation.

What is this? Ahead of us. This can't be right. What are we seeing? None of us say a word. Barry makes a gurgle from his chest. Alan slows, rolls to a stop. It's like we see it, but can't *see* it in terms of what it means and requires.

Tom Dillon and a big man crouch behind the hood of a pickup. The big guy I don't know. They're parked in a driveway before an open garage – must have backed in. The remodel looks like it's had a total face lift. The back of the pickup has a big white box. Tom Dillon and the big guy are waving at us, making the universal signs for stop or get back.

Alan pulls off to the side, rolls down his window, leans out, calls, "What's up?"

Tom Dillon yells, "Gunfire from the house!" He's pointing at the cute little job. It has nice front windows and a carved wooden front door. The window on the left, nearest the door, is broken. Tom yells, "Get down!"

This house was supposed to have been abandoned. I check my list, go over the address. It matches! Looters!

Alan puts the truck in reverse, backs away slowly.

Barry goes, "Damn. Damn!"

Alan turns it off. He says, "I'm gonna go see what's up. No point in going for help until we know what's going on. You guys stay here." He opens up his door, sneaks out, then, keeping the door in front of himself, he leans backs in. "Let me," he says and reaches behind me for one of the rifles.

I duck.

Alan says, "Be right back," and he's gone.

I scoot over to the driver's side.

Barry says, "Almost impossible to get someone out of a house when they don't want to. Unless you got tear gas. Which we don't. Well, I don't know. No telling what Lucien's got. We can't burn them out."

"No, we can't."

"I was kidding."

"It could be looters," I say, "who knew about the house, then stayed too long."

We study the house, can't take our eyes off of it.

Barry says, "They broke in last night before our guys got here. Then they lost track of time, fell asleep, woke up to find our guys outside. Whoever checked on this place last night never saw a thing."

"We can't have all this shooting. It's one thing to defend the town, but to fight among ourselves – "

"Agreed."

Tom Dillon, Alan Ripple, and the big guy – "Who's the big guy?"

"That's Bob Pauley. He's okay. Monster, huh?"

The three of them are hunched down before the pickup. Alan hustles back to us. I scoot over. He gets in the truck but leaves the door open so he can hold the rifle out of the cab.

He says, "The guy assigned to watch this neighborhood last night, well first thing he did was check out the houses. You know, just looking 'em over, peeking in windows. He reported in right away this house had a garage full of supplies. He sent a runner back. That's why

Tom and Bob showed up early, to load it up. But when they got here, the security guy, name of Saul, told them he'd seen movement inside the house. Tom and Bob went to check it out, while the guy went over to check on the other two abandoned houses nearby. Anyway, Bob and Tom couldn't see anything. They looked in all the windows. They knocked at the door. It was locked up. They'd loaded the first box on the truck, when they heard a window break. That's when the shooting started. Rifle fire from the house. But pretty wild. Like the person didn't know anything about firing a gun. They got behind the pickup. They tried talking to whoever was in there shooting. Got no response. They were just huddling here trying to figure what to do next, when we showed up."

I ask, "What do they think? Did the people who owned the house come back? Looters?"

Barry says, "We get backup. We have to. Surround the house. Go in. It's the only way."

Alan says, "We'd have to shoot whoever's in there. Nah, no more shooting. And if people had come back through the fog, we would have heard. The guys at the roadblock would have seen them. Some poor slob knew about the supplies these folks had, so took a chance. Now he's scared stiff. Thinking he's been caught. No telling what he'll do."

I say, "What do we do?"

Alan says to me, "You're the mediator. Right? Hey, don't look at me like that. That's what you told us. You wanna try to talk to him?"

"Yeah, get shot trying," says Barry.

"Sure," I say. "We can't go running for help – we

are the help! Ha!"

"Let's go," says Barry.

Barry throws open his door and I follow him out. Barry leans back in for the other rifle, the .22. We bend over and hurry to the others behind the pickup. Alan follows. Barry explains to Tom Dillon and Bob Pauley. They make funny faces.

Bob Pauley says, "Be careful!"

I stand up by the pickup's lights, but stay hunched over a bit, head down. Wish I had that bullhorn. Will the person inside be able to hear me?

I yell, "I'm coming out! No shooting! My name is Pitka. You probably've seen me around. You know what Pitka means? It's Slavic for tiller, like farmer. We're all farmers now, right? We're in this together. So far, no harm done. So let's just talk. Can you hear me okay? Do you understand?" I take a step away from the truck.

The house's front door rattles. I try not to jump. The door's going to open –

Barry calls in a husky voice, "Get down!"

Tom goes, "Watch it!"

I stay where I am and the front door opens and there's a naked baldy standing there with a rifle in its arms.

A voice comes from the hole in the head that stands for a mouth: "No goody! Slap shot shot! Come! Don't! My house! My house!"

I scoot back down in a kind of shock. Baldies can

talk?

Alan and Barry are prone, in shooters' positions, guns ready, aimed, steady. Barry stammers, "What do we do? What do we do?"

I say, "Does anyone know who lived here? I left my list in the truck. Could it be the same guy?"

Bob grunts and goes, "Yeah, naked as a jaybird, talking like a retard. And no nipples. Check it out! No junk, no hair at all. It's one of them."

The baldy kind of staggers from the door onto the porch. It's making awful gurgly crying sounds. I don't like looking at it. Its face – well, its head is all wrong. It's like a practice head of dough that was fashioned by little kids, or people who didn't understand the basic human face. And the way the thing jostles and waves the rifle – the rifle goes off! Not even aimed at us.

Bob says, "Hope Saul knows to stay down."

Tom explains, "He's over at the other houses."

Alan grimaces. "Suppose there's baldies there?"

Barry says, "Somebody's gonna get hurt."

I shout, "Hey, watch that! Somebody could get hurt. We're not here to fight. Put down the gun. Put down the gun! You can't be shooting at folks."

Baldy goes back in, shuffling, crying –

I say, "I guess we could try to capture it. Bring one in, figure it out."

Bob goes, "Them ain't human!"

I say, "I know, but we need to know. How did it get here? God – what about the other vacated homes? Now, I'm worried! Oh, no, suppose – "

Bob says, "Arnie Soles lived here before. He used to work for the county. Did a gig in the army, too. The Nam. A double dipper, you know? Worked on that little house twenty years, then some. Wanted it just right. Then he retired. Then shit hit the fan. He left yesterday. I did jobs for him. Couple times. He was okay. He was human. Nipples and everything." Bob liked the man.

I ask, "He lived alone?"

"Oh, yeah," said Bob.

Gunfire! Gunfire! Where's it coming from? Behind us! Everybody glances at each other, but also leaning out, straining to hear. It can't be good. More gunfire plain as anything.

Alan says, "Now what?"

Barry says, "Baldies – betcha anything."

Tom says, "Neighborhood watch?"

Alan says, "Could be."

I shake with it. "They're shooting back! Baldies with guns?"

Bob goes, "Double damn. I ain't got my piece. Tom, you said I wouldn't need it."

The gunfire stops. What's happening? We are dutiful as hell.

Tom says, "How would I know? We didn't know

what was going on. Didn't expect this shit."

Gunfire again. Then it stops.

I say, "We better find out. For sure, people are getting the word downtown. But in the meantime, Barry, you stay here with Tom and Bob. Does the other guy, Saul, have a gun?"

Bob and Tom shake their heads. Bob says, "He's got a bow."

Alan says, "Oh, great."

"You guys stay here. Me and Alan will go see what's going on. But watch for that thing with the rifle. It could get out a lucky shot."

Tom jerks back, nodding towards the house: "Speak of the devil."

Barry mumbles, "We're gonna have to – "

Sure enough, the baldy steps from the house and out to the porch with a wide, sloppy gait, swinging its arms, trembling, spasming. The rifle hangs down from its right hand, barrel on the porch. The rifle wavers, back and forth with the thing's shakes.

Barry snickers. He says, "Look at the way it holds that weapon." The baldy manages to get down on one knee, bringing the rifle up. "Is it aiming that rifle? Looks like it's getting serious."

Tom says, " Damn." He turns his head wearily from me to Alan. "What the heck is that thing doing?" He's a husband, a dad, a decent guy. His big head is puffy from lack of sleep. People like his forthright manner, so that means they like to depend on him. He's one of those types of people who feel obligated to live up to expectations. You're glad to have him around in an emergency. He rises to the occasion. He whispers, "What the hell?" Then: "It's like a horror movie – living in a scary film." He heaves an angry sigh and the baldy fumbles and drops its weapon.

Barry's focused, aiming, perfectly still. He says, "I got 'im. Should I take the shot?"

Tom looks startled. Like all of us. We don't know what to do. No one wants more violence. What the heck are baldies? If they're not human, then what are they? What are they doing there?

Barry says, "I never liked them scary movies. Uh-uh. Go on. We got this."

Alan and I scurry to our truck, bent over so far it makes my back hurt. We get in. He puts his rifle back in the rack. He gets the truck going. He backs down Star Avenue. All the way. Alan swings the truck in to the turn: we head out.

"Where to?" says Alan.

"I don't hear anything now. Wait, wait." I stick my head out the window, can't hear a thing. A drop of misty moisture falls on my forehead, like a sick cloud kiss. October on my mind! "It stopped. Where's the next houses in the canyon? Let me check the map."

"We'll head up the canyon."

Us and them. But we don't even know what *them* are. Shouldn't that be the first law of warfare: know what your enemy is? We don't even know the species. So we shoot 'em on sight; or, well, wait 'til they do something first to deserve being slaughtered. If they deserve it, then we're off the hook. We have to figure this out. The past, *the great before* left us a bunch of natty old suitcases. Samsonite memories, useless baggage now, of before ways of doing things, before ways of making sense.

We head west, up the canyon. This part of the canyon is narrow. To our left, the south, there is one layer of houses then the steep wall to the bypass on top. Our right side follows the arroyo, the ditch, and there are a couple layers of homes beyond that. There are also big cottonwoods through here where the vultures used to perch. A guy on a bike pedals down the canyon toward us. I don't recognize him, but Alan waves him over.

Alan calls, "Murray, what's up?"

The young man in sweats leans into Alan's window, gasping: "The abandoned houses from yesterday all have baldies! Crawling with 'em. Every single house that belonged to folks that left yesterday. Freaky. Plus, these baldies are picking up guns and shit left in the houses. Knives, bats, tennis racquets. I swear! I saw it! I'm going downtown to report. Runners got word back already."

"Anyone hurt?"

"No. Mainly, they don't seem to be able to use guns. Like they can't aim. Looks like every house people left is occupied. If a house had a family of three, there are three baldies in it. Total crazy! I mean, what were they expecting? That we wouldn't notice?"

Alan says, "Go let 'em know. We'll head up to lend a hand."

Murray shrugs, shakes his head. "Nobody knows

what to do." His sweaty face beams with energy. Maybe I have seen him around. At the library? He inhales deeply, nods. He pushes off from the side of the truck, starts pedaling his way down the canyon.

Alan takes off. We move up the canyon slowly. Pretty soon, the canyon opens up to like a bowl, and we come on a few cars parked in the middle of the road. Clusters of people by the cars. Mainly men, weapons in hand, at the front. They wave at us. We wave back. No one knows what to do. We can read the giant question marks of their expressions.

Alan stops, turns off the truck. Several side roads branch off here. Lots of possibilities. The next houses on the list are right around here. Some up Spring Canyon on the south side, then Locklin on the other side, the north, has two. A little funky park, Garfield Park, a couple blocks up, has young people, couples with kids. People mill, debate, threaten, with their makeshift weapons – like garden tools. Families wield rakes and hoes. Everybody's in windbreakers and jackets.

I say, "What are we gonna do?"

Alan says, "What are our options? We can kill them. We know we can do that pretty easy. Or what? Let them live in our neighborhoods? Don't think so. How do we get them out? Make them leave? Ask in a stern voice?"

"We could exile them?"

Alan hits the steering wheel with his open hands. "We have to get some people to go to the gate up on the bypass and tell those people to take them back. They have to stop sending them over. Nobody wants to go near the gate. I don't blame them, but now we don't have a choice."

"I don't know. I don't know."

Alan looks around, scanning, twisting to see all around us. He says, "Well, we don't have to worry about parking anymore." He gives a dry, fake laugh. "Let's see what's going on."

In this small canyon bowl, surrounded by mountains, people gather to commemorate their fate. Options are limited. People are practical. But it's not right. It's too easy?

Side canyons connect by narrow roads winding between stone walls, brick walls, concrete walls. People filing down those roads. Everybody heard the guns.

Around us: a guy on a motorcycle shows off his pistol to a few other men, who also have pistols. People on bikes. People on foot. A skateboarder in his twenties roars down a hill with a rifle slung over his shoulder. A bearded guy, with an ancient looking shot gun cradled over his arm, uses his other hand to stroke his beard. A woman with a deer rifle, all in camo, camo bandana.

I stumble: "I guess we should get out."

Alan says, "You'd think Lucien would be all over this."

I plunder: "Must be busy...or they're already here."

"There *were* abandoned houses down town, the Gulch, too, so they might have their hands full. Well, Frankie brags she's got like a hundred men and women. Yeah, they gotta be around."

"One step at a time."

"Yeah, Frankie's super organized. Ten teams each

with a leader. I'm head of mine. Frankie and the top dogs coordinate schedules." He sighs. "It all seemed easy, you know. Supposedly, more training one of these days. Yeah, Frankie's a trip. But organized."

"We have to help."

We get out of the truck.

It looks like it's going to rain, but it doesn't. I can hear a car honking down the canyon. No more gun shots. Kids' lilting voices, always close to laughter, call out challenges and greetings. Nobody seems too worried now. Must have been up a side canyon. There's that Bean boy. I had to check on his family, home visit, back in the day, when I was a social worker. His family left, I think. He stayed. He's carrying a sword.

"I'm gonna go talk to those guys," says Alan.

Down Spring Canyon, one of the side roads, leading here, Fred Stanley comes leading a group of woman warriors. The women carry guns and adzes. I can see a pair of shears.

"Fred Stanley," says Alan, coming back. He keeps his arms at his sides, but the veins and muscles in his neck stand out in relief. "Hope Fred doesn't go nutty on us. That's his neighborhood defense group. And that guy over there? In the thick of it, by the biker doods? That's Don. He's one of Fred's main guys. Shit. This is going to get complicated. Hope you got your meditation hat on. We'll have to talk to them."

"Mediation."

"What?"

"You said meditation. No meditation right now.

Maybe I should start a class."

We join the crowd, asking what's happening. Getting the down low, edging our way to Don, keeping an eye on Stanley. This Don is tall, rough looking, needs a shave. He wields a wicked looking sawed-off shotgun. Like ones I've seen on TV. The ones bad guys carry. Bad hombre! Why did he stay? He looks like a thug weasel heavy from the 1950s that hangs out at garages and drinks Jim Beam in *Coca-cola* bottles. He's a leader here, or else everybody's afraid of him.

Don nods at Alan, looks me over quickly, says, "All the homes vacated yesterday are occupado. No vacancies! Bunch of baldies in their place. Some of them have guns, but they don't know how to aim. They be yelling and slobbering. Really sick. Just acting spooky crazy."

I say, "Every single house that was left in your neighborhoods?"

"We got the list, too," says Don, "so, yeah, the ones up here."

Alan tells him what happened on Star Avenue.

Don asks, "Did you kill it?"

"We decided to wait," I interject. "On account of we heard gun shots, so we wanted to see what was happening here."

Don nods, smiles. He points to Stanley, fast approaching. "Our man! Yeah, there was some shooting," goes Don. "We got it under control."

A guy standing next to Don in camo, short, with a bowling ball in his stomach, and a holstered pistol at his side, demands, "Take 'em out! What else can we do? Shoot 'em! We can't let them stay here. We got 'em, cleaned out our neighborhood for reals."

I go, "Wait." But don't know what I'm saying –

Another person throws up, "Wait for what?"

Fred Stanley has joined us. "We know what we're doing. Don't need no advisors."

Don says, "No way we're letting them things stay in our neighborhood."

I murmur, "What do they want? What do they think they're doing here?"

Don says, "Who knows? No way they're welcome. No way they're staying. Can't really round 'em up either. I mean, without *deflating* them."

Fred Stanley will not be ignored. He shouts, "What do we care what they want? We saw what they did to Oscar." He and his minions officially glare. Now he pushes it, all anxious, aglow with righteousness: "Besides, ya'll are in *our* neighborhood. We got everything under control. We don't need any help. Sure, the security guys were back up. Appreciated! But unnecessary. Tell 'em we got it covered."

Don says, "Right on, Fred," and nods. He snickers.

Alan says, "Fred, we got to agree on what we do. This affects all of us."

"We got it under control!"

Don yells, "Halt!" like an ass: "You got no right. Man said for you to clear out."

I'm starting to see they made a choice, not just to stay, but preserve their stupid, 19th Century, machismo ways.

Don goes, "We got this shit under control. Already took care of things up Spring Canyon. Fred's all over it."

Fred Stanley is chipper, tight, wiry. He blasts, "Secure! We take care of ourselves. We know what is necessary."

Don says, "We're taking care of business. You and those security guys, thanks for the help. We're good."

I blurt out, "What did you do?"

"Let's just say that any house recently vacated in our neighborhood is vacated again."

Don says, "We blasted them. So did your security boys. Couldn't have done it without them. That's a joke."

Fred says, "How can you kill that which is not alive? Self-preservation! They don't belong here. Not in our neighborhood."

His female warriors shout support. Don whoops!

Everyone turns to watch yet another old pickup coming up the canyon towards us. When it's close enough, we can see it's Councilman Martinez driving with Officer Latta in the passenger seat. They park by our pickup, get out. Latta's wearing his uniform.

Where has he been? Haven't seen him a couple days. Folks were wondering yesterday, looking for him during the *Deportation*.

He calls out hellos and people greet him back. He

strides over to us talking all the while: "We got the word downtown. But we been having baldies up that way, too. And folks took care of 'em. Maybe a tad premature. Cause those baldies were acting different. We got the doctors and scientists thinking on it. I mean, we can always get rid of the baldies. But maybe we should try to talk to them."

Don smiles at Latta and nods, sputters with it: "Fred decided what to do. We took care of bidness, officer!"

Latta, strong and crisp in his uniform, as though nothing can irritate him, holds his arms up, palms out and open. He says to Fred and Don, "We're trying to have a civilization here. Okay? Requires folks to talk it through, come to a decision together. Know what I mean? Well, I guess it don't matter now." Latta turns from the two, calls out to the crowd in general, "I think everyone should stay put the rest of the day. Just go back to your homes and lay low. They don't all have guns. And none of 'em can use a gun. But just to be on the safe side. And if you got some good ideas, or questions you think important, bring 'em down to the convention center. Maybe we can get together this afternoon, figure this out."

Don says, "Nothing to figure out. No more meetings."

Fred goes fast, "We already figured it out. We have everything under control, officer. And no way we're hiding in our homes when those things are running around. Clean it up! It's our duty! Protect our homes!"

Something's not right. It's too easy. The baldies must have known what'd happen. Their controllers knew. Whoever built them, made them, concocted them. Maybe the baldies didn't know they'd get shot. Then what's their purpose? Trying to colonize our town? Doesn't make sense.

These rocky canyons have been our hideaway. Canyons in canyons! Boulders and cliffs, stairs and paths, crisscrossing the hills. New life in the canyons now – they are alive, aren't they? Maybe not. But why would they be sent here? What could be their purpose?

Councilman Martinez, a tall fellow, seems nervous. He squirms, working up his courage to say, "Where's the security guys?" He yells some names, "Rios!" "Langan!" I don't know most of the names. Young men, one woman, in the crowd make their way through the people to Martinez. They all have guns. Sheepish is the word that fits their tight, downcast faces.

Martinez says, "Everybody okay?"

One of them, a young man, says, "For sure! And we got word out right away, soon as we saw the places were occupied."

Officer Latta says, "What happened?"

They shrug, glance away, tuck in their guts.

An older security man says, "These folks were upset with their new neighbors." He can't keep from a throaty chuckle. He goes on, "So we helped them out. All of us did. Couple homes up that way, Spring Canyon, Then, one back that way, up Locklin." He points.

Officer Latta, very sharp, says, "You'll have to help them clean up then. The mess after they're shot. We don't know, could be toxic. Who knows? We don't want that stuff stinking up the place."

People yell, "Yeah!" "No problem!"

Fred and Don beam.

Martinez steps, stops. "People! This is getting crazier by the day. Each day the curtain goes up on more unbelieveableness. Something's not right. Hey, I was underground, I seen the supplies come back in the bomb shelter. But...but folks say there is no magic." He shakes his head, frowning, looking away. "Somebody is doing this. First, we make our choice, then they let us go, then right away they send in these things. What's up with that? They know we can kill 'em easy enough. They know we will. Then why? See how crazy? It's gotta be somebody pulling the strings. All this shit coming from some place."

I say, "I think everything's gonna depend on us figuring this out. It's the only way we can be sure we're safe."

Don goes, "We're safe!"

Alan says, "Security guys can help you clean up."

A little girl, dressed in sweat shirt, corduroy pants, and sneakers, pushes in to our midst, just as folks begin to wander off. The girl has a stick and when she stops by me, she holds it out in front of herself, bottom pressed to the ground. The stick is taller than she is.

She says with a grown up urgency, "If all the empty houses get filled up right away, then maybe the things are here all the time. And we can't see them."

Officer Latta nods. He smiles at her. He says, "Good thinking."

I say, "What's your name?"

"Didi," she says, striking her stick down hard in

front of her.

"What's that?"

"Christmas tree from last year. We found where a man kept a lot of them. All these Christmases. I cleaned it myself. With a knife. But it's still got sticky spots."

"Christmas trees?" says Latta.

"Daisy says Christmas trees are good choices for sticks, on account of they are *supple*. That's what Daisy said. All the kids have sticks," says Didi.

A far off scream! We jump! We search for the source. More screams! Across from us, coming out of one of the side canyons that has a winding road going up it, people. A man in the front has something in his arms.

Everyone is at attention. There's a breathless, terrified silence, as most must realize what they are about to see. We've divided the world between Coltrane and everything else: and every time everything else comes to visit, comes to stop by a sec...there is tragedy. The air is redolent with the smells of smoke, fear, and panic.

Didi sizes up things and runs for it, heading down the canyon to report.

The man with his awful burden is close, people are looking, then turning away to scream and puke.

A little girl's body...pushed in...caved in –

I've never seen anything like it. At first, I am all intellectual and clinical, wanting to see for myself. But it's too much.

We're all screaming now –

## Clay Mason

*looking down the Thylacine's throat*
*canyon cliffs morphing fangs*
*mountains are incisors*
*sharpest monster teeth*
*rock formation skyscrapers*

Lope, lope, lope, back from the tunnel – gun shots! Already in the ditch, and I will cease touching my face. My face! Face face face. My head's getting big! I finger my belt loop to rub. Rub-a-dub. No rope this time, that few days ago exact same steps, same breaths. Now, no rope-a-dope. Now, a different no rope. There's repeats, unfolding dimensions – this is not that. This is Planet Coltrane. BAM! Everyone freaks, shoots, leaves, stays. We decided! Monsters come in. Here they are! Gunshots! They fall. They die. They deflate. Jump rock to rock, avoiding accumulation. I wonder: what is the name of our solar system? When will it collapse? We orbit each other for gravity. Destroy all planets! Destroy all monsters! Pink rays! Scooby rays! I'm over here.

The tunnel stands secure!

It's like a 24-7 party up there at the tunnel, people all charming and appropriate. Hold the tunnel! Cots. Snacks. Plenty of water. Kids up there. Like it's jolting back memories of life in the caves. We all know the same things, we have the same images. But I am not they. We decided to stay. We changed. The weather changed.

Gunshots ahead! I'm coming!

*gray skies*
*gray eyes*
*gray skies*
*gray eyes*

Her gray gunfighter eyes! And we ventured... adventured into the depths, into the void of ping pong balls...together...

Down Mule Canyon in the ditch, I transmogrify. A kid on a bike shoots by never suspecting. I know what to do. I have a stick, a knife, and this new invention around my soul, elasticity – a sling.

*trickle of water*
*wetness feet*
*boys her own age, boys her own age, boys her own*
*age.*

The Indian tobacco is blooming. I think I smell Chinaberry. It can't be, way too late in the season. Didn't they go extinct with the Trilobites? Smell of stinky feet. Re-invent humans! Human stank. I can smell the past, the future...the future smells like mental illness horse pistols. Kids are used to not bathing. Kids crave *Dirt.*

Gunshots!

I never played games. I mean, I never had a smart phone or a computer. At school, we used computers. Mom and Dad kept it real. They kept it close to the bone. Bone Bonetron Boner –

What do I smell like? Why can't you smell yourself?

I know what Daisy smells like – she smells of Moloch and Freya.

The ditch is invisible so I am –

Rock to rock, Sacred Datura to horehound patch. A dirty masked moth! Moths in October? Moths are messengers. Moths are guardians. *Opuntia!* Cactus, good to see, covered in spines. Fingers mild. Then covered in spines, spiny spiny spiny. No one can threaten the kids because they will fight back with their sticks, the way Daisy taught them.

A voice cuts through: "What you doing down there?"

"It's a free country!"

"You watch out for baldies!"

How can I explain to this security dood, who can't be more than seventeen, with what looks like a .22 lever action – oh, great! How can I explain to him that I was the one who discovered the baldies? How can I tell him that I got just what the doctor ordered?

I unwrap the sling from around my shoulder. I go, "Sling."

He pulls around his rifle, shakes it at me, goes, "Koolio! You got it going on, pardner!"

Yes! Yes! Yes! to requests! Going on, going on, going on. I can be this or that.

Ever since the pink ray. Ever since the silver ball. Daisy cobbed one. I wouldn't have. That's the difference in our smell.

Boys her own age, boys of the Stone Age –

I am not his 'pardner.' So I keep going. He must be

on patrol. Baldies all over the place. That was the damn radio show people were talking when I took off. In all the houses people left. Makes sense.

How did they get in? Past our guards and roadblock? People be shooting their sorry asses, left and right. What does Daisy think?

Last couple nights I stayed at my folks' place. It had been pillaged. Vandalized! Ha! Joke's on them! No loot for looting, that's for sure. We are all marauders now. What did they take when they left? My people. No one will know when I turn fifteen. No one will know how pitiful a pillaged house can be. That's not true: we all know now.

I must be getting close to the first group of houses with baldies, because there's traffic overhead. Voices. A motorcycle. People shout but I can't see them. I have weapons, they have weapons. We are deployed!

I guess I can climb out.

I do what I can. I do what happens to me.

Types among us. The swagger of their weapons walk. Then frantic PUs clutching their rakes and hoes. Couple Wooks. Ewoks laying low in the caves.

Where I come out, the road is wide with close houses on either side. A canyon going up, due north, has its own side road. Lots of side canyons.

"What's going on?" I ask.

A lady says, "Up Spring Canyon, they had to take out baldies in the vacated houses. Other places too."

A man next to her says, "I was there. Fred Stanley

saying we should take care of our own neighborhoods. That's why I came back."

The woman says, "I was there, too. The councilman and the police officer said we should wait or try to talk to them."

A bunch of people laugh and make jokes.

There's a house up there that's occupado. Family of three. Three baldies. At least that's what the word is on the street.

We go to investigate. Mi gente. Take the side road, a bundle of people, no line or order, weapons pointing in all directions. It's a little house, wood with a metal roof, like so many that dot the hillsides. It's got a porch. A driveway. One rose bush, some lilacs. Looks cuddly normal. People stay back, keeping their eyes on the place. Watch the watching. Kids from Daisy's are here – scouts. Families stay on the road, near me. Wooks giggle like hyenas.

The couple houses by the baldy house seem quiet. Empty? Nope! Because the front door of the nearest neighboring house bursts open and a little boy, a human boy, with black hair, in shorts and a sweat shirt with Pooh bear on it, comes running out. He runs right over to the baldy house, goes up to the front door and knocks.

People around me start yelling, "Get away from there!" "What are you doing?" "Get back!"

Wooks moan away like it's the end of the world. A PU spits. A little boy bites his stick.

Is this the way it's supposed to go? Where's security? They must be here, some of these guys.

The little boy's family tears out of their house to see what's going on. Ma screeches. Da calls his name, "Victor! Victor!"

Dad zooms for the house. He carries no weapon. Defenseless. Meanwhile, the door opens for the little boy and the baldies are there, three of them, two big and one little. They grab the little boy and rip. Next thing you know his black-haired head is sailing through space to daddy who catches it.

Hands. *My hands do not belong here*, da thinks.

He – I is thirsty and forgot a water bottle. Toes tense twitch. Fingers jump hurt. Plenty of plenty. He thinks he's gonna puke. I don't puke. Last time I puked was July 4, 2025. Something to do with Trilobites? He thinks thinks thinks, *this could not happen.*

I smell smoke. I smell puke. I hear voices.

Can I talk to myself, or will everyone know?

**Didi Grebe**

> *STICK ALERT!*
> *everyone knows*
> *what to do with a stick*

I've seen baldies. They are completely uh-uh naked. You see everything. But they're like doll bodies – smooth as ice cream. How do they tell themselves apart? Maybe it's just one voice talking in to their heads, telling them what to do, like when you're playing dolls. These don't seem so much like dolls.

Screams are scary. Especially from adults. Claymason calls them PUs. Parental units. Because they dress funny. And smell goopy. Claymason. Claymason. He's dropped his sling trying to get it out. He looks as white as a baby. Everyone does, except for the lady PUs crying, who have red blotchy faces around wet red eyes.

Screams!

The three baldies are screaming, too, walking away from the house, from that little boy body parts. I guess we come apart easy. I am not – I do not come apart easy. That walk they do like a drunk they do. Only their screaming isn't as scary as it is disgusting, with lots of slobber and stuff spraying. Don't spray it, say it! They're coming down the drive way, right towards us. At least they're not carrying guns. All the guns are on they.

"Shoot 'em!" goes a voice. "Take them out!"

"Wait! Wait! We're supposed to wait!"

"Wait for what?"

"Shoot 'em!"

"They killed that little boy!"

"Wait! What are they doing?"

"Why should we wait?"

"Here they come!"

"They're attacking!"

"Wait! They don't have weapons. This is different.

Maybe they want to talk?"

Claymason gets his sling going, stone in place, then stops. He doesn't know what to do. He hasn't been at the house for two days. Daisy sent out scouts to keep an eye on him. They reported the sling. They said he talked to himself. Maybe that's what happens when you're older and turning in to a PU?

Wow! These baldies are different. They're pink-white, whiter. They have more face, not so globby. They have two little dots on their chests like they got pretend nipple stickers. Something's going on between their legs. I don't even want to know – or look. Bumps between their legs. You can tell it's a man baldy, then a woman baldy, and a baby baldy. They're still crying, getting closer. Maybe they're going through baldy puberty?

People draw back. We face them. No one shoots. Guys stay out front with guns aimed. A lady yells at them something like 'what do you want?' Are they going to talk? I watch the cry baby baldies get to the main road. Now they're moving down the middle of the road towards downtown. Why is everyone waiting? Well, they're not actually attacking. They are crying and gurgling, with faces sicky sticky sickly. They have blood on their hands and arms. Little boy blood. Really gross.

Trucks and bikes take off ahead of the baldy parade. People on foot run on ahead. Nobody shoots them. The baldies stay in the middle of the road. People follow alongside, but on the sidewalks, then a big bunch behind. Pretty soon, we meet more people, who've got their own baldy problems.

I always have to look real close to see if my PUs are there on account of they want me back. To come back home. And I don't want to.

Yikes! Scary! More baldies stumble down side roads from these canyons, towards us on the main road. No one shoots. Our baldies who ripped the little boy's head off are waiting for them. They know each other? They're joining up? The PUs say we should try to talk to them?

We head up the canyon picking up people, more security guys, some old people, more kids. More baldies! Some of these baldies carry guns, rifles. But they are not firing. Security guys stay close to them. One baldy has a hatchet. He could throw that hatchet and cut a kid in half, like they did to the little boy. How come they're letting them go after what they did to the little boy? I didn't know that little boy. But he's dead dead. One baldy has a butcher knife. I don't know where they got them. But none of the baldies carry sticks. Kids all carry sticks now. I have two.

Baldies join up with the baldies in the middle of the road. There must be a zillion baldies now, male types, lady types, little kids. And they're heading up the middle of the road towards downtown. All the people escorting them.

There's Daisy! She and Claymason are talking. But they're on the other side of the road. I don't know what they are saying. I bet Daisy is asking about his new sling. No, no, I bet they're talking about baldies.

Baldies are crying. Snotty slobbers. Total grossness. Occasionally, one gives off a screech that might be a sick bird. Or twisted metal guts. Sometimes they make a sound and you could swear it's a word.

Then, the security guys start yelling, "Crossfire!" "Crossfire!"

They want everyone that is human to be on one side of the road, so when the shooting commences, people won't be blasting each other. Smart! They're smart.

People rearrange themselves, crossing the road, yelling out hello and what's going on. More baldies join the parade. But the main road's kept open, so they can keep going. I guess everybody thinks they're heading back to the gate?

Now, there's gotta be fifty naked baldies going down the street, between the empty stores and shops and restaurants that will never open again. I could go in there with money and get stuff, when I was a kid. Like dolls. Or candy. I wanted a Trilotat. My parents wouldn't let me get one because people were afraid of what they could do to your mind. Daisy and Claymason are ahead of me. Everybody's watching baldies. Glued to the sight of them plopping down the road. One false move and they will get it. I wave my Christmas tree at Daisy, but she doesn't see me. Everybody is upset. You can tell by the way their faces show so many faces. Baldies have one face.

They're coming up to the post office plaza by the convention center. There's a truck parked right there in the middle of the road. In front of the truck, the mayor, Frankie Lucien, Officer Latta, Margaret Pitka, and the councilmen who stayed.

**Frankie Lucien**

*trap*

*gotta be a trap*
*it's too easy*
*not to be*
*something's not right*
*self-preservation, etc*

We got security guys in the windows of the upper stories all along main street. Up on the roof. All men who can shoot straight. They know how to take out a target. I can see their rifle barrels sticking out. We're covered!

Enfilade!

Only way to clean up this mess.

Now the baldies stop in front of us at the plaza. Maybe twenty feet from us. The ones with weapons are scattered through the group. Not a single weapon is raised.

If they surrender? It don't matter –

Folks are hanging back. All on one side of the street. Not getting too close. Folks are quiet. They watch as they've never watched before. They are ready for it. To do what must be done.

The mayor calls out to them, "Where are you going? What's going on? Are you going back?"

No answer. Some gurgling. Baldies are made of snot. It leaks out of their empty, awful faces.

The mayor tries again: "What are you?"

No response. Not a peep. A wail cuts above the baldy crowd. Are they singing through their degenerate pie holes? Cries of utter despair. They're offering themselves up? They gotta know what's going to happen.

Are they crazy? Can they think? They're not human, that's for sure. They stand there, shuffling from bare foot to bare foot. Targets. That's all they are. Some seem to have nubby beginnings of fingernails. They're gross. Stringy clear liquid stuff slimes down the fronts of their faces onto their fronts, covering their chests. Little nipple dots there now, too. Bulgy parts between their legs. That's new. They're just gross.

The mayor tries again: "What do you want? Who are you? If we move, will you keep going and leave? Do you understand what I am saying?"

**Margaret Pitka**

> *if I prick my skin*
> *I bleed*
> *if I prick your skin*

I step forward to the mayor and Frankie. I don't want to. I ignore Frankie and the others' fierce whispers to watch out. They think I'll wreck this? What can be wrecked now? I told them I'd try. Don't I have to? It's what humans do.

Who speaks for baldies? Who speaks for dead baldies?

I raise my voice: "We don't want to hurt you. We don't want to fight. But you killed a child! And others. What should we do? Can you talk?"

Susan Kell is over at the bank at the corner,

leaning behind the brick wall at the entrance. Suddenly, she rushes over. She takes my hand. I can see Frankie doesn't like this one bit. The councilmen looked confused. Officer Latta and the mayor offer grim nods.

Susan Kell yells, "Say something!"

A wail serves as an answer.

Susan Kell pulls away from me, takes a step towards the baldies. "You killed children! These people are going to shoot! Do you understand? They're going to shoot!"

I've never seen anything like it. She is courageous. She is a fool. Then, I think or realize, that makes me one, too. We know what these things do. They know what we do. It's suicide. It's like suicide by cop, because they know what we are forced to do.

## Mayor John John Placido

> *clamor*
> *means*
> *rise to the occasion*
> *push back*

We have changed.

But we never had kids. We wanted to. We decided against it. Now it's too late. I can see kids in the crowd. They carry sticks. They are tough. They fight back. We all do. We do what we have to. Natural law! The kids have changed the most, I think. What people do, when necessary –

Frankie's eyes dart away from Ms. Pitka and Ms. Kell. He releases them from her gaze. The councilmen have no hope in their faces. Officer Latta's eyes won't leave the baldies. Now the Pitka woman looks like she's losing it. She's breathing funny. So is Ramsey. He's gonna blow –

"What do we do?" I cry. "Folks, we gotta do something and fast!"

Ms. Kell says, "Let them pass! Let them go back!"

No one answers. So much for leadership. The baldies hold, standing there, shuffling, dripping, the occasional wail.

### Officer Oscar Latta

*I didn't call on death*
*it called on me*

Is that how that goes? I think it's a poem. By someone famous. Death stops by. Death comes over for tea and strumpets. Death touches you forever. It leans its stick on you, inserts thorns, bristles. It leaves its stink on you. The pressure is always there. For the rest of your life. The awful inevitability of Death means more Death to follow. Here comes Death!

"We don't want to fight but we will. Tell us what's

going on?" I try.

A baldy man near the front, with a rifle sloppily banging at its side, hobbles forward. Susan Kell pulls back fast. Margaret Pitka makes a weird rattling sound as she cringes. Frankie stomps forward, rifle ready. The councilmen shake. I can see them shaking.

The baldy stops and stares at me. That head! I mean, sure a vague face, but no presence, like a person would have. Are those eyes or sensors? Empty stare, like a zoned-out druggie. I stare back. I will not flinch. Then a voice erupts. No, spurts from the head. It's slobbery talk:

"We we we we we give you you you you ting ting ting to fight...to pose...to release?"

It's the worst voice I've ever heard in my life. It's ugly and scary and sad like a pathetic car wreck screech imitated by a rabid cat. Like you don't want to look at where that voice comes from. Don't want to see what makes those sounds. I can hear the way the people in the street, and those next to me, inhale sharply, ready to gag or bolt. Also, I can hear the question mark in that voice, the way the sounds go up, so what does that mean?

The baldy man who spoke sputters and mutters some more, but I can't make out a word. I glance at Frankie and Mike, gripping their rifles like life preservers. Crossfire! Gotta be careful. Pitka and Kell are going to run. I can see it in their faces. But these kids – I'm thinking *all these kids...*

There's no escape now. Ugly demands it. Sounds of gross demand it. Only one thing left to do. They're making us do this. It don't make no sense, but it seems necessary? See the way my voice goes up even in my head, when I make a question?

The baldy raises its rifle and fires before it's even all the way up. The bullet hits the asphalt and ricochets. But the baldy keeps firing. The drool or spit or ooze is really flowing –

A tidal wave of reaction then, and for me in slow motion, as all these weapons open up, and the mayor hits the ground.

## Councilman Michael Ramsey

*all of a sudden*
*hell*
*breaks loose*

With baldies firing weapons, even without aiming, we are forced. We have no choice but to shoot back, but only at the ones with guns. Then the other baldies attack! Knives and axes and rolling pins are brandished by the limping, straggling baldies. All the while, they grind their mouths, whimpering out those awful wails, then an occasional word sound. But never fear, cause folks open up right in their ugly fake faces. Wailing intensifies, then abruptly stops.

Because the street, now, is all baldies going down, shrinking, melting away, deflating right in their tracks, into gooey messes.

Good thing so many guns around. Bad thing that some who chose consolidation left behind guns for baldies to find.

They're awful shots. None of us are even grazed. I don't think they got a clean shot out at all. Our people are great shots. We been practicing.

## Didi Grebe

*claymason*
*claymason*
*claymason*

All the shooting in the world, all at once, sounds like war. This is war now. No pretend. No hold backs. Total war.

I stay close by claymason. At first, I think he's going to use his sling. But, instead, like me, he just watches and is grossed out forever and ever. I don't know where Daisy is. She has a knife. I hold on to my Christmas tree. But none of the baldies come close to me.

I bend in closer to claymason and take his hand. At first, he's surprised, and I think he will pull away. I tug him to the brick edge of a building's wall, like an entrance to the alleyway. Good place to watch. He comes with me. We don't want to miss a thing. Our eyes are glued to nastiness. But we don't have to be up close. I don't want any of that yuck goo getting on my clothes. Thousands of baldies fall to the ground. Thousands of bullets fly through the air. Baldies flatten out like gooey pancakes. They just do.

The guns get quiet like.

Clay looks down at me finally. I think he likes me. We're friends and everything. "Thanks," he says.

"For what?" I go.

He's all: "Look! There's Daisy." The way he says her name is real cute. He walks back to where we were, around the building's edge to the street, to Daisy, who is sharp and tense as an eagle I can tell.

I take steps back. I can walk backwards. Don't want no more to see it. Hold on to my Christmas tree. Tight. I stay up close to the bricks of the building. I count bricks: red, red, red – that's three.

Then, this is what I see:

I'm huddling at the brick edge of a building right by Main Street, and I can see real close, but to the side, in a boarded up doorway, couple buildings over, a little baldy curled up there. Baby baldy. Not too far, near me. Must have got separated from the other baldies. Its parents? I don't know if they have parents. Maybe they come out of an egg. Like lizards. Or birds.

All of a sudden, from the street, two kids, Roland and Cassie, come running. They see me, motion for me to come and help. We move over close to see the baby baldy. We come in slow so as not to spook it. It's like we're hunting snipe, like claymason told me a story about. We come in slow and careful. They have a blanket and everything. The two of them are holding that blanket like they are going to toss it. How can I help? I feel funny and don't want to touch a baldy, even a baby baldy. They toss the blanket. We go in to grab. Baby baldy don't fight backs. We wrap it in the blanket.

Cassie goes, "I saw it first. I told Daisy. She wants

it back at our house. We're taking it. Come help."

Their eyes meet mine, and we're all scardey cats but won't let on. I'm thinking, Daisy gave them a mission? How come she didn't tell me? Roland is nine, and he got the disc. Cassie is nine or ten and can beat me up.

Now I'm thinking, and I'm trying to send an ESP message to Cassie and Roland. But I don't think they hear.

# THE EIGHTH DAY

**Scotty Paulson**

> *artists*
> *the disappointed legislators*
> *of the world*

No resistance. Beauty is right here in front of me. The artist is on time. Today, in my studio at Central School, this time is all times, even without electrics. No candles. Open the windows, breathe in the miasma. Light the work, work the light! Joy of change met with change. These junctures impose superimpose on SHE. She sits on the bar stool with long bare legs dangling like a beautiful spider. Cute feet. Central School is still and stuffy. This early only a few people around, and they are echoey as edifice mice. Outside gray, Central School gray, studio gray. The only thing not gray is the pink pink pink of Reyna Cueva. I like to photograph her at dawn. Time for an excuse. The cure is essence. Joy of cantaloupe juice.

All at once, right here, all of history, that time in Coventry, my first touch where the rhubarb grows. May

Belle and I traipsing down the hedgerow, sweaty and dusty and laughing; and young as sin and twice as ducky, snarking into a tidy shuttered store's entrance. A slot, a sleeve, a hidey hole, momentous in a moment. We stood close. We breathed each other's breath, and liked it. Suddenly, nowness, newness, my surroundings glaze my eyeballs: Reyna. I'm back in heaven with a camera.

In Coventry, her real name was Francis, but I prefer May Belle – sounds so American!

Everything sharp. Beauty smells like fresh fruit. Earth is known for its amazing fruit. There is cartoon time. There is solid time. This time, Coltrane in the 21st Century, *Café Terminus*, end of the line – *All aboard!* back and forth, time travel is real. False teeth are real – I put them back in. I peer around my studio as though I've been gone. When I work, I go. In my studio Reyna is life imprimatur who must be worshipped. She's a New Age visual artist, and I have never been able to figure what that means. But no matter: we are outrageous.

Once upon a time, there was no time, there was only moo cow to pluck. So, rise from my knees, lay aside camera. I remember being very small and staring into wood grain, say of a board in the wall, and seeing faces. They were the faces of my story books: heroes, beasts, princesses. Right there – if I stared hard, I was invited in. The artist stares at the wood grain, sees the faces, annotates, reverberates. Inspiration indulgence. And today, *Café terminus*, working the Black Iron Prison like it *is* the last trope in town. Nothing else worked: not religion, philosophy, or science. Art is a way to beam.

Reyna is poised for take off like a gangly bird. She goes, "Scotty, you're the best! I gotta go."

"Where to?"

"The light in my studio, what there is of it, it's not an...elaborating light. But right now it should be good. Or at least illuminated." She smiles. "I need light. At least for a little while."

"Light."

She jumps off the bar stool. "You have a tissue?"

"Tissue, water, snacks." I toss her a roll of toilet paper. "We live on snacks."

She says, "End of the world, go with the flow." She blows her nose.

"No where flow. Was that always it? Our victuals are nutrition lumps. Our brains are portals. Too easy? Too cliché?"

"Not really." She shakes her shoulders. She's one of those women whose every movement is a ballet of swans. Her breath puffs, "I'm working on a giant flower painting. Flowers are keys, a way in, a way out, a link that opens up bloom. Blossom. Think of all the species that bloom then die."

"We don't even know whether we are still in the world."

"Maybe we're dead, right?"

We both answer: "No!"

She's ignited loud and clear. Her tall form pulses. "You are not a cynic." Her hair is messed up. Her eyes are moist. She raises her head, decrees, embellishes, "This is what you always wanted, right?"

"Confirmation of alternative universes only comes

from living in one. I reside in a Black Iron Prison. You live in a giant flower."

"You come to the calyx."

"Nuzzle petals?"

"How could we leave here, right? Our inhabitation? More than home: cynosure. But after yesterday? And the day before that! And the day before that! Each day is a crisis of crime."

"Genet says 'criminogenic.' Civilization forces us to be criminals."

"You're writing a poem. I can tell. Just don't make it all about yourself. What do we want to hear now?"

"What we knew was here all along."

"I feel good. Right now. Yesterday?" She shrugs dramatically. "Those baldies? Yesterday was gross."

"The whole town, yesterday: the massacre of glub."

"Don't ruin my buzz. When can I see the prints?"

"Someone should have filmed it. Yesterday. We got batteries! We should be filming everything. Our archives! Wouldn't it be typical, long after this is over and we're all gone – ha, some visitors stop by, find the film, can't figure how to run it. No batteries."

"Immortality?"

A sigh and a shoulder roll. "One day at a time, like the drunks say. Besides, batteries apparently last a lifetime." Goofy grins, we shrug as one. "Or else how will we record these final *Amens*?"

*"Amen!"*

Reyna goes, I go. I exit the building, walk around Central School to the back where it slopes down to City Park on stairs and paths through the anise archipelago. No one knows why anise continues to thrive when so many plants succumb. So our town at the end of time smells like licorice. I go around City Park from the top side. Empty street. Smell of grease and anise. Head up the Gulch like I know where I'm going. No way going downtown. I know what that greasy smoke is from. Some kids with sticks go by on a horse. A woman on a bicycle shoots past me. She's wheezing. The kids atop the horse yell to her. Centaurs! People who stayed busy surviving this day. Here we go, getting through – surviving this day.

I could use a cup of tea. A biscuit.

Check my pockets. Nothing. I carry nothing. No weapon. No stick. No pistolero! No pen, or pencil, or camera.

The Gulch goes rough, dirt road. Fewer domiciles and those that hunker around here are dilapidated. Will they stand? Will a giant come and fart and squash them? A heavy hairy hand descending from heaven to do the dirty work? Fee-fi-fo-fum! I smell the blood of an Englishman. Bare rocky walls now, with swoops and slopes. Twisted weeds. Dead trees. Scenery. The eyes love scenery. More trees in boulder cracks, rending the pure stone. Seed heads of weeds look pretend. A rabbit peeks from an agave. One head, two eyes – cozy real. An orange-winged wasp goes by. I pull back. Let it go on. No resistance. Some big blue bird is yammering Xantippe style. Outside in the country, as Woody Allen famously observed, one has to contend with 'moths in the screens.' Then one sees manzanita have muscles. Muscles flex in hepatic rage. This is edge town, edge bite. There's the house the kids took over. The last one on the road. I slide over, go stealthy. Approach caution –

Two little urchins, a boy and a girl, pull a wagon loaded with plastic water bottles out the front door. They're positioning it to get down the steps from the house's front porch. Which they do. Then they yank and pull and push the wagon and its booty up the dirt road, boy in front pulling, girl in back pushing. Then they switch positions. They have a baseball bat lying in the bottles on the wagon. Who would rip off a couple kids? Cute little dirt balls. I slink into the gloam. They go right by me.

Maybe the old house at the end of the road has a well?

All that water. A fortune. Trade. Barter. Reciprocity?

Everybody stocked up on supplies. Or said they did. Energy bars. 'They last a lifetime!' Gotta get disciplined. Gotta stay on top of the water and calories uptick. I am in charge. I've stocked up on moments to the bitter end.

We'll host happenings at the end of the world! Events! Masques! Ribaldry! Everyone will perform! Gargantuan exhibitions! Final art! Survival art! Calyxes! Sticks! The children can do heroic stick art. We'll dance, we'll paint, we'll sculpt, we'll declaim into the wilderness.

I'll sneak over to the kids' house. Take a peek. They must be up. We don't need alarm clocks now, we need light.

Guards? Watchers?

No sign.

So slip along the road's edge, huggy buggy bushes, and, because of the way the kids' house sits back from the road, no one should be able to see me. All nonchalant, I saunter, I plunder to the rear window. Fold into a bush in a rocky defile. Scope it out. I'm a little fellow. I'm very close.

Someone's here already! A woman. She's scrunched down under the back window, stretching her neck up to peer over the bottom ledge. It's a woman I've seen before. Faintly fortyish, glasses, bottled up, plump in a good way. She's sharp. On. Definitely professorial. A leading lady. She's peeking, peaking, piquing!

I join the female, scrunching in close to her. She jumps, falls back. Her face is red. Her eyes are wide. She touches her glasses, pointedly looks away. I hold a finger to my lips. She nods in slow motion. My legs are uncomfortable. I sit back, drag my legs around to a more comfortable position. The two of us stretch our necks, leaning forward, so we can see in. One inch of open space along the bottom of the four-paned window, so we can hear some, too.

She says, "You stink." She gives me an appraising look. I start to whinny but swallow it. I like her right away.

Let the rumpus begin! This is what we saw:

## Susan Kell

*The Ruins of Time build Mansions in Eternity.*

Margot Pitka is a leader. She has clarity. Seems indomitable. Horrors don't bring her down. She won't let them. She welcomes them. She is disciplined. Challenges, she says, are: opportunities. For what? For perfection? She says, 'to live fierce.'

Last night, after things calmed a little and the clean up fires were under way, we talked. I'm on no sleep. What did we talk about?

She told me she thought we were still alive and on Earth. So it was simple really: continue, endure. Man will endure, the whole Faulkner eternal verities stratagem. I tried to interject the paradox, the contradictions, the impossibilities. The horrors. She said, for sure. What else is new? We see it now, she said. Up close. All laid out before us. But it's what's been going on a long time. Baldies, I queried. Our senses work overtime, fine tuned, now, she said. Extreme experience – it's still our universe. But yesterday, the baldies, I pleaded.

*Does the Eagle know what is in the pit?*

She said it was never a question of what is there to do. It was always, how far do you want to go? And those who stayed, she said, were those who already had a commitment to go far, far, far.

*Can Wisdom be put in a silver rod?*

I felt guilty being glib. I felt jaded. I felt I couldn't feel any more. I am not heroic. I have no confidence, no certainty, no fierce. I have dreams.

My energy: sordid, solid, soiled, common, daft,

deft, frugal. Small.

*Joy and Woe are woven fine*
*A Clothing for the Soul divine*

I don't know. Commitment in nowhere is all I know. I didn't want to give up my rapture. Routine can get you so far.

*Exuberance is Beauty*

Up all night inventorying my exuberance. Lists. Fails. Itineraries. Programs. Long term goals.

At the first gray light of dawn, decide to walk. Over the mountains from Howell, down rocky trails that finish at the end of the Gulch.

Furies at work?

*In Futurity*
*I prophetic see,*
*That the earth for sleep*
*Shall arise and seek*
*For her maker meek*

The children's hour has come, their crusade to fix what we perverted. Their neurology sizzles like *Pop Rocks.*

I don't know why I'm here. I know Daisy Piper is here. Some of the boys from the high school. Then, little ones. Their parents must be in a state. But I guess not. I guess they are adapting and want their children to handle this their own way? I suppose teacherly instincts intuit me here. I snuggle down in the rocks. I am invisible. I am open. When some kids with a wagon load of plastic water bottles depart. Don't know the kids. Third or fourth graders. I careen in my hiding place, so as not to be seen. I keep low, legs folded in.

An animal plops down next to me!

I carry no weapon! Defend, offend!

At first, I think it's a dog. Nope. Man-dog: man-beast. He reminds me of a childhood glimpse of a weasel, small and pointed and fierce. The wee beastie fled from a disturbed bush when da was hedge trimming. I'd thought it was a rat at first. But it was too long and sinewy. It had a lovely brown coat. Its energy was distinct, not ratty at all. Aha, this is not a weasel, it's that British artist who won all the awards. Little guy, grinning at me maniacally. I push up my glasses. He winks at me. I know how I blush in surprise. He must think my head's going to pop. Or I have blood pressure problems. He shrugs. I shrug. We rearrange ourselves, settle down, slowly stretch up our necks to see. He stinks and I tell him.

Maybe I should carry a weapon.

We see: there's a little girl with glasses filling plastic water bottles from a five gallon jug. I know her! Samantha? Samantha what? Maybe ten? That would put her in fourth, I think. She's so focused on her job.

We're looking into the kitchen. It's small. Sink and cupboards to the left piled with bottles and boxes. Supplies. Small wooden table on the other side of the window already covered with plastic water bottles. Lots of water! To the right of Samantha and the jug, a closed door. Bathroom? Utility closet?

The kitchen opens to the living room past the front door. A bunch of kids gathered in a circle there, around a round table, with some kind of equipment on it. Maybe a mechanical device? That's weird, because there's no electricity. The living room is knee deep with pads and sleeping bags. The young people are busy, busy –

Daisy Piper, Tenny Luna, and Bennett Tilson, I recognize from school. Then a bunch of little guys. Bennett Tilson is in the middle kneeling by the mechanique on the floor. Daisy is talking. Tenny leans in to help Bennett. I hear someone mutter 'heavy.' They seem to want to move it, arrange it, unless they were trying for the other *heavy*?

I hear Bennett say, "Windows closed?"

"Yes," exclaim little voices.

"We'll see then," Bennett says. "Cassie!"

A little girl comes over to Bennett with a small suitcase. She swings it to him. Bennett takes it, makes room on the table in front of him for it, opens it.

Immediately, a white disc, like a *Frisbee,* emerges. It rises sluggishly, going straight up! Bennett quickly tosses something over it, some kind of cloth, and rope or string. Rigging! It continues to rise, taking the rope and cloth with it. Then it stops, as the rope and cloth are extended as far as they can.

Funny kite in the kids' house!

The little girl Cassie says, "Better than the rat cage."

Another kid goes, "I found the suitcase. Huh, Daisy?"

Bennett pushes the suit case off to the side, then fusses with Tenny on the device in the center of the table. A black machine. Tenny growls. Daisy asks if he needs help. More heavy talk. They're trying to set the machine up in the right position? Daisy bends around, trying to help. Lots of tugging, pushing, while the kids silently watch. They get the machine up on its end.

Tenny says, "Straight up. No lateral motion. Disc in position. We're ready, boss."

"Good," says Bennett. "Don't move! Let's see if there's some kind of connect – "

Daisy leans back on her heels. She calls, "Sammy, it's time!"

The girl by the water jug opens the top of the jug, stabs a fish net into its depths, pulls right up, a ping pong ball in her net. She brings it to the living room.

The big piece of equipment is set the way they want it. The bulgy parts, knobs or whatever, are visible. Tenny's still grappling, holding it in position. Bennett takes the ping pong ball from Samantha. He places it in a precise spot, like an indentation in the black machine's top. They seem to be going for some kind of preferred positioning.

"Okie dokie, sports fans," says Bennett, "let's see if this does anything. Let's do this Budinski thing!" He moves his hands over the projections of the black metal machine, almost like he's playing a musical instrument. Tenny struggles to hold it in place. The machine tapers at its end to like tubes or maybe legs to stand on. But they've got their set up set up. They've got it 'aimed' – black machine, ping pong ball, floaty disk on top.

A light comes on from the machine, but not shining from it, exuding from it. We all gasp, kids and voyeurs. They're so intense at their work, they don't hear us. A soft bluish glow emanates around the black machine. The blue glow climbs, weaves straight up, like a blue glow snake, to the disc. Contact!

Odd light, more of a sparkle?

A little voice calls, "What's it doing?"

Another goes, "What's happening?"

Bennett says, "That's what we're trying to find out."

Daisy says, "Just make sure you can turn it off."

Bennett moves his hand over the black bumps of the machine, its protuberances, and the light goes off. His hand flutters some more: the light goes back on.

Tenny whoops: "You got it going on, bro!"

Now it looks like a chain of blue glow, from the black machine to the disk. The blue seems to congeal? Thick light? The disc glows now through the cloth like it's been turned on. It's been simply hovering there, now it starts to spin.

This is it! What I been waiting for. What I knew was coming. Fear not! Embrace the curdled light. This is beyond science and sense. Blake counted dreams and prophecy in his tool kit. My tool kit uses dreams as kindling.

There's a knock at the closed door in the kitchen I thought was the ukulele closet. It's directly on the other side of the window where we squat. The little girl, Samantha, turns from the light show and hurries to the closed door. The other kids glance at her but are too engrossed. Bennett and Tenny and Daisy only have eyes for the blue column of light and the spinning disc. Samantha raises her hands, palms out, and makes *back, back* motions with her hands.

Fast, Samantha calls, "Daisy!" She rubs her nose and wipes her mouth, and I can see her hand shaking.

She's gone up on tip toe.

"You okay, Sam?" asks Daisy.

"Knocking at the uh-uh door," says Samantha.

To Bennett, Daisy says "Hold it like that, just like that!"

She and a couple of the kids make their way for the kitchen. Samantha uses an index finger to point to the door, jerking out the code scouts know. Daisy goes to the closed door. The kids with her hang back. More knocking.

A little girl hands Daisy a fork, saying, "Here. Just in case."

Daisy takes it. "Thanks, Didi."

"Well, yeah, cause – " blurbs Didi.

Daisy opens the door and there's a little girl in there wrapped in a towel. She has dark hair and eyes. No eyebrows. The little girl says, "I felt it. I want to come out. I could feel it. We're going to be best friends."

Daisy and the kids have huge eyes. Didi jumps back to the sink and grabs her own fork. Samantha cringes. Daisy and the little girl in the closet are locked in each other's gaze.

I think it's Tenny who calls out, "Be careful! Watch it! You know how strong they are."

Bennett adds, "What's going on?"

Samantha and Didi go, "She changed!" "She changed!"

The little girl says, "Can I come out?"

Bennett calls, "What's going on, Daisy?"

Tenny says, "Turn it off. This thing is heavy. We can't hold it forever. I'll get the disc."

Off! Bennett does. The bulky black machine is lowered to the table. The disc stops spinning. Tenny hauls it in like an indoor fisherman. He pulls it down then gets it back to its suit case. Bennett holds the suit case. They get it situated. Done!

Tenny and Bennett and the others still in the living room come over to the kitchen.

All eyes are back on Daisy and the girl who has taken another step.

She looks – it's a baldy! She looks handmade or just made or – from yesterday? One of the new lot?

What are these kids up to? A little girl baldy!

The Brit next to me is wheezing to hold in his laughter. I glance at him curtly. He leans into me to whisper judiciously, "And the children shall lead them!"

"It's impossible," I whisper.

"Deranged," says the Brit. "We are witnesses to events of biblical proportions. This changes everything. This is the realm of Oz, of Nephelococygia."

Tenny and Daisy stretch out their arms and herd the baldy girl back to the room, like they're corralling llamas.

When she's back inside, the kids make whooshing noises.

The baldy whimpers, "I want to come out."

Daisy says, "We'll get you some clothes and talk about it, okay?" She closes the door.

Samantha pushes at her glasses, says, "I didn't know what to do."

"You did fine," said Daisy.

Tenny says, "What's going on?"

"She's changed," says Daisy. "They're changing."

Didi says, "Changed back to a people! Maybe she's nice now?"

What is happening here? What are these guys doing?

Are we seeing things? Hysterics? Hallucinations? A bit of spoiled potato? Ergot in the old grain? What have we just witnessed?

Daisy continues, "She looks more like a little girl."

Another little girl standing by Daisy raises her hand.

Daisy says, "You don't have to do that, Cassie."

Cassie says, "She looked like Moira. Moira was in my class. But she and her family left. Couple days ago, with the others, when the druggies left."

Tenny says, "So this baldy's trying to imitate her? Like fricking pod people?"

Bennett slaps his hands together. He's barely able to contain himself in place. Jittery, fidgety: "It happened –

she knocked just when the light came on! She felt it! That's what she said."

A little boy goes, "What are *pod people*?"

A voice *behind* me, loudly, says, "What are you guys up to?"

The Brit and I swivel around fast. It's Clay Mason. He's got a broom handle in front of him, holding it with his 2 hands in a defensive pose. He's got a thin rope coiled over his shoulder and a wicked looking knife belted at his side.

"Admiring the scenery, lad!" goes the Brit.

I go, "Hello, Clay."

We stand by the window. Tenny raises it. He goes, "Having a party out here?"

"Look who I found peeking," says Clay.

Daisy says, "Hey, Ms. Kell."

"Hi, Daisy."

Tenny says, "So you saw?"

Clay Mason says, "Saw what?"

Tenny says, "Dood, you been missing out. We been experimenting."

"I been staying at my folks' place," says Clay. "Watching for looters. Even though there ain't much at the house. I mean to loot. But I'm back now. Just in time."

"Hey, Clay," says Daisy. She seems flustered all of a sudden. "So much to tell you – "

Clay looks away fast, starts to convulse – no, it's a nervous twitch, like a tic, but he inhales, breathes, gets control, and it stops.

These kids are overflowing.

Tenny says, "Dood, we been doing fine without you."

The Brit goes, "Well, aren't you going to invite us in for a cup of tea? And a biscuit."

Daisy hands him a plastic water bottle through the window. "Here," she says.

I go, "What's going on, Daisy? We saw the little girl in the closet."

Samantha goes, "It's not a closet."

Daisy says, "It's not a little girl."

I ask, "Don't you think scientists and doctors should be involved here?"

The Brit explodes laughing: "Why? These pollywogs have as much chance at figuring this out, than they do. Probably more. They don't bring a lifetime of preconceptions to the table. We've crossed over: the Black Iron Prison demands a rat's ass. We'll keep your secret. Promise. Cross my heart."

Cassie says, "Show them the item."

But Tenny, Bennett, Daisy, and Clay, and the little ones are watching me, as though they understood what the Brit meant, and are waiting for my confirmation. Now they seem to wear halos. Every single one of them is robed in light. And I'm really thinking this is it, the cerebral aneurysm that shreds my senses rapturously before blowing.

Daisy, staring through the window at me, her eyes probing, finally speaks, her voice slow and practical: "We have an item, too."

"We saw many items," I say.

Clay says without a smirk or question, "We have to trust you."

I say, "We'll keep your secrets."

"Good," goes the Brit, fingering his water bottle, getting off the top, humming all the while, to take a drink. He sighs. "Scotland Paulsen at your service, guv'nors! You can call me Scott. Or Scotty. Now, my young scallywags, you must share. Tell all! We don't want to miss a thing. The disc, the ball, the baldy child, the black machine. And we will reveal all, too, tell you every bloody secret of the adult club."

Daisy says, "Thanks, I guess. Ms. Kell – "

Scott won't stop. "Good work! Really good show. Glad to know you're on our side. Be warned: machines bite. The machine is everything you are not."

I force myself to say: "Daisy, I don't know what's going on here. I'm not sure what I just saw. I don't know anything anymore. If I ever did. We're all stressed. But you have a baldy – a little baldy girl. You know, that brings up many issues."

Cassie explains, "It's an experiment."

I continue, "And this machine – the black thing, what is it? Where did it come from? Too many questions,

I know. Sorry. What's an 'item'? I'm afraid to ask."

Clay says, "You're doing fine, Ms. K."

Bennett says, "You might as well come in so we can talk proper."

Tenny says, "We have theories."

"I must know them all," declares Scotland Paulsen.

Tenny says, "Come on, go around."

Clay and I walk around the house with Scott following us, making odd huffing and puffing sounds. Is he okay? Are we freaking for reals? The 'ruins of time'! The porch is busy with luminous orbs, crowded into Daisy, Bennett, Tenny, and the little ones.

"Do you want to come in?" asks Daisy.

Scott bows and steps up to the porch. "Thought you'd never ask, milady." He bows with a flourish this time.

The kids giggle. Daisy glances to me, and I nod. The little girls, Cassie and Didi, take each of Scott's hands and guide him inside. Didi is trailing and before she enters, she looks back at me and says, "Are we in trouble?"

I go, "Of course not!"

Clay mutters, "I can't wait to hear these theories."

Tenny says, "We'll make 'em sign an oath in blood!"

Daisy interrupts: "Chill!"

We're inside, standing around the living room, high stepping carefully to avoid sleeping bags and pads. We approach the table with the black machine and gather around it. It is our idol, but not to worship. To banish? To mastermind?

Scott says, "Looks like it's made of licorice. Licorice device!"

Didi blurts, "Clay found it."

Cassie adds, "Then they pulled it back in the wagon."

Didi says, "Roland and Amy took the wagon this morning with water for trade." She nods her head solemnly.

Cassie blurts, "Me and Roland found her. The baldy girl. I think her name is going to be Moira."

"I saw it," says Didi. "I helped. Swiped her right off the street." She pauses, searches our faces, then: "Plus, Roland got the disc."

"For experiments," explains Cassie.

"Smart kids," says Scott.

"Do you know machines, Mr. Paulsen?" asks Bennett.

"Oh, no, no. I'm an artist. The machine stopped! Throw in the sabot! The machine is the enemy."

"Unless we can use that machine," says Daisy.

Tenny goes, "Like for defense, or even a weapon."

"We're trying to understand capabilities," says

Bennett.

"Clay found the machine. Tell them, Clay," says Didi.

Clay has the oddest presence: he steps back a moment, stepping back from the present, as though invisible or he thinks he's invisible, then he comes forward, takes a step forward in to the now, head low, eyes down: "I think we were at the end of the road, way way up the Gulch, past here. Where it's a dirt trail. And I saw something." He powerfully shrugs then: "Baldies were setting it up. They were positioning the black thing on a cliff so that it faced out to the Gulch."

I say, "How did you get it away from the baldies?"

Daisy smirks. Tenny burps. Bennett goes, "Kids got skills, abilities, we took care of it."

I have no clue where this is going. "Did the baldies look like they knew what they were doing with it? The baldies we've seen couldn't do much. Was it a different type of baldy?"

"We all pushed it back in the wagon," says Tenny sharply. He's a handsome young man of confidence and poise, now with lightning bolts shooting from his eyes at Clay.

Clay doesn't care. He doesn't want to talk now.

I prompt, "They were aiming it up the Gulch – what for? What does it do?"

Clay says, "Disc, machine, baldy – they're related."

"Items?" says Bennett.

Scott turns from the circle and the black machine on the table, as he's noticed something else of interest in the living room. Against a wall in a corner, a bunch of sticks. Maybe 20 sticks leaning there. "Sticks?" he asks. "Very nice! Your regular forest turned to Birnam Wood."

Didi says, "Christmas trees. 'Splain sticks to them, Daisy."

Daisy smiles and says, "People been saving their Christmas trees for awhile, before they stopped selling them. I guess for firewood? Mementos?"

"But we went around," says Didi, "and traded they for water. Tell 'em, Daisy."

Daisy says, "Christmas trees tend to be fir or spruce. Cleaned up, they make dynamite walking sticks."

"A walking stick can be anything," says Cassie.

Didi goes, "Poke! Poke!" acting it out.

"For sure," says Daisy. "Everybody gets a stick. A walking stick. We can imagine what else they can be. Seriously, what people first had was sticks, the Swiss Army Knife of cavemen. I read even chimps pick up sticks."

"Pick up sticks!" goes Didi.

Daisy goes on, "I guess, in the beginning was the stick. Sticks make sense. We have to look at everything now as though it could be, maybe, something else. So these sticks – "

"Capabilities," says Bennett.

Daisy finishes, "As far as parental secrets, Mr.

Paulsen, we're not too worried. All that stuff was about authority, wasn't it? Control. How we had to listen. Some of us had our whole family leave. Others still have their parents around. But it doesn't matter. Authority, now, is just what has to be done."

"Pokers!" cries Didi.

Scott says, "Your story could cure the world. Philosophy of Sticks! Well done!"

I insert, "What's the item?"

Daisy is a presence. She's opened herself, a throughput.

Clay says, "All items come from the same place. Items. At least, that's what we think. That's what I was trying to say. What we got here are the tools of the bads. And we never seen anything like them. Don't think anybody has. They're like clues we gotta figure out."

"How so?" asks Scott.

Clay shakes his head. He steps forward, back in the circle, reaches out to pat the black machine. "To understand these clues, first we got to know they're gonna be surprising. Unexpected. We have to know the...code that explains how they work. Their directions? What – how they work."

"So what do we know?" asks Daisy.

Bennett begins, "When you put the ball on the machine in that spot, blue comes on, and the disc spins, and the little baldy girl looks more like a real girl."

I wonder, "It's projecting? Making us see things – it changes how we see?"

"Maybe it turns on a whole set of things in our brains," says Daisy.

Capability is daunting. "But if they can make us see things!"

Didi says, "When I was little, in the dark, we used to get flashlights and hold them under our chins to look spooky."

"Exactly!" says Scott.

Cassie says, "Daisy, Didi's talking too much."

Didi says, "I am not!" Right away, Cassie gapes.

Daisy leaves the living room and Tenny opens his mouth, "Anyway, something comes out of the machine that can change how things look, or turn things on. So, like a signal. EM, right, Bennett? Plus, plus, plus, those scouts over the divide saw something like this, a black machine, at that attack, when the truck released the discs. So, so, so, two of them. How many are there? Do they have them all around us?"

Daisy calls back to us, "They're not machine guns."

Clay says, "Some kind of masking? Camouflage? Or something deeper that is affecting our minds?"

Didi says, "Great Wall of China? A virtual wall? I used to play games with my brothers."

Scott says, "Smart girl! They'd need to place them strategically to maximize affects. Like lighting a show, for the best overlap."

"To do what?" I ask.

Bennett says, "If we hadn't taken this one...well, maybe...we wouldn't have seen the baldy march down the street yesterday, maybe they would have looked like those people they replaced, and we wouldn't have been able to tell."

Daisy returns with what looks like a small laptop or pad. She says, "Cover up the machine."

Bennett and Tenny wrangle a cloth, like a table cloth, on top of the black machine. Daisy places the small case on top. She fusses with it and it opens. Oddly shaped, red plastic folds and compartments, it looks like...

Cassie says, "It's a *Transformer.*"

"Uh-uh," goes Didi, her voice rising.

"Bennett," Daisy says, nodding to the boy, "you do it best."

Bennett leans in and, too fast for me to figure, he bends and snaps and folds and unfolds the case. "This is the rocket ship configuration. At least that's what we're calling it. Because it looks like a rocket ship."

## Scotty Paulsen

*she was a phantom of delight*
*inside her rocket ship space ship*

I'm up front in the command module. I have seen plenty of WW2 cockpits. This one is big. I'm standing with the girl. It looks like a hoity-toity cockpit, with huge computer screens. Windows or screens? Screens or windows? Fuck sakes! I'm dead and inside a computer!

Colored dots run across the screens. Colored geometric shapes. Ah, infographics!

Which way. I am not – I have no idea how to focus properly. Daisy, next to me in the cockpit, looks equally bewildered.

She gasps, "What is this?"

"We're inside," I say. "Just for now. We got in, we can get out."

"It's like the mine. The other space – "

"I don't know. But if we're talking, I mean, it's sure to pass. We're not threatened. It's a timing thing."

"Only us? Why us? What's on those screens? Are they computers?"

"I can't figure it."

"It's a map?"

I turn vaguely to Daisy then vaguely to the 'front' to the screens. This is not movement, this is stretching focus. "Map? Explain."

She raises her arms and uses her hands to point at the colored bits on the screens. Her arms and hands make marks in the air. Traces appear on the screens. Light trails. Patterns left behind on the screen. Contours. Clearly, a map emerges on screen, in air. Her hands have long fingers with light bulbs built in, I guess. She's into this. Nothing fazes her. She adapts, she adjusts. She speaks in every gesture. She takes two breaths, then a third, then lets it out steadily before she speaks:

"See these, the way they set things up, scale. But not the usual way. These like a big L. The L is the canyon. Town. Coltrane."

"And the big four? The four red markers?"

"The one here is right where the highway gate thingy is."

"You think gates? They're gates?"

"We really don't know what they are. But makes sense. Should we be getting back?"

**Susan Kell**

*a world in a grain of sand*

Clay yells, "Here they come!"

Bennett says, "Oh, great, Tenny, you better – "

Tenny goes, "No, put away the item."

Cassie sputters, "Show 'em what else it can transform to!"

Daisy interrupts with, "Maps!" She's looking around, eyes wild. She glances at Scott. She goes, "How long were we – no. Yes, put away the item, Ben."

I move over to Daisy, offer her a hand. She takes it. We all go look out the front door. Except for the little Brit, who stands there with narrow eyes in a daze. He could be melting. He could be cogitating. He could be having an infarction.

The steep rocky hillside on the other side of the road from the kids' house experiences mini- avalanches, cascading stones and sand, as the source, teenagers, slide down the hillside, leaning back to control their descent.

Scouts must have alerted Clay.

Four of them: Sam Bean, Tom Thoms, Tim Solvang, Andrea Samson. And they are armed with axes, poles, and one rifle. They are disheveled, pale, dirty – dirty faces, like they been licking messy ice creams.

Clay goes, "They been scavenging supplies at empty houses, looking for pills, shit like that. Daze, we gotta give them water. Well, anyway – "

Daisy says, "We don't have any pills."

We're all on the porch now. Scott joins us, looking deliriously somber, his goofy smirk replaced by a resolute countenance. The children have saved him!

Sam hails us, "Behold, ripture upon us! Apocalypse beckons. Am I right? Its messengers have arrived!"

Daisy releases my hand, strides down the steps toward them but stops. "What do you guys want? We're kinda busy right now. We have water if you need it."

Sam howls, "We need nothing! We got everything. What more could we want, boys and girls? This here isn't the rapture, it's the – "

The others call out as one, "The ripture!"

Sam moves towards Tenny, confides, "Tenny, I thought you'd like that. All kinds of poeticals!"

"Come on, Sam," goes Tenny, "get some water and go."

Andrea Samson is a pretty, dark-haired girl, keeping her hatchet to the side. She's tall, big, but by no means fat – fully fleshed. Girls walk in gold. The boys in lighting bold. They're seekers, looking for trouble. They want to scavenge our fears. Roil them, roll in them. Andrea shuffles over to Daisy shyly, looking away. She says, "Hey, Daisy. What are you going to be for Halloween?"

Sam calls, "Every day is Halloween now! I keep telling that to sister but she won't listen."

Cassie says, "Halloween is for babies."

Clay laughs for the first time. He says, "This year, for Halloween, we go as ourselves."

Sam goes, "Wow! Caveboy making with big brain talk! Ooga booga. I think we should all go as homicidal maniacs.""

Didi says, "I'm not a homo – "

Daisy puts her hands on her waist, elbows out, then she cocks her hips. "What are you guys doing?"

Andrea says, "I'll take a water. I'm thirsty. Thanks, Daisy. You guys."

Sam orders, "Break it up! Break it up! This ain't the *Love Boat*, boys and girls. This here is an island of

Purgatory before perdition's pearly gates. So what do you think of Ripture?"

Tenny shrugs, smiles. "I can see you are ripped, man. I don't care. Come back when you want to help."

The Brit goes, "Well done! Positively anarchy. Say, by the way, where does all this water come from?"

Sam points, jumps in place, scolding, "Teacher's pet! Teacher's pet! What kind of experiments you guys doing in there anyway? You got Bennett, you got Clay. Why Daisy, you gots yourself a boy toy band of geeks!"

I clap my hands together, assert, "Class! Children, time to settle down. The bell's going to ring!" I pause. They're all wide eyed, glaring at me in disbelief. Even the Brit. I go, "Gotcha! Oh, come on, what did you think, I was trying to pull rank?"

The little kids go in the house to fetch water for the four high school kids. Sam, Tom, Tim, and Andrea drink.

**Jacob Derry**

>*Robinson Crusoe*
>*Natty Bumpo*
>*Davy Crockett*
>*self-reliance*
>*is not*
>*self-interest*

"Nothing alien is human to me," slips out then:

"Well, if you don't look snug as a bug in a rug! Morning, scout! You know me? Jacob Derry, the catapult guy. The bow and arrow guy?"

Here, I take my bow from my shoulder to show the kid. I have to duck my head and shoulder in to get the bow around the quiver of arrows. I rattle the bow before the kid in his notch in some rocks on the south slope of the mountain from the tunnel.

"Hey," he goes weakly. He moves, an awakening chrysalis. Faster, he comes to attention...at least, wakefulness. "What time is it?"

He's embarrassed! We've already had a full dawn blow out uptown while this scout was living large.

"Let me get you updated so you'll know why I'm here. I guess we should wait on the full story until we join your partner. The game is afoot, grasshopper! Adventure calls! 'Grasshopper' isn't much of a name – "

I pause.

He goes, "Josh Ryan. People call me Ryan. I got some more instant coffee. Just had mine. I can make some more?"

He unfolds from the rocks, pummeling then squeezing his sleeping bag into a puff ball. "The other scout is on the other side of the highway. Marley."

"Ought to let that dry out, Kemosabe. I mean, Ryan. Just throw it over the rocks. Sure, instant coffee, it is!"

He stops, looks around in a bewildered manner,

tosses the bag over the rocks. He fixes his boots and gets busy at the camp stove at the other end of the rocky defile from where he laid his head.

I reassure him, "The Grand Poobahs of Coltrane, those with 'ideas', are cogitating! After a big morning. They made a discovery. Discoveries are dangerous things. In the wrong hands, they tend to trouble. But in our capable hands – well, let's just say we rise to the occasion. Why wait? But I'm getting ahead of myself. I do that. You'll have to keep me on track."

He's pouring bubbly water into Sierra cups. He mixes in the coffee powder. He hands me a cup. I grunt, sip. I slurp my coffee. "Good and hot. Thanks."

"Sure," says Ryan. "Power bar?"

"Don't mind if I do," I say, taking one from him. We sip our coffees and munch our power bars.

He says, "What's this about?"

"You know the last house before the fog? Down this way?"

"Sure, Marley and me been down there."

"We're going to play a little visit."

"With your bow and arrow? We got guns."

"Bows and arrows are recyclable."

"You can make new arrows? What about that catapult? You some kind of Special Forces guy?"

"Nope, not at all. Let me tell you a little story, Ryan. So you'll know where I'm at. After all, we need to trust each other. Ever been to New Mexico, over by Hatch?"

He shakes his head, muttering, "Maybe went through there when I was a kid with my parental units."

"Yeah, know what you mean, no one travelling much anymore. See, my family was in the steakhouse bidness. No special forces for me. Never even went in the army. No college. None of that. Just the family business. Family made a fortune. Four steakhouses across southern New Mexico. Damn, we had it good! We cornered the jalapeno market for the whole region. That's power. Ha! The do re mi just pouring in. What happened? Trilobites happened, everything changed. Besides beef production got iffy. There goes the neighborhood. Double ha! Caught the wife in flagrante with my best bud, my partner. No, I didn't shoot them with a bow and arrow. But I got out of there. Something kinda snapped. Whole world falling apart, family going nuts. All I'd ever really done was take care of myself. No wonder she ended up hating my guts. Rich guy, white guy, tough guy beliefs. Like we got this extra credit. Total bull. My needs! My privileged stance? Men are such cowards.

"I fucked up. Needed a reboot. Moved out to this shithole a few years ago. Art town? Bozo town! No problem! No matter to me. Consolidation came up. Consolidate? As if! They give you food, water, shelter, clothes, health care, and entertainment. What else could a person want? Or need? That's the clincher, right?

"Survival ain't enough. Not just survive, excel. *Be here now,* like the Buddhists say. Take what you need, leave the rest. I can garden. I love Bar B Q. Build a catapult? Why not? Hell, being left alone in Coltrane's worth it. We hunger for anonymity, don't you think? But anonymity on our own terms. Coltrane's perfect. You got your Mexicans, your arty types, your gays – who cares? A good place to start over. To learn my p's and q's at last. No matter how much moola I had, I knew shit. Easy to give up on what doesn't work. Now it's what do I know, what can I do. So, sure, build a catapult. Beg females to forgive my sorry ass."

"Wow," goes Ryan, "Not quite sure, but sure I get it. I'm a scout, just as important as the next guy. Yeah, survive plus. I used to play a lot of Internet games."

We drink our coffee to the grit, munching our power bars. Ryan cleans up, wraps up the camp stove, hauls in the sleeping bag that has been trying to dry in the first morning stirrings of gray light that substitute for day now.

Ryan shrugs. "You haven't explained what this has to do with us perimeter scouts?"

"East, west." I wave my arms in those directions to show him. The bow is eager. "East, west," I continue, "it only makes sense. Edges. Borders. Corner posts. Follow me?"

"Not a clue, Mr. Derry."

"Ah, don't call me that. The will of the people – no, our humanity calls us to explore. Isn't that what connects us who stayed, what we share? So, no titles. To hell with mister. Shit, let the Grand Poobahs worry it through. Action! We need action – right now. I figure we'll just mosey down to the west side. Over that way. That fogbank. Our end zone so to speak. See what's there."

"The house at the very end is weird: the way its front is in the clouds, and its back sticks out of it, like on our side."

"Now we're talking, scout! Let's go take a look see at this house, because the folks in town are stymied. We got to show 'em. And guess what I got?" I reach into my pocket and pull out the cell phone. I hold it up.

"They don't work anymore."

"A cell phone that takes pictures. It still photographs. And guess what? The mining company has generators. And guess what? We, the people, have confiscated those suckers. We got a couple computers we can power up to talk to this cell phone. Then B2B we got a good chance of sharing our look see with the folks."

"The generators can run computers?"

"Right now, they use them sparingly. Generators go through a lot of gas. They got one generator hooked to one of those battery rechargers, keeping folks in flash lights, I guess. But this should work."

The boy ducks back in his rocky retreat and pushes stuff around. He comes back up with a 12 gauge.

"You got shells for that?"

"Eight."

"Know how to use it?"

"For sure."

"Let's get going."

"The other scout, from the other side, Marley, we like to meet every morning on the road just down that way."

"Good man?"

"She's only fifteen."

"That's perfect. Getting a late start today, huh?"

The scurry down the rocky mountainside is uneventful. Two fat ground squirrels, colored the same monotonous gray and brown as the rocks and gravelly dirt, gape at us, then give piercing chips, then disappear in the tumble of rocks. I'll have to remember where they are.

Ryan is good in the rocks. He's fine tuned, geared up. Wiry young man, used to the outdoors, used to scrambling through rocks and brush. He's letting his natural billy goat guide his feet.

When we get to the road, the other scout comes out of the brush from the other side. She's smaller than Ryan, shorter, but, also, like Ryan, fit, eager, exuding adolescent confidence.

She keeps her eyes on me.

Ryan says, "This is Jacob Derry. The catapult guy? He's got info for us about that house at the end. You know, the house in the clouds. Half in, half out? You know which one I mean. We're on reconnaissance."

She says, "'House in the clouds?' Whole front in the fog – that one?"

Ryan nods enthusiastically.

She goes, "There's nothing there. We checked it. People left a while ago. What's this about?"

Ryan says, "We never get too close. But, for sure, it seems empty."

She moves over to me, hand extended. "Marley Sumner."

"Jacob."

We're copacetic now. My team! Eager beavers! So, I go, "Is this a good time?"

Ryan says, "To de-brief us?"

I snort. "Take it to a whole new level."

They look at each other. Suspicious? I'm going too fast?

Marley says assertively, "We can't be in trouble. Okay – sure, we're getting a late start today, but so what? Things are quiet."

Ryan rolls his eyes. "We had a couple of their trucks go through a few days ago. Well, everybody knows about that. We know what it's like to face baldies."

They glance at each other again, and this time a streak of confusion.

I gotta clear this up before we get there. "Can we talk and walk at the same time?"

Marley says, "Let's go."

We head down the highway, walking right down the middle of the road. I'm going over the rifle slung across Marley's back. It's a single shot, bolt action .22. I have my bow. Ryan has his blunderbuss. So how are we going to do this?

"So, so, so, meanwhile, back in Storyland. Let me back up a tad. You know those meth addicts who came back from the clouds? They offered a last chance for people to leave. What was interesting about their story was how in the fogbank they described a gate. Some kind of crazy ass gate. Not a regular gate, like you'd see at a ranch around here. It was a long, one pole gate that stretched across the road, maybe the pole was metal. Behind, beside the pole, kind of cubes, a couple of them. Squat square deals. But the most interesting thing, in the middle, there was a big, J-shaped pipe gushing water. They said it looked like a waterfall. Just a torrent of liquid. They thought it was water, pouring from this J pipe. Guards, maybe, posted back there, too. Uniformed guards, but not baldies or uglies. Humans, they thought. They couldn't tell how far the clouds went back."

"Forever," says Marley. But maybe I didn't hear her right, as she's walking faster than us so slightly ahead.

"I heard about the waterfall," says Ryan.

"Well, how much water's around here? Mines used it up. Who knows what that stuff is?"

How long can we stay on the road? Should we be heading in to the brush? We're out in the open! They're easy going scouts, but I don't think reckless. I know we make easy targets out in the open like this.

I go on, "Anyway, I don't know what it is. Water? Poison chemicals? Sheesh – who knows? But last night – back to our story, conferencing, communicating, cogitating, the Grand Poobahs figured, 'someone needs to go talk to those guards. See what's up.' Course, no one wanted to go. How could their safety be guaranteed? And seeing as how the druggies got to the gate and maybe were sedated? Some kind of gas?"

Ryan says, "We stepped in to the fog stuff. Plenty

of times. Huh, Marley?"

Marley calls back, "No effect." She keeps walking.

"Well, that goofball councilman, Michael Ramsey, said they had some kind of airtight mining suit on display at the Mining Museum. Turns out the folks who know about such things said the suit was a pressure suit for mining rescues. A relic. No one knew whether such an antique deal could possibly still work. But it was worth taking a look at."

Ryan says, "I'd like to see that thing!"

We're close now. I got this creepy flushed feeling like something's going to happen. If the baldies were harder to kill, I'd probably be less excited?

Marley stops, turns to me: "What does this have to do with us scouts out here at the edge?"

"Let me finish. Turns out the old pressure suit wasn't in terrible shape. I mean, it didn't work anymore, the pressure controls, all that stuff was kaput. It had O2 tanks but they were empty and we didn't have any spares. But what we had was one of those portable O2 units that heart patients and asthmatics use, and a guy could have that O2 unit over his shoulder and still fit in the suit. We could make it pretty airtight: amazing what duct tape can do. They worked on it all night."

Marley says, "Who did it? Who went?"

We resume walking, my eyes back and forth between brushy thick cover and approaching sniper lookouts.

"Frankie Lucien volunteered. We got her one of those O2 units and got her in the suit, closed it up. Duct tape! Voila! Good to go. She wasn't especially comfortable but it wouldn't be a long trip. She had a safety line hooked around her waist so we could pull her out. She carried a big manila envelope with all our notes, from the mayor and council, from regular folks too, asking what the heck was going on. Who were the uglies? Who were the baldies? Stuff like that.

"We got her up to the fog on the highway in the back of a pickup at dawn. Yeah, just a bit ago. Hardly anyone around. She gave the ol' thumbs up routine and walked into the fog."

Gray light over dense forest farther back from the road. It's close. We're almost there. The scouts keep their eyes straight ahead.

I snort. "Know what my note asked?"

Ryan says, "Uh-uh, what?"

"I asked what the deal was about the weather? All this gray, the fog that is not fog."

Marley says, "So what happened?"

"Frankie Lucien walks out about seven or eight minutes later. She couldn't breathe, getting too hot and flushed."

"She's ok?" asks Marley. "She trained us, you know."

"Oh, yeah, she's fine. She gave the envelope to one of the human guards and the guard took it. But the oddest thing was how the guards reacted: they laughed at her. They don't know her, they weren't laughing at her in particular we don't think. She said they were giddy, fall on the floor laughing, so hard. Just belly aching laughter.

She thought they were human. *Homo saps.* They didn't wear masks. They seemed to breathe easy. And there was a gate. And in its middle, a gushing current from a big upside down J pipe. Lucien asked them what the gushing pipe was. She asked them what was so funny. Maybe they couldn't hear her through the suit."

Marley asks, "No answer?"

"Nah, but the guard took the envelope. Lucien thought he'd nodded when she told him to see it got to the people in charge, but maybe he was laughing so hard she couldn't tell."

Marley says, "People are saying there's been a war. And outside of town is so hot now we're lucky to have stayed."

"People say a lot of things."

She goes on, "People think everything's changed out there, but somehow we're okay. Because we stayed."

I shrug. "All them stories assume our staying was a good thing."

"Isn't it? We're still here," says Ryan.

I query, "Are we keeping them out? Or are they keeping us in?"

Marley says, "A government experiment? I don't know. I don't think anybody on planet Earth knows how to make baldies."

I ask, "So from space? ETs?"

Ryan says, "It's gotta be supernatural or super science."

"We don't know. But you're right. We are still here...week into it. Still here."

Marley says, "You know Daisy Piper? She has that kids' house up the Gulch. She's a teenager. Well, one of the little girls up there, Cassie I think her name was, she said she thought we were all in one of those snow domes. You know, the clear plastic domes you shake and it snows on some little Christmas scene?"

Ryan says, "Why were they laughing so hard? What was so funny? The old pressure suit? I don't get that, like they were making fun."

Pretty soon the way the road goes down and twists, we can see the fogbank plain enough. It cuts clear across the road, this wall of fluffy gray and white, like a chunk of sky fell down right here. The mountains here open, widen, not nearly as steep and close as farther back. We strike out from the paved road and head on a trail that used to be a driveway through madrone and manzanita. I'm following them. Blue jays joke at us. I give them the finger. It's good to be off the road. The trees and brush go over a slight swell that ends up before a clearing. We hang back because the house is close, near enough to see: boxy ranch style, front half in the fog, and back half out of it, in the clear, with the trees. We don't see any gate. No J pipe gusher. The back looks like the regular back of any suburban house. Cement patios go around the back. A good flat roof. At the top of the walls, all the way around, just below the roof, a clear space, maybe a two foot strip along the top. Glass? A ribbon of window that goes all the way around. Glass or plastic, but transparent. Perfect for our needs!

We're hunkered down, scanning our target.

I ask, "Do you know who lived here?"

The scouts shake their heads.

"Was the house here before?"

They glance at each other a sec, then back at me and shrug. Ryan says, "Think so."

Marley giggles. She says, "I don't know. Looks like a house. Hey, how come you had a catapult anyway?"

Ryan answers, "Dood, ol' man Steakhouse here got it going on. He can make anything. Totally Leet!"

Marley says, "I still don't get it. Why – "

"Focus! East/West! East side on the highway has a gate, so what about here, West side?"

Ryan says, "You figure there's a gate on both sides."

"East/West."

Marley says, "What about North and South?"

"One thing at a time. Did you ever get closer?"

Marley says, "Looks empty to me." She picks herself up, starts strutting towards the house, fancy as you please.

Ryan goes, "Wait, wait! We gotta have a plan!"

I call back Marley. "I'll tell you all about my catapult after. For now, see over there, those big trees? Oaks. We use the edge of the clearing here, follow it for cover over to those oaks. What we do, we sneak around quiet from here, staying in the brush. By the oaks – that's about close as we can get and still have cover. It'll be what? Like thirty feet to the house. Less. See what I mean?"

"Got it," says Marley and dodges around Ryan and me, taking off slinky style, keeping to the brush, towards the big oaks. Ryan and I follow behind. We're quiet. We're careful. But any kind of basic surveillance would have made us by now.

We get to the trees. It's a good spot. I climb up into a tree to about six feet above the ground.

I say, "Marley, you stay there, at that tree with your pee shooter. I'm up here with my bow. Easy shots. We got you covered, Kemosabe."

Ryan says, "What do you mean?"

"You're going to sneak up to the house and take photos with my phone. You know how, right? Maybe through that space along the top of the walls. Me and Marley, we got you covered. That cannon of yours ain't much good except for close work. Just leave it."

Ryan stares in disbelief. He goes, "No, not leaving it." He gulps, says, "I'll need a ladder."

Marley laughs.

I say, "It'll be easier to run without it."

Ryan goes, "No, I mean it."

Ryan keeps the shotgun around his shoulder. Marley pushes into the tree trunk as I suggested. She goes on one knee, positions.

"Ready," says Marley.

I toss Ryan the phone. "Just snap away, at

whatever you see."

"Sure," he says, flipping it open, jabbing and touching at it. "No bars."

"Easy. In and out like the wind. Marley's .22's perfect for baldies. As long as she's a good shot. See what you can see, Ryan."

"I'm an excellent shot," says Marley.

Ryan goes, "I'm off!"

Instead of following along the edge of the brush to dash for the house with some cover, he makes a cometary thrust straight on from where we are to the back of the house. He huddles up, scrunches over to the nearest wall. He slowly moves to the south corner. He stands up, stretches up to peek through the top clear space. He can just make it on tippy toe. Tall boy! He holds the phone there and starts moving along the wall towards the cloud bank. He's got his arm out and up with the phone and moves along slowly.

"Uh-ho," goes Marley.

I see them: three baldies pop out of the fog that starts/ends in the front of the roof. They're coming in across the roof, taking the high ground above Ryan. Well, starting over means you have to learn for yourself. Starting over means understanding new intentions. We got three seconds before they're on Ryan. They're grossly white and unformed, naked, pinky, and they're moving in that stupid stagger across the roof. We realize Ryan can't see them. My arrow gets the first one, the one in front. It deflates in a squishy mess. The .22 starts pipping pocking and the other two sink to the roof.

Ryan turns, watching us. He's about halfway to the front of the house. He's not taking pictures now. He's looking towards us for confirmation – what the hell's going on. He can't see the baldies but he must have heard the .22.

I wave at him. Give him the thumbs up. I wave him back to photography, miming clicking pictures with my free hand. He's got to keep going. And he does. Gets back in position, close to the wall, arm extended and up with the phone. He takes more pictures. He's near the fog now, almost to the front of the house.

Now three more baldies appear on the roof at the same place, moving right away towards Ryan. Plus, three other baldies come around the corner from the side of the house we can't see, but which Ryan is approaching. These are patio monsters, coming right for Ryan. They're slurping across the patio. Baldies on the patio, baldies on the roof! Blast them!

Arrows fly! The .22 keeps firing. Hope she has enough bullets.

We got it covered!

The nasties directly in front of Ryan do a nasty squeal. Do they register how it's going up top on the roof? Remorse? Anger? Knowing what's in store. Behind the three patio baldies, an ugly appears – this is new! The controllers, the handlers! Tumors all over its body. Ugh. Yuck. But the ugly hangs back. Is it overseeing things? Is it in charge? Ryan's got his shotgun pulled around. He takes it easy, smoothly, in control – no panic.

Kerplow!

Dang! That thing is loud!

Two baldies collapse, start their deflation process, while the ugly screams and staggers back into the fog. Was it hit? Could be for sure: that cannon lets out a lot of shot, that would go through a baldy like an arrow though a balloon.

Good thing the baldies aren't packing. Too easy? Learn to make a catapult, and you're a hero! Learn to take on baldies, and you feel like an exterminator.

I call out, "Ryan! Get back here!"

Ryan spins around and runs for it, shot gun swung back over his shoulder. We've taken care of the baldies. Got our picts. Mission completed. I drop out of the tree. Marley is hightailing it away, through the brush the way we came in. I wait for Ryan, slap his shoulder, and we get going after Marley.

Ryan says, "Hang on, I gotta reload." He stops, fusses with his shotgun, cracks it open, reloads.

We go on and Ryan's breathing hard and trying to squeak out words. I make it out: "At the top of the walls, the clear, the space, wasn't glass. I don't know what it was. I could feel it and it was weird. It went all the way around. Hope the pictures work."

I'm waiting, hanging. He needs validation. "You got some photos, I'm sure."

He pats his pocket. "Think so." He shudders, looks grim, sick, uncertain. "Don't you get it? The clear strip went all the way around. How – how was the roof...it must have been holding up the roof."

## Daisy Piper

*best things in life are free*
*everything else is $19.95*

When you start over, you're a hunter/gatherer, a forager at first. You gotta learn how to check things out, find what's usable. When you start over, and things are crazy, you still have to figure what. Be realer than real. Pick up sticks. You learn how to play well with others.

We never had to do to be. I mean none of us middle class kids ever had to do anything to make anything happen. I mean earn our keep, prove our worth. I mean, the options we had to fill up the day were set. Kidness routine. Now we have to do what happens – all over it.

After the strangest dawn ever with Ms. Kell and the Brit, Clay Mason and I get to the convention center by late morning. It's a total zoo, people inside, outside. We left the house, kids doing their thang. All items accounted for. The girl in the closet seems safe but we don't really know. Cassie and DiDi are keeping watch over her with forks. The disc, the black machine, the pong and its case are tucked away. If any PUs show up, it's strictly hush hush. Bennett's in charge. Scouts are out. Water traders hit their beats.

Kids tell stories to explain things. And they are very observant, so there's a lot of stories, a lot of explaining. They watch me very closely, when I tell them a story. They watch Tenny and Clay. Little kids, older kids, all kids have to learn to listen to each other again. Seems like we haven't for a long time. Tenny has lots of stories. Clay not a one.

The kids say that when Clay and I are working on a problem we enter *Clay-sy space,* which they say is very intense, but they can tell what comes of it, like when we figure what to do. Clay and I communicate in our own way. Maybe this is because we felt the pink ray and the ping pong ball space? No, I feel like me. No intruder in my head! We'd know. He helps out a lot. He's jittery quiet, like he's holding it together. Clay has to be alone a lot. I guess he works on things then. I don't know. It's his choice. I like it when he's around.

Tenny and I don't communicate as well, because he thinks I'm just a girl. He wants to be a hero, I think. He likes to act, like take on roles. Try them out, how far he can push it. He's coming around, helping more, pitching in without having to be told. Everybody has to help. The kids depend on it. Coltrane depends on it. Parents? They're on their own.

All of a sudden, my stupid nothing life is shot out of a cannon. I feel things I've never known before. Like what happened between me and the Brit? What transpired? How were we selected? Where did we go without going? *Why us?*

The number of PUs, plus security, and Ewoks approaches MAX. They heard something. Something's up! They're packing the sidewalk, little groups talking and gesturing. More inside. It's always busy at the convention center. The so called 'community offices' are here. Adults expect organization to run things. Plus, now, the basement is kinda like the community chest. All the accumulated extra stuff is kept down there. Car parts taken off roadblock cars. That kind of thing. Maybe some gas down there? Another part of the basement has the bomb shelter supplies – that stuff we brought up from the mine. I guess it's for when everything runs out?

The mining company has these generators they've brought in and set up. They keep them in the basement because they make so much noise and their exhaust is awful. You have to keep a window open all the time. Mainly, so far, they've run power cables from the basement to a couple offices. One has a recharger. One leads to a couple computers. They been trying to see if they could access the Net, if there still is one. Nothing so far. Nothing out there, or the devices can't pick it up.

We work our way in. We do kid magic among PUs. Invisible at first, then a nuisance, then WTF are they doing here. A few other kids around. I recognize them from school. A scout scurries among the people, gleaning, gleaning what she can overhear and see. It's Amy. Inside, people keep their weapons down, out of sight. I've got my stick. Clay's got his sling. We keep them close to our bodies. It's warm inside, and noisy, and stinky, all these bundled bodies. We figure right away where everyone is trying to get to. One of the office spaces – it's the room with the computers. Maybe they're just obsolete now, old fashioned PC towers. Or, maybe, they're streaming the next installment of *Celebrity Chef.*

Clay doesn't like all the pressing closeness. I let him take my arm. He's holding my upper arm just below the shoulder. I guide him. I whisper into his ear, "Ground control to Major Tom!"

We can hear the belching of the generators in the basement, as we weasel in. Yup, computers on! I used to hate crowds or ignore them or avoid them. We're connected now in ways we weren't before.

I see the mayor. Whole bunch of folks: Margaret Pitka, Frankie Lucien, Councilman Ramsey, that police officer who stayed. And smack in the middle, nestled among them in the sacred computer office, Sam Bean, beaming like a rock star. The crowd gives, we swing, we move in. We step back. Clay holds on.

Wow – two computers lit up. They're on!

Clay whispers in my ear, "Items!"

I nod, avoid a shove, trying to hear and figure what's going on. He lets go my arm. I hear his, "Major Tom!" outcry. No, he's Major Tom, I'm ground control!

We mingle, mix. Loud voices. Sam Bean giggles. Standing behind the computers and their operators is Jacob Derry, the catapult man. Bow and arrow guy.

Mr. Derry goes, "Marley and Ryan were staunch in the thick of it. Fine scouts! They should get some kind of honorific for what they did."

"Am I ground control or you?" says Clay in to my ear, his lips close to my ear.

Jacob Derry's supposed to be 70. What does he know that gives him such confidence?

Talking all at once. Councilman Ramsey is getting excited. He pronounces loudly: "We all been blooded now. Whole town staunch. Last couple days."

The computer guys, two mega nerds, one from the high school computer lab, the other I don't know, are working away at the keyboards. They both mumble that the computers seem fine – operational. The high school computer nerd – I think his name is Mr. Putnam, has a cell phone he's connecting to his tower. He goes, "It's working."

Jacob Derry says, "Quality isn't great. I couldn't see shit when I tried. But something there. Maybe you can enhance them? Lighten them up?"

The other computer guy says, "This machine has an enhancement function. I'll try."

We watch the download like we've never seen such an interesting thing. Like we've all missed our devices so much! Like the simple event of downloading, witnessing a device in action is somehow pleasing. Mr. Putnam unplugs the cell phone and hands it to the other guy, who plugs it in to his computer. "Okay, I'm downloading."

Mr. Putnam says, "Can't see much. They're too dark. Blurry."

Jacob Derry says, "Lighten them? Can you do that?"

"Not much I can do with this computer." Mr. Putnam pecks some keys, makes a face.

Clay remains close to me. He bends in to me again. His eyes go big.

Mr. Putnam says, "This is about good as I can get it."

The other computer guy says, "Look at this."

His monitor has images of cloudy dark blurs lightened up enough to make out shapes. A room. Inside a room. Figures. Life forms. Not much detail.

The mayor says, "No gate."

Jacob Derry says, "Can't tell."

Computer dood's' working the system's photo options, tapping away trying things. A vague room with human shapes? Walls? Tables? Some kind of standing surface, transparent, like a glass bulletin board? Figures clarify, now. For sure, human shapes. They're uglies.

Councilman Ramsey bursts, "Uglies!"

The whole room is a gasping hive of funny breathing.

The enhanced photos start moving across the monitor. Most are useless, can't see a thing but blobs. Then one comes up: we see the front of the so-called house from the inside. So-called because now we can tell the whole front of the house is open and in the fog, with a vague gate complete with vague upside down J pipe, gushing a waterfall.

Jacob Derry says, "I knew it! East, West. They got us blocked in. The fog's ersatz. Ersatz, I say!"

I go, "East, West. What about North and South?"

Everyone's looking at me.

Clay points back at the monitor. The new picture is much brighter, and it shows the gate more clearly with its boxy cubicles or platforms at the sides, and in the center that upside down J pipe with gushing, right into a hole beneath it. This picture has more uglies and –

"There it is!" someone gasps.

"The waterfall!"

Jacob Derry goes, "It's not a waterfall! What is that
– "

But the next photo flicks in at a funny angle, away from the front of the place and the gate, more to the side. Some light. And there's an ugly there standing in front of the glass sheet, what looks like glass. The rectangle of glass is ten feet across and six feet high. There are dark lines drawn around the transparency with red dots scattered in and out of the curving lines.

I've seen this – something similar?

Margot Pitka says, "Can you make a hard copy of that?"

"Sure."

Someone else says, "Can you clean it up any more?"

"Some." The computer guy hits some buttons, the printer activates.

"What do you think?" asks the mayor to no one in particular.

The room has gone fairly quiet. Faces are excited. I don't feel a lot of fear or panic as much as a desperate *oh, not again!*

Councilman Ramsey says, "This can't be good."

Jacob Derry says, "That glass, whatever it is, with those lines. Looks...I don't know, looks familiar?"

I cry out, "It's a map! It's a map of the world but it's turned upside down!"

The monitors go blank and dark. Power failure. We're all thinking fast. Didn't realize how much light the monitors threw out. Now it's creepy in the crowded office.

Flashlights snap on!

Clay, close, whispers, "The red dots, then, they're –
"

"It's that girl!" somebody yells.

I find him right away, the man who yelled, Mr. Mead.

Clay is again whispering, "The red dots, they're – "

Margot Pitka inserts, "That doesn't help."

Mr. Mead says, "That's the girl that went underground with us. She got hit by the pink ray. She always knows what to say. I'm just saying."

Margot Pitka says, "Michael's right, we all got blood, or goo, on our hands now. Whatever it takes to survive. We need everybody."

The mayor looks like he's sick, or terribly uncomfortable. Maybe he wishes he knew what to add right now. He's probably having a hard time keeping out of his noggin, like we all are, the slow mo action film that is our collective memories of *The Day We Defeated Them*. We were all involved. We were maniac baldy slaughterers. Gleeful? We just slaughtered them. And it was gross.

Jacob Derry seizes the joy: "Upside down map – why?"

I shrug. Clay says so everybody can hear him, "From space, point of view is arbitrary."

"You're saying – " someone begins.

Councilman Ramsey bristles forward, gets behind the guys at the computers still trying to turn them back on. Someone runs to check with the generators. The councilman faces the crowd.

Flashlights rule!

He says forcefully, "East, West. North, South. We're cut off!"

A voice from the crowd, a woman, goes, "We're surrounded."

Another voice adds, "A cage?"

Another: "Zoo?"

Still another: "We're all dead, and this is Purgatory."

A woman asserts, "Fuck that! Who cares? This is what we wanted, what we chose. We can deal with the occasional baldy."

It's a thought, a guess, a suggestion, a question, and no one knows its answer.

Jacob Derry says, "All we gotta do is turn the picture right side up. Did it print? Do you have a copy?"

Mr. Putnam is nearest the printer. He examines it, then shows how there's a piece of paper half way through. He pulls it out. "Wow," he says.

I struggle closer to see. Jacob Derry and Ms. Lucien are holding it upside down. Each has a side of the paper, grounding the sacred document.

Frankie Lucien declares, "Hold it, everybody. The half that came through is what was on the bottom of the glass. So we hold it like this. It is a map! Plain as day. She was right."

Fred Stanley, from the canyon neighborhood groups, has pushed in to see. "The red dots, then, are places on the map?"

Everybody's trying to see. People start yelling to take turns.

Officer Latta says in his adult voice, "Take it easy, folks. We'll all get a turn. But it's our only copy, so be careful."

Fred Stanley is backing up, arms up and out, announcing, "Leave it alone! That's what I say. Maybe we shouldn't try to figure out their plans. Maybe we'll just draw more attention. Will this help us survive? Not hardly any red dots in North America anyway."

Someone goes, "So maybe the red spots have something in common?"

I've been checking it, calculating, visualizing, so have to say: "See where this one is. It's gotta be us. Coltrane."

Voices surge. Doubts, questions, jump through the heavy atmosphere in partial light like bolts of human lightning.

Ms. Lucien says, "It may be us. So what's going on here that's common with these other red spots? Gotta be. Probably. Folks that stayed? That didn't get consolidated? Fred, we can't leave it alone. Don't you see? Besides, how could we stir up any more trouble than what we have already? We stay sharp. We're on top of it. It's what we gotta do."

Officer Latta says, "Necessity guides us. Know what I mean? Look, I'm no public speaker, so bear with me, but I know we're all feeling the same thing. After all, like Margot said, we all been through this. And this could be important. We get the power going again, we see what this is. We've been threatened. We responded. What else can we do?"

Clay whispers in my ear, "The closest red dot to us is in Mexico."

Ms. Lucien says, "We send a team beyond the gate. See what happens. They could find out what the hey is going on. What the new rules are."

"Too dangerous," the mayor squeaks. "You barely got back. They thought it was so funny there at the gate. Remember? We can't ask anyone to take the chance. Too risky. They'd either get laughed out, or they'd get changed like the druggies."

"We don't know that," says Ms. Lucien.

Some college boy, who's been hanging about with two or three other people who look college age, says, "We'd try it. Look, even if we didn't come back, and ended up in some consolidation," he shrugs. "You know, it's like six of one, half a dozen of the other."

Funny how not many people that age stayed. Just a few. I don't see them around hardly.

Dr. Stevenson, who has a disc, and supposedly a physics guy, steps forward to speak after examining the half page of map. He says, "Whatever anyone thinks, whatever we do, we have to know what we are dealing with. 'The new rules', exactly! There do seem to be new rules about where we can go, how things work. None of that was gone over when we agreed to stay."

Everybody nods.

He continues, "One thing we have to be clear on is that this is like nothing that has ever happened. I don't think we're in Purgatory. Unless it's in some science fiction format. I'm talking the uglies, their flying craft, the baldies, the things we've seen...the discs."

Margot Pitka adds, "And the things we've done."

He goes on, "The disc is amazing. It can't work but it does. It can't be from this Earth right now, but where else could it come from?"

# THE ELEVENTH DAY

## College Kids

*And what costume shall the poor girl wear*
*To all tomorrow's parties*
          - The Velvet Underground

Millennials made geeks and nerds cool. It's because we're techno savvy. So why would a couple college kids choose a Red Dot rather than consolidation which is totally techno?

We are waging a chill war with these riffs, as we hide in the brush and rocks in front of the last house on the Gulch. We walked up the Gulch before dawn, all the way until we could see the house, when we ducked for cover. Those kids are there. That girl who made the Connection. They say they have a lot of supplies. We came down from our place on OK Street and figured it was worth a look. So just being careful...vigilant. We have no weapons. We have no intentions. We know a riff when we see it. We think they have something going on we should know about. Isn't there knowledge to be had in other ways we haven't imagined? We know we have to be sharp – pro-active. We have to get our petrified brains up and running. Reboot. We know there are no easy resolutions.

Three of us college students, Raleigh, Jenny, me. There must be more. There's hippy kids our age. Druggies. But still we three suggest a clique. First of all, we don't even like each other. Parents, families gone. We may have gone to high school together, but not well. Those kinds of nerds. We went to different colleges, me to one, the others to a different one. And both colleges closed down, or went totally online. We three came to the conclusion that our chances at the American dream via a college degree were meaningless now. No future. Day One we happened to run into each other. Maybe we recognized the sighs emanating. We remembered the horror of high school. We settled into her place, as it was bigger, had more supplies. We consolidated right here in Coltrane where we grew up. No biggie.

Why did we stay? We didn't really like our families. Never got along. They didn't care. So, college was pointless, dreams of making it pointless, the lust to accumulate heaps of filthy lucre, too, pointless. We didn't have a lot of razzamatazz and poignant uploads, which were millennials' main perks. College was a like a filtering system for human sewage. Our work, our politics or religion, were just not 'right' enough. We were relegated to consolidation with all the other sewage. The US leads the world in consolidation. Plans for the future for humans have always been wrecked by humans. We are the wild card. No superpowers. Here we are. 'It' is our big chance. Only chance? The best and only way our times offered? How do we rise to the occasion? With networking and social media kaput here, we are primal elements. It doesn't matter, we guess. We consolidated right here in Coltrane where we grew up.

We'll become peeping toms led to the wallop that will fame us.

Hey, walk into the fog, pass the gate. Consolidation awaits! Everything out there in the consolidated experience – total connect! Fed, clothed, gamed, dead.

Here, total hoarding is de rigueur, not just a riff on reality TV. Money is stupid. Position is unnecessary. Protein Bars worth more than gold. None of us that into food or drinking, like partying. Water is fine. Power bars are fine.

Is this the way? We snicker down here like rats hoping for insight. We were virgins.

**Roger Mead**

*if they're not doing anything*
*then they can't complain us watching*

Me and Bob Pauley and Barry Hilton come over the hill from the old water tanks. There's trails up there, easy to find, even in the dark. All through the hills, trails from peccaries and people, I don't know. We're in the rocks on the other side of the dirt road from the last house on the Gulch. We're packing, but we expect no trouble. Just came over the mountains for a look see.

Ever since my family left, I've had these feelings. Like worries about what's gonna happen. There's something off here, and with that girl. What are they up to? What does she know? We have to keep watch. It's up to all of us. Everybody's saying that.

My fam. Why did they leave? To get away from me? Because it was too damn hard. Just wore a person out trying to make it day to day.

Bob Pauley shifts on his knees, falls back on his big bum. "Well, if we're gonna be here a while."

Barry Hilton is stretched out on his stomach on a flat rock, with his head just peeking over the top to see the house. "It's dawn. They should be getting up."

Bob says, "Funny how empty the streets are at dawn. Nobody rushing to work. Back in the day, I avoided dawn much as I could. Now? Not so much."

Barry answers, "Hell, you avoided work period."

I shuffle around, keeping down, checking how much cover we have. I go, "We've not here causing any trouble. Just a look see. Keep an eye on things. If they're not doing anything, they can't complain us watching."

Bob asks in a funny husky whisper, "What do you think they're doing?"

Barry snickers.

I say, "Like Fred Stanley said, drawing attention to all of us. That girl. Is that what we want?"

Barry says, "Some kind of trouble makers over there, you think? Them's stirring things up?"

I nod solemnly. "Could be endangering us all."

Bob goes, "It's cold. Never used to be this cold

before."

Barry says, "We get snow in October. You know that."

Bob says, "Remember them snow ball fights we used to have at the Divide? Giant battles!"

I remember! "Remember that time me and Rupert rode in the back of Sam's pick up, loaded with snow balls, and we went right down the middle of the road into town, all those kids lining the street, heaving snow balls at us. We ruled! And no one hurt, no one cared. That was a good time."

## Susan Kell

*I must create a system or be enslaved by another man's.*
- William Blake

Apocalypse is good for losing weight, says Janet Gorey. How long can we live on power bars? And keep our girlish figures? And hiking before dawn to the last house on the Gulch is mucho healthy. I get stronger every day. The last part of the hike, I had to keep to the sides, in the rocks. I snuck in like a mongoose. Now, I'm beyond the house, but up the side of the hill, in the brush and rocks – good view.

I keep thinking, what are the kids thinking? Where do they get all this water? They have power – yes. Is this what raw and pure creativity looks like? Is this the mythical *new*? Something I've never encountered, at least at this depth. How to learn this? How to learn how to learn this? What is knowledge to them?

Startling what Daisy comes up with. What is she coming up with? Insights!

These kids are making a real break from the Before. They've organized themselves for safety and justice in ways they invent every day. This is the way it would have to be. And they did.

I have no weapons. Family is gone. I have an illegal cat but no food for it now. Mr. Blake has taken a sabbatical. He'll visit, I believe, just to be courteous. Maybe he'll bring me a rat.

If the kids are thinking in a new way, are they changing? On their own, in this context, where does it lead?

I'd like to think I helped. Prepped them. Blake, Keats, all the way to Yeats. I'd like to think the Humanities teach us how to think. We used lit as our guinea pig. We learned how to frame an issue, research it, figure the options, the POVs. The kids had a primer then. I helped!

**Sam Bean**

*All chicks do is smoke your weed.*
    - Tom Tom Thoms

Finally, we left Eliana's, me and Tom Tom, to the gnashing of teeth, the rip of silk and flesh wounds, because we were bored. Hedonism is a flimsy thing. Novelty is king. Routine is a stupid prole. We're off on an adventure. We're on the lookout. I have my sword. Tom Tom has a stick – the versatile mop handle.

We ran out of weed. We had cabin fever. Supplies seemed low. Too many of us in the house. We kept bumping into each other. I need a bath. Tom Tom needs the ol' mojo back, as he's been down. I think he needs somebody to tell him what to do. I don't.

We sauntered, wandered, plundered, explored our way here. It was still dark. But we've been up and down these trails so many times, it was simple. My sword led us here. Up above the house at the end of the road, we can look down, see everything, as the light pumps up.

What is it about this house at the end of the road that gives off energy?

Vibes!

I think we're dehydrated. I'm getting weird vibes. I know Tom Tom is dehydrated, because he likes to brag he doesn't like water. Its taste. Duh. What does water taste like? Well, bang! Here we are, I think it's time to share...share and share alike.

**Scott Paulsen**

*Art is $hit!*
     - Hugo Ball

What is an *Art Town*? An art center? Art in America is like flying pigs. I guess an older continental affectation – the art town. In this country, art towns across the Old West! An emblem of sophistication? Art borne in isolation geography. The light, the quiet...the exposure here. Ha! No exposure, no audience. Art town, finally, meant tourist town, meant tourist trap...meant art is dead. Which the locals resented: elitists, they declared.

The locals have learned the word, *poseur. Flaneur.* The Avant-Garde did not replace God. Tourist dollars did. Us*urpation is delight.*

Art beyond consolidation.

That's so cynical.

Young artists on fire, batting about, flailing arms, seizing – burning burning burning. The middle-aged artist is enthralled, steeped in his lucky filters that make beauty the really good time after all. The old artist makes muscle art, moose art: this is what I have to say, and this is the way I say it.

Getting to the place of clarity –

Outside is a gray moth sticking to my eyelashes, then sand and grit peppering my toes. Cold, too...wet chill.

Nature means cold, dirty toes!

Ever since I witnessed those kids at the end of the Gulch, I have been certain: here is a key. What happened to me and the girl was perfectly unsurpassed. I am clear about what we might do.

<u>A grand finale performance at the end of the world!</u> And the children shall lead us –

Meanwhile, back in America: money talks, talent walks, glamour, fakes, phonies. Consolidation is immolation. As gaudy and unreal as a hippo cowboy.

It's bloody Burton back to the source of the Nile, all over again. Mutual stupor. Swatting tsetse flies. 'We shall not cease from exploration' – my last chance...

That's why I chose to trek over this morning, getting my sandals scuffed, my nose drippy, my toes gritty. Ha! This is the way the world ends, not with a bang but a sniffle.

Ahoy there, mates, in the ground gray world!

Shall I stay back? What is this hiding thing about? I'm hiding a hide in a hiding. Where *do* they get all that water? My second recourse to hiding?

## Didi Grebe

*kids with sticks*

If I stand in the screen door not moving a muscle, no one knows I'm here except Cassie and Amy. But I can see everything. The bads must think we are asleep. Cassie and Amy climbed out the back window by the bathroom that doesn't work. We have an outhouse. It has spiders.

They are circling around while I keep the focus. That way I can keep all eyes right here on the screen door.

The five groups across the road are spaced out

enough that I don't even think they know each other is there. If I draw a line connecting through the five groups it makes an ear. Looks just like an ear. The way they are spaced in a half circle with a bump at the bottom. Like a human ear. Ears have ridges and spirals so they look a little bit like a curled up baby in those pictures inside a womb. I have a womb.

I can color and stay in the lines if I want to.

Why do people spy? What do they want? Will they try to hurt us?

Cassie takes the low side, Amy takes the high side. I can see Amy standing behind a girl who suddenly – all surprised notices a girl with a stick behind her.

*Sticks!*

Cassie's doing the same thing: standing behind hiding people who jump around when they discover her.

*Ninja girls!*

They want our secrets! Or why else would they show up today? Today, when we're doing it!

I push open the cranky screen door.

"We gots you surrounded!" I yell, and start laughing. "You might as well come out. We see you. We can see you! Every last one of you."

Cassie goes, "We see you!" She's pointing, too: point! Point! Point! Point with her stick!

Amy, too, says, "We see you!"

I call out so they all hear, "I'll get the others," as

five bumps on an ear stand up straight up people. That high school boy has a sword.

I go back into the house and bump right into Bennett Tilson. "Spies!"

He's eating a cookie. Wipe your mouth! He spits, "Kokoman?"

I nod really hard. "I'll get Daisy," but she's right there. Claymason behind her.

I tell her. "Me and Amy and Cassie found spies all around the house in the shape of an ear. Like a big ear. They must know what we're gonna do."

Daisy puts her arms around me and my stick. "Good work! You're really excited. What's that 'ear' listening to? Nobody knows what we're gonna do. Show us what's going on."

"Come on."

We go outside on the porch. Claymason and Bennett Tilson are with us but follow after us. I count the people standing outside.

There are ten people standing in the road in front of the house. They're in jackets. Some people wear hats and caps. Cassie and Amy are the end ends. I didn't count them with the ten.

Bennett Tilson acts tough though he's a puny guy: "Poachers! What do you want? What are you doing here?" Like he's making a joke of it. Good plan! Smart cookie.

That high school boy with the sword says, "We want in."

Daisy says, "Cassie, Amy, come and help Didi get water for our guests."

A PU, who I can tell Daisy doesn't like on account of the way her eyes squinch when her eyes touch on him, says, "What do you know we don't?"

Cassie and Amy are up on the porch with us now. I say, "Daisy, I should stay. I have a stick."

Cassie and Amy go into the house.

Daisy says, "I don't know what you mean, Mr. Mead."

The big guy with him laughs and slaps at himself. He could be a giant with a tiny head.

The teacher who was here before steps closer to the porch. She says, "Hi, Daisy. Hi, you guys. This is embarrassing, but I guess we were all spying on you this morning. You caught us fair and square."

Claymason says in his scary voice, "What do you want?"

The man Daisy doesn't like says, "You seem to draw attention to yourself."

Cassie and Amy come out with their arms loaded with water bottles. They step down to the road and give one to everyone there. All ten of them.

Daisy, says, "Mr. Mead, you expect me to know what you are talking about. Maybe you're having a conversation with yourself, but you think it's with me. This is our place. We're okay. Why would we draw attention to ourselves? Nothing is going on, other than the crazies we all know are going on. Have a water. We're allies, all of us in Coltrane right now are."

"Here, here," goes the funny old man with the accent. He's a little bigger than me.

I would draw 'attention' in blue – with blue microscopes, blue telescopes.

Bennett Tilson says, "What did you expect to find here this morning?"

Tenny comes out rubbing his eyes. He doesn't have his shoes on yet. He's got bare feet and it's cold. How will he get his feet on now? I don't think he will like spies. But he knows the high school boys.

"What's going on?" asks Tenny.

Bennett Tilson says, "Can't you tell? Three guesses! We're having a party? We're playing a game? We're being invaded?"

The high school boy with the sword goes, "And you weren't invited!"

Rude!

"Hey, Sam," goes Tenny, nodding to him. He points at the two boys and girl sorta in the middle of the line of people in the road. They look older than high school kids. "Who are those guys?"

"I don't recognize them either," says Claymason.

Baldies!?!?

But they're not PUs, or Wookies or Ewoks. They step close to the porch a couple steps. They say together, "We're from here." They look at each other and burst out laughing. Real embarrassed type laughing. They look back at us and again say at the same exact time, "We've been away at college but came back because we chose to stay." They laugh some more. Other people are laughing. The high school teacher lady. The little elf man with the accent. But I think it's nerves laughing.

The giant hollers, "I need coffee! Nothing going on here, Roger. Let's go. Thanks for the water."

He and this other man make as if to leave, but the guy Daisy doesn't like calls them back. "Hey, we're allies. Let's see what's going on."

The two men look like they don't know what to do. Or don't like the suggestion. They shuffle together, inch by inch, real slow, real close, to the other man. I can't hear what they say. They stay.

The high school boy Tenny called Sam whoops and says, "We're wasting time here. Let's cut to the chase. You guys know as well as we do, you're gonna invite us in. We're here to sign up, Captain! We want in."

Tenny goes, "You gotta be kiddin'!"

Amy yells, "Scram!"

Cassie makes bump noises with her stick on the porch, then she ducks inside.

It's time! We got things to do, places to be. No more fooling around!

Daisy says, shrugging her shoulders, "Sam, Tom Tom, it's gotta come natural. You can't force it. Know what I mean? We gotta trust you without a doubt so there can't be any goof on it. You and your toy sword."

Sam says, "Tom Tom's gotta stick? I know how you guys are crazy for sticks. But, sure, understood: we have to prove ourselves."

The man Daisy doesn't like says, "Gotta trust allies."

I stamp my stick down hard on the porch, too. "Thump!" and say, "Kids have sticks!"

"Want us to leave?" asks the high school teacher.

The college kids are slinky, sinky, slidy. They're not spies at all. They give up so easy. They got nothing from us. We gave them nothing 'cept water.

We are ready for adventure!

Cassie comes outside with the little baldy girl as though it were for sure happening, and this is the way it was going to go, with Cassie super hero queen of sticks in the middle of the army.

I think Daisy isn't going to say anything at first. Claymason says something about being too many. The college kids look back.

Clay-sy space for reals!

Tenny yells, "They'll interfere!"

## Scotty Paulsen

*Was this the face that launch'd a thousand ships,*

*And burnt the topless towers of Ilium?*

I call out to the kids on the porch of the last house up the Gulch, "Crikey! You blokes up to something!"

This stunning young woman sparks gray good eyes. The kids glance to her for direction. Two doods around the same age as the gray-eyed eminence: sallow creature with a chip on his shoulder big as a loaf of bread holstered to his neck; then the athletic, cute one is pure satyr, with goat hooves. A slip of a girl – I believe the one they had holed up in the closet, is with another little one. A girl with a stick is front and center.

The Gray Queen steps away from the porch, approaches me dramatically, like she is about to bestow knighthood. She extends her hand to me. I take it, clasp it with two hands, smile and snort. She takes her hand back.

For we have touched the fabric of dream, together. We were chosen. I cannot forget the taste of her dreaming.

"I'm Daisy Piper. You were here the other day with Ms. Kell. We had an experience."

"I'm Scotty. How could I forget our magic? Time to pay the piper. A scenario, if you will. These are your minions?"

The brash, good looking boy sputters over. "Daisy, come on! These are sightseers! They're not coming."

Daisy goes, "This is Tenny."

"Scotty," I say and do a little soft shoe.

Tenny says, "I remember. Nice to meet you, but we were just taking off."

His buddy, whom he called Sam, yells, "Where we going?"

One of the miners says, "We're coming too."

The college kids mutter, "Back up. We're back up."

Ms. Kell says, "Can we go? Scotty and I should both go. We were both here the other day."

The big boy on the porch comes over. He slinks. He holds back. He's got a storm cloud over his head. He says, "'Scenario?'"

Daisy says, "This is Clay. And that's Moira over there with Cassie. You know Didi. And that's Amy."

I recite: "Daisy, Tenny, Clay, and Moira. Cassie, Didi, Amy. Perfection itself! This should work! Perfect for the scenario!"

Tenny says, "We were just leaving, dood!"

What are they about? What's up with the chosen ones? Unless they are about to – indeed: let us talk scenarios. Embrace the scenario. No inhibitions.

I translate: "Scenario: trajectory, narrative. Linearity. See what I mean? But non-objective story spirals. The Grand Finale spirals!"

Now, Tenny scratches his head perfectly. "Well, that's clear. Dood, you're giving me a headache."

The miners are restless. The college kids are chomping their bits. The minions want close to Daisy. Close to Daisy –

Daisy stops. She interjects, "We're taking off on a

scout." She waves up the canyon. "That way, to the North."

Clay says, "I'll explain along the way."

Ms. Kell asks, "Should we all go?"

Sam, a cave child with a rock for a brain, yelps, "I ain't going nowhere with you creeps, until I have some breakfast."

Daisy says, "Bennett, Didi, get these guys some power bars."

Didi says, "I'm going, too. But I was going, too, Daisy. Cassie's going!"

Tenny says, "Everyone take water. We should bring extras. Come on! Duh gear. Gear up! Take a minute!"

A couple kids head back inside the house. New kids come right back out.

...scout...scenario...I am a camera...

Daisy explains, "We have to get our sticks." She goes back to the porch. The little girls get in close, all around her. They imbibe her essence. She comes back around with a sharp stick, Cassie and Moira behind her. Cassie already had a stick, but not Moira.

The boy, Bennett, distributes power bars to the high school boys who are content gobbling them away. A few of the others accept the gratuity.

Daisy is near me. "You need water?" I show her the one the girl gave me. I have a sip. She says, "You should take an extra."

She has a huge knife strapped to her side in a big leather scabbard.

Tenny and Clay come out. Clay has a pistol holstered to his side. Looks like a movie prop. Tenny's carrying a slim rifle, I would guess a .22.

Tenny says, "Well, if they're coming." He slings the rifle over his shoulder on its strap and dances to the porch corner where a stash of sticks is kept. He selects a couple sharpened broom handles. He brings one to me and one to Ms. Kell. "Everybody needs a stick."

We start off.

Clay leads, then Tenny. Daisy, holding the hand of the Moira child, follows. Moira's vibes are extreme. She's not what she appears to be, but I don't know what that means. Ms. Kell, Cassie, and Didi come next. I bring up the rear with my broom handle and the three miners and three college kids.

I like the name *Moira*.

Clay makes a popping gurgle sound, comes tearing back down the line, and he's walking stiff legged, as though he's got the gout. "I need a stick," he says. "Pick a stick. Pick a stick." He's going back to the house! "Just in case – case...case." He runs by –

Cassie yells, "Clay-sy! Clay-sy!"

Daisy goes, "Don't, Cassie."

Moira looks like she's never going to make a sound. As though her mouth is drawn on. Her small oval face...doll like.

The rocky road narrows. We slow. The canyon

comes in close, walls to either side of us. Now we're moving up a wash through rocks and debris. Stub my toe! Stub my toe! Trees up ahead on one side, two or three big ones, opposite a sheer rock wall.

Clay reappears, running back with a stick, panting, and when he's close, he calls out, "This is the place, Daisy."

Ms. Kell asks, "What place? What happened here?"

Our parade clots up. Clay and Daisy look around, checking the rock wall and trees. There's a rope in the tree, tied up high. Tenny, bored, bounds over to the wall and hoists himself, spider crawls right up, rifle over his shoulder on its strap. Cassie's yelling he's a monkey. Moira is still.

I say, "Scenario! What to do at the end of the world but celebrate of course. We get the entire population of Coltrane. We get everyone out at the park. And the children shall lead! We will conduct the Grand Finale! Perfection itself. The ultimate act. See what I mean? You're the stars of the show."

Daisy stares. Finally: "Not now, okay? Focus here now. Rope's still there."

Tenny from up top shouts, "Yo, scouts! Nothing up here, you guys. No baldies, no rattlesnake."

Ms. Kell pops, "What rattlesnake?"

Clay gets up close to the tree with the rope. He's staring at it, figuring. "Herpetologica," he mutters.

Daisy closes in to me and says, "Scotty, I'm glad you are including us. You know. 'Scenario's' like the story, right? So we definitely will get into that."

Tenny scurries down, begins, "You know what happened to Ms. Lucien up on the highway. At the gate? And you got to have heard about Jacob Derry finding a gate with those scouts out west of here. East, west. East, west. Get it?" He's making flailing motions, pointing, like an orangutan. "So it only makes sense: north, south. North, south. See?" More pointing in the opposite way. "It only makes sense to check up this way, to the north."

Cassie sings, "North, south. North, south."

I gasp. "Intuitives! Of course! What are you expecting, oh great sensei?"

Clay says, "Another gate. I'll get my rope later. I thought I got it. I thought I got it. I don't remember though. Let's go."

I point to Moira. "What's with her?"

Daisy says, "We figure she can help."

I must look deranged because Clay moves between us, says softly, almost in a whisper "This is the first place baldies showed up. We spotted them. Right over there." He points towards the wall. "Up there, at the top."

That miner mouth goes, "I missed that. No secrets! What about this spot? What were you saying?"

"We fought back," says Tenny. "He had a rattlesnake."

Ms. Kell asks, "I don't think I want to know about the rattlesnake. What day was that? The first time you saw baldies?"

I can't resist: "Perfect! Non-objective theatre! You're all naturals. Of course you had a rattlesnake! You know what they say in the theater, kids and rattlesnakes grab all the energy, all the attention."

Daisy says, "There's no one here, we should go on."

Curiouser and curiouser –

We walk up the creek bed some more. The quasi-ersatz-path has us lined up. Me at the end this time. We get past the narrow canyon, the canyon opens. Rocky walls pull back. Hillsides give on to mounding fields, bordered by trees. And the fog. There's the fog! The going gets slow as we mince between boulders and rotten logs. The kids think it's a game: they're all bouncy, smiling. Ms. Kell and I take our time, but watch closely, trying to catch their secrets. Secrets we have forgotten. Secrets we've never known. It doesn't matter, time goes on. Knowledge is knowledge, openness is all. The mountains close but foggy. The streambed wash trail, or whatever you call it, *arroyo*, goes right down the middle of the clearing. I suddenly realize we're in a bowl, cut by this ditch down the middle. The wash gets deeper, has steep sides. We can see over the sides. We should climb out. Grass and brush along the banks. Plenty of sticks. We climb from the wash and follow alongside it. Ahead of us, right up to the fog, actually in the fog, touching the fog, a log cabin. A long low wood and log cabin with a flat metal roof. No windows or doors that I can see. All log. Log rhythm. But it's far enough that I can't see clear. It looks like a fake log cabin, trying too hard. Like an art project?

"There's a cabin up there," says Tenny.

We gather together, Daisy in our midst. A chill touches down on our nose tips, even little Moira. We stare at the log structure.

A miner voices: "Whose place is that?"

Another one responds: "I been up this way a million times." He shakes powerfully. "Uh-uh, this is new."

It sits at the base of a mountain of fog. Mountain tops peek through the fog up high. High. High. It looks like the front of the cabin, the side opposite from us, must be right in the fog. We're looking at the back of the structure.

Tenny's studying the site with binoculars.

Daisy encourages, "What do you see?"

Tenny growls, "Looks like a log cabin."

Nobody knows how long it's been there.

"But it wasn't here before?" asks Clay. "I mean, before."

"I say," says Tenny, "we get closer. See what's up."

"Surely, someone lives there," says Ms. Kell. "We don't want them to think we're spies or marauders."

The miner speaks, "Why not? What else are we? Nah, don't worry. A friendly gesture, townies checking up on them."

Daisy says, "I don't think that's a regular log cabin. But we'll see."

One of the other miners and a college boy try to say something across each other. The miner goes first: "What Jacob Derry saw, and what was in his pictures, well, this looks awful similar. Fog and all. The way the fog has the front of the house."

The college boy adds, "I saw those, too, the pictures and everything. But that house had been there a while. I think."

Sam says, "Ah, maybe this is a fixer upper!"

We walk on. We have the wash to our right. The cabin's on the other side, past the wash, then ahead of us. We're close. I notice there's no chimney. I don't see any windmill or out buildings, or any of the other, typical piles of accumulated trash.

We stop again, cluster. Tenny uses the binoculars. "Nothing," he says. "I don't see a thing."

Daisy says, "Me and Moira, we'll cross the wash, we'll walk up that way. You guys hang."

I ask, "What's going on? What's all this mystery?"

The big miner quips, "Nothing to see here! I'm ready for coffee, jefe!"

"Why are you bringing Moira, Daisy?" asks Ms. Kell. "She seems – "

Clay looks surprised then agitated. "Daisy, you should take the pistol. Just in case, Daisy. Daisy."

He likes saying her name.

Daisy shrugs. "Gotta stick. We'll be ok. Anything happens, you guys are right here."

The boss man miner, or at least their main spokesman, says, "I don't like this one bit. What are you thinking? What's your plan?"

Daisy says, "Tenny, explain it."

Daisy, clasping Moira's little dough hand, moves to the edge of the wash. They begin going down, leaning back, sliding to the bottom. Daisy uses her stick for balance when she has to. Moira seems in free fall, as though gravity has no effect on her. Or she's light as a feather. They cross the wash and clamber up the other side. They're walking to the cabin now, hand in hand.

Ms. Kell says, "Tell me that little girl is in no danger."

Cassie says, "No danger. Just clay-sy."

Ms. Kell says, "Tell us what's going on? We have to know."

The miner fellow speculates, "Too late now!"

The college girl says, "I can't believe they're just walking over – "

Clay says, "Moira – "

Tenny interrupts: "Let me tell it! Moira's a baldy! We caught her, raised her, everything."

"You did not!" gasps Cassie.

"Are they safe? Is this safe?" I ask. "I'd hate for any of our players to be at risk."

Ms. Kell clasps her stick with white knuckles. "As though any of us are not at risk. Civilization is supposed to minimize risk."

The college girl clamors, "Wait! You're saying – you guys raised a baldy?"

The big fellow makes noises, shakes his head side to side. "Down the rabbit hole, hoss!"

Cassie says, "Me and Roland caught her in the street, when all the baldies came down to get killed."

Didi says, "I was there. I helped."

"That's a little girl!" exclaims Ms. Kell.

Daisy and the little girl have paused near the cabin. None of us like it. There's something ballooning the vibes to odium. The pregnant dawn is bloated with monsters. One sentient entity is all you need! There she is!

The miner aka boss, or the main voice, says, "You guys up to some stuff. Wow. Baldy kid? That's – I mean, what were you thinking? Okay, 'nuff of this nonsense, time for the adults to take charge."

I change the subject: "You think there's a gate there, at the log cabin. That's what this is about?" Clay and Tenny both nod vigorously. They glare at me joyfully, eyes torn from Daisy. Happy soldiers! "And Daisy and Moira over there, what's that? You blokes gotta share! Tell us. We're approaching a non-objective climax."

Clay says, "Not yet."

Ms. Kell says, "Daisy thinks she can negotiate. Doesn't she?"

Tenny pulls the binoculars away from his eyes and says, "I don't like it either. We should at least get to the other side."

The miner proclaims, "We can make a line. Ah, geez. Who decided this? How comes she's just doing this all la-de-da? That ain't no baldy child!"

Sam plops, "Be prepared!"

The college girl says, "Spooky! Like a set up? You know?"

"Keep watching them with those things," says Clay, "so we know right away if they're in any trouble." Clay thinks, too many peeps, too many onions, I mean opinions. I mean onions –

Tenny raises the binos. Daisy and Moira are going in way too close –

Ms. Kell asks, "Is the little girl in danger?"

I go, "Child safety, you know, part of the code. Audiences hate children in peril. Parentals being what they may. Killer to our scenario. But I'm a pragmatist."

Tenny lowers the binoculars, glances at me, "How do you know she's a child?"

Clay whisper shouts, "I see! Someone! The cabin! On the side, near the back, in the fog!"

Tenny adjusts the binoculars, announces, "Someone coming out."

Clay goes, "Ugly? Baldy? I can't tell."

Tenny shakes, "We should get to the other side."

Clay says, "Take it easy, see who it is."

He looks. "It's not a baldy. Wow! Another one coming out, following behind. Right out of the back there from the fog. They're giant beavers!"

The miners are very adult, get into action. They have weapons out. They're ready to save the day! The high school boys huddle to the rear, ready to bolt. College kids digging it.

Clay says, "Let me see!"

Tenny hands over the binoculars.

I'm watching Daisy and Moira because they're stationary. Standing there. Can they see what's coming? They must!

Clay says, "They look kinda like people but they have these giant beaver tails like making a cape behind and over them."

Tenny exclaims, "Swear to God, look like beavers to me. I mean, the front is basically like a furry person, but the big flat tail."

Ms Kell is trembling. She stumbles out with: "'Beaver'?"

Clay has the binoculars. When do I get a turn?

Clay says, "I don't know, maybe they're furry or maybe they're just brown in front. Maybe that's not a beaver tail. Maybe it's something else. I can't tell." He swings the binoculars away as though he's going to toss them. At the last second, he hands them to me. "Look."

I focus in and Ms. Kell yelps, "We got to get them back here."

Miner commander concludes, "We'll head over there. Back up. Make sure the young ladies are okay. I've shot beaver before. Go down nice and easy."

Clay says, "We don't know their intentions."

I go, "Do we have intentions? Giant beavers, whatever, so random, so clear."

Ms. Kell speculates, "They're going to have intentions, and they are not going to be good."

I exclaim – can't help it, "Giant beavers! Come on. The game is afoot. The moon is down."

Walking from the log cabin's corner in the fog, two giant beavers steadily step towards Daisy and Moira who...are waiting for them. They can't help but see them coming. The girls clutch each other, at the approach of the creatures: two man-sized figures, small heads, bulbous curvy bodies, big feet and legs, small hands and arms. They look like bears? Except for the capes or tails or covers across their backs. Beaver tails or fleshy capes?

Beaver people! Beaver people! Workers! Dams! Tree cutters! Bark eaters!

Daisy and Moira are stuck in their tracks. I'm looking at their backs. They're holding hands. Daisy's other hand, her left, holds her stick upright. She has a small backpack on, over her pullover. That's where she carries the extra water. Moira has no backpack.

The beaver people stop. They are pretty close. But the beaver people's hands are empty. Daisy has a stick. They stand apart from each other, maybe ten feet. Daisy's talking to them. We can tell she is. She's animated. What is she saying? What's she saying? Speaking up for the whole planet! Do they understand? Are they responding? Daisy makes awkward gestures, using her stick.

Cassie blurts out, "She has nipples. Now she has nipples."

Tenny chortles. Ms. Kell says, "What do you mean?" She grips her stick so hard!

"The little girl, Moira, has nipples."

Clay says, "Let's get on the other side of the wash."

The big guys and the college kids go first. The miners want to take over. They move awkwardly with their pistoleros out. The rest of us scat to the edge, slide and slither down the bank, cross the rocky bottom, then up the far bank. I have to pull myself up, but I manage to hang on to my broom. Army on the move! Daisy's minions! The troops. Men and guns. Girls and sticks.

Nothing is happening. They're standing there examining each other. Daisy doesn't seem to be talking. Silent negotiations? Telepathic tête-à-tête? Are they responding to Daisy? Sprechen Sie Deutsch? Did we miss the beaver people's subtle gesture that enunciated the secret of existence? Our one and only chance? Then, from the back corner of the so-called cabin in the fog, where the beaver people emerged, baldies pour out. I mean, lots of them. In a stream. Naked, white, pink, run of the mill baldies, like we've seen all week. The beavers turn and waddle back to the cabin. You can see the cowling or cape or beaver tails from behind much better. They make a shield.

Baldies stream right towards Daisy and Moira. The baldies are not running because I don't think they can run. They have this art deco shuffling dance gait that eats up distance.

Daisy and Moira hold on. We can hear Daisy shouting. What's she saying. How do you scold beaver people? What do you say to baldies? 'Hey, we got a baldy child, and we'll give her back, if you leave us alone?' Was that the negotiation? But the beavers disappear around the corner into the fog. The baldies are too close. Daisy!

Ms. Kell yells, "Daisy!"

Clay takes it up: "Fly, Daisy! Fly, Daisy!"

Daisy and Moira turn and run towards us, hurdle of baldies close behind. Well, I wanted to be part of the Children's Crusade. Here I am with a stick.

The miners are moving out deadly, talking among themselves. The college kids wait for the rest of us to decide what to do.

We want to charge in to save the day. Our sticks are eager. Good for close work, baldy to person to death kinetics.

The miner dood orders, "We got this, folks! Stay behind us. We're gonna set up a line and have us some target practice."

Tenny's down on one knee, next to them, rifle ready to go. He aims. Clay takes a position. The three miners have their pistols out, arms extended. A line of firepower!

Ms. Kell is back with me and the rest, holding her stick like a spear.

Tenny yawps, "Wait until you see the whites of their eyes!"

Clay gurgles, "This isn't a game! Wait until Daisy and Moira are out of the way."

Ms Kell yells, "We have to help them!"

The big miner says, "Like shooting rats in a barrel!"

His superior says, "Wait! Wait! Until the girls are clear."

Daisy and Moira are clear now, and bullet country ejaculates.

Tenny fires the .22 which pops like a toy, but a baldy goes down. The four pistols and firing and firing, and baldies are falling. Same dissolve, same deflating skin of ooze and primordial mess. They keep firing. Their cannons blast out our ears then echo in the mountain bowl.

The big guy goes, "Running low on ammo. Didn't expect this shit, Roger." Again, he fires.

Lots of firepower to dispatch measly baldies.

"They're almost back," cries his leader. "Hang on!"

Daisy and Moira make it to us. Daisy's eyes sizzle gray. The little one looks the same...maybe?

Daisy says, "They looked like beavers."

The baldies hold back, they're stalling. Don't like a wall of bullets?

Clay says, "We should get back. To the other side of the creek. That'll slow 'em down."

The college girl insists, "I'm outta here! Let's go! Come one. Let's get out of here."

Ms. Kell rasps, "We have to get out of here!"

Daisy says, "I tried to talk to them. I told them who

Moira was. I tried to make contact. I told them we knew about the underground. Then all the baldies – "

What 'underground'?

Ms. Kell asks, "Did they respond? Did they say anything at all?"

Tenny busts out, "Is it a gate?"

I diplomate, "Clay's right. The better part of valor...egad. You and I and me broom stick aren't going to be terribly effective at slowing baldies down."

Daisy says, "You'd be surprised."

Cassie yammers, "Kids with sticks!"

Tenny and the other fusiliers pick them off. Grand annihilation! Random carnage. Tenny's having quite the time. He yells, "There's too many of them!"

Carnage nihil obstat. Carnage adovada.

"Don't get your panty hose in an uproar, lad! You're doing fine! Stand fast! Bullets away!"

"Pistols aren't good for this," says Clay. "I mean at these distances."

"True," says the big miner. He keeps picking them off with his pistol. I don't want to look at it. Or where the bullets go. "You know how much practice it took me?"

Casual carnage. Discussion carnage. Effective as hell.

The miners discuss firearms, loads, accuracy. They say the best pistols ever were made in the former Czechoslovakia.

"They're cannons,' I say, "bombards for buffalo."

Daisy lets the girl's hand go, twists her backpack off her shoulders. She opens it, takes out the case that looks like a laptop I saw before. The same case they had at the house when Daisy and I shared our unexpected displacement. She unfolds it. She's been practicing. She intones, "This is the ray gun configuration."

She raises it up, looks down the barrel, figuring how to aim the thing.

Tenny says, "Hope Bennett remembered to keep the black machine on."

Daisy goes, "Only one way to tell." Daisy fires or pulls the trigger or pushes the button.

Nothing.

Time to get out of here! The army is neighing and stomping in place. College kids appear gaudy sanguine. We're all looking around at our adventure, trying to decide which disbelief this is. Next, Clay notes first: "The baldies!"

We had all checked right away when she pulled the trigger, and there had been no change we could see. We looked all over, the melted onslaught, the fake cabin. Now our eyes go back or switch forward or glitch prosaic, and boom! The last baldy...baldies...their forms. They feel different. Because baldies close by, the last few, are transparent, fading outlines. They flicker depth, heft, flicker back to empty outlines. See through cartoons dissipating in the air. Insubstantial baldies, regular baldies, distant baldies. Stagger from the cabin. More? Less? Something this thing we thing is slow –

Tenny whoops. "It's working!"

A college boy gurgles, "I'm going to throw up."

Cassie screams out in triumph! Then, cries: "Look at Moira!"

The college girl cries, "They're changing! Oh – ah! Something terrible is happening."

Moira is see through, transparent, a window. Daisy takes her hand. Cassie grabs her other hand.

"We have to hold her here, Daisy," says Cassie.

"What's going on?" whimpers Ms. Kell.

We vacate: we scoot down the bank, cross the bottom, climb up the other side. New baldies? Are there more now? And closer? Why is it so hard to tell? We reach our side we just left, and the new and old, the improved and regular baldies fall, tumble, slide down steepness – clumsy lads!

The big miner says, "You think they'll follow us?"

The other miner, the older one, says, "We got 'em. Nothing to see here. Baldies a baldy."

Cannons wreck and make the battle. The baldies have trouble going down the bank and actually start deflating on their own from the rough slide alone. Maybe a sharp pointed rock pricked their fish belly pink white integument? Awful empty faces. Looking into a baldy face is looking into an unformed mask over a scrim.

The big miner describes, "They're following, all right."

Clay says, "Daisy, I don't know if you should use that thing anymore."

Daisy packs it up, puts the ray gun in her backpack. Cassie and Moira are next to her, still holding hands. Maybe Moira is an iota more substantial.

Clay continues, "You and Moira, Didi and Cassie and Ms. Kell, get out of here. Take her back. We might still need her. Go on! We'll hold them off."

The college girl cries, "Me too! We're going!"

"You got any ammo?" asks Tenny, glancing around, from high school boys, to college kids, to miners – a regular phalanx of typology!

"For sure," says Clay, hoisting his stick up high!

Tenny says, "Take the old man with you. Without a gun, he's not gonna be much help."

Clay says, "Scotty, leave your stick, okay? In case we end up needing it. Okay? And when we're out of ammo?"

We take off. We go and go and go, away from the brouhaha, heading back, down the ditch, follow it back, the way we came. We are half running, half stumbling, half skipping, back, away, the way back, the way we came.

The best told tales of innocents!

"Fortified by victuals, we are here to slay the dragon, mi'lady," Falstaff expounds.

## Tenny Luna

*NEVER SAY DIE*

The hero is methodic in his choice of target. We must hold! They will not pass! Baldies come and go. Punctured and deflated. How many are there? Replenish! Sure, I have no ammo. Sure, rifle goes over my shoulder. Buck knife time, up close.

Clay is wailing about something.

Sticks at work! Puncture, deflate. We get 'er done. Done. Daisy and those guys are out of the way. What're we waiting for? Git, git, git! What's Clay yapping about?

Clay: "We gotta get to a strategic spot. See what's going on. Find a stronghold we can defend."

Me: "What the hell you yapping about? Use the fricking binoculars to see! They're slowing down. This is easy. Check it out! Let's go! Let's get outta here!"

The other guys are starting to move.

Clay demands, "We have to make a stand!"

"Dood," I cackle, "there's no more of them. We won! Boom! We're done."

It's true. No baldies left. No sign of beavers. Okay. A few baldies off to the side, creepy confused, the lopsided crawl. They've learned the power of the gun. They're afraid of us. They're things. Like in gaming.

CHRIS DIETZ **339**

What did Daisy think she could accomplish with the little girl baldy?

The men mutter. The oldest one says, "We're outta here. You guys, too. Let's clear out."

The college kids already are.

Clay goes, "Well, I'm heading over there to those rocks."

He heads out, pistol in its holster, Scotty's stick in his hand, and he scrambles to a rock pile behind us. Always a handy rock pile in the desert. Fine.

Sitting ducks. Fish in a barrel. WTF. What's going on here –

Total shooter game. I glance at Clay climbing to the top.

Oh, great!

Flickering baldies all around us, clustered weird now, and grabbing.

Where'd these baldies come from? We're surrounded! We're seeing things! I yell, "We're seeing things! It's not real."

Pistols! Final bullets. The doom! Stick in hand, scramble to stab. Check out Clay's rocks. Baldies stop, stand among us. Suddenly, no more grabby. Adults with knives doing the dirt work. Dumb baldies! Flickering baldy faces show nothing – places where features tend to go. This is like a total game. I glance back at Clay who's climbing to the top of his rock pile. Oh, great.

Now, they're grabby grabby again. And strong!

Changed baldies! Altered baldies. The college kids get clear and run for it, high school boys behind them.

Do they have a strategy? Are they getting messages, telling them what to do? Dumb baldies! I inch over to the rocks to see what Clay is doing.

I climb up, go, "Now what?"

He grunts. "Wait and see. They're different. They're acting different. When Daisy turned on the ray gun, something happened. Then, I'm thinking the beavers did something to counter the ray gun. We have to see what's going on. They're up to something."

Baldies hold up the big man, grasping him from all sides. They've hoisted him aloft and he's screaming, and his buds are all around the uplifted, stabbing, puncturing, penetrating best they can. But they, too, are about to be overwhelmed. Bunch of baldies come down the creek trail holding Sam aloft, and he's yelling like a banshee.

Clay calls out to the baldies. Baldy heads peek on our side. Looking our way. Clay yelps, "Hey! We don't want to fight! What do you want? Who are you?"

I yell, "What are you?"

I'm up in the rocks above Clay now, blinking my eyes rapidly, trying to get the flicker to stop.

Clay gives out another super, "Hey!"

And it is immediately answered by another super cry: "Hey!"

A baldy spoke? Moira could spoke –

Loud enough an outcry answer, it knocks Clay

uneven, unbalanced, because he's sliding now, going right down the rocks, bumpity bump, right into baldies! Where's his stick?

"Clay!"

I throw rocks at the baldies.

They're leaving. They're taking the three men, the three humans.

They don't seem to be hurting them. They're not tearing off arms or anything. Screeching dies down.

Six baldies have Clay up in the air and they're taking him.

A reflection on the ground, at the base of the rocks, catches my eye.

Sam's fake sword. Still, it is sharp.

I'm down. I'm in the thick. Dance of death! Jabbing and jabbing. It doesn't take long for the baldies to be smooshing away into piles of goo, allowing Clay to get away.

I slide and hop away with him. We don't dare say a word.

# THE TENTH DAY

**Mayor John Placido**

> Hang in there, baby!
> *as seen on posters*
> *with teacup cats*
> *struggling to hold on*

The convention center is headquarters, I guess you could call it. Bunch of people already here. I never used to like getting up in the dark. Regular committee people, security people, bunch of folks volunteering in the supply rooms. We're trying to organize, get an inventory going. They're firing up the generator already, to get the recharger working. Check emails – I'm kidding. Plus, there are a few extra men about who Frankie Lucien picked for today's adventure. For today's mission.

Everyone is hushed, talking in low tones. Everyone is sleepy?

Frankie Lucien and Officer Latta are standing before a table laden with firearms and ammo. They're going over these weapons, checking them out. At least that's what I think they're doing. Councilmen Martinez and Ramsey, and Janet Gorey and I sit beside each other at another folding table opposite the guns. Janet is cleaning her glasses.

What is an adventure? I'm not going on any adventure. Adventure has to do with danger. You can't actually have an adventure without danger. But back in the day, adventure also meant fun. I am no seeker of danger. I've been tried, I've been tested. Right now, I believe we're on track. We listen, we learn, we respond.

No coffee.

The last couple days Coltrane has been arguing about what to do next. All we been doing. The old process of majority rule has evolved to other forms now...we adapt as we go...adjusting. Consensus, sure, but also some kind of snowballing necessity seems to guide us. We're going on. Doing it.

We're going for the south gate, which according to the best estimates has got to be at the saddle in the mountains just below Mt. Baldy, tallest peak of the Apache Mountains.

Councilman Ramsey says, "I left my camp stove out front. Boiling water for tea. It should be done. You all want some?"

Martinez, Gorey, and I all make anxious pleas for tea. He goes to check it out. Janet goes to fetch cups.

Councilman Ramsey comes back fast, but no steaming tea pot, just a cold one. "You won't believe it!" he cries. "My Coleman stove is gone! Someone just picked it up and took off with it. But they left the pot. See?" He hefts it to show us.

Officer Latta and Frankie Lucien wander over to commiserate. Officer Latta says, "Come on, somebody just borrowed it. Maybe they thought it was being tossed out?"

"It was lit, warming up the water!"

Frankie says, "Looting! We got to keep a handle on that."

Ramsey fumes. "Where were your security guys when my stove walked off?"

"I think someone borrowed it," says Officer Latta.

"Oh, gah, don't be so naive!" Ramsey is disgusted.

"Since consolidation," says Officer Latta, "our sense of ownership has changed."

"That's a lot of crap," snaps Ramsey. "I want my stove back!"

We hear the door open in front, turn to see who it is. Whether they're returning Ramsey's stove. Daisy, Clay Mason, and a little girl walk over.

Daisy says, "We need some security guys to help us find some kids."

Frankie Lucien says, "Whoa, whoa. Tell us what's going on."

Daisy frowns. I've never seen this girl mad. She looks it now. The others, too, are upset.

The little girl steps forward right away. "Some kids went to the north gate yesterday and haven't returned."

Councilman Ramsey bursts with: "Oh, great! Stirring up more trouble. I mean, you kids – "

"Hold on," says Officer Latta. "Let's hear what she has to say."

The little girl holds out her hand to Officer Latta. "I'm Cassie. Remember me?" They shake. She goes on: "Me and Daisy and Moira and Ms. Kell and the old man came back before the boys." She counts them off on her fingers. "Then Clay Mason came back. Tenny. But Sam and the giant man never did. We waited last night. I fell asleep. We thought they'd be here by morning. They aren't."

"Have you checked their homes?" asks Officer Latta.

Clay Mason nods. Daisy looks away.

The little girl, Cassie, says, "Baldies got them. We need to go back to the north gate in case the beavers let them go."

We glance at each other. Officer Latta moves closer to the girl, kneels. "Thanks for telling us, Cassie."

She adds, "We're 'fraid the beavers got them."

Councilman Ramsey coughs. "What's this about beavers?"

Frankie Lucien says, "Sounds like you guys had your very own expedition. So there is a north gate? Then our mission to the south gate is all the more important. We've got this going right now. I'm just waiting to fill a few slots. We should be back in a few hours. If they haven't turned up by then, we'll send out a team."

Councilman Ramsey repeats: "What about beavers?"

Cassie says, "Giant people beavers."

Councilman Ramsey squirms. He proclaims: "That does it! All kids need to go back to their parents. We can't have a bunch of orphans running security operations."

The young people stare at him but just for a second. They look away like he's got a booger on his nose.

Cassie says, "It's too late." She shakes her head. "We're not orphans."

The kids want to rescue their friends. We figure they've found the north gate. With giant beaver people and baldies. If their friends got caught, they're probably already dead. Or worse. Changed into something like those druggies were, who suddenly were all eager for consolidation. Daisy Piper says these guys would never go for consolidation. She says they are 'crucial' citizens to our survival.

Frankie Lucien and Jacob Derry think we have to know what we are up against. And if there is a south gate by Mt. Baldy, it will prove we are 'not in Kansas anymore.' That's what Jacob Derry said. As though that explained something. Frankie Lucien argued that Derry was right, which was pretty funny on account of how these two hardly ever get along. If there is a south gate, now that we know there's a north, east, west gate, then we know we are up against odds beyond government capabilities...beyond the forces of consolidation. This is a crucial consideration for making future plans. Oh, that doesn't cohere – but it's what we got...

We got nothing.

Others argued, wouldn't a mission provoke 'them', add to heightened tensions? Retaliation? We are not geared for war. We are not ready for much in the way of defense or offense. We been lucky. Let's not push that luck. Shouldn't we hang tight and keep on the alert and avoid gates, baldies? Beavers?

A certain logic.

A leader offers guidance. Responsibility for the decision. We have scouts. We are doing what we can. Holding it down. But, sure, probably not good to stir up more tension.

I say, "Hey, everybody. Look, we been struggling with this all week. We don't want to bring down retaliation. But we can't let boys be kidnapped either. So a compromise solution? Frankie Lucien leads some guys to check on Mt. Baldy. If there is a gate there, then, like Frankie said, we know what we are up against."

Councilman Martinez says, "What does that even mean?"

I answer, "That we're enclosed. We're surrounded. Right, Frankie? Oscar?"

No one answers. Finally, Frankie says, "Time to muster." She goes to gather her men. Officer Latta goes with her.

Pretty soon, they're getting together, Lucien, Latta, Martinez, then Tom Dillon, Roger Meade, Ramon Salazar, Saul Palmer with a bow, and Phil Nately. I don't know Saul Palmer or Phil Nately. But Frankie vouches for them.

Jacob Derry comes in and stands in front of the men. His tall frame and big head is stiff and delirious. He's a whack job! He raises his arms over his head and says, "All the old rules need not apply. New paradigm. New way!"

Janet Gorey says softly, barely audible, "That's not new: it's assuming it's all negative like men always do. So we have to fight."

Someone snaps, "Wargo assumed positive!"

Janet Gorey holds up her hands, "Now's not the time to debate. We have something to do. We have people who will do it. We will do this thing."

Councilman Ramsey waves his hands around, then says, "Come on, folks! Mayor John John's right. This is a compromise. No compromise is perfect. We'll find the boys. But first things first: we'll have a little look see, scouting operation up the mountain. We'll be back in plenty of time."

Daisy says, "You do what you want. They're our friends. They're depending on us. Maybe there's still time. Maybe we kids should have gone back for them already. But we didn't have enough guns. Or ammo. We need ammo. You go for the south gate, we'll get them."

Frankie Lucien says, "We'll be back before you know it. Ten men is what we need."

Jacob Derry grunts, "Ten? You commander?"

"You want the job" asks Frankie.

Jacob Derry stalks away, shaking his head. "I be outta here!"

Frankie says, "Officer Latta is coming with us. Tom Dillon, he's a vet. Councilman Martinez knows how to handle a rifle."

Frank Stanley steps up to the firearms table. "I'll go. I'll represent my neighborhood. It's important. It's only fair. I don't want to. I have to."

Councilman Ramsey says, "Geez – don't start! Frankie, what do you think?"

Councilman Martinez says, "I know the way up. We used to climb up there, race to the top."

Stanley chuckles, shrugs. "Drink some beers."

Frankie Lucien says, "Some miners volunteered." He nods to Meade and Salazar. "We have a solid group."

Clay Mason kind of pushes in front, faces Frankie, says, "I got a .22. I know the way, too. I'll go, too."

Before anyone can object and say a thing, Daisy Piper asserts, "He's faced baldies. Fought them. He can go."

Clay races off to fetch his .22.

Everybody seems grim or tired or scared. Now, word will spread. Coltrane will know what its folks are doing. Daisy Piper will return to the last house on the Gulch and prepare for her mission. All over the hills and steps and walls of Coltrane, peeps will be hunkering down in their cold, damp homes. They'll stoke up the fireplace, then re-count their supplies for the hundredth time.

Jacob Derry calls from the front door of the convention center as they muster and he skulks: "Full frontal? Kidding, right?"

## Oscar Latta

*War – what is it good for? Absolutely nothing!*
- Song from the 70's

*by the book*

We used to race up these mountains like there was no tomorrow. Like there was no incline either. Now it seems straight up. And the trails disappear or lead nowhere. Martinez and I can't find shit, then we think we have them, then they're gone. Pig trails. Animal trails. Where are the pigs? But we get going, all bunched up, then spread out in a ragged line. I can tell Frankie doesn't like it. We're barely up and she calls us over.

All over the world people are choosing one thing over another. Maybe the red dots on the map mean places like Coltrane. Places where the choice was not consolidation. But why those towns? Didn't any city, even mid-sized city, rise up with a collective no? People make decisions every day. We stayed. Who else stayed? What's connecting these little towns of defiance? Defiance?

Martinez puffs, "It's changed. Rain, erosion, I guess. Unless I don't remember anymore. Exactly where the trails were. You remember, Oscar?"

"Old age." I tap my head, swipe at my nose.

Clay Mason pivots, calls to us, "Starts up higher. We'll find it."

Frankie Lucien looks over her troops, men and weapons, small packs, water bottles, knives on hips, in boots. We're the real deal. Panting. Starting to break a sweat. I know Roger Meade, and I went to school with Ramon Salazar. Ramon's a bit puffy, let us say. Now, he's puffing and sweating. I know Tom Dillon and he's been a real help all week. Good guy. Saul Palmer, I don't know. I've seen Phil Nately around. I think I got him speeding out of the tunnel in the last year. Stanley is Stanley. Frankie Lucien looks a bit disgusted.

"Don't matter about trails," she says. "Look, we gotta have a plan. We go into this careful, see. No rush or contest to see who can get to the top first. What we're gonna do is have a few guys at point. Up front. One goes over here to the left, one goes straight up like we're doing, up the middle. A third guy goes over on the right. Then the bulk of us follow the easiest route up. Two guys bringing up our rear. Back up. Tom, I want you back there. Just in case. Reinforcements. Everybody got it?"

Martinez swings his deer rifle around from his shoulder to clasp its barrel in front of himself. He says, "Cover's so irregular, rocks and the way the mountain slope is, it's hard to see."

Frankie Lucien says, "For gosh sakes, don't shoot each other. Know what you're shooting at."

Tom Dillon says, "Who's in back with me?"

Lucien points to Salazar. "Ramon, why don't you go with Tom."

"Got it," says Salazar. He has a deer rifle on his shoulder and a bowie knife on his hip.

"I know the way," says Clay Mason. "I'll go point."

Lucien looks over to me, says, "Oscar, I was hoping you'd be up front."

"Course," I go, nodding to Lucien, then: "But he's been at one of the gates, so sure, he leads, I'll follow, at the – on the left side. That way." I point to the left, the east.

The boy nods and looks like he's talking but I can't hear what he's saying.

Phil Nately sniffles, cradling his deer rifle in his arms, and says sharply to the kid, "I guess we all shot a few baldies. What did you do?"

Clay Mason says, "I shot enough baldies to know a good shot will go clear through two or three at once. If'n they're in a row."

Saul Palmer says, "Bull's eye!"

Frank Stanley has been standing off to the side. He comes in abruptly, demanding, facing Lucien. Stanley says, "I'll go on the right." He holds a shotgun over his arm, pointed down. His eyes are red and glassy. He's not panting though.

Lucien looks at me and I shrug. Lucien says, "You should have a rifle. Maybe, Ramon will trade with you?"

Ramon Salazar pffts out a quick, "No way."

"Good enough," says Lucien. "Then, Oscar on the left, Clay in the middle. Point. Let's get going. Take it easy. I don't want anybody getting so winded he can't aim straight. Or can't control his weapon. Nice and careful. Deliberate. And if you have to shoot, mean it. No screwing around. I'll head up the main group in the middle."

"How much longer to the top?" says Stanley, stretching back his head, neck curved out, big ol' Adam's apple bobbing like a fishing bobber.

Clay Mason says, "If we take it easy, less than an hour."

Lucien nods. "All right, then. Another drink for the

road, let's get."

The whole group pulls out water bottles, sloppy toasts, and drink. Tom Dillon and Ramon Salazar hang back, slide, walk, go on down a bit, Tom talking to Ramon. The rest of us are fanning out.

Clay Mason says, "If we find an easy way up or something, we should signal you guys, right?"

Lucien wipes her mouth. She's got a deer rifle on her back, slung over her shoulder. She's got a military issue .45 in a holster on her hip. She puts away her water. "Sounds good," she says.

Clay Mason says, "So what's the signal?"

Lucien raises an arm, holds his hand out, open, fingers spread. "Means a good path, not too much climbing. If it's super good, thumbs up will do." He re-folds the fingers of his hand and makes a thumbs up gesture. The way her fingers splay I can tell she's got the arthritis.

Stanley cries, "Let's get going!"

Clay Mason says, "What if we spot trouble?"

Lucien makes a fist. "Universal sign," she says.

Stanley says, "Come on."

Clay Mason starts up, moving fast, agile, over rocks and boulders like a billy goat. Stanley takes the right side which is steeper, slowing him down. I head off to the left. Not too bad.

As you get higher, there are like steps. I guess you could say Mt Baldy is in layers – terraced. Are all mountains like this? These are supposed to be volcanic. Or upthrusts. Now I can't remember what Mr. Weller said in Earth Science back in the day. Here, there's pinon and juniper, lots of agave with sharp points. The problem is each layer offers a limited view up or down. Gray-blue rock bulges out, breaking away to form cliffs. We have to skirt them and find the in between way where it's easier to climb. It's slow. Our trails used to just zigzag straight up! It'll be hard to keep the bunch together.

This could be crazy. A big mistake. What else can we do? We gotta do something. How to proceed! By the book! What fricking book? Anyway, who knows what to do? We do. These circumstances are beyond any book.

Training kicks in. I'm huffing now. But it becomes automatic: lean, reach, stretch, step, groan. Up the mountain –

They call these small mountain ranges in southeast Arizona *sky islands*. The name has a romantic flair. I imagine mountain islands floating over the desert. Floating mountains, floating cities. People up high, who refuse to come down. Why would they want to? Geology fixed this landscape over millions of years. Much, much later, we gave it a vibe and a story. When we're gone, who will tremble at the geology?

I don't know if this is right. I mean, going up the mountain this way. I watch where I put my feet, pull up, bend around and through a bush. But I've got to offer my leadership and skills. These guys' lives are in danger. They're taking a chance. It's my job, it's their risk. No one has ever experienced...no one ever expected a week like this. I'm wondering where it all leads.

Leaning over, crab walk up a crack in the mountain. Push through manzanita, the little apple. No apples today. Well, the little dried up ones that fill javelina poop. Avoid stickers, spines, muddy spots. Drops. Head over a bit by some colored rocks, red and orange. Outcroppings. Not so chilly, but where's the fog? Slippery rocks.

I know why they call them *sky islands*, so, yeah, up here in the sky for sure. In the cloud realm. Keeping the order, protect and serve. This is the way the mountains look: straight up from the desert and damage, to pure rock heaven. The range is an island. We, islanders –

**Frĕd Stanley**

*There is no time for those without anxiety.*
- (I believe that's Kierkegaard.)

I remember a mountain in Colorado Liz and I conquered one summer when we were young and chipper. We had camped the night before at the bottom of the mountain. When we got to the top, we looked back and saw our tiny tent like a postage stamp in a softly pastel meadow. It looked like heaven. We'd dry humped the night before. Liz was not my wife. We never married. I never married.

In my neighborhood the ladies look to me –

– for blame!

I didn't want this. Neighborhood as some sacred unit of Coltrane space. I didn't intend on moving to a neighborhood of women. But I will defend my home. And

my    neighbors.    It    seemed    to    make    sense    to
compartmentalize for security.

But I didn't ask for this. Who knew what would
work? Our canyon outpost! The ladies insisted. I thought
they'd find it annoying and ironic that a man represented
them.

I will show them now. I will scramble up this
mountain, making it to the top, then they will respect me.
My physical prowess. Between them runs a fiery, raging
righteousness. Together, I do not know, I am wondering,
they are fulfilled claiming the righteous mandate.

Too steep!

I    cram    through    branches    almost    slipping,
scratching my hands. Catch a root, climb up and over.
Fingers snarled and blooded. I am on top of the world. The
neighborhood is solvent. The man has proven his worth.

Liz was not my wife. But she was the longest, my
only long-term relationship. It was like living with a
visitor from a different dimension. I yearned to play
steadfast husband. I played the fool, the doofus, the hurt
little boy, in a forest of nyloned legs and high heeled feet.

Slip down a few feet. Wait. Catch my breath.
Review what's ahead. Then turn around and glance down.
I can't see anybody. To my left, no one. To my right,
nobody. Cut off. Alone? I am clear and it's all a mistake.
Today, I'm mountain climbing, tomorrow I'll be sky
diving. Yesterday, I shot monsters.

Keep going. Cement it all together. Pull up on a
bush. Scrape my hand some more. My delicate fingers
shredded. The shotgun bounces on my back. It's heavy.
It's going to leave a mark. It's my grandpa's. He taught me

to shoot. I wouldn't trade it for anything. There's a lip ahead. If I go up and get over it –

**Clay Mason**

*Items?!?*

Evidence everywhere I turn. Evi-any-dense proof...this is the way...way, way, way. Fingers fingers play and spider. I am in the zone Daisy selects – she learned me.

This mountain cracked on account of a mine blast at the turn of the last century. Jagged crack on top like an EKG. My boots in crumbly, crumbly. Every step must mean it. If I step on a crack, I'll fall on my back. Crumbly, crumbly. Straight to the deep, deep tunnels beneath, where the dinosaurs roam.

Daisy thinks we can do about anything. She dreams of a better world. She is a better world. She's a girl. What's the deal with girls? Why do I feel – what do I feel? Or is it just Daisy? She thinks things happen when we let them. She thinks our constant, or my constant, fretting crumbles things. Then she thinks that's okay. What happened with the old dood – she won't let me in. She acts so tough. He's all mush. Momma, sistah, boss. She's real worried about them boys.

Alley oop!

Pull up, into a crouch. This is easy. I been training for this. On patrol! It's a game, it's not a game. It runs us.

It never does. Practice patrol makes real patrol practical. One foot up, sidle over to the left. Ease up, on. Easy as pie.

And if the kidnappers bite the dust? If the baldies have their way and tear them to bits? Daisy won't let that happen. Time must standstill flash-forward: time times time skips: this time no time means my time: squeeze time out of a toothpaste tube. Long enough to get this done, then for a getaway – enough time when you have a girl involved.

Anywho, who's worried about those dumb shits? If that was what the creature critters were going to do, tear them to bits, they would have done it right away. They carried me away. Dood saved me. Tenny. The others need saving, or they're binging, or partying. Those boys are boys. Boys. What about the big one? No doubt about that. I told Daisy.

Step, step, step around. Head up. Count the cliffs that look like faces. One makes a Trilobite monument. One makes a nippled boob. One, two, three, up, up, and the way is sailing: if I go over this mound. Almost a trail. This way was the right way! Glory! Crumbly, crumbly, crumbly! I found it! The easy way.

Trilobite! Be proud!

We're invaded. We're conquered. We're playing it out like kids.

I move to the open and turn around. Not so fast.

Where are the others? I perch, scanning.

I stretch hands over head, give two big thumbs up.

Can anyone see me?

I'll be the first one up that's for sure.

The way the mountain bends and breaks and cracks makes a saddle between the two biggest peaks. I'm right below the saddle to the side. From here, I can't see much. Coming up, I could see the saddle but not a lot. I am aware of it. The saddle goes off to the left. It sweeps over to hit the other mountain which must be Number 2, second biggest in the Apaches. What's its name? Can't remember.   I'm in between boulders – suitable cover, but not too bad. Ahead of me, a rough stretch to the saddle, but not too bad. Mt Baldy right here, beside me, on top of me, shrouded in white fog. But not too bad.

Solid white on top. Can't see beyond the white.

Pull myself erect. Scramble to the saddle!

Not so fast –

Twenty feet from me on the saddle, but set back so impossible to see climbing up, a gate! A gate. A gate in the fog. I didn't see anything like this at the beaver cabin. But this is just the way those guys and Ms. Lucien described it. Solid rods – beams, making a gate, the J shaped pipe. Gush! And right in front of this gate, extending out of the ground, as though they are mostly buried: two tops of what must be spherical shapes, the top halves of spheres, kinda bluish tint. Doesn't look like metal? I don't remember anything like this being described.

I duck to the right fast as I can. Get away. Up the side of Mt. Baldy, hugging for cover, picking through rocks. Climb higher. Good cover. I'm zooming up, close to the fog. Whatever it is. Mt. Baldy, real fast.

*Protect us, mountain! We've tried to know your beauty and power. Help us with these outsiders.*

Spheres? What do they do? Structures! Nothing like this before. They're buried there. They gotta be big. I gotta let the others know. Walking right into a trap?

I hear a whoop! A human whoop! That's not our signal.

I spot Mr. Stanley way down, on a little ledge. He's got both arms above his head, waving his arms. On the other side of him, further over, up on the Number 2 Mountain, I see the policeman. He's waving his arms over his head.

They changed the rules! Humans!

I do my signal. Fists up!

They both head for the saddle. Did they see me? What did their signals mean? How much of the saddle can they see? I couldn't see the gate from below. Can they see the tops of the half buried spheres?

I check the gate. The sphere tops are expanding!

What!

Complex, complex – this can't be right...or good. They spin. Yup – they're moving, they're spinning. They're coming out. They're digging themselves out, emerging from the rock and dirt they've been buried in. They emerge, they spin faster. They're spinning faster and faster.

Daisy, Daisy, protect, remember. Because this can't be good.

Quickly, I climb out of my hidey hole to get a better look and prepare for another signal. I know it can't be good. Wish I had a walkie-talkie. *Talky walky.* I give a big whoop and make my hands into fists and hold them high. I thrust my fists up and down to amplify the signal.

The main group appears like magic, as they step from brush and rocks. Do they see – can they see? Suddenly, there's a bunch of guys below me on the mountain. They're near where Mr. Stanley was.

Mr. Stanley and the policeman are right out in the open. I don't know if they can see the spheres and gate from where they are. They're also glaring at me. Frankie Lucien and her men have eyes on me.

Two spinning spheres have emerged, and now they emit a lightning bolt each. The blue glowing light crackles right at me. I fall back into the boulders: protected! It's easy. I just fall back. Lightning bolts strike the boulders. Tremendous impact! My ears black out. I see blue glow flickers around me. My hearing's gone! I'm huddling in a cleft of boulders about to pee my pants. Smells funny now: chemically.

I can hear something! Scraping, plodding? My ears come back! I bend forward, inch my way over to peek. It's the sound of rocks and boulders bouncing down the mountain. Uh-ho, uh-ho, landside! Look out below! The landslide hits me peeps. Dumb spheres!

I shake my head to clear it. Is my head sticking out like a target? I duck, cringe, make terrible faces. I come back, barely peeking over. The spheres spin so fast now.

Two more bolts flash out. I jump back, then realize these lightning bolts are aimed elsewhere. How the bolts curled around and down the saddle I can't figure. It's impossible. Lightning bolts can only go in straight lines, right? These had to have curled. I can't tell what the first bolt hit. But the second bolt hit the rocks and brush in front of Mr. Stanley and he is cut in half. I don't want to see that. I can't see that. I can see his legs and waist hiding there in the brush. His top half is in the open. Where's the policeman?

I unsling my .22, chamber a round, check the safety, and get to work. I hit both spheres but it's hard to tell whether the bullets have any effect.

Two more bolts slice at me!

I'm down! Down, down, down!

Huge explosions! I'm pelted with rocks and debris.

Hunkered down, waiting for it to be over –

Again, my ears are funny but come back to the sound of more rock slides, boulders of all sizes kicking up as they bounce down to the men.

The spheres glow, spin, flash. Too many lightning bolts now. It could start a fire. Are our guys okay? I can't tell. I shoot the spinning forms: first one, then the other, then I realize more bullets are hitting, too. Spinning is throwing.

They're big fat white-blue spheres of spinning light, risen from their holes!

Our guys! Shoot back!

## Frankie Lucien

*the idea of war*
*is not to die for your country*
*but to make the other son of a bitch*
*die for his country*
*Or something like that from General Patton.*

When the first explosion hits our ears after the blue flashes, we aren't able to see what's what. Where it comes from exactly. Where it hits exactly. I figure the boy has bought the farm. He had been signaling us. He made it up that mountain fast.

I push on ahead with Roger Meade and Jimmy Martinez near me. Saul Palmer and Phil Nately are behind us. Latta and Stanley ahead of us. We realize it's coming from the saddle. What's up there? When the next explosions hit near us. Blood and gore rain down on us. Saul Palmer and Phil Nately scream and scramble away, sliding, falling. Running for it. Nately drops his rifle. Palmer drops his bow.

Jimmy Martinez stares at me. His eyes are wide. He's covered in blood and bits. I guess we all are. Must be one of our point guys blown apart.

I don't see Roger Meade now, as I crawl fast straight ahead, then duck for cover. Martinez follows. I take in the mess of what's left of Stanley. I move over to some boulders for better cover. Get in tight. Jimmy Martinez makes it in next to me. We stay low. Better view for sure.

I hear .22 pings.

He's alive!

Dang! If that boy isn't having at them!

A couple more lightning blasts hit up on Mt. Baldy again. Debris showers down. Didn't expect I'd need ear plugs.

Jimmy Martinez brings me back, whispering, "I think that was Stanley." He's wide-eyed, chewing his tongue to get some spit going.

I ask of both of us, I go, "You all right?"

He nods, turns his head and pukes. I nod.

I slap his back. He comes around, gets his rifle down. We crawl to opposite ends of the rock and peer out. Up top the saddle, two lit up spheres, spinning. They look like gigantic Christmas ornaments. Big! We can see them. Just enough. They've risen up.

Gunshots! Men are shooting! Jimmy and I start shooting. All's right with the world.

Rifles to our right, in the rocks, I make out Roger Meade and Tom Dillon and Ramon Salazar. Latta on our left, firing. We keep firing.

Roger Meade hollers to who the hell knows, "That boy up there, he was one of them! One of the kids that went underground with us. He and that girl, they're always first, always in the know. Up to something I tell ya!"

"Keep firing!" I yell.

## Clay Mason

*my reptile brain*
*likes spirals*
*to wind me down*
*wind me in*
*I like helixes*
*I like spinning, glowing, erupting sphere*

Flashing bolts! Explosions below! Stop! Stop this!

Those men are going to be blown to bits, and I, hunched back here, gone fetal. Gotta move –

Out of ammo.

Peek.

Too loud! Too windy!

The slope looks like a shooter game. Men are forced to scoot about for cover, and they fire when they can. Fools' war. They have seconds.

Peek spheres going mad. Spheres spinning so fast, so glowy, their tops have opened, and it looks like a column of heat and fire coming out. Exhaust? Exhaust pipes! So all a person needs to do –

Geology in the day time.

Lucky, lucky, lucky! So much to choose from. Boulder buffet, all shapes and sizes. Rocky, rocky, rocky. Here, come to daddy!

Good heft. Solid. Not crumbly. Granite?

Granite!

Position.

Brace.

I'm up, up, high in the rocks. Over them, the one closest to me, doable. I got one shot. Work it out. Set it up. Do it done. All I gotta do is step out, keep tight, lob me baby boulder. Choke that fricking exhaust pipe!

No time is all time.

Flow into it. Plow it. Lob!

Back to cover.

A hit, but to the side.

It's gonna slide down the sphere!

No! The spinning – the spinning is pulling it in.

Bingo.

Blast!

I think I died and came back a mushroom. Totally fungal, osmosis death. Paralyzed. Filled with filaments. I think I blacked out from the shock wave. I have no clue. But my slowly returning ears offer something new now – stillness. This time it's so quiet. Quiet. Everybody's dead. The spheres stopped. The one that took the rock looks no different from its mate. But they are off. Shut down. Extend my tentacles –

Baldies start coming out of the fog beyond the gate. From the beyond, from the beyond gate, beyond them, baldies start coming out. One, two, then three at once.

Been there, done that! Here they come!

I get my .22 up again, aim, and click. No ammo.

Baldy, baldy, baldy!

Baldies aren't real. Daisy can make them fade away.

Waste of resources! Waste of space, waste of –

Why can't I get my thoughts to make them fade away?

Daisy used the 'item' and it liked her?

Whoever's behind baldies wants us to do this. It's so easy. I guess baldies have no value?

This is like the shooting gallery at the beavers.' Our guys made it!

Then the shooters hold off, cause the baldies are acting weird. Different. As they've been doing a lot lately.

What's the point?

Slimy baldy messes around the gate, then over by the spheres. The baldies left, then the new ones are proceeding along, straight to the spheres. Wonder if the guys down the slope can see this. Ah, they're climbing closer.

Rockpower did the trick. Caveman art. We beat them back.

The baldies give us a show. What's the point? They circle the spheres, and heave ho! Pick 'em up! They lift them. They're hauling them away, past the gate, into the fog.

*Let 'em go!*

Did we win? Can't be. What would Daisy think?

What do I think? Think, think...thunk.

I hear a husky voice emit a piercing war whoop.

Then, quiet.

I come out of my boulders, scatter down to the saddle. I wave to the men below me. They wave back. There were ten of us, I think. How many now?

Frankie Lucien waves me over. She calls out, "Come on down. Not safe up there."

It seems clear. Now. I start down, sliding, taking it easy.

With me, there's six of us. Ramon Salazar and Roger Meade are on their bellies, rifles fixed in front of them, watching the gate. They're ready. On point. They don't even glance my way.

The others standing nearby talking. I go over to them. I get a lot of shoulder slaps. Lucien stares at me.

She goes, "What were the spheres? You ever seen them before?"

I shake my head, find my voice. I realize I'm shaking. "Lightning bolts came out of the tops. Never seen them before. Or anything like it. Maybe in the movies. Have you?"

Councilman Martinez says, "That first day. Remember the big metal sphere?"

Ms. Lucien says, "Could be." Then, fast: "What did you do? We couldn't see. But we assume it was you."

Prone Roger Meade cackles, "Of course it was him.

He's a monster killer!"

Councilman Martinez says, "You were so lucky you were in the rocks. They couldn't get you." He's got blood on his head, in his hair, on his shoulders.

The policeman says, "They weren't expecting you. What did you do?"

Ms. Lucien's got blood over herself too.

I explain, "I threw a good-sized rock down its exhaust on top. I figured it was like the exhaust pipe. Thing like that, all that spinning. Friction. Builds up a lot of heat."

Councilman Martinez nods, mumbles, then, "Now what? We know there's a gate up here."

Roger Meade calls again, "Boy's a hero. Saved the day. No way we could have lasted much longer."

"Four gates," says the policeman. "In each direction. It's gotta mean something."

Ramon Salazar turns his head to glare at us. He goes, "Let's get out of here. We know now. So let's git!"

Roger Meade adds, "What do you think it means, boy? I want to hear what you think it's all about."

Ms. Lucien says, "We have to clean up."

Ramon Salazar gets up on his feet. He slaps at his belly, shakes his head. He says, "Ah, hell. You mean – "

Lucien says, "We got friends to take care of. We can't leave Stanley's legs up here for the coyotes."

The policeman says, "We still got coyotes? I'll do

it. Anybody want to help?"

I look over to Mr. Meade. I remember underground. He thinks something is going on. Like me and Daisy got insights. He's afraid of Daisy. I think most men are. I say, "Whoever's controlling the baldies, letting them loose and stuff, is testing us."

Councilman Martinez says, "Are we passing the test or failing it?"

The policeman pulls his pack around, opens it, pulls out a couple big black garbage bags. The heavy duty kind.

Ramon Salazar goes, "Wow, you thought of everything. Let's do this."

"Also," says Ms. Lucien, "pick up dropped weapons. No point in leaving a good weapon behind. Nately's back down there." She points.

Ramon Salazar says, "Man, those two came rushing by like a chupacabra was on their ass!"

Frankie Lucien says, "We won't mention it ever again."

I move over by the policeman and the councilman gathering parts. Scorch marks. Mini-craters. Little bits of red something. I don't even cringe. I help with the other guy, too.

The policeman finds Stanley's gun, a shot gun.

They start down, sharing the burdens. Meade gives me a last, lost long stare, then he goes. I'm watching all this and I realize Daisy is the Sun.

Lucien says to me, "You ok?"

I nod.

The policeman calls back to us, "Well, I guess, we're okay!" He gives a fake laugh. "We got 'er done today!"

Ms. Lucien heads down, taking it nice and slow.

I stand, get my rifle reloaded with the clip Lucien gave me. I am about to start down.

I have an urge to say bye to Mt. Baldy.

Urge-surge-purge.

One last look. Check it out. Just to make sure. And funny the name of this mountain, and the battle just fought. I mean the name of our adversaries. Daisy would like the irony. Sam would make a joke. He better be back by the time I'm down. Dig it.

When I'm up in my boulder hidey hole again, I fit my rifle next to me. Lean out so I can see the gate and the holes where the spheres were, the whole area splattered with baldy goo.

Yeah, baldy goo...

Light has a sparkle. Or my sparkle? Flickering, sparkling – what the heck. An aura. Scotch tape a penny to my forehead. Ma used to do that for the migraine. Looks weird. I guess I didn't notice before the way the light fickled my pickle, didn't bother rhyming it. Here I am. Now I utter. *Mist midst.* Before the white, puffy fog, a gnarly chemically smell.

When out of the distance –

From the gate –

Movement, form, shape – uh, ho, here comes another one!

I should signal!

They'll hear my gun –

...whoa, whoa, whoa...

...it's not a baldy. It's a guy. It's a naked young guy who's passed the gate now, all furtive like, like he knows he can't stick around here, the way he's looking around, scared like, but, yes, intention, too.

I get my .22 on him. Clean.

no wait

He kinda skirts the spheres and goo, careful like, picking his way. But hauling when he can. The way he's looking around – then, he's over the saddle. He's got dark skin. Maybe he needs a shave. I'd guess twenty-five, maybe. He's slipping, falling, but he's getting down the mountain.

He sure doesn't look like a baldy.

He's naked. He's got his junk. All the right parts. Including nipples on a hairy chest.

I decide to follow him –

*Born in 1951 in the Ozarks,* Chris Dietz *is a writer, teacher, and a birdwatcher. Currently, he lives in Bisbee, Arizona, surviving a catastrophe.*

Made in United States
North Haven, CT
06 July 2023

38631338R00232